First Year

First Year

Barbara Schnell

iUniverse, Inc.
Bloomington

First Year

This is a work of fiction. All of the characters, names, incidents, organizations, and dialogue in this novel are either the products of the author's imagination or are used fictitiously.

iUniverse books may be ordered through booksellers or by contacting:

iUniverse
1663 Liberty Drive
Bloomington, IN 47403
www.iuniverse.com
1-800-Authors (1-800-288-4677)

ISBN: 978-1-4620-1263-3 (sc)
ISBN: 978-1-4620-1264-0 (ebook)

Printed in the United States of America

iUniverse rev. date: 6/1/2011

On a tropical August evening in eastern South Dakota I sat on the front steps of my house, sipping Diet Pepsi and contemplating the cornfield across the road. The sun was a big orange ball hanging over the cornstalks but the wind was beginning to rise. It had finally cooled off enough so that I could stand being outside; I'd be able to open up the house soon. Until then I'd enjoy the cooing of mourning doves and the soughing of the breeze. Bob'd be home for dinner shortly but it was too hot to cook. Good thing I got the phone service hooked up today. I'd be able to order a pizza.

"Yoo hoo, Mrs. Anderson! Yoo hoo!"

Mrs. Nelson from next door was standing in her driveway waving frantically. Oh man, I'd hoped I could avoid her if I stayed in the front yard. Normally she spent her time bent over her back garden, her big pink polyester-draped butt a valentine for the neighbors.

"I've got some more tomatoes for you, Mrs. Anderson," she yodeled again. She was wearing a too-tight tank top and the skin on her upper arms was flapping. *Geez,* I thought, irritated at having my peaceful mood disturbed, *if she weren't so heavy she'd be airborne by now.* She'd even scared off the doves. And I had absolutely no desire to talk to her because Mrs. Nelson was a vicious gossip. I'd found that out the day after Bob and I moved in.

"You know she had men in there all the time," she'd whispered about Mrs. Swenson, the wife of Dr. Swenson, Bob's engineering professor and owner of our house. It sounded to me like Mrs. Nelson was trying to

1

make a scandal out of grad students so I'd futilely tried to change the subject. I finally ran inside the house to escape her.

Today she trudged over, pulling a wagon with a bushel basket half-full of tomatoes.

"Hot enough for you?" she began the ritual conversation.

"You bet," I said with a resigned smile.

"Well, you know, it's not the heat, it's the humidity," she chanted.

"You bet," I returned, right on cue.

We'd completed the opening hymn so she began her sermon. "I hope you can use some more tomatoes," she said, leaning into the basket and grabbing three in each large hand. She straightened with a groaned "oof duh", waited until I bunched my T-shirt into an improvised apron, and dropped them in. "Fritz always puts out a dozen plants and we can't use everything that grows. Now you take some of these here, slice them up, and put a little sugar on them. You're such a skinny thing we have to fatten you up," she chortled and various parts of her shook. I smiled and wondered how she managed to stay so...chubby. If her garden was any indication she worked hard and ate a lot of fiber.

She continued her prattle about recipes and I understood how she stayed so robust. "Now I like to take a few tomatoes and chop 'em up for my mac and cheese. Have I given you my mac and cheese recipe yet? Well, my Fritz just loves it..."

Her mouth was off and running so I let my mind wander. Marilyn had invited Bob and me out for the weekend at her cabin. I could save the tomatoes for then...

My attention returned to Mrs. Nelson when she moved in uncomfortably close and lowered her voice. "You poor thing. I heard all about that student business. It wasn't true, was it?" she asked sympathetically but her eyes gleamed avidly. I thought about blasting her with a few well-chosen comments about curiosity, old cats, and why the Eskimos put their old women on ice floes instead of social security—and the wisdom of that practice—when the admonitions of my Midwestern mentor, Connie Schwartz, surfaced.

"Stevie," she'd said, frowning in amused exasperation, "it's not wise to say the first thing that comes into your head. And it's not necessary to win every confrontation. Take a minute to decide what the consequences of your words or actions are worth. You're a smart girl and if you make it to my age without being shot" (Connie was only eleven years older than me but she acted like a generation separated us) "you'll be a truly admirable woman but you need to work on your impulse control."

After reflection I'd decided Connie had a point so now I swallowed my nasty comments and silently counted to ten. Mrs. Nelson was a neighbor so I had to be nice, I guess. She seemed lonely so it wouldn't kill me to put up with her bad breath and spite for a minute or two. And she did grow great produce.

When I failed to respond with anything other than an inward stare Mrs. Nelson changed tactics. "That Ricky Anderson, he always was a trouble-maker. I don't think he has any business teaching though between you, me, and the fencepost," here she leaned in again and whispered, "he's pretty much finished at the University." She waited eagerly for my reaction.

"I wouldn't know anything about that," I said coolly.

"Oh," she said, disappointed. Then she brightened, "Tell me all about Hollywood. Is it true…"

From her questions, I was pretty sure she got her information from the tabloids so I zoned her out again—which seemed to frustrate her. She wanted to gossip and I was the only neighbor who hadn't ducked out in time. Mrs. Nelson forcibly recalled my attention by grabbing my arm and hissing, "And Mrs. Olafson, in my church? Well, I heard that her third daughter…"

I didn't know Mrs. Olafson or her daughter—they weren't Lutherans—and whatever Mrs. Nelson was saying about them was probably fiction anyway. I told myself that I was paying for my tomatoes by pretending to listen and planned what I'd do with my big, red, juicy treats. Maybe I'd slice one of them up tonight and put Italian dressing on it. Bob hated tomatoes—he wasn't too wild about Mrs. Nelson either, for that matter—so he'd bitch but I could always peel a sack of carrots for him. Or I could drop some off at Connie's and report how I'd managed not to over-react to a stupid comment. She'd probably pat me on the head and give me a cookie.

I wonder what would have happened a year ago if I'd had a buddy like Connie to advise me about my impetuous rush into marriage. Leslie, my best friend in L.A., was just as young and stupid as I was so I didn't pay much attention when she tried to dissuade me. Knowing me, I probably wouldn't have listened to Connie either—assuming, of course, that she would've recommended caution.

Not that I regretted marrying Bob—well, not today anyway. Let's face it, if I'd been smart and cautious I would have missed out on a lot of adventures. On the other hand, I'd have missed out on a lot of crap, too. But don't you need crap in order to mature? I read someplace that life slaps you around until you learn to duck. But I could have learned to duck in Los Angeles; God knows I got slapped around enough there. And if I'd stayed in L.A. maybe I'd've become rich and famous. Ahhh, I probably would've ended up dead in a ditch. Of course, on the other hand...

chapter 1

"Stephanie O'Neill, you're up."

I grimaced and waved my size sheet, Polaroid, and headshot. The casting assistant grabbed my paperwork, glanced over it, nodded briskly, and marched out of the room. I followed slowly. After looking at the storyboard and reading the copy I was offended at the idiocy of the advertising world. Who did they get to write this crap? Had they no shame? I knew I didn't; I was about to do my best to sell it. As I walked to the video room running inane lines through my head I remembered all the years I spent studying Chekhov and Ibsen for my Master of Fine Arts degree. The academic life doesn't prepare you to sell panty liners—not that I have anything against panty liners; I just don't think they're necessary. I change my underwear every day. But I had bills to pay and if acting like I needed crotch protection—other than a .357 Magnum—would earn me some money…

I smiled brightly into the camera and chirped, "I love that fresh feeling!"

Man, did I feel stupid. And what's even worse—I was lousy.

I worried as I drove back to my condo in Hermosa Beach. Was I losing my grip? Had I really been that bad? Nyaahh, it had to be the writing not me, I rationalized. The excuse gave me courage to call my agent, Heather. I reported that the panty liner thing was a stinker and did she have anything else in the pipeline?

"Stevie, I'm so glad you called. I need a Hispanic woman for an action film that calls for some nudity. Now, before you say 'No' right away, just listen. It could lead to something interesting and I personally feel…" Blah, blah, blah.

Before you get your shorts in a snarl about my last name and this Hispanic business let me explain: My mother was a Morales from Texas and my father was an Irishman from the Old Sod. I have dark curly hair, brown eyes, even white teeth, and can play anybody in the known universe except an Aryan. Hitler would have gassed me.

"Heather," I sighed into the phone, "you know how I feel about nudity."

"I know, darling, you've told me before but you only have a few more years to make the big money. If you haven't done it by thirty you probably won't. You've got to get your foot in the door."

"It's not my foot they want to look at," I pointed out.

But Heather was ready with an argument. "Listen, you only have to do it once…" More blah, blah, blah.

I've heard it all before.

The feminist in me says that all this frontal nudity crap is just that: Crap. Do you see Tom Cruise letting his little dangler hang out in front of God and everybody? I don't think so. Why is it that if you're female, 25, and reasonably good-looking, the film world thinks disrobing is a plot point? And that's a purely rhetorical question. Everyone knows the movie industry is directed at prurient teenage boys.

"Heather," I interrupted with my usual excuse, "you know my chest isn't all that great. I'm under-qualified for the role. Don't you have any Playboy bunnies who don't mind showing their boobs as they're being blown up?"

Heather paused then said forcefully, "Listen carefully, Stevie, you're running out of time."

I'd heard that before, too. "Heather, it's creepy and embarrassing," I said.

"Well, if you're so sensitive I don't know if there's any future for you in this business," Heather said threateningly. This was not surprising, Heather always closed with a threat. "Should I submit you for the film, or not?" she finished.

For once in my life I took a deep breath before I said anything stupid. I'm a nobody. An educated nobody but a nobody, nonetheless. I needed an agent and Heather was the only one who'd shown any interest in me.

"Listen, Heather, I don't think it's good for me but I'll give it serious consideration and get back to you," I equivocated, then hung up and scratched the ears of my cat, Pudgy. It appeared she and I were in for another quiet evening at home. I love my cat but every now and then you need to talk to a person. So I called my friend, Leslie, who has the condo across the hall.

"Les, it's me," I said when she answered. "I think I hate my life…"

"Again?" she interrupted. "Well, come on over and we'll talk about it."

Leslie Williams is maybe the only real friend I have in the world. We're both new to Hermosa Beach; she bought her place six months ago, right after I bought mine. She's about my age, single, and also searching for her niche in life. We both like to talk and we both have nicknames that are considered sexually ambiguous. There our similarities end. She's tall, willowy, and blond; a WASP from Philadelphia. I'm, well, not short, but shorter, compact, and a runaway from patriarchal Catholicism. She has an MBA in Finance from Wharton and is now working for the local PBS station as a lark. I have an MFA in theater arts from Cal State Northridge and I work for money. Les' parents are making the payments on her place and probably consider her California adventure an amusing bohemian interlude before she takes her rightful place as chatelaine in a mansion with a career in charity work and motherhood. I'm an orphan, make all payments on my own, and consider my Hermosa Beach condo the nicest place I've ever lived in—as well as a good investment, of course. Les is personable, witty, and says she likes to hang with me because I'm brave but she mistakes bravado for bravery; I just have a lot more practice tap-dancing on land mines than most people. But I'm glad she likes me. I trust her to feed Pudgy and pick up my mail when I can't. And there're not many people you can say that about.

"Most women would love your life. I came to Los Angeles to live your life," she declared after I'd unburdened my frustrations on her living room couch.

"I thought I'd love it, too," I grumped. "I'm beginning to think I should have gone to law school."

"You're just down because you had a bad audition," Les consoled. "We have to get you out of the house. What do you want to do?"

"I don't know. What do you want to do?"

"I don't know. You're the one who's depressed. What do you want to do?"

We sounded like the two guys in *Marty*. I had no ideas; I just sat slumped on the couch. Les had little patience for such blatant self-pity. "We can always go to the grocery store," she suggested. "Maybe we'll meet someone cute. I need bananas anyway."

"I've had enough discussions with guys about produce," I returned impatiently. "I want to do something new, meet someone different...I want...Oh, geez, I don't know what I want."

"I've been telling you for months you need to get out more. You know, experiment? Even if it's short term, it wouldn't hurt you one bit to have a man in your life. Honestly, you're going to grow shut."

She had a point. I'd been celibate about a year now, which unsurprisingly enough, coincided with the anniversary of the death of my last romance. Les found my celibacy ridiculously cautious and I thought Les' sexual philosophy foolhardy. The fact that intercourse and AIDS were connected had apparently not penetrated her psyche. She seemed to think a trust fund would protect her from anything. I put more faith in a good condom. My last sexual partner, a fellow actor—who else did I meet, fercrysake?—claimed that I didn't trust him when I insisted on using protection and complained, "Stevie, I can't feel anything!" He was right about me not trusting him; I'd never found much reason to. And if he didn't feel anything, well, that was only fair; neither did I. He was more in love with his mirror than with me. I didn't miss him one bit when he left and I swore I'd never date another actor. And I haven't. Of course, I've haven't dated anybody else either.

This is not to say I'm a lesbian; I'd probably be better off if I was.

But Leslie had a point about rejoining the human race. I was tired of spending most of my free time watching TV with my cat. If I didn't connect with a human soon I'd have to invest in something battery-operated.

"Well, maybe you're right," I reluctantly agreed.

"Great!" Les exclaimed. "Let's go for a drink."

"Okay, but no sports bars!" I warned.

I had a good reason for my objection. Early in our friendship Les confessed that she was having a terrible time meeting guys. "I always see them in cars," she complained. "They have to get out of them sometime, don't they?" She gave the problem some thought and came up with a strategy. "When you're hunting big game you hang out by the watering hole," she decided. "So let's go find a bar. The guys have to get out of their cars to get in the bar, even if it's only to pee. Smart, huh?"

"Les, I am not going to stalk men and trip them as they go to the bathroom," I stated firmly.

"Stevie, sometimes you're so literal," she returned witheringly and waved the local free paper in my face. "I found an ad for a bar in West Hollywood. Look at the picture! This could be the place for us."

I stifled a grin. West Hollywood is known as Boys' Town…but one that has nothing to do with Father Flanagan. Les was crestfallen when I told her it was probably a gay bar.

"Darn, and the guys in the picture looked cute, too," she said wistfully.

"They're probably gorgeous," I agreed. "It's one of life's little tragedies that they're not even remotely interested in us. As a matter of fact, you should consider them competition." I snickered at her look of dismay, and added, "Welcome to Los Angeles."

Les finally decided to try her luck at a local sports bar. "It's Monday night and there'll be a football game on the tube. I bet the place'll be packed."

"But I don't know anything about football," I protested.

"We're not going for the game," she returned shortly.

Well, she was right about the place being packed with guys. Les and I were among a handful of double X's (chromosomally speaking) brave enough to force our way in. And it was loud. Huge bellowing Y people stood shoulder-to-shoulder staring at TV screens scattered around the bar. And since Les and I were smaller and lighter than the men we got shoved around and stepped on. We finally squirmed through the crowd and wedged ourselves onto vacant stools. We screamed our beer orders at the bartender and then gave up on conversation; there was no way we would have been able to hear each other. Having nothing better to do, I finally decided to watch the game on the TV closest to me.

Now, the only sport I ever played was field hockey, which I was forced to take in high school to meet the PE requirement—and I never bothered to learn those rules either. The point of field hockey seemed to be running around for an hour with a stick in your hand and, if you perspired and panted enough to suit the instructor, you got to go home with your teeth. It soured me on team sports generally.

But here I was at a sports bar watching football. Well, how tough could it be to figure out? None of these people seemed to be mental giants and if they could understand it, I could too. I watched intently.

One little guy in a blue and white uniform ran backwards as the others scurried around. The guy on the barstool next to me started yelling encouragement. On TV one big guy in an orange and white uniform jumped on the first little guy and flattened him. My neighbor groaned and drained his beer. Apparently, something bad had happened to the little blue man. Then another little blue man kicked the ball and all the people on the field jumped on it. A man in a striped shirt indicated that the orange side got to play with it and the action started again. Both sides got in circles, broke up, did something with the ball and they all fell down. At this point the man next to me was frothing at the mouth in excitement. Finally, one orange man managed to run quite a distance before being mashed. My neighbor jumped up, gasped something about 'Down', and knocked my beer on my lap. He didn't apologize, probably because he couldn't hear me swearing at him—or maybe because he could. Les hauled me out of the bar before I could get in real trouble. It's a problem having the personality of a T Rex in the body of a bunny.

I never did learn the rules to football.

Les always giggles when I bring up this story. "Okay, no more sports bars," she agreed. "Hey, I know! I read about a jazz place in Hollywood. We've never done that before."

"Do you like jazz?" I asked dubiously.

"No, but it sounds cool, doesn't it?" she said ingenuously.

Well, it did sound cool. I knew very little about jazz myself but it seemed like such a sophisticated sort of thing to do I was willing to go along. I'll try anything within reason once.

So we went to the Vine Street Bar & Grill, clear over in Hollywood. The club was crowded so Les and I sat at the bar, sipped wine, and listened to a quartet. To save calories I decided I'd have a glass of wine, a glass of water, a glass of wine, etc., until my bladder blew up. I was still working on my first glass of wine when the band took a break but it seemed like a good time to get a head start on any leaks. I left for the bathroom and stood in line, waiting impatiently and kvetching with the other women on the shortage of stalls as we did our snake dance down the hall. I'd reached the point where I was blocking traffic when a tall, blond man came out of the men's room. I was turned away, loudly commenting that the management needed to hire a woman to design toilets, when I felt a light touch on my shoulder and heard a soft, deep voice say, "Excuse me?"

I turned, looked up, and got jolted by a pair of clear, blue-gray eyes surrounded by the kind of white you normally only see on bathtubs. I was a tad stunned so I just gawped at him and said, "What?"

The skin around the blue-gray eyes crinkled and the full, wide mouth below them smiled. He gestured, "I'd like to get through."

"Oh sure, I'm sorry, go right ahead," I babbled and stumbled out of the way. At least I didn't wet my pants.

When I returned to my bar stool I related the whole sorry encounter to Leslie. "I feel so stupid. The one time I run into an attractive man I'm standing in the pee line," I said in a minor orgy of self-disgust. "The best thing that can be said is that I wasn't clutching myself."

Leslie waved her hand. "Relax. You'll probably never see him again anyway."

Somehow that didn't make me feel better.

The quartet started again and I sipped my wine moodily. What the hell, I was just out to hear music and be cool. I wasn't out to impress anybody. The goal had been to get out of the house and be entertained; I would meet that goal. I lifted my chin, determined to enjoy myself.

Of course, the fact that you're not cruising for men doesn't mean that some drunken, obnoxious piece of sub-human filth won't take a fancy to you, proceed to ruin your evening, and make a spectacle of himself. Not necessarily in that order.

The two stools next to me had been vacated by a couple and replaced, both stools, by a balding, overweight, very drunk man.

"Buy you a drink, honey?" he belched beerily in my direction.

I smiled coolly, said I was through drinking for the evening, thank you very much, and turned to Les to simulate a conversation. He wouldn't take the hint, though. He grabbed my arm to turn me back to him.

"Hey, good-lookin', I'm offerin' to buy you a drink," he slurred.

"And I already said thanks but no thanks," I replied as I tried to extricate my arm.

"What's the matter? Ain't I good enough for you?"

As a matter of fact he wasn't but I'd done my best to be civil. I could feel his fat, sweaty palm through the sleeve of my dress and I'd had enough. Personally, I think that a woman should be able to sit in a bar, have a drink, and listen to some music without being physically and verbally assaulted by the brain-dead of the world. Well, I'd been taking care of myself for a long time and a fight didn't scare me. My Irish and Latin were both up and I was taking a deep breath to begin an attack when I felt a hand on my shoulder (different hand, same shoulder) and a vaguely familiar deep voice saying, "I thought I recognized you. I was going to call and tell you I was in town. Imagine seeing you here. You've got to come over to the table so we can catch up. Excuse me, friend" (to the drunk) "this is the sister of my college roommate." It was the tall blond man with the blue-gray eyes. I grabbed Leslie's arm and he directed his attention to her. "Well, I haven't seen you in years either…" He continued his patter as he freed my arm from the slug's grip and led Leslie and me to his table. He seated us, returned to the bar, got our drinks, and returned, all without losing his smile or getting into a fight. Very smooth.

As he left to retrieve our wine Leslie asked, "Is he the guy by the bathroom?" I nodded. "I can see why you got so weird. He's cute," she murmured.

"Shut up," I hissed and composed myself as he returned. He placed the glasses on the table and sat down. "Thanks for bailing us out," I said sincerely.

"Oh well," he shrugged, "I hate to see women hassled."

"Were you watching us?" Leslie asked him, with an amused glance at me.

He looked startled for a moment then even in relative dark of the club I could see him blush. "Well, you, I…" he stammered.

"He was just helping out two women, that's all. Right?" I said to spare him and stuck out my hand. "My name's Stephanie but my friends call me Stevie. And this is Leslie. We both thank you very much. Don't we, Les." I kicked her lightly under the table to encourage her agreement, ignored her look of outrage, and turned my attention back to him. "Can I buy you a drink? You know, thanks and all that?"

"Oh no, that's not necessary," he replied, recovering. "More than happy to help out."

The music started again and we all settled back to listen. I caught Les sneaking peeks at him and I caught him sneaking glances at me. There was a lot of sneaking and peeking going on. I again offered to buy him a drink, which he again gallantly declined, but he bought me one (Leslie refused his offer since she was driving). There wasn't much conversation because of the music.

During the next break Leslie excused herself to the Powder Room—the first time I'd ever heard her use that euphemism. Since she hadn't had much to drink it was pretty obvious it was just an excuse to let me flirt.

The two of us sat silently. I waited for this guy to say something. I figured if he was brave enough to stop a drunk from bothering us and smooth enough to do it without a fight, conversation wouldn't be a problem. But he concentrated on his cuticles.

The wait went on with me sitting there expecting the come-on equivalent of the Gettysburg Address and him picking his fingers. Uncomfortable, I finally took the initiative. I cleared my throat and said, "You haven't told me your name."

His head popped up and I got another good look at those eyes. "I'm sorry. It's…Rob Anderson," he said. I wondered at the small hesitation.

"Pleased to meet you, Rob Anderson. Remember me? Stephanie O'Neill? Also known as Stevie?"

I expected him to say suavely, "I hope you'll let me call you Stevie. I'd like to be your friend", or some variation thereof. He said, "I'm pleased to meet you, Miss O'Neill."

Miss O'Neill? The last person to call me that was the receptionist at my gynecologist's office and she was from the Philippines. I got the feeling he wasn't from around here.

"Are you visiting Los Angeles?" I asked to jumpstart the conversation.

"Oh no, I live here."

The end. No further information was forthcoming.

I was baffled. Was it worth the time and effort it would take to see if there was a personality hidden in that attractive hulk? He glanced up at me quickly and looked back at his fingers. I got a shot of those eyes again; intelligent eyes, rather shy. Shy? Of me? How flattering. Maybe this guy had potential if I could pry some words out of him. I redoubled my attempts to make him talk. "And what do you do…uh… what should I call you? Mr. Anderson, was it?"

"Just call me Rob."

"If you call me Stevie," I replied with a Groucho grin.

"Okay."

He smiled into my eyes again. Even the cartilage in my nose melted as I smiled bemusedly back. I enjoyed the moment before I remembered my responsibilities as icebreaker.

"And you do…what?" I continued.

"I'm an engineer."

"What sort of engineer?"

"Civil." Thud.

This was getting ridiculous. I felt like I was talking to a computer. Wait of minute, maybe he was hiding something. A woman living alone like me has to be careful who she takes up with so I backed off and said quickly, "I'm sorry, I don't mean to pry."

"No! That's okay! Go ahead and pry!" he said, sounding slightly panicked.

I eyed him. I was having a little trouble reading this situation. I'm not patient by nature and I was afraid I'd seen the best this guy had to offer. Then it hit me that I was the one who should have gone to the Powder Room. Maybe he was miffed because he was attracted to Les and got stuck with me. A wave of disappointment washed over me closely followed by pique.

Les came back, seated herself jauntily, and beamed at us. "So, where were we?" she sang.

"We were just leaving," I said as I grabbed my purse and stood up.

She looked at me blankly but obligingly got up again. I threw a couple dollars on the table explaining to Mr. Anderson that they were for the tip. I was being petulant and unreasonable but I couldn't seem to stop myself. Leslie was making excuses when I got control. Okay, so maybe he wasn't interested in me but he'd saved my butt and he deserved better than being pouted at. And maybe Les would have liked him. I was mean-spirited, childish…and ashamed.

"I'm sorry," I said to Rob Anderson, "I'm acting badly and I apologize." I turned to Les. "Do you want to stay?" I asked her with as much charity as I could muster.

Les looked at me like I'd lost my mind. "No, I'm ready to go if you are."

Mr. Anderson just sat there looking confused. Then he stood up. "I guess I haven't been very entertaining," he said to me and I smiled wryly, "but I was just trying to figure out how to get your phone number… without being too pushy," he finished in a blurt.

"You want *my* phone number?" I asked.

"I thought that, well, since you seem to like music, maybe, well, maybe we could go to the symphony or something. But I don't want you to feel pressured or anything. I mean, I know you don't know me or anything but I'm not dangerous or anything and, you know, if you wouldn't mind or aren't busy or anything..." His speech dried up under my gaze.

I hesitated for a moment, looked at Les who raised her eyebrows and shrugged, and turned back to him. His face had a slight sheen of sweat. He seemed harmless enough.

"Sure, why not." I quickly wrote my name and phone number on a cocktail napkin and handed it to him. He put it carefully in his wallet and removed a business card.

"Here," he handed it to me, "just so you don't forget who I am."

I put the card in my purse without looking at it. "Thanks." Now they were both looking at me expectantly but I didn't know what to do. Sitting down again would be ridiculous. A quick exit seemed like the only option. "Well, be seeing you. Ready, Les?" We walked out, leaving him standing, and drove home in Les' Volvo.

"That, without a doubt, was the strangest attempted pick-up I have ever seen," Les commented en route. "What's the business card say?"

I dug it out of my purse, turned on the interior light, and read: "'Robert Anderson, Department of Water and Power, City of Los Angeles.'" I frowned. "Department of Water and Power? He told me he was an engineer!"

"The city needs engineers to map out sewer lines and that sort of thing. He's probably legit," said Leslie.

"Anything's possible," I said doubtfully.

Leslie smiled. "What are you going to do if he calls?"

"I'm not going to worry about it." I mused over the card then put it away, out of sight and out of mind. I forgot all about the guy and the card.

A week later I got home from the library to find a message on my box: "Stevie O'Neill? This is Rob Anderson. We met at the Vine Street Bar and Grill? I was wondering, well, I mentioned the symphony and I have two tickets and I was wondering...well, I know it's late to ask someone out for Saturday night but if you'd like to go..." He sounded like he was strangling then managed to leave a phone number.

Of course! The guy with the great eyes and no verbal skills. I called

Leslie. "Remember that guy at the bar last week? The one who saved us from the drunk? Well, he just left a message asking me to the symphony," I announced.

"I didn't know you liked classical music," Les said, surprised.

"Maybe I do. I've never really listened to any," I said.

"Oh," Leslie said, nonplussed, then asked, "So? You going to go?"

"I don't know," I said uncertainly. "He seemed nice but for all I know he could be Ted Bundy's evil twin. Besides, he doesn't know how to talk. It could be an absolutely horrible evening."

"Meet him downtown," Leslie advised impatiently. "That way he won't even have your address. And you won't have to worry about talking. You're not supposed to talk through the music."

"Yeah," I said unconvinced.

"And the best argument of all is," here Leslie paused impressively, "what else do you have to do? Your cat can survive one Saturday night without you. Honestly, you make such a big deal out of everything. A good-looking guy just asked you to a concert; you don't have to marry him!"

"Okay, okay, I'll go," I said. "What should I wear?"

After we thrashed out the wardrobe question I called Rob Anderson and told him I'd love to go to the symphony with him. He sounded vaguely pleased even when I told him I preferred to meet him there. I hung up before he got too tangled up in his tongue and I started regretting my decision.

I had a date for Saturday night just like a normal person! I just hoped Pudgy wouldn't feel abandoned. I'd leave the TV on so she wouldn't miss the 60's sitcoms she liked so much.

chapter 2

Saturday I got dressed up in a casual gray jacket, black slacks and running shoes, and parked in the Music Center garage. I checked my make-up in the rearview mirror, smoothed my hair, admired the effect, and walked up to the Dorothy Chandler Pavilion. Rob Anderson was standing on the steps outside the doors, scanning the crowd. I didn't remember him being so tall. He looked big and a little forbidding compared to the people around him. I also didn't remember him being that good-looking, I mused as I trudged up the steps. He was positively dapper in a suit and tie and I was positively underdressed compared to him, I noted uncomfortably as I waved to get his attention. His eyes lit up and he ran down to meet me.

"Have you been waiting long?" I asked.

"No, I just got here myself."

We stood, smiling and nodding at each other, a little stupidly. The difference in our heights was even more daunting when we were on the same level. Maybe it was because I was wearing flats but I had to lean back to look up at him.

"Six foot three. Why?" he said when I asked.

"No reason," I replied and mentally vowed to wear heels from now on—or start learning the lyrics to *Follow the Yellow Brick Road*. "Well, should we go in?"

"Oh! Sure." He pulled two tickets from his jacket pocket. "I don't know how good these seats are. I got them last Wednesday."

The usher directed us to the fourth floor, second balcony. Our seats had absolutely no legroom. It was like flying coach—the only thing

17

missing was peanuts. And we were so high up the pigeons were worried about us. We could see the orchestra but it was basically just a black blob in the distance. These were not great seats.

I tried to cross my legs but quit when I kicked the woman sitting in front of me. I finally splayed my feet out so I could keep my knees together without getting a cramp. Rob was even worse off because he was roughly twice my size. He hunched his big shoulders around his knees and smiled at me weakly.

"Do you come to the symphony often?" I asked. I wasn't trying to be sarcastic; it just came out that way.

Rob smiled ruefully—he had a whole repertoire of smiles to take the place of words—and said, "Not on Saturday. Look, this is terrible. If you'd like to leave…"

"Oh no, we're here now. I might as well see what it's all about."

The orchestra started out with a weird little ditty by somebody I'd never heard of. It was all clanks and tinkles; there was no recognizable melody and you couldn't dance to it. The audience was so full of coughers it sounded like a TB ward. I huddled in my seat wishing I'd never come.

Then they played Beethoven's Emperor Concerto. It started off slow and soft and then turned into a party. No music I'd ever heard made me feel like that, almost exultant. At the end I had a silly grin plastered on my face. I turned to Rob who'd been watching my reaction. "How come I've never heard that before? It's wonderful!" I exclaimed.

Rob said, "I'm glad you like it. I grew up with Beethoven. My mother played it every night before we went to sleep."

We smiled at each other delightedly. Conversation be damned, contact had been made. We didn't even fight over the armrest during the second half of the program. Rob gallantly volunteered to hold my hand—if I had no objection, of course. I didn't. My arm fit snugly inside his. He wasn't huge anymore, just big enough to fit comfortably around me.

After the concert he offered to buy me a drink. "It'll have to be downstairs," he said apologetically. "I took the bus because it's such an expensive hassle to park here."

"I've got my car if you'd rather go somewhere else," I offered.

"Tell you what," he said, "how about if we go to my place and pick up my car. I can lose this tie and get into something more comfortable. Then

I'll take you to a piano bar in Old Pasadena. How's that sound?"

I'd spend my formative years in the Valley so Pasadena sounded like an adventure to me.

"But we take my car, okay?" I stipulated. I wasn't about to get trapped with someone I didn't know very well without wheels. The fact that he was big enough to knock me on the head and take the car and me didn't filter through my little brain.

I followed his directions and in ten minutes we were at his Echo Park apartment. I'd never been in this neighborhood either. Funny how you can spend your whole life in a city and not know much about it.

I hesitated when he invited me in while he put on a sweater but curiosity won out over caution. You can tell a lot about a person by how they live. He seemed to sense my distance and the reason for it because he was careful not to crowd me. Which was hard in his tiny studio.

I stood in the doorway briefly taking stock. Rob Anderson was either in training to be a Spartan or a monk. The whole apartment consisted of three rooms: a tiny bathroom, a tiny kitchen, and a tiny living area. In the living area were a desk and chair, a couch (a hide-a-bed, I assumed), a tiny color TV, and a monster stereo system perched on a brick and board arrangement. He had one floor lamp by the couch, and a table lamp on the desk. Two ties hung off the doorknob of what turned out to be a closet. Everything was so small I felt like Gulliver. I can't imagine how someone his size tolerated it.

I sat on the couch and looked around some more as he rummaged in the bathroom. He had a CD collection of half classical music, half rock & roll. A large pile of magazines was right next to me on the floor so I ruffled through them: *Time, Stereo Review, National Geographic, Playboy* (on the bottom), and *Car & Driver*.

There was a portrait on the desk that showed an unsmiling couple in their sixties. All they needed was a pitchfork to be a reasonable facsimile of Grant Wood's *American Gothic*.

Rob came out of the bathroom and grabbed the jacket hanging on the desk chair. I gestured to the picture. "Those your parents?"

He grinned. "Yeah. We can't get them to smile in front of a camera. It makes for a depressing picture."

"It does look like a mug shot," I agreed then gulped. He just laughed, thank goodness.

I surveyed his cell again trying to think of something charming to say. "You're so neat," I commented gamely.

Rob laughed again. I seemed to delight him. "It's not much, is it," he said, "but it's cheap. Let's go. You know how to get to Old Pas from here?"

I didn't, of course, and since he'd earned a measure of trust by not immediately jumping my bones I offered to let him drive my Miata. "But only if you know how to drive a stick," I warned.

His face lit up at my suggestion. "Stevie, just give me the keys," he said confidently.

It was a wild ride up the Arroyo Parkway. I don't mean to imply that he took unnecessary chances but he put the car through its paces. He wound it out in every gear and took joy doing it. Compared to him, I drove like a little old lady. I sat in the passenger seat, white-knuckled, through the curves. I guess he noticed I was a little pale around the gills. "Don't worry," he shouted over the whine of the engine, "I'll get us there in one piece."

He whipped into a minuscule parking space, led me to the bar, and ordered me a gin-tonic. The exhilaration of the drive had worn off his shyness and I didn't have to work hard at all to pry information out of him. I found out that he did in fact work for the City of Los Angeles as an engineer and specialized in hydraulics. He told me that he was 27 years old, had grown up in South Dakota, and had been in the Marines.

"The Marines?" I interrupted, unsettled. Weren't they supposed to be the gung ho psychotics of the armed forces? "Why'd you join the Marines? Did you want to like…kill people or something?" I asked with an uncertain smile.

He returned my smile, amused. "I spent most of my time as a clerk," he explained. "I needed money for college. And the discipline didn't hurt either." He continued with his recitation. He had gotten his Bachelor's Degree at South Dakota State University and was working on a special water project for the City of Los Angeles. He was a registered Republican ("A Republican!?" "I know; it's not politically correct.") and had never been married. His parents and three married older brothers still lived in South Dakota. He was a real solid citizen; not the type that I'm normally attracted to—probably because I'd never met one before.

He sipped his beer. "I don't usually talk that much. Your turn. Tell me about you."

Usually I didn't listen that much and I wasn't sure where to start after all that.

"Well, I'm a Democrat," I began.

He blew that off. "I figured. Are you originally from California?"

"Yup. Angelino born and bred," I said.

"You must like it here."

"I guess so. I've never really spent time anywhere else so I haven't got anything to compare it to. Well, I lived in Texas because I have relatives there but I was only there about a month because I couldn't stand…" I broke off because I didn't like getting this personal about myself. "Never mind, it's not important. What else do you want to talk about?"

He seemed faintly surprised at my abruptness but he obligingly switched topics. "So tell me what you do."

I told him about my MFA in theater, my part-time teaching job at a community college, and the trials and tribulations of a struggling actress. He looked impressed.

"I thought you looked familiar. I bet I've seen you on TV," he said with a pleased smile.

"Probably. I've done some commercials."

"Have you done any movies?"

"Small parts in lousy films." I shrugged. "I call them lousy because I ended up on the cutting room floor."

"It sounds exciting. You must like it."

I swirled my drink around. "I thought I would. You know, when you're in college you do great theater, plays by Tennessee Williams or Eugene O'Neill. You get to be a person. But that's college. The movie parts I get sent out for are either prostitutes or mommies. They're all one-dimensional characters, mostly all victims, and they're all supposed to get naked. It's pretty boring. And I won't strip so I don't get cast a lot." I sipped my gin-tonic.

"Why don't you just do theater?" he asked.

I smiled wryly. "No money. And I have the same problem with professional theater. The stuff that's being produced these days, at least in Los Angeles, has to be cutting edge, which means nudity. Apparently, it's in the writer's handbook that if you have a woman in a play, she has to spend a certain amount of time prancing around in the buff. And let me tell you, those stages are cold and drafty. You could get pneumonia up there. But, to be fair, the current theater scene has become an equal opportunity exploiter. Everybody has to take off their clothes, not just the women. I almost feel sorry for the men with their whozits hanging out. One of those cold drafts hits them and their genitals shrivel up like a chicken neck and two acorns. Not very impressive." I surprised a yelp of laughter out of Rob and I grinned impishly. "I hope you're not shocked."

"Maybe a little bit. But it's funny."

"Well, I always say if you can't laugh about things you'll probably end up jumping off a building. But, really, I hope I didn't offend you. Sometimes my mouth takes off before my brain engages," I apologized with a droll look.

We smiled companionably at each other until Rob found another subject that interested him.

"That's a great little car," he started. "But it seems sluggish. When's the last time you had it tuned up?"

"Tuned up?" I asked blankly.

"Yeah, tuned up." He looked at me narrowly. "You know what a tune-up is, don't you?"

I find that sort of question condescending and chauvinistic and I was going to reply tartly that, of course, I knew what a tune-up was— except that I really didn't. I'd heard about them on TV, of course, but I had no idea what was involved. This was the first car I'd ever owned, it had taken me forever to learn how to drive it, and I hadn't gotten around to reading the maintenance section of the owner's manual. I knew all the catch phrases so I could talk a good show but that was about it.

I was still trying to think up a good response to the tune-up question when he interrupted with, "When's the last time you had the oil changed?" From the expression on my face it was obvious that I didn't have a good answer for that little chestnut either.

"It still runs," I muttered defensively.

"How long have you had the car?" he asked incredulously.

"About a year. I don't know what you're getting so excited about. I wash it every other week."

I got a brief lecture about car maintenance. Not taking proper care of your car, in his opinion, was analogous to not taking care of your body and could have the same disastrous results.

"Okay, okay," I capitulated, "I'll take it to a mechanic when I have time."

"Tell you what," he said patiently, "I'll come over some weekend and do it for you. As it is, I'll worry about you being stranded on the freeway." And he shook his head.

Part of me was irritated at his assumption of command because he clearly thought I was incompetent. Another part of me was starting to hum *Someone to Watch Over Me.*

"Whatever," I said and checked my watch. "Wow, it's getting late and I've got a long way to drive. We'd better go."

He drove back to his place slowly like he wasn't in a hurry to say goodnight. I was getting set for the wrestling match I was pretty sure was ahead of me when I tried to get my keys back. When Rob parked in front of his apartment I briskly jumped out of the passenger seat and ran around the car. I stood with my arms crossed loosely in front of my chest and was smiling coolly, ready to fend off any unwanted clinches as he unfolded from the seat.

"It was fun tonight," I said pleasantly as I held one hand out expectantly for my keys.

"Yeah, it was," Rob agreed and handed the keys over without a quibble. "I'll call you about the tune-up," he said and held the car door open for me.

This man was a revelation. There was no chance of him getting in my drawers, I was borderline rude, and he was still a gentleman. Maybe decency wasn't dead in the world after all.

"I'd like that," I said. Was that my voice? I hadn't sounded so sweet and dewy since I was sixteen.

"Good." We shared an awkward pause. "Well, goodnight then."

I got in my car, he closed the door firmly, and I drove off. In my rear-view mirror I saw him standing there, watching me, and I grinned goofily. Warm fuzzies were cuddling in my stomach, which is distinctly uncharacteristic. Cynicism, anger, contempt; these were all familiar emotions for me after dates, but warm fuzzies? The Iron Woman in me felt a patch of rust coming on.

All the next day I waited by the phone expecting to hear from Rob. Nothing. Monday, still nothing. Tuesday, I got distracted by a callback on a beer commercial, which I took as a great compliment. Beer ads specialize in pretty women and I was flattered to be considered in that light. My feminist side scolded me for allowing myself to be used as a sex object; I should insist on being appreciated for my mind. *But let's face it, honey,* I told my feminist self, *ain't nobody paying cold hard cash to admire my mind.* I find a mild case of schizophrenia common in most women my age.

Wednesday, I was notified that I had the beer job which shot on Monday and Tuesday of the next week. I still hadn't heard from Rob but by then, I'd given up on him. I scolded myself for allowing myself to get so goofy. I'd been alone for so long I was probably imagining virtues in Rob Anderson that he didn't possess. If he didn't call again I'd survive; he was just another man who hadn't followed through. Life could be worse. I had my classes to teach and my laundry to do. My agent wasn't being snotty with me, I still had Leslie to play with, and Pudgy helped keep me warm at night. I went to the library and checked out some bodice-rippers.

Sunday the son-of-a-bitch called. I was pleasant but cool after he identified himself. Rob could tell that all wasn't as it should be.

"Am I interrupting something?" he asked.

"Not really," I said loftily.

"Maybe I should call back later."

"Depends on what you called about," I replied, undercurrents rippling through my voice.

"Are you mad at me?" he asked cautiously.

"Me? Mad at you? Why on earth would I be mad at you?" I said with my best Noel Coward airy laugh.

"Perhaps I called too soon. I wasn't sure when a good time would be. I know you're busy and I didn't want to bother you."

What we had here was failure to communicate. I'd been pissed off because he hadn't called soon enough and he was just trying to be polite. I thawed considerably.

"I'm sorry, I guess I expected…" How was I supposed to finish that? That I expected him to be on my doorstop with concert tickets last Sunday (that he didn't have my address was beside the point); that I expected my condo carpeted with roses; that I expected him to battle a dragon for me on a white horse; that I expected a damn phone call much, much sooner?

"…nothing," I finished lamely.

"I was hoping you were free sometime this week," he continued.

"This week?" I dithered. "Well, I'm shooting a commercial tomorrow and Tuesday…"

"Really!? What for?"

I told him the brand of beer, that I actually got a few lines, and that if it played nationally I could earn megabucks. He crowed and congratulated and made much of me. And if that doesn't cause your kidneys to flow into your pantyhose, nothing will.

"Let me take you to dinner Tuesday to celebrate," he suggested and I graciously accepted. We made arrangements for him to pick me up at home—yes, I gave him my address and directions on how to get there—and we regretfully parted to pursue other aspects of our respective lives.

I immediately called Leslie. She listened to my excited babbling calmly.

"I don't want to pop any bubbles," she said, "but I don't understand all this excitement. You told me yesterday that you'd probably never see him again and now he calls and you're all nuts. What's with you anyway? You hardly know the guy."

That stopped me. What was with me anyway? In the cold light of Leslie's rationality my reaction was inappropriate. I didn't know what to say.

"Shut up!" I mumbled and went to bed. I'd worry about my lunacy later. I had a long day ahead of me.

The shoot went smoothly. I was in a buoyant mood and didn't even object to my costume of T-shirt and short shorts. The only bad moment came when the director asked the costumer if they couldn't get a padded push-up bra so I looked like I had 'something'. *I had 'something' all right*, I mentally snarled, *they just weren't of zeppelin proportions*. But I rose above it. I didn't even get mad when the costume lady asked me if I'd ever considered installing implants. Installing—what a word for it. It sounded like she was talking about putting two washing machines on my chest instead of silicone sacks. I politely told her no and she tsked tragically like I'd rejected chemotherapy. You gotta love the business.

I paid particular attention to the actors on the set. If my response to Rob Anderson was the result of mere neediness I'd probably go bonkers over them, too. They were handsome young men, not particularly bright, but very charming. We had some laughs but nothing went twang. Curiouser and curiouser.

Tuesday night I got home in time to switch from heavy camera war paint to street make-up, change clothes, and feed Pudgy. Rob rang my bell punctually which was good; it'd been a long day and I was hungry. Rob looked impressed when I let him in—not with me, with the condo. My townhouse was a two-story, three-bedroom, two-bath place. It had a fireplace, formal dining room, and a breakfast nook in the kitchen. It was light and airy and even had a small yard.

He looked around in appreciation. "How can you afford the rent on a place like this?"

"I own it," I said.

He looked surprised. "You must be more successful at acting than you let on."

"Maybe I'll explain over dinner. Let's go, I'm hungry."

He led me out to his car—an eight-year-old Buick sedan. My gallant knight was going to whisk me away in the chivalrous equivalent of an oxcart. Now, most twenty-something men I knew didn't drive family cars. I don't consider myself a snob—all right, I'm a snob—but a Buick sedan went right on the debit side with Republican membership. I was disgusted with myself for wasting a week being in such a stew over this man.

I am not a well woman.

Then he opened the passenger door for me, got me settled, and shut my door before going around to the driver's side. My opinion of him did another whipsaw. Not only do most twenty-something men not open the car door for you, you're lucky if most parts of you are in the car before they take off.

"I thought we'd go to the Charthouse unless you'd rather do something else," he said.

"Fine with me," I agreed and we putted off in the Buick.

"You've kept your car in good shape," I commented, attempting to be charitable.

He glanced over at me and smiled teasingly. "It runs. I bought it from my dad two years ago when he got a new one."

He bought his father's old car. What was I to make of this new information? This could mean a) he was poor, b) he was cheap, c) he had weird taste in cars, or d) none or all of the above.

"Oh?" I said encouragingly, hoping he'd tell me more.

He stopped at a red light and turned to look at me. The amused look in his eyes told me he knew perfectly well what I was getting at. "I'm saving my money to go back to school," he explained.

I hate getting caught in my finagling. "You must think I'm awfully nosy," I apologized.

"I'm flattered that you're curious about me, Stevie."

We exchanged a smile. I decided to sit back and let him unfold in his own sweet time. He seemed to have broken the sound barrier so it wasn't up to me to poke and prod and pry. Besides, I was tired.

Shooting a commercial doesn't look difficult but keeping your energy level controlled and up, take after take after take, takes a lot out of you. It felt good to sit back and sip on a glass of cabernet. Rob was attentive but not intrusive, capable but not overbearing. I was relieved that my initial positive impression of him had been correct.

He asked me about the shoot and I rambled on about that until our table was ready. He asked me questions about my teaching, my MFA— just general stuff. He was a great listener which is terrific because, even tired, I'm a great yakker. He laughed at my silly stories, admired my initiative, and just seemed interested in me generally. Which was a real departure for me. Most of the men I've dated want me to flatter and listen to them. It was fun being on the other side and definitely good for my ego. We were having coffee when, looking a little uncomfortable but determined, he said, "I know it's none of my business but this has been on my mind since I saw where you lived. How do you come to own such a nice place? And your car isn't cheap. Teachers don't make that kind of money, especially part-time ones, and you said that you didn't earn all that much acting. So tell me; how can you afford it all?"

"Why? You want to 'borrow' money?" I asked with a side-long look at him. "Most of the men I meet at least wait until the third date to try to get cash out of me."

He seemed shocked. "I would never ask a woman for money!" he declared.

That's what they all say. I sipped my coffee and stared at him. "Just wondering why you want to know."

He met my eyes levelly. "I was just curious. Now I'm sorry for asking. Would you like an after-dinner drink?"

Okay, the man wasn't after my fictional millions. He just suffered from perfectly normal curiosity. If I could pry I guess he could, too.

"You know what? Since you're driving I would like another glass of wine. And to pay for it, I'll tell you the whole silly story," I offered.

I flagged down the waitress and ordered. He just had more coffee. We waited until she brought the wine and I started.

"Well, my mother was a Latina from Texas, I look like her..."

"She must have been a beautiful woman," Rob murmured.

"She was," I agreed, smiling. "And my father, I think but I'm not sure, was an illegal immigrant from Northern Ireland. Anyway, my mother's family were good traditional, Catholic control freaks who had Mom's life all planned out for her. They disowned Mom when she married some poverty-stricken nobody like my Dad and left home for California. Which doesn't seem to have bothered her much. She always went her own way. I guess Dad must've gotten legal when he married Mom because I don't remember any trouble with the INS. But I never had any contact with any extended family either. Anyway, Mom and Dad had a bar and grill out in the Valley. Dad ran the bar—figures, doesn't it? Irish and all that?—and Mom was in charge of the restaurant. They owned that property and we had a nice little house. I was an only child and, boy, did I make out. I remember Christmases, Mom and Dad would..."

I found I was having a hard time talking.

"Throat's dry," I said gruffly to Rob and turned my head away. He didn't say anything. He didn't try to grab me and moan over me. I mentally blessed him for his restraint.

"Listen, we can talk about this some other time," he said quietly after a moment.

I sipped some wine and said, "That's all right. I'm told it's good to discuss this sort of thing. Of course, the people who say it usually feed off other people's misery and are full of shit. But I suppose it's possible they're right."

He nodded so I plunged on.

"See, my parents were killed in a car accident when I'd just turned sixteen. Drunk driver. It's sort of ironic. They were on their way home from closing their bar. I got the call at four o'clock in the morning." I had another sip of wine. "Well, to make a long story short, they both left good-sized life insurance policies, the business, and the house. I sold the real estate, bought the townhouse, and invested the rest. I paid for the Miata out of my own earnings. I'm not rich but I'm doing all right."

I smiled cheerfully, trying to lighten the atmosphere, but he still looked puzzled.

"But you were only sixteen, didn't you have a guardian?" he asked.

"That's another ugly story. The authorities contacted my mother's family in Texas. They weren't interested until they found out how much money was involved; then they took me in. See, the idea was to turn me into a good tortilla-making incubator while I "contributed" toward my upkeep with the cash. I lasted one month with them then ran back to California and petitioned the court for adult status. The court allowed me my freedom as long as I agreed to their choice of school and assigned an attorney to be trustee of the estate. For a fee, of course. But I figured better the attorney than the familial sharks. The attorney turned out to be pretty honest and only took what was legal. When I turned twenty-one, the bulk of the estate reverted to me and you see me as I am now, educated, in possession of a condo and a car, and struggling the rest of the time to make ends meet. I learned long ago not to touch the principal. So, anything else you want to know?"

He pushed his coffee cup around. "What do you do at Christmas?"

"Have dinner with whatever friends don't have family obligations. Or Jewish friends. Christmas doesn't mean much to them. I've even just gone to a movie and had dinner with my cat. Have you met Pudgy yet? She's a great cat. We're each other's family."

He pushed his coffee cup around some more. "You've really had it tough," he said finally.

"Just for a couple of years. Don't waste pity on me. There's a lot of people who've had it a whole lot worse."

"What do you do when you get sick or in some sort of trouble? You don't have anybody to fall back on."

"Sure I do. That's why God made friends...and money. You'd be surprised how independent that makes you."

He obviously didn't believe me. "No down side at all?"

Sympathy was nice but this was getting a little ridiculous. This was a date not a sensitivity session, after all, so I looked him right in the eye and said, "Not really."

He backed off, thank God. "Sounds like it works for you."

"It does." I finished my wine. "Well, it's been a long day and I'm tired. Are you ready to go?"

"Anytime you are."

He paid the check and we left. We talked of inconsequential things, like traffic patterns, on the way. I was priming myself for a goodbye scene. I know, he'd been a perfect gentleman at the symphony but this was the second date. Time for a big move. My gut feeling about this man was that he was decent but my experience warned me...Well, in my experience the act at the front door involved some heavy-duty maneuvering, particularly if the man paid for dinner. The quid pro quo seemed to be satisfactory sex, at least on the man's part, a shower, and possibly breakfast if the man found you worthy. I was tired, over-fed, owly, and emotionally drained from my stint in the confessional. Besides, I'd made it a policy not to part with sexual favors after one dinner. I've read that some prostitutes command $300 per session and I've never had a meal that cost anywhere near that.

He parked on the street and walked me to my door.

"You're quiet," he observed.

"Just tired," I said, mentally girding myself for the whining and guilt tripping when I didn't invite him in. It takes a lot of concentration to shut a guy down without ending up with a broken jaw. I could evade the Roman hands and the tongue thrust down my throat like an undigested oyster, I encouraged myself and checked my mental focus. Yeah, I was ready. I had my keys out, ready to unlock and run. Rob appeared thoughtful during the short walk up the sidewalk.

I unlocked the door and turned to him, all defenses up. "Thank you for dinner, Rob, I enjoyed it."

He put his hands on my shoulders, looked into my eyes, and said, "So did I." He leaned forward and kissed my mouth firmly but briefly. Then he stepped back and asked, "Can I call you again next week?"

Wait a minute. He'd done it to me again. Where was the clutching, the oyster, the whining? You get your mind all prepared for something awful and when it doesn't happen you feel like you've stumbled. I was so flummoxed all I could do was nod and mumble, "If you really want to."

He tipped my chin up, kissed me again, and said, "I want to." Then he walked to his car.

You know, he could have tried a little harder. Dammit, now that I didn't have to kiss him I wanted to. On the spur of the moment I called out, "I thought you were going to fix my car."

He stopped and turned back to me. "How about Saturday?"

"It's a date," I said. By God, he'd get some kissing then.

chapter 3

I really needed to discuss this guy and his unusual behavior so the next day I bought a six-pack of Diet Pepsi, a big bag of Nacho Cheese-Flavored Doritos, and waited for Leslie to come home from work. The minute I heard her key in the door across the hall I was out like a shot, on her couch, and offering her what was left of the Doritos. As she put her briefcase down and helped herself to a soda I described every word, every look, and every move of my date. "He's such a gentleman, he never even tried to do anything!" I said munching Doritos furiously until another thought occurred to me. "Maybe he didn't want to. Is there something wrong with me?" I asked.

"Stevie, you'd probably have tried to kill him if he had tried something," Les said helping herself to handful of chips.

"Yeah, but he didn't know that!" I argued.

"You'd be surprised," Leslie said dryly. "You're pretty obvious sometimes. Besides, this guy sounds like he's been around the block a few times. He probably wouldn't be happy just necking with you."

"Mmmmmmm," I murmured and munched. Then Les' slighting tone percolated through my self-absorption. "I wouldn't be happy just necking either," I declared. "I'm not in high school anymore. Maybe I want to have sex, too."

Les looked amused. "You, have sex? You?"

"I'm a normal woman with normal needs," I said defensively. "It's time I left the convent. He's a nice guy. You yourself said he's cute, and you yourself said I was going to grow shut. He's coming over to fix my car this weekend. I'll get him then," I decided.

"What's wrong with your car? I thought it still ran," Les asked.

"It does. But he says it needs a tune-up and oil change and he offered to do it. Isn't that sweet?" I said with a smile. "You know, I should do something nice for him."

"Sleeping with him's nice," Leslie commented.

I gave her a withering look. "That's for me," I said. "Think of something nice for him."

"Take him out to dinner," Leslie suggested. "Men always like food."

"That's so impersonal," I objected then said, "I know! I can cook dinner!" Then my face fell. "But I don't know how."

Leslie eyed me in disbelief. "I thought your mother had a restaurant."

"She did. But she said she never wanted me to end up in a kitchen like her. So I never learned to cook."

"You could always get a cookbook," Leslie said reasonably.

I perked up. "Yeah!" Then my face fell. "I don't have anything to cook with either," I admitted.

"I guess we better go shopping," Les said and stood up. "It would help to know what you're going to make. Then we'll know what to shop for."

I stopped, perplexed. "I don't know." I looked at Les expectantly. "You're a WASP, Les. What's something your dad would like?"

"Roast beef and mashed potatoes," she said promptly. "And boiled vegetables and apple pie. But that kind of cooking's not easy," she warned.

"It can't be that tough," I said slightingly.

We went to Macy's and bought a box of pots and pans, a pie plate, a rolling pin, and some bowls. As we shopped we got into a long philosophical discussion about male/female courting rituals. According to Leslie the masculine version involved wrenches, screwdrivers, and grease. The feminine equivalent came out of the kitchen.

"You're a perfect example," Leslie lectured. "He's changing oil and you're trotting out the pots and pans. To my knowledge this is the first time I've seen you exhibit any signs of domesticity. You must really like this guy."

"You're full of shit," I retorted. "What cookbook should I buy?"

We argued whether demonstrations of affection through specialized tool usage were cultural or genetic until we went home. We never did settle the question.

I spent the week cleaning and studying my cookbook. The recipes didn't sound all that tough. I enlisted Leslie one more time to help me make out a grocery list. Then the only planning left was personal protection. I wasn't on the Pill because my sex life had heretofore been limited, to say the least, and I didn't want to put any more hormones in my body than were absolutely necessary. My fantasy life was rich because I read a lot of books but my personal experience had been limited to a few unsatisfactory boyfriends.

"I have a diaphragm in a drawer somewhere," I told Leslie. "I guess it's time to dig it out and make sure it still works."

"Don't bother, you'll never go through with it," Leslie taunted. "You're too afraid you'll catch something."

"I will too do it," I said indignantly. "I just don't know if I should buy condoms or some sort of spermicidal jelly. My last boyfriend carried condoms in his wallet. But what if Rob doesn't?" I thought feverishly. "I guess I better buy some of everything just in case. But what if I get into an accident on the way home from the drugstore and the ambulance people find all this stuff in my purse? I'd just die. And what would Rob think if I have it all on hand? Will he think I'm a skank?"

My mind was squeaking around like a gerbil on a wheel. Dating's gotten so complicated these days.

Leslie and I decided that Rob should be in charge of the condom. I suppose I should have called and told him but I had enough on my mind. I finally found my diaphragm and checked it for holes. I washed off the spider webs, dusted it with talcum powder, and left it in the bathroom.

Rob pulled up in his Buick on Saturday about noon. I nervously met him at the door, not quite sure when or how to begin the seduction—or dinner, for that matter. Rob didn't seem the least bit interested in me, he was all business. He announced he was ready to go to work and asked for the keys to the Miata. Then he went right back outside and pulled a pair of overalls out of the trunk of his car. Honest to God, they were real, grease-stained, patched overalls. He pulled them on with as much reverence and seriousness as if they were vestments and he was a priest preparing for a holy ritual. Rob then removed tools from his trunk. He grabbed his 'real jack' (my jack wasn't good enough) and spread his tools out on a clean towel. I didn't know whether to be relieved or disappointed that he hadn't grabbed me so I asked if there was anything I could do to help. He answered absently, "No, you'll just get in the way" and lifted the hood of the Miata.

Good enough. I went to the kitchen to unpack my pots and begin my trial by fire as hausfrau. I rolled up my sleeves, opened my cookbook, and got to work.

The pictures in the cookbook made everything look easy and I felt confident in my ability to duplicate them. This wouldn't be that tough for an educated person like me. After all, how many housewives do you know with Master's degrees?

I decided to make the pie first. That way, you see, it would be out of the way and I'd have room for the roast in the oven. Besides, the picture was so pretty it made me hungry. The cookbook said to "blend the flour and shortening with a pastry blender until the mixture resembles large peas". If you didn't have a pastry blender supposedly flicking two knives would do the trick. Well, I didn't even know what a pastry blender was so I grabbed two knives and 'flicked'. You know, you can flick with your two knives all day long and not get anywhere; I finally ended up mashing the shortening and flour together with a fork. My mess didn't resemble large peas—hell, it didn't resemble anything in the known universe—but I threw the water in anyway. Five tablespoons of water didn't make any discernable difference so I kept adding more water until things stuck together. I looked in the bowl doubtfully. The flour mixture seemed a little gluey but what did I know? Ahh, it'd probably turn out "light and flaky". It better. I peeled the apples.

Then I tried rolling out my sticky dough. It stuck to the rolling pin, it stuck to the counter, it stuck to everything it came in contact with. I was almost weeping with frustration by the time I got it rolled out and fitted into the pan. When I threw the apples in and covered them with crust my pie looked like a sweaty fat woman's thighs—sort of white, shiny, and lumpy. But ignorance is bliss and I was confident my pie would bake up like the picture in the book. I did make a mistake with the oven, though. I forgot to turn the knob from broil to bake. I caught the error halfway through the cooking process but the top got a little dark. Maybe Rob wouldn't notice.

It seemed like a good time for a break so I wandered out to see how Rob was doing. He was standing next to a big tub of black gunk.

"That's the old oil," he said in response to my questioning look.

"Looks disgusting," I commented.

"It is," he agreed forcefully. "You have to change the oil every six months or three thousand miles."

"I'll try to remember," I said lightly and watched as Rob did something to the engine with a wrench. He had beautiful hands. The fingers were long and slender but strong. He had the hands of a sculptor. My mouth went dry and my face got hot. To cover my confusion I picked up a tool and asked, "What's this?"

Rob took the tool away from me and replaced it in its spot on the towel. "It's a gap gauge and please don't touch anything."

"Okay," I said and sidled closer to him pretending to be interested in what was under the hood. "So. What are you doing now?"

"I'm changing the spark plugs," he said patiently. Sort of.

"And where are they?"

"Stevie, I'm busy. Don't you have anything to do?"

"I was just going to ask you when you wanted dinner. I'm making a roast," I said importantly.

Rob's face perked up with pleased interest. "A roast? Gee, you didn't have to do that. But I should be finished in a couple hours," he said.

"Well, good. I guess I better get back to work." I wandered back to the kitchen.

The next few hours were pretty hectic. I removed the pie to make room for the roast. It didn't look at all like the picture. I guess I should have caught the mistake with the broiler knob earlier. My pie looked like a tiny manhole cover. I shrugged despairingly. Nothing I could do about it now except hope it tasted better than it looked.

The cookbook said to put the roast on a meat rack and cook it for twenty minutes a pound. I'd forgotten how much the thing weighed and I'd thrown the wrapper in the garbage and didn't feel like getting my hands dirty retrieving it. I estimated the weight; it seemed like five pounds or so. I decided to cook it for two hours just to be on the safe side; I'd read stories about the diseases you can get from undercooked meat and didn't want to take chances. My book suggested a meat thermometer if there was any doubt about cooking time but I didn't have one and Leslie wasn't home. Hell, I didn't have a meat rack either but what earthly difference would that make? I threw the meat in a stockpot, tossed it into the oven, and moved on to the vegetables. I peeled three potatoes, washed my beans, peeled some carrots, and left to take a leisurely shower. I was going to be as gorgeous as possible. Not only was the meal going to be picture perfect, I was too. None of this housewifely frumpiness for me.

By the time I got myself put together and the table set I was running a little late so I turned the vegetables on 'high'. When I thought to check the roast it looked like a 70-year-old Beverly Hills tanning freak, poor desiccated little thing. I must have misjudged the weight. I also overcooked the beans. These early disasters rattled me so badly I tried to save time by pouring the milk on the potatoes while running between the refrigerator and the stove and I tripped over Pudgy who was being helpful underfoot. My mashed potatoes became vichyssoise. When I tried to make gravy I ended up with a pale liquid of flour and water because the roast I chose had no fat on it; what little grease there was stuck the roast to the bottom of the pot. My gravy looked like gruel.

Rob was seated at the table, scrubbed and hungry from a hard day of playing mechanic and looking expectant when I came out of the kitchen with a bottle of wine in my hand. My perfection of make-up and dress was as destroyed as my dinner. I think I looked like I'd been through hard labor and given birth to a monster. Which in a sense was true. I plunked the wine on the table and poured us each a glass.

"I think we better order a pizza," I announced grimly, refusing to meet his eye.

Rob sipped his wine, looked at me carefully, and asked, "Can I see?"

"Yes, but if you say anything or laugh I'll kill you," I warned him.

Rob followed me to the kitchen and looked at the crispy critter of a roast stuck to the bottom of the pot. I was obviously embarrassed and ready to blow, and he seemed to know he had to choose his words carefully.

"What happened?" he finally asked.

"I think I cooked it too long," I said through my teeth.

Rob nodded. His eye lighted next on the "mashed potatoes". He picked up a spoonful and poured it off. He was honestly puzzled.

"Mashed potatoes," I explained.

"Oh! I guess they got a little thin."

"Well, I was in a hurry because I didn't time things right and I was running across the kitchen pouring milk into the pot and Pudgy got underfoot and I tripped and too much milk got poured in and now the potatoes are too runny. So shut up."

He turned to my gruel. "And this?"

"That's gravy."

He picked up a carrot stick and munched. Fortunately, I'd just peeled the carrots so they were still edible. I saw him glance at the pie, flinch, and look away hurriedly.

I was standing there, spoiling for a fight, waiting for the snide comments I was sure were coming.

"Stevie, have you ever tried cooking this kind of a meal before?" Rob finally asked.

"No," I bit off the word. My body language was saying, c'mon, boy, do your worst, give it your best shot, I'm ready for you. C'mon, put 'em up, put 'em up.

"Well," he said finally, "I'm touched that you would make the effort. And the next time you want to try something like this, we'll do it together. But Stevie, I want you to know I really appreciate the thought."

He patted my arm kindly and my defiance and irritation popped like a balloon. I'd stood over my disaster, combative as hell, ready to tear him a new asshole, and he thanks me for ruining his dinner. Plus, he fixed my car. You gotta love a man like that.

Rob was looking wistfully at the roast. He probably hadn't eaten since breakfast so I hesitantly offered him some yogurt. He looked repulsed so I joked feebly, "I didn't cook it, it's probably edible." I poked the roast. "Have you ever seen anything this awful? It looks like King Tut after a bad night." I waved my hand at the carnage in the kitchen. "We might as well laugh. It doesn't do much good to cry," I said giving him permission.

He obliged with a big smile. I smiled back bemusedly, admiring his wide, mobile mouth. He poured more wine and we laughed together. We howled at the potatoes, we screamed over the gruel, we chuckled over the beans, and the pie left us breathless. I don't remember laughing that hard with anyone before—especially at my own expense. But he was laughing at my jokes, not at me. And there's a big difference.

I finally stopped laughing to wipe my streaming eyes. "You want to go to bed now?" I asked him.

Rob looked a little taken aback at my abrupt invitation but pulled himself together quickly. "Okay," he said agreeably.

I led him into the bedroom. I guess I was radiating lust because he abruptly opened his arms just in time for me to walk into them. We kissed. And you know what? There were no fumbling hands or undigested oysters. I specifically remember thinking how good he smelled. Imagine that, liking the way someone smelled. I was enjoying the kiss so much I didn't think about spit or germs, which is normally the only thing on my mind. Wait a minute...spit and germs. And consequences. Time to disengage. I reluctantly pulled back.

"I have to go to the bathroom," I mumbled and hurriedly left. Why is it, I thought sadly as I inserted the slippery diaphragm with shaking hands, books never talk about sordid details like birth control and disease prevention? Because it's stupid and embarrassing, that's why. I spent a lot of time washing my hands; I didn't know how to face Rob. And how in the world was I going to recover the mood?

When I finally got up the guts to return to the bedroom I found Rob had retrieved the wine from the dining room and was standing by the bed, sipping. He smiled when he saw me and offered me his glass. I focused on his hands again. He was wearing a polo shirt and I could see the tendons corded on his forearms. That was so cool. I felt a strong urge to touch him. Lack of mood was no longer a problem. My hormones surged and I think I remember salivating. You don't need to know what was happening at the other end.

I quickly walked to him, touched his arm reverently, and he pulled me into another kiss. Then he undressed me slowly, admiring the view on the way. I apologized for my small breasts. He cupped them in his hands and kissed them.

"They're beautiful," he said simply. "They're perfect with the rest of your body."

By God, after years of being treated like an unsatisfactory dairy cow by the people in my profession that simple compliment almost brought tears to my eyes. The words of approval gave me the courage to undress him. He was long and lean, rangy not bulky. His shoulders were broad and his stomach was flat. He had a slight matting of hair on his chest; it was curly and fine. He tasted slightly of salt.

He picked me up without effort, placed me gently on the bed, and then, well, sex isn't a spectator sport. But we had throbbing this and pulsating that. He was even better than my books; I had my first non-literary orgasm. That was cool, too.

I think God made sex so you'd have something fun to do when you're hungry. It takes your mind off your stomach. Thank you, God. But when we finished Rob's stomach rumbled to remind us we hadn't eaten so we ordered a pizza. I found a bathrobe and Rob put on his pants so we'd be presentable when the food showed up and we went into the living room to wait. Rob eyed the fireplace. "I know it's warm out but how about a fire? I was a Boy Scout," he said, "I can get one going in no time."

I think he was just trying to figure out something useful to do but it sounded romantic to me. "Sure. Want to eat in here? I'll get the plates and stuff," I offered.

He had the fire going by the time I got back. We sat on the couch quietly and watched the flames while we waited for the pizza. I didn't have to yak to mask discomfort and he characteristically didn't say much. I thought it was nice just to be together but he fidgeted a bit. I figured he was just hungry. When the pizza came he insisted on paying for it. He scarfed down two pieces while I picked at mine. By the third piece of pizza he slowed down and started fidgeting again. All his bodily needs had been satisfied so there must be some thing on his mind. I chewed and waited expectantly for whatever was bothering him. He finished his slice of pizza and started on a fourth. Man, this could go on all night.

"Something on your mind?" I prodded.

He looked at me, puzzled, and made a waving gesture between us. "What was this?" he asked.

"I thought you knew," I said and smiled. "You've obviously done it before."

"No, no," he said and took a moment to get his thoughts together. "See, when we went out before you were so skittish I was afraid to touch you. I took it slow so I wouldn't scare you off. Then out the blue you haul me off to bed. I don't understand."

"What's to understand? I changed my mind," I said simply.

"Just like that?" He snapped his fingers.

"Well, no, it took a week." He still looked uncomfortable and I thought I had a pretty good idea what was bothering him. I'd probably make him blush, I'd probably blush myself, but if you can't talk to somebody about contraceptives you have no business having sex with him. I said shortly, "Look, if you're worried about me getting pregnant, don't. That short trip I made to the bathroom? Birth control break. So don't worry that I'm trying to trap you or anything."

He looked momentarily relieved then alarmed as my tone of voice sank in. "I didn't mean to offend you. But I'm glad you brought it up. See, I have a condom with me. Not that I planned on anything but well, you know the Boy Scout motto: Be Prepared." He glanced at me. "Unfortunately, I got...distracted and didn't use it." He took a deep breath and plunged on. "I just want you to know I had myself tested for AIDS recently and I'm clean."

My jaw dropped and I had to snap it shut before my pizza fell out. "You had yourself tested? Why?"

"Well, I'm no virgin. I was hoping we'd get together and I wouldn't come to you if I wasn't healthy. I just want you to know you don't have to worry about disease."

I was a little amazed at the confession. He treated his body like he would a car, periodic diagnostic checks and careful maintenance. Too bad I didn't plan ahead like that. I murmured shamefacedly, "I just worried about getting pregnant. I've never taken an AIDS test. But I've been to my gyno since the last time...well, you know. I had some sort of blood test but I don't know if they looked for that."

Rob said matter-of-factly, "Something probably would have shown up. Besides, it's a little late to worry about it now, isn't it?"

Of course, the nuts and bolts discussion had squelched any further romantic thoughts. We finished up the pizza and I suggested we eat the ice cream I'd bought for the pie. I didn't know what to do with him anymore. I sighed as I grabbed bowls and spoons. Maybe we could make fudge and sit in our jammies. Oh yeah, he didn't have any jammies. Well, he could sit in his underwear. I turned on the TV and we silently sat together on the couch and watched a cable movie as we ate ice cream.

Pudgy chose to put in an appearance and jumped in Rob's lap; he stroked her gently. The fact that she showed up at all surprised me. When people visit Pudge normally scurries under the bed and stays there for the duration. She's a one-person cat and that person is me. I couldn't believe she let him pet her. I was so touched by the picture the two of them made that I snuggled up, too. Rob used one hand to scratch

Pudgy's chin and the other to stroke my neck. The poor man couldn't eat his ice cream. He deserved a reward for his kind ministrations.

"How about if I get tickets to a play for next week?" I asked suddenly. "I could go through the paper and pick out something I think we'd both like. Or maybe there's something you have in mind?"

"No, you know more about it than I do. But let me pay for the tickets."

"You always buy dinner. It's my turn…"

We went on in the vein for a while. We sounded like those two Warner Brothers gophers: 'Oh no, no, no, after you.' 'After you, I insist.' 'Oh no, no, no…'

We compromised: I would buy the tickets and he would buy dinner. He smiled down at Pudgy and quit rubbing her to eat some ice cream. I watched his hands as the spoonful reached his mouth. He sure had a lot of good parts and admiration for them made carnal thoughts rise again. I'd been out of action for a year; I had a lot of time to make up for. I put Pudgy on the floor, took Rob's surprised face in my hands, and kissed him firmly.

"Do you need time to digest or you ready to go back to bed?" I asked.

"Ohh, I think I could handle whatever came up," he said solemnly as he put his bowl and spoon down and stood up quickly. "Race you!"

We had fun making love this time. The urgency was gone and we took our dear sweet time. Afterward, I asked him if he wanted to spend the night.

"I'd like to," he said. "But I didn't bring a toothbrush."

I offered to let him use mine. I figured after what we'd just shared I couldn't possibly get any more germs. I found it amazing how relaxed you can be around a man, especially one you really like, once the sex is out of the way. We were past the tension stage and were acting like friends with a few modifications, like a lot of touching.

I fell asleep that night spooned against him, his arms around me, his breath on my neck. The subject of the condom never came up again. Maybe that was an indication that this was more than a mere roll in the hay for him. I sure hoped so.

Leslie was outside stretching after her morning run when I kissed Rob at the door as he was leaving. The way she grinned I knew I was in for an interrogation. I insisted on bagels and coffee first. "He ate most of the pizza last night," I explained. "I'm ravenous!"

"Pizza!? What happened?"

I made her wait until I got home with a sack full of bagels and cream cheese. Then in between bites I described my culinary nightmare. "That's the last time I ever try to cook!" I concluded.

"I don't want to talk about recipes, I want to hear about the sex!" Leslie said and leered.

"It's sort of personal," I squirmed.

"Since when has sex been personal? This is Aunt Leslie you're talking to," she said then stopped herself. "Oh Stevie," she clucked, "are you getting serious already?"

"Of course not! It's too soon. I'm too busy. Besides, we have nothing in common." I was a little too vehement in my denial. Leslie just raised an eyebrow at me in derision.

"So how was the sex?" she asked softly.

I tried to be cool and sophisticated and ended up grinning goofily. "It was great. Hey, let's get a paper. I told him I'd try to find a play he'd like, something innocuous. I don't think he'd be comfortable with the current crop of homoerotic art that's going around. Geez, sometimes I'm not comfortable with it. Maybe there's something decent at the Taper. He's familiar with the Music Center so he won't be intimidated. And it's reasonably mainstream; the actors'll probably keep their clothes on at least most of the time. I hope so anyway. I don't want his theatrical virgin cruise so be a total blowout. Do you think Wednesday's too soon? I don't want to seem like I'm in love or anything. I'm going to wear heels this time. I think I look too short in flats."

Les listened to me babble and watched me dither in disbelief then announced, "Sounds like you're in over your head already." She stood up. "Well, I need a shower." She sniffed in my direction. "And so do you."

She was out the door before I could throw a bagel at her.

chapter 4

───────────────────────────────────────

Rob dozed through the play—he said he'd had a long day at work—so I volunteered to stay at his place that Wednesday. He was delighted to accept. He offered to buy me dinner on Friday and we had so much fun we spent the entire weekend together at my place. In the following weeks that was our pattern; we'd spend Wednesday night at his place on his crummy little hide-a-bed and Friday, Saturday, and Sunday we'd sleep on my comfortable king-sized bed with Pudgy. Being with him was relaxing. He didn't talk much but he liked to listen to me yak. That's what he said anyway. I chose to believe him and yakked away.

I even took him to the library with me—something I'd never done with a boyfriend before. They'd have thought I was weird. "I always spent a lot of time in libraries. They were sort of a second home," I explained shyly. "There're not a lot of safe places a teenage girl can hang out and a library was always one of them. Besides, all that reading gave me a real edge in school."

"You don't talk like the average 25-year-old," Rob agreed. He read a technical journal while I selected some novels. I found myself gravitating toward science fiction instead my usual collection of bodice-rippers. With him around I didn't need my sex written down for me.

Leslie was a little distant until he fixed a defective outlet in her condo. Then she fell for him, too—in a platonic way, of course. On Saturday mornings Leslie and I would do his laundry and he'd wander around with a set of tools tightening loose hinges and fixing leaky faucets.

After a month of this Rob and I'd lost our individual identities, at least as far as Leslie was concerned. She went to movies with Stevie-and-Rob; she ate pizza with Stevie-and-Rob; she watched TV with Stevie-and-Rob. Pudgy had gotten so used to Rob she followed him around in the morning begging for breakfast.

Once Leslie casually commented on all the time we spent at my place and I said, "His studio is too small. That hide-a-bed must have been designed by Torquemada. I prefer comfort."

"I mean, don't you think you're spending too much time together so early in the relationship?" she asked cautiously. "Don't get me wrong, I like him a lot and I can't believe everything works in my condo but… well…aren't you moving a little fast?"

"No," I said shortly. "As a matter of fact, I'm thinking that he should move in here. If he didn't mind the commute he could live like a person. There's really no point in keeping that crummy little studio." I frowned and nodded to myself. "Yeah, I think it's the right thing to do. It's my birthday next week. I think I'll bring it up then."

Leslie muttered something about bull-headed Leos. I ignored her.

On my natal day I met Rob at the door; he was carrying a small cake box. I told him I had a proposition for him.

"Can it wait? I've got a surprise for you." He went to his car and returned with two wrapped presents. Nobody'd made a fuss over my birthday since my parents died and I got a little misty. Then I focused on the presents and my natural greed won out over nostalgia. I love presents. Some jewelry or killer perfume would be nice.

Rob sang *Happy Birthday* in a surprisingly nice baritone voice and I cut the cake. We each had a piece and then got down to the important business. He handed me the first present, a good-sized box, with a flourish. I kissed him, exclaimed over the pretty wrapping, and ripped it open eagerly. It was a dust-buster.

"A dustbuster?" I asked blankly.

"I wasn't sure what to get you and that's what my mother asked for last Christmas. I know you don't have one and it's something you can use to pick up Pudgy's spilled catfood," he explained.

"A dustbuster," I repeated.

Rob could tell by my expression that my level of enthusiasm for the dust-buster wasn't what he'd hoped for so he pushed the other present toward me. This package was small and slim. This could be the jewelry. I smiled at him and eagerly opened it to find a certificate and a plastic card—from AAA. I looked at him and smiled carefully. "Triple A?" I asked.

"It's a three-year membership," he explained. "I know first-hand you don't take care of your car so I snuck a look at your wallet to see if you belonged to an auto club. You spend so much time on the freeway I worry about you. What if you broke down and couldn't reach me? I know it's not glamorous but it's something you need…" he faltered to a stop.

I sat there, looking at my dustbuster and Triple A card, trying to summon up some proper gratitude. Rob looked stricken at my expression. "You're disappointed," he said.

"No, no. These are very…practical gifts," I protested weakly.

"It's just I've never bought anything for a woman except my mother," he explained.

Oh yeah, Ma Manson of the photograph. I just bet she'd like a dustbuster for her birthday. *She probably asked for rat poison or bug spray, that was practical, too,* I snarled mentally.

Then I pulled myself together. Where were my manners? My last birthday party had been ten years ago. It seemed silly to spoil this one with pouting. Rob had spent some thought and effort selecting gifts he thought I could use. I might have preferred a Rolex but a watch won't do you much good when your car breaks down. Rob was concerned about my safety, which meant he cared what happened to me and that's worth more than a watch I could have bought myself. Once I finally figured out what was going on, I was so touched I got tears in my eyes.

Rob started to panic when he saw the tears. "God, Stevie, I'm sorry. I'll take the dustbuster back. I'll cancel your membership to Triple A. Whatever you say."

The whole situation was getting ridiculous and I started to giggle. Actually, it was sort of a sob giggle because I hadn't gotten over the teary thing yet. Which gave me the hiccups. Rob got me a drink of water and a Kleenex.

"Thanks," I hiccupped after I'd blown my nose. "Forget about returning the presents. They're just fine and thank you very much." I carefully blotted under my eyes to preserve the mascara, then said briskly, "Tell you what; why don't you move in with me?" Rob's eyebrows went up and his mouth dropped open. He didn't seem able to say anything so I pressed ahead with my arguments. "You know we spend a lot of time together and I really enjoy being around you. Doesn't it seem sort of stupid to have separate apartments? I have lots of room and your place is pretty awful, no offense but it is, so…you know…you want to move in with me?" I finished in a rush and waited expectantly.

Rob still didn't say anything. He just ran his hand over his stomach and looked troubled.

"If you're worried about money, don't be. You can pay the monthly maintenance fee or something," I added. He just sat silently so I hurried on, feeling like a fool. "I know it'd be a long commute for you and I don't want to pressure you or anything. It was just a thought really…" I finally dried up. "Rob, say something."

He sighed and said, "Stevie, I've never felt this way about anybody before."

My heart went cold. There was a big 'but' coming and I was pretty sure I wasn't going to like it. Boy, the minute you put yourself on the line something awful happens.

"But?" I prompted.

"I don't know how to tell you this," he muttered and scrubbed his hand through his hair.

"Don't tell me; you have a wife and four kids. Right?" I asked sarcastically.

"No! Nothing like that," he said impatiently then stopped again.

"Then what?!" I demanded. "You're dying and have six months to live?"

He looked shocked. "Of course not. Where do you get these ideas?"

I flounced on my chair and almost broke my tailbone. "What?! Tell me! You better tell me, I'm starting to get mad."

"All right! Calm down!" He started pacing around the room and began, "You know I'm working on a special project for Los Angeles. Well, it's almost done. I begin a Master's program in hydraulic engineering in September."

"That's great! Where you going? Caltech? UCLA? What's the problem?"

Rob ran his hand through his hair again. "I'm going back to Brookings. South Dakota. Where I got my undergrad degree. It's a good school, I already know most of the faculty, and I got a TA job. I can't get that kind of a deal out here."

I sank back in my chair, stunned. He was leaving. For South Dakota. He was leaving me. I looked up at the ceiling, took a calming breath, and asked, "It's July now. When were you planning on telling me?"

He had the grace to look uncomfortable. "We don't talk much when we're together."

He had a point about not talking. Our relationship was pretty hormonal.

Rob knelt next to me and took my hands. "I would have told you earlier but I never dreamed I'd get involved so fast. Hell, I never dreamed anyone like you would ever even go out with me in the first place. If I'd told you earlier you'd probably have dumped me and I wanted to be with you," he confessed. He rubbed his thumb over my index finger and said softly, "I know your life is here. You've got this great career" (I grimaced at that) "and I didn't think moving to South Dakota would appeal to you." He looked at me hopefully. "Would it?"

I looked at him bleakly. Move to South Dakota? The Outback? Let's get real here. "I can't see it myself," I said miserably.

"I figured that's how you'd feel," he admitted. He was silent for a moment then returned to his chair and sat down heavily. "Well, I want to be fair to you. Do you want to break it off now?"

My stomach curled up at the thought of it. I just wasn't ready to quit having fun and orgasms. But I pondered the offer. I didn't want him to go but apparently I couldn't stop him. So for my own sake I should probably make the break now. But could I stand being in the same town and not seeing him? I didn't think I could handle that either. On the other hand, could I stand to get even more involved knowing he'd be leaving soon? My gerbil cage of a mind was starting to squeak again. This was like dealing with a terminal illness.

What the hell, I decided, I'd rather spend as much time with him as I could. We'd have one of those bittersweet, heartbreaking experiences that romantic authors are so fond of writing about. Professionally, I could use the pain as a sense memory if I ever got to play Ophelia or Juliet or some other suicidal broad. And maybe he'd weather-strip my windows before he left.

Rob agreed with my decision. We'd spend his last days in Los Angeles together—at my place so I wouldn't ever have to sleep on that horrible couch again. "And maybe I can get you to change your mind about coming with me," he said with a wan smile.

"Hell will freeze over first," I assured him and changed the subject. "Show me how to use this dustbuster thing," I suggested. I had already learned that one of the quickest ways to divert a man was to plug in something that makes noise. Works every time.

Rob moved his bits and pieces of things into my condo, which took about fifteen minutes. All he owned were his records, his clothes, his electronics, and his parent's portrait which was now transplanted onto my mantelpiece. The only problem we had was when Rob insisted on paying the monthly fees, insurance, and taxes on the place. He said it was the least he could do.

"I'd pay the mortgage, too, if there was one," he declared.

He was so cute. Well, I couldn't have him pay for everything, that wouldn't be fair, so I lied about the amount; I told him it was half what it really was. He never knew the difference because I got the statements.

It seemed like Rob had been with me forever. He was even warmer in bed than Pudgy, maybe because he covered more territory. And he never encroached on my space because he was working a lot of overtime finishing up his project. He'd come home about nine and we'd enjoy the rest of the evening curled up together listening to music and reading— he read technical magazines and I stuck to novels—or watching TV. I had the best of both worlds; warm feet and no bother.

Of course, all this domesticity was making the approaching separation even more depressing. Although I had so much else to be depressed about it was hard to fit Rob in. I was notified in early August that due to budget cutbacks my teaching job was being phased out.

I went over to Leslie's to get some sympathy. "I can't believe all this crap is happening to me," I groused. "It's like the fates are telling me I should go to the Tundra with Rob."

"Oh please," Les said impatiently. "You don't belong in South Dakota."

"I don't belong anywhere," I said bitterly. "Here, the Anglos look at me like I'm going to drop a little brown welfare-recipient right in front of them. And last week some La Raza guy screamed obscenities at me because I didn't speak Spanish. He said I was brown on the outside and white on the inside."

"He called you a potato?" Les asked, amused, then muttered "Sorry" when I glared at her.

I brooded for a minute then said, "You know, maybe I need a change. I've never really been anywhere or done anything. And I'm tired of everything here. The newspaper is all about rape and murder; sometimes I just want to cry. That's no way to start your day."

"So don't read the paper," Leslie said impatiently. "Besides, you can't get away from crime; it's everywhere."

"Okay, then how about I'm tired of the high cost of living. Do you know what I pay for car insurance?" I asked. "And now I don't even have a steady part-time job—I don't know where my next paycheck's going to come from."

Leslie stared at me. "You're talking yourself into something here and I don't like it. You're always telling me not to do impulsive shit, now it's my turn. For your own sake don't do anything drastic."

I was shocked. "Leslie, I always think things through carefully."

"Oh please," was all Leslie said.

The end was near. Rob was leaving in a week. I kept waiting for him to renounce his plan for higher education or at least declare his undying love for me, but, characteristically, he said nothing. He didn't even try to talk me into going with him. He'd just look up from his magazine and smile mournfully at me. He seemed to be waiting for a declaration from me but I certainly wasn't going to say anything. A tough heroine never tells the guy she loves him until he says it first. I was getting more depressed by the minute.

Well, moping gets really boring so Rob suggested a movie might cheer us up. We drove my Miata to Santa Monica, parked it on a side street—Rob didn't believe in paying for parking—and walked a block to the theater. Rob ate popcorn and I stewed.

As we walked back to the car, I noticed a running Honda parked next to my Miata and two figures in my car. I stopped dead in my tracks and grabbed Rob. "My car's being broken into!" I gasped and pointed.

Rob's eyes followed my pointing finger, fixed on the Miata, and his eyebrows climbed. It's not often you actually see your girlfriend's car being ripped off. Then his eyes narrowed and he took off for the car. "Stay back," he ordered over his shoulder.

The hell with that; it was my damn car! I ran right behind him. Looking back, it was curious how we split up. Rob automatically charged the driver's side and I went to the passenger door and gave it a yank. A fat Hispanic man looked up from trying to remove my radio and, in a heavily accented voice, snarled, "What the fuck you want, bitch?"

That really pissed me off. Not only was he eviscerating my automobile, something I'd worked very hard for, he was insulting me. "It's my car, asshole," I snarled right back.

The criminal sneered at me, pulled himself out of the car, and brandished a knife. Now, I want to point out a few shortcomings of civilized indoctrination. Had I known then what I know now I would have kicked this guy in the stomach, or someplace even more debilitating, before he got into position to attack. Instead, stupid, law-abiding me waited until he managed to hoist his medium-tall, two-hundred-and-fifty-pound bulk from the seat and swing a knife around. My attention left the hairy stomach slopping out of the gap between his T-shirt and pants and focused on the knife. I guess as knives go, it wasn't all that big but standing there unarmed it looked like a machete. What to do, what to do. Fortunately, I was carrying a purse with a long shoulder strap so I swung it around and hit him with it as hard as I could.

I could tell this really surprised him. He hadn't expected a woman half his size to put up a fight. Encouraged, I kept swinging my purse and dancing around to make myself a harder target as I yelled insults. I floated like a butterfly and stung like a bee. Actually, I buzzed like a bee and stung like a butterfly but you do what you can. He'd called me a bitch, well, fine; I can call names, too. I editorialized at the top of my voice about the criminal's personal hygiene (or lack thereof), his ancestry (ditto), and any other horrible thing I could think of. I think I hurt his feelings. I sure hope so.

As I danced and screeched I heard the sound of scuffling and some swearing over on Rob's side of the car but I was too preoccupied with my own situation to pay much attention. I finally noticed the getaway car starting to roll away. Rob told me later that the thief had managed to twist away from him and jump in the Honda. He tried to drive off so Rob jumped into the passenger seat of the getaway car and continued the fight.

I heard a voice yell out, "Get out of my fucking car, man!" And Rob's basso profundo return, "Fuck you!"

As I continued my defense I quickly glanced over to see Rob and his thief exchanging blows in the front seat of the Honda. Then the driver's door opened, the thief was rolling on the pavement, and Rob was slowly driving down the street from the passenger seat. This left me with both thugs. I didn't like the odds so I bashed my criminal one last time with my purse and ran down to the only lighted building on the street, a fire station. The thugs started to chase me but stopped when they noticed their vehicle gliding away, then they chased the Honda instead.

This whole scene had taken place in about forty-five seconds; apartment lights were starting to come on and the firemen were congregating in front of the station in response to all the yelling. I ran up to them and panted that my boyfriend was being chased by armed men and would somebody call the police, PLEASE.

I stood in front of those men, gibbering, panicked, out of breath, and trying to explain what had happened. The firemen were calm. They're trained for emergencies, I guess. They listened to my incoherent yammering and tried to quiet me down. One of the firemen patted my shoulder and said, "Miss, we've already called the police. Why don't you come inside and wait."

"But they're chasing Rob and they've got knives!" I protested, almost in tears. "I have to go after them!"

"You can't do anything by yourself. You just come in and sit down and wait for the police," said the kind fireman and grabbed my arm so I couldn't take off.

We stood arguing. I was just about to whack the fireman with my purse when a white Tempo pulled up. "Your husband's okay," the driver called out. "He's out in front of the theater but he can't leave the car. I was driving by and saw the fight. I followed your husband and made sure he was safe. He said to tell you everything's all right." Then the Good Samaritan drove off without giving me a chance to thank him or explain that Rob wasn't my husband.

The firemen took me into the firehouse and gave me a cup of coffee. Caffeine was probably the last thing I needed right then but I appreciated the gesture. Rob came running in as I was wrapping my shaking hands around the coffee cup.

"I can't stay, I have to get back to the car," he panted. "I just wanted to make sure you were all right."

"I'm fine but what…?" I tried to ask.

"I don't have time to explain," he interrupted me. "The Honda was hot-wired. I'm parked in front of the theater so come there when you're done here."

"But…"

"No time. I have to get back." Rob ran off.

I looked at the firemen helplessly. They poured me some more coffee.

A police car showed up in five minutes. I'd been telling the whole ridiculous story to my firemen but I started over for the policemen. The firemen nodded along at the familiar parts but the cops obviously didn't believe a word I said. I didn't blame them much. I wouldn't have believed it either if I hadn't lived through it.

"Where's your car, ma'am," interrupted one of the policemen.

I led them outside the fire station and pointed—to an empty space. "Oh no," I breathed, "my car's gone."

"You're not having a good night, are you, ma'am?" the policeman observed. Boy, that had to be the understatement of the year. When I told them Rob would corroborate my story, they put me in the back of their patrol car and drove me to the front of the theater where Rob was waiting with his own complement of skeptical police. He was standing between my Miata (God knows why but he'd driven it to the theater after talking to me at the fire station; too bad he hadn't bothered to tell me) and the still-running getaway car. I ran over to check him out. Rob's burglar had tried to use his screwdriver as a knife and Rob had a ripped shirt and a gouged rib as a result. Fortunately, his wound was a long gash instead of a punctured lung but I felt sick when I realized how bad it could have been.

Rob finished his version of the story and all four policemen stepped aside to confer. I was asking Rob if he wanted to go to a hospital and he'd assured me that the monster gash was just a scratch when the policemen came back. One of Rob's cops said to me, "Why don't you tell us your side."

So I did. The policeman all listened quietly at first. They could hardly think we'd stolen the Honda; we were the ones who'd called them, after all. Then I noticed all four of them grinning. I'd gotten to the point where I was describing the thug as he got out of my car brandishing his knife when I was distracted by one of my officers telling Rob's cops, "You won't believe this." Then my officer apologized for interrupting and urged me on. "Go on. Tell them what you did next," he said.

"I hit him with my purse," I said simply. All four officers broke up.

I couldn't understand the laughter; I'd protected myself with the only weapon available. I looked at Rob for sympathy but he was grinning, too. "This is not funny," I said to all those men. "This isn't funny, is it? I don't think this is funny."

I inspected my broken window to preserve what little dignity I had left as the police ran the license plate on the Honda. They tried unsuccessfully to contact the owner of the stolen car but got no answer. The car had to be towed to the police impound area for safekeeping. The owner, poor slob, not only had his car stolen, he'd have to pay a fee to get it back. Oh well, the police tried. I could afford to be charitable now that I'd ceased to be the butt of everybody's amusement.

Rob and I filed a report on my vandalized vehicle. The police explained that the chances of catching the perpetrators were slim to none and after lecturing us about how lucky we were that our particular attackers hadn't been armed with guns, they warned us that "in future, let them have the radio, it's not worth risking your life over". They left us with a broken window and a messed up dashboard, but in possession of the radio and car. Hooray for our side. I bet the thieves had to take the bus.

"They must have been real amateurs," Rob said as we drove home. "A pro would have had the radio out in thirty seconds. Hell, a pro wouldn't have taken a Miata radio in the first place."

"That's supposed to make me feel better?" I asked.

"Well, Stevie, it could have been worse. They could have slashed the top instead of breaking the window. The window is cheaper to replace."

"Lucky me," I said glumly.

I was in shock. I didn't start to shake until we got in the house. Rob took a hot shower with me and made me drink a glass of wine to offset the jitters. He had some wine, too. He was in worse shape than I was; he'd been injured, after all. I bandaged his wound and gave it a kiss. Time would heal Rob's body but I wasn't sure about my psyche. I sipped my wine moodily.

"I'm beginning to hate this city," I muttered angrily. "It's getting so I'm scared to go out of the house. I'm ready to put bars on my windows and I don't want to live that way! I'm tired of producers asking me to take my clothes off! I don't even have a part-time job anymore! My life is crap and it's getting worse all the time!"

Shock had been replaced by anger. I wandered around, screeching and waving my arms, until I ran out of breath and energy.

"I'm so tired of everything," I sniffed, close to tears. "You're leaving, it'll cost a fortune to fix the car, and I have no career!" The sniffs turned to wails and I threw myself into Rob's arms, sobbing against his chest. The Iron Woman needed a break.

Rob held me, stroked my hair, and murmured into my scalp. When my sobbing subsided to hiccups he held me away from him and looked intently into my face. "Are you sure you shouldn't see a doctor?" he asked.

"No," I sniffled. "Thanks anyway. I love you."

"What?!"

"Nothing. I just said thanks," I said quickly. I was appalled at my blurt. Only extreme shock could cause me to launch my emotional cookies like that.

"No, I heard that," Rob pressed. "Did you mean it?"

I hung my head. "Yeah, I guess," I admitted. Well. I was twenty-six years old and had finally told a man I loved him. I'd lost my emotional virginity. Now what?

"Thank God, I thought I was the only one," Rob said in relief. "This probably isn't the best time to bring this up again," he continued, "and I would never have mentioned it except we both, well, you know, we love each other now, so please, won't you come back to South Dakota with me?"

I didn't think he was ever going to ask again and now that he had I wasn't sure what to say. I goggled at him.

"You know," he coaxed, "my parents don't even lock their door at night."

"Don't they have anything to steal?" I sniffed and swabbed my face with the back of my hand.

Rob smiled. "Sure. But there aren't as many thieves."

"Must send 'em out here where they're protected," I muttered savagely.

"Something like that. I'd sure like to have you back there, Stevie. I didn't know you were such a tough little character." He chuckled. "I couldn't believe the way you fought with that guy." He laughed until he noticed my look of outrage. "I'm sorry. I shouldn't laugh. It's just that you're so small and he was so big. He looked like a St. Bernard being attacked by a rabid Chihuahua." He chuckled again admiringly then sobered. "Seriously, will you come with me?"

"Well, I've got property. I can't just pick up and leave," I said, tempted.

"Sure you can. Hire a management company to rent it out for you." Rob took my hand and kissed it. "Come with me," he said again.

He seemed like the only rock I had in an increasingly hostile world. Oh, what the hell. "Okay," I said.

"Are you nuts!?" Leslie shrieked when I told her.

"Probably," I admitted. "But I'm going anyway."

"I knew you were going to do something like this," Leslie muttered and starting pacing. "Did I or did I not tell you not to do anything drastic?"

"You told me," I agreed and hung my head.

"Then what in the world are you thinking?" she yelled.

"Quit yelling at me," I said mulishly. "I know it's probably stupid but I'm tired of being left behind by the people I love. This time I'm going, too. So just shut up about it."

Of course she didn't, especially when she found out I'd agreed to marry Rob.

"You haven't been rational since you met that man," she declared, "but even you aren't crazy enough to marry him. You barely know each other!"

"He says his mother wouldn't understand us living in sin," I explained. "He says he's taking me as his wife or not at all. And I'm going."

Leslie lectured, she pleaded, she even cried at one point up until the day we went to City Hall to get legal. But my mind was made up. I asked her to be my witness on the big day. I said I needed a friend.

As we waited for the judge, Leslie challenged Rob. "I still don't understand why you two can't just live together. Aren't you a little old to be afraid of your mother?" she asked him. "What if Stevie doesn't like the Dakotas?"

"South Dakota," Rob corrected her. "And maybe she will like it. It's not any worse than L.A. Better in a lot of ways. I'll have my Master's in two years then we'll see what happens. And I'm not afraid of my mother, this is the right thing to do." His smile took the sting out of his words but he obviously wasn't going to let Leslie bully him.

The feuding over my head halted when the clerk called our names.

"You can always get a divorce if you can't stand it," Leslie hissed to me as we went before the judge. "A marriage license is just paper. Nothing's carved in granite."

On that positive note, Rob and I were married by the Justice of the Peace. Afterward, Leslie went to work and Rob and I went home to finish his packing and consummate our marriage. Sex had been Rob's primary argument in my decision to marry him. It was a potent argument.

Rob left the next day. We were both a little weak in the knees when he got into his Buick loaded with his worldly possessions. He gave me a hug, a long passionate kiss, and my final instructions.

"I'll call you every night while I'm on the road," Rob said. "It might take me a while to find a place for us to live but I'll start as soon as I get there. Your car is in good shape for a cross-country drive but I left a list of things to have checked before you start. You better contact some management companies about renting the condo but don't give them a date until I have everything taken care of in Brookings. God, Stevie, I miss you already," he said and hugged me again. "I want you with me as soon as possible so start getting ready to come. I love you."

He got in his car and drove away.

I stood at the curb, waving, feeling bereft. Then I went inside to sit with Pudgy. The feeling of loss was replaced with dismay.

What the hell had I done?

chapter 5

I went back to watching TV with Pudgy at night. It was hard to believe I was a married woman; the last few months seemed like a pheromone-induced haze. Rob called every night he was traveling so I didn't forget about him but I didn't really miss him all that much either. Life was pretty much what it had been before Rob entered my life—except all the faucets and drains worked. He'd been a handy little devil to have around.

"Maybe I got caught up in lust," I mused to Leslie.

"You think?" she asked sarcastically.

My new status was brought home to me when Rob called from Brookings. He sounded exhausted. As we spoke I could hear children screaming and a woman yelling in the background. Rob said he was surrounded by his parents, his three brothers, and their wives and respective children.

"Mom wants to talk to you," Rob said and the next thing I knew I was speaking to a woman.

"Hello, Stephanie? I'm your mother-in-law," she caroled.

"Nice to...talk to you, Mrs. Anderson," I gulped.

"Bobby tells me you're an actress and half Mexican. Is that right?" she continued.

"Well, yes, I'm an actress and my great-grandfather came from Mexico," I affirmed hesitantly, not sure whether I should be pissed off or what.

"Isn't that interesting? We've never had anybody from the stage in the family before. And I guess I'll have learn some Spanish," Alice said chattily. Lord, she seemed like a cheerful sort.

"Mrs. Anderson, that's really not necessary because I don't speak…"

I was interrupted as she said, off, "Bobby, quit trying to take the phone from me. I'd like to talk to my new daughter-in-law." Back to me. "Although why you two were in such hurry to get married is beyond me. We could have had a lovely ceremony at the church if you'd waited."

I heard some clunking sounds and Rob was back on the line.

"Mom's just excited about meeting you," he said.

"Sounds like it," I said dryly.

"No, really, you'll love each other once you get to know each other," he assured me.

"I'm sure she's very nice," I hedged. I was bothered by the Mexican remark. Rob and I had never really talked about my Hispanic background because it hadn't seemed important. Now it seemed important. "Rob, is there going to be a problem about my ancestry?"

"What do you mean?" he asked absently.

Time to take the toro by the horns. "How does your mother feel about Hispanics?" I asked.

"I don't know that she feels anything in particular. She doesn't know any."

This, of course, was a perfectly rational response but I've never known racism to be rational so I kept at him. "What about what she said about learning Spanish?"

"Oh, she's just trying to make conversation. As a matter of fact," Rob continued, "my folks are so ready to like you they want to know if we want to live with them until I get my Master's."

"Rob, that'll take two years, maybe more," I protested.

"Yeah. Isn't it great of them to offer? We could save a fortune."

"Listen, Rob, it's very nice of them to offer and thank them for me but I don't think it's such a good idea," I said, trying to keep a grip on myself.

Rob ignored me and continued hurriedly, "We'd have the basement all to ourselves and Mom could teach you to cook. We could save all the money we'd spend on rent and buy ourselves a house when I graduate."

"Rob, I already have a house…"

"I know, but that's your house. I never felt right living off you."

"Well, I wouldn't feel right living off your parents!" I was speaking through my teeth at that point. Rob must have heard my molars grinding together through miles of fiber optics or maybe he just got distracted because he didn't pursue it.

"Listen, Stevie, I'm beat and the family's all here. I just called to say I'm here and I'm fine. I miss you and I'll talk to you tomorrow." He was gone.

I'd accepted the move to the Outback but I hadn't given any thought to in-laws. I'd assumed that since I didn't have any close family ties Rob was the same way. I mean, I knew his parents existed, I'd had their portrait sitting on my mantel, after all, but Rob never said anything about them. I'd assumed it was a nice, civilized, arm's-length relationship. Apparently I was wrong. And that Mexican crack...Was Rob's mother really trying to be understanding or was I walking into a snake pit?

I went over to Les'. "I have in-laws," I announced, discombobulated.

"Well, did you think Rob hatched?" Leslie drawled.

"He wants us to live with his parents," I continued and flopped on her couch to assimilate this new development.

Leslie's eyebrows arched. "That's not good. You want some wine?"

"How hard is it to get an annulment?" I asked when she handed me a goblet.

"I don't know," she returned. "I think you're not supposed to have had sex."

"Well, that's out," I said and she snorted. "How about a divorce?" I continued.

"You stand to lose a lot," Leslie said judiciously. "California's a community property state. Did you guys sign a pre-nup?"

"No," I said glumly.

"You better tell me what happened," Les advised. So I did. She listened intently.

"You know, Stevie, I don't think this is worth getting nuts about. Not yet anyway," she said when I finished. "Rob's just finished a four-day drive. He's exhausted and he's surrounded by his loving family; anybody'd be a little stupid under those circumstances."

"What about his mother's Mexican remark?"

"Maybe she was just trying to show you how tolerant she is." Les swirled the wine in her glass and smiled at me. "When you told me your background I didn't know what to say either. I'm sure I made stupid comments trying to show it didn't mean anything to me. You know, melting pot solidarity? You probably thought I was awful because I sounded stupid even to me. But I meant well. Most people are clods not bigots. Don't go looking for racism where none is intended."

"Why in the world would Rob think I'd want to live with his parents?" I continued, perplexed.

"He probably doesn't. But his mother wants him around and boys and their mothers have very strange bonds."

"He should have told me about all these strangers he's related to," I said angrily. "They weren't part of the deal. I don't think I even want to go now."

Leslie looked at me in amused disgust. "You don't even know if there's a problem yet and already you're talking about jumping ship. I hate to say I told you so but…I told you not to rush into this marriage. If you had no intention of living up to the agreement why in the world did you tell the J.P. you would? Now it's going to cost you a fortune to get out of it."

"I live up to my agreements," I retorted, stung. "I just think I was misled."

Les raised a derisive eyebrow and taunted, "Should have thought of that earlier. You're a wife now. You have to be supportive." She grinned malevolently. "It's your job."

"If you sing *Stand by Your Man* I'll deck you," I threatened.

Leslie giggled and poured us both more wine.

The next day I was still debating whether or not to tell Rob that I'd changed my mind—nothing personal but I was obviously insane when I'd married him and maybe it would be better to call it off—when Heather called. "A producer told me you were rude to him," she shrilled on the phone.

"Did you give that guy my phone number? Heather, the first thing he asked me was my bra size. All I said was that it didn't really matter because I was dealing with concavities. Then I said it was none of his business. But that's the truth; I wouldn't call it rude."

"I'm not going to be able to give you away," Heather declared and hung up in a huff.

Heather's call settled my inner debate. I wasn't a teacher. I wasn't an actress. I was a stripper that refused to strip so I guess that made me… nothing. Was anything keeping me in L.A.? It didn't seem so. There was a reason I'd married Rob although I couldn't think what it was at the moment. I'd given my word; I'd make it work. I just wasn't happy about it right now.

Rob called. "I found us a place today," he said. "The only problem is we can't move in for awhile. See, one of Dad's Kiwanis buddies is evicting some guys and they won't be out for a couple of weeks. But we can stay with the folks until then. And the best part is I can afford it. Isn't that great?"

"Yeah, great," I agreed feebly.

I guess my lack of enthusiasm finally got through to him. "What's wrong?" he demanded. "Aren't you happy about this? You can come out right away." My silence dragged out. "Stevie, you haven't changed your mind or anything, have you?"

I didn't have the heart to tell him I'd been going through my 'one-hand, other-hand' business ever since he left. He'd figure out soon enough that I didn't need a husband, I needed a psychiatrist.

"Nope," I said bravely, committing myself. "I'm on my way."

This was my true vow of marriage. The fifteen minutes at the J.P.'s had been just…well, being agreeable. I got busy. I'd worry about "staying with the folks" later.

I found a management company that promised to take care of my property. I contracted a moving company to move my furniture. I told them I didn't have an address to give them just yet but they said it'd take awhile to get it to the Midwest anyway. I could call the head office when I found a place to land and they'd deliver then.

I called Heather. "Heather? This is Stevie O'Neill. Hey, I'm sorry to tell you like this, but I got married and I'm moving to South Dakota."

"What!" Heather shrieked. "You can't leave just like that! I've spent a year bringing you along!!"

"Why, Heather," I said, quietly sarcastic, "I didn't know you cared."

"I care about my wasted time!"

"Well," I said, grinning manically, getting ready to hang up, "you won't have Stevie O'Neill to waste your time any more."

"Go to hell," she said shortly. I almost said I was afraid I was doing just that.

I called Rob and told him I'd be leaving California in a week and was having my furniture shipped. Rob objected to moving the furniture. He said it was waste of money.

"It's my money and I want my own stuff," I retorted. He quit arguing.

I spent the next week saying good-bye to people and places I loved. Which basically meant I sat in the library a lot and bothered Leslie. The time came to supervise the loading of all my furniture into a moving van. Great, now I didn't even have a bed, so Leslie offered me her spare room. We spent my last night in Los Angeles reminiscing and carefully outlining my route on a map. With my sense of direction I had to be careful I didn't end up in Canada. Then we got maudlin over ice cream.

"I'm going to miss you," she admitted. "Life's never dull when you're around."

The next morning I put a suit bag, a duffle, and Pudgy's port-a-potty (for hotel use) in the Miata trunk, the crated-up cat in the passenger seat, and then looked around at the condo complex. "I spent almost a year here," I commented to Leslie. "And the only thing I'm really going to miss is you."

"Oh, what's the big deal? We'll be calling each other all the time. You won't have a chance to miss me 'cause I'll be on the other end of the phone," she grinned but the effect was spoiled by the tears in her eyes.

We hugged each other, sobbed a little bit, and Leslie finally pushed me into my car. "I guess this is the '90's version of the covered wagon, huh," she said. It was a pretty feeble joke but I appreciated the attempt. Saying goodbye is pretty depressing.

"I'll call when I get there," I promised as I put on my sunglasses.

"You do that. And say 'hi' to Rob for me," she said as I started the car.

"Will do," I promised and backed out. I could see her waving in the rearview mirror as I drove off. I cried until I got stuck in traffic. Then I swore a lot. Rob said there was no traffic in South Dakota. Good. I'd miss traffic like a toothache. I found myself humming the theme to "Green Acres" as I wended my way out of Los Angeles and thought of Eva Gabor; I hoped my hair didn't start looking like a bad wig.

I took I-15 through Las Vegas and drove until I got someplace in Utah the first day. Then I found a cheap motel and died. Driving cross-country was a lot tougher than I thought it'd be. I'd tried driving with the air-conditioning blasting and the convertible top down but that only lasted about an hour. I got one hell of a sunburn and baked Pudgy. The heat dehydrated me even after I put the top up I so bought a six-pack of Diet Coke. That took care of the thirst problem but then I had to pee. After some experimentation I managed to discipline myself to two-hour travel increments. I'd have a soda, stop and pee, and drive, drive, drive. I had to make sure Pudgy had water and made the ghastly mistake of letting her out in the desert to relieve herself. Of course, she ran away and I had terrible time chasing her down and stuffing her back in her box again. Before starting out the next day I found a pet shop and bought a collar and leash so Pudge couldn't make like a lizard and waste time on me. She ended up on my two-hour bladder schedule, too. I allowed her five minutes to get out on the leash, pee (or whatever), and back in the box she went. I was in a hurry to get into the mountains where I hoped it'd be cooler.

For anyone who's never taken a cross-country drive take my advice—don't. The interstate system across this great country of ours is why God made airplanes. There's nothing but miles and miles and miles of miles and miles and miles. I'm told if you get off the interstate there are lots of interesting and educational things to see and do. I saw truck stops, concrete, and tumbleweeds. I don't know how truck drivers do it.

And speaking of truck drivers—I was leery of them because I'd heard about their depredations on TV; you know, running single women off the road and raping them? I figured I could outrun them if I had to but I felt very insecure traveling alone with only a boxed-up cat as protection—which is no protection at all.

About 8:00 p.m. on the second day of my backbreaking, eye-watering, soul-searing drive I stopped at a truck stop someplace in Wyoming for coffee. I wanted to get in a couple more hours of travel before I stopped for the night but I was tired and needed a caffeine jolt. Unfortunately, all the booths in the "family" section were full. The only spot open was a stool in the truckers' section. I thought about moving on but I really needed a break and I figured, what the hell, how much trouble could I get into with all these people around? I resolved to say as little as possible, avoid eye contact, and scream rape if one of those big, burly men made advances on me. I strode to the stool confidently and ordered a sandwich and lots of black coffee. Nobody said a word to me or even seemed to notice I was there. I quickly cleaned my plate, downed three cups of coffee, got up to pay my check, and waited my turn for the cashier. Two truckers standing behind me started nudging each other and clearing their throats. *Uh-oh*, I thought, *here it comes. Act tough and if that doesn't work, scream.*

The shorter trucker cleared his throat again and asked gruffly, "You looking for a ride?"

I was civil but aloof as I replied, "No, I have my car out front. Why?"

Both truckers shuffled their feet for a bit before the taller trucker explained, "Well, most people sitting in this section are either truckers or hitchhikers. You sure as hell, pardon me, ma'am, don't look like a trucker so we figured you was lookin' for a ride. There's a lot of crazy people out there on the roads and you can't be too careful. So if you was lookin' for a ride we figured we'd give you one." They shuffled some more, looked at the ceiling, and cleared their throats again.

Even in my exhausted haze I could tell these men were trying to help out what they perceived to be a damsel in distress. And their gruffness wasn't rude, it was shyness. The media had prepared me for pillage and rape on a Peterbilt scale and instead I found the knights of the road—unwashed and unshaven but decent and gallant. I smiled gratefully at them. "Thank you. That's awfully sweet of you to offer," I said.

That seemed to embarrass them more so I paid my check, wished them a safe drive, and left. I let Pudgy have a pee break before starting again and told her about the encounter. "You know what, Pudge? Maybe living in the country is going to be all right." I slept like a baby when I stopped for the night.

I was a lot more relaxed as I tootled through Nebraska on I-80. Instead of concentrating on my fears I started paying attention to things around me. Without my noticing it the country had turned to prairie— which is just another form of desert to my way of thinking. From where I was on the interstate all I could see were the concrete road, blue sky with lots of billowy clouds, and miles of tall grass. After the wall-to-wall people of Southern California the landscape was intimidating but there was just enough traffic to reassure me that I wasn't alone in the world, although I saw more cows than people. When Pudgy and I stopped at rest stops for our pee breaks I noticed that the few trees scattered around had obviously been planted. Natural groves occurred next to rivers but since there weren't many rivers there weren't many trees.

The radio stations were different, too. I found very few classical stations—as a matter of fact I only found one outside of Omaha, but then I wasn't looking too hard. I found mostly mainstream pop and country-western. I bellowed along with the pop tunes to keep myself awake.

It was hard to stay aloof at the rest stops. Most of the people using them were traveling from one point in the Midwest to another and were generally a convivial, garrulous bunch, which was unsettling after the West Coast. In Los Angeles, people tend to avoid conversation and eye contact and hurry to wherever they're going. At the rest stops in Nebraska folks would wander around to stretch their legs, pour cups of coffee for themselves, offer cups of coffee to other travelers, and exchange information about each other. I raised quite a stir when I got Pudgy out of her box, attached her to the leash, and carried her to the litter area.

An older couple watched in amazement as Pudgy fought her leash then settled down to do her 'business'. They were so flummoxed they put down their coffee cups, stopped smoking their cigarettes (that's another thing; people smoke in the Midwest), and stared.

"Doesn't like the leash much, does she," the man finally commented.

"Not even a little bit," I returned.

We all watched intently as Pudgy defecated, sniffed it, made one little scratch to cover it, walked away to the extent of the leash, then started biting at her collar frantically. I started dragging her back to the car. The woman couldn't stand it anymore.

"Why don't you carry her?" she suggested.

"Because her butt's dirty."

That stopped them both for a minute, then the man said, "Little lady, why don't you have some coffee with us and let the cat clean herself up. Mother, we have another cup, don't we?"

The woman dug an extra cup out of a picnic basket and poured me some coffee. "We don't have cream or sugar," she apologized.

"That's fine. I drink it black," I said and sat down with them.

I was to discover that coffee, black, is the Great American Drink in the Great American Desert. I couldn't understand how these people stayed so calm with so much caffeine in their systems until I sampled their brew. It was weak as dishwater.

The man extended his hand to be shaken. "I'm Tom Himer and this is my wife, Marlene. We run a little plumbing supply business back in Hastings. We're taking a short trip to visit our daughter in Iowa." They beamed at each other and looked at me expectantly.

"Uh...I'm Stephanie O'Neill and I'm going to meet my husband in Brookings, South Dakota," I said as I shook Mr. Himer's hand.

"And what does Mr. O'Neill do?" asked "Mother" Himer.

"My husband's name is Rob Anderson and he's a grad student at South Dakota State University," I said matter-of-factly.

"But you don't have the same last name?" Mrs. Himer looked vaguely horrified so I hurried to explain.

"I'm an actress and I kept my name for professional reasons," I said.

The Himer's thought about this for a few minutes then Mr. Himer concluded, "So you must be from Los Angeles." He pronounced Angeles with a hard G.

"Yes, that's right," I smiled.

"That explains it."

"Explains what?"

"Putting a cat on a dang leash. Only a Californian would do something like that," and he threw his head back and laughed. Mrs. Himer chimed in agreeably.

They weren't being offensive; they were just following a behavioral pattern I came to recognize in older Midwesterners. They'll tell you everything about themselves, I guess because they have nothing to be ashamed of, and show absolutely no hesitation about prying into your life. They'll prod and advise and suggest and meddle and then, just when you're ready to murder them, they'll offer you the shirts off their backs. They don't watch much television because they find other people so interesting. "Besides," Mr. Himer said, "there's not much on our minister would approve of. I'd rather go bowling than bother with the nudity and canned laughter those Hollywood people put on the boob tube."

I exchanged farewells and good wishes with the Himers who told me to look them up if I ever got to Hastings, stuffed Pudgy in her box, and drove off. I now had two human-interest stories to tell Leslie and I treasured them both. I felt like quite an adventurer.

I stopped at a Motel 6 in Omaha and continued the next day up I-29. According to my map it was only a four-hour trip to Brookings so I took my time. I slept late, ate a leisurely breakfast, and took off at noon. I braced myself when I crossed the South Dakota border. I made one last rest stop north of Sioux Falls to check my make-up, comb my hair, and get my courage up. I felt like a mail order bride. I hadn't seen Rob in a couple of weeks and I wanted to make a good impression. I also knew he was probably in class and I didn't want to call his parents' house until after five.

As I drove toward Brookings I noticed that the speed limit was 65 and nobody exceeded the limit. What little traffic there was stayed at 65 mph or below. And I didn't see any highway patrolmen. This was my first indication of how law-abiding the residents were. I also saw very few foreign cars; these people bought Detroit iron.

My first sight of Brookings was unprepossessing. There were no tall buildings. A water tower and a brick pillar were the only things projecting above the rolling prairie. To the right of me was a gravel pit and to the left were mobile homes. Oh well, I consoled myself, the best part of a city is never in the outskirts.

I'd agreed to call Rob from the local Holiday Inn and I'd almost driven past my exit before I saw the big sign off to the left standing over a two-story building. I managed to get off the interstate and pull into the parking lot. I peed Pudgy one last time and went into the hotel bar. It was only 4:30 so I thought I'd have a drink before I made my call. Not only would it kill time, maybe it'd calm my nerves.

There were only two other customers besides myself. They stared curiously but made no attempt to bother me. I seated myself on a stool and ordered a tall gin-tonic. The bartender was another one of those friendly, talkative souls.

"You're not from around here, are you," he said as he put my drink in front of me.

"No, I'm not."

"I'da remembered you if I'd seen you before," he assured me.

"Umm," I murmured and sipped my drink.

"Yeah, I remember all the good-lookin' women," he grinned. "You here on business from Minneapolis?"

There didn't seem to be any harm in telling him my story. "I'm joining my husband. He's a student here," I explained.

The bartender looked at me sharply. "Say, are you Stephanie Anderson? Bobby's wife?"

"O'Neill," I corrected. "But yeah, I'm married to Rob."

"Well," he chortled. He didn't slap his thigh and say 'Dog my cats!' but the effect was the same. "Bobby told me to keep a lookout for you. He's been shittin' bricks...excuse me...real worried about you. Does he know you're here?"

"I just got in and haven't called him yet. I thought I'd wait till after five to make sure he's out of class."

"No problem. I know where he is. I'll give him a call right now."

Any protestations from me that I wanted to wait and call him myself were disregarded. "Yeah," the bartender said into the phone. "She's here. Just sat down. Yeah. Yeah. Okay. I'll tell her," he hung up the phone and said to me, "Bobby'll be right over. Oh, and the drink's on the house. Welcome to Brookings."

Of course, I panicked. I ran to the bathroom to check my face and hair again (why do women always do that? It's not like anything has changed in the last half hour) and steeled myself. "You will be charming and you will not make a fool of yourself," I told my mirror image and went back to the bar to wait.

I'd just seated myself, smiled self-consciously at the grinning bartender, and taken a long pull on my drink when Rob appeared in the doorway. I kept forgetting how good-looking he was.

He crossed the room rapidly saying, "Goddamn, Stevie! I was worried sick about you. Nobody's heard from you since you left L.A.! I even called Leslie to make sure you weren't dead!"

You know you've been on your own too long when it doesn't even occur to you that someone might be worried about you. I tried to apologize for being thoughtless but I didn't get much chance. Rob grabbed me and kissed me and spun me around—just like in the movies, with a grinning bartender as the audience. It was so cool. Boy, was I glad I hadn't chickened out. For the moment.

chapter 6

When I took a break so I could breathe I got formally introduced to the bartender. His name was Al and he'd gone to high school with Rob. "So what's next?" I asked Rob after I'd shaken Al's hand and accepted his congratulations on my marriage and another welcome "home".

"You have to meet the folks," he announced. "Where're you parked? You can follow me over."

"Now?" I asked. "Can't I check into the hotel or something? I've been driving since noon. I could use a nap."

"You can take a nap later. Mom can't wait to meet you. She's had the family on alert since yesterday. We're having a big dinner for you tonight. She put a roast in the oven and was calling everybody when I left the house."

"But I should at least drop off Pudgy and my luggage in our room," I objected weakly and presented the argument I'd been preparing ever since I left Los Angeles. "I thought it'd be a good idea if I stayed at a hotel. Don't you think so?"

"The folks want us to stay with them until the furniture comes," Rob said.

"But I can't just camp out on them; I've never even met them," I protested. "And I have Pudgy and everything. I can't ask them to put up with…"

"Relax! They know all about the cat and it's no problem. Stevie, it's only until the furniture comes. That's what families are for."

To put up with foreign brides and livestock? It seemed a little above and beyond the call of parenthood to me but I felt a headache starting so I didn't argue.

"Okay, if you're sure it's all right," I surrendered.

"I know it is. You're going to love it here, Stevie, it's nothing like Los Angeles."

That's what I was afraid of.

We caravanned over to the Anderson homestead. Rob's dad and older brother were down at the hardware store—the family business—but his mother was home.

"Stevie, this is my mother, Alice. Mom, this is my wife, Stephanie," Rob announced formally and presented me to a short, round, curly-gray-haired woman in bifocals. Her big smile made her almost unrecognizable from her mantel portrait.

"I'm so happy you're finally here," Alice exclaimed, giving me a brief hug and a peck on the cheek. "We've been worried sick about you! A young woman driving cross-country by herself like that…Anything could have happened to you! Bobby's going to have to teach you to use a telephone!" She continued scolding as she led me into the living room and seated me in a doily-covered easy chair. "I know you're one of those independent young women but you have a family now and we worry about you." She pressed a glass of iced tea and a homemade cookie into my hands.

Rob patted my shoulder indulgently. "You'll have plenty of time to teach her some manners, Mom."

I almost choked on the cookie. I turned to glare at Rob who had one of those 'My wife, I think I'll keep her' expressions on his face. He wilted slightly under my scrutiny so I turned back to his mother. "I appreciate your concern and I guess it was thoughtless of me not to call but I didn't have any trouble and it didn't seem necessary, Mrs. Anderson," I said as smoothly as I could around the cookie.

"You're one of the family now, Stephanie, just call me Mom," Alice urged.

Mom? I wasn't ready for that yet. "Well…" I hedged. "Would it be all right with you if I called you Alice?" I asked, disregarding Rob's frown.

She looked slightly taken aback but recovered quickly. "All right, if that makes you feel better," she said. Then she got down to the serious business of finding out just who her baby boy had married.

She asked me about my antecedents (Mexican and Irish, of course; she knew my parents were deceased, "You poor thing! Orphaned so early!"), my educational background (MFA; I scored some points with that), and my professional background (she'd seen some of my commercials and was impressed at my implied earnings; more points scored).

"But I guess I have to start a new career now," I concluded. "Rob says the University has a liberal arts department. I have some teaching experience. Maybe I could find something there."

"As long as it doesn't interfere with your home responsibilities," Alice qualified with a smile and a pat. I guess I passed the inquisition because she excused herself to the kitchen. "The whole family's coming over to meet you. Bobby can get help you get settled in until they get here," she called back over her shoulder.

Rob obediently followed me out to my car. "What was that crack about manners?" I hissed as I grabbed Pudgy's box.

Rob took my luggage out of the trunk. "I was just teasing," he protested as he led me back inside. "Don't be so sensitive."

Sensitive? I felt a nerve pinch behind my eyes. My headache got worse.

We went through the kitchen on the way to the basement so I took the opportunity to introduce Alice to Pudge. "You can store the litter box in the garage," Alice suggested. "I'm sure the cat will be happy to stay outside."

"I don't think that's such a good idea. Pudgy's an indoor cat," I demurred. "Rob said you wouldn't mind if she stayed in the basement. I'll make sure the litter box is cleaned out every day so there won't be any smell," I hastened to add. Okay, I fudged the truth a little; all litter boxes stink. But I couldn't throw Pudgy outside. God knows what would happen to her. There could be bears or wolves or coyotes or something.

Alice looked at my fuzzy friend doubtfully as Pudge peered out of her carrier. "I guess that won't hurt. Maybe she'll be good for catching mice," Alice said hopefully.

"I don't think she knows what mice are," I admitted. "Food, to her, is round and comes out of a can."

"Oh…well…" Alice said vaguely and she went back to her stove. Rob and I went downstairs.

"Your mother thinks I'm a flake," I said to him.

"Relax, you're being paranoid," he retorted.

There was no closet in the basement bedroom so I hung my suit bag on the rack provided and sighed. "The whole family," I echoed Alice. "Already."

Rob was unworried. "You have to meet them sometime."

He was no help at all. He'd been lucky; there were no in-laws for him to meet so he couldn't understand my trepidation. Alice, on the other hand, noticed my nervousness as soon as I reappeared in her kitchen to offer my help. She patted my arm, assured me that all the family would love me, and said, "I know city people like a drink before dinner but I wasn't sure what to get. Bobby said you drank gin every now and again so…" she reached into the cupboard under the sink and triumphantly pulled out a half-pint of Gordon's. "Surprise! Would you like some gin?"

"Oh, Alice, I'd love a gin-tonic," I replied gratefully. This would be my second drink in two hours but I justified it because this was a special occasion. Besides, it's not like I'd be driving anywhere—unless Rob pissed me off again.

"Tonic?" she repeated, sounding confused. "Bobby didn't say anything about tonic. I just bought gin."

Well, I don't drink very, very dry martinis under even the most stressful of circumstances, so I tactfully passed on the gin. "Maybe another time," I said and Alice accepted that. Approved, even.

"Bobby can show you around," she said to her son. It was an order.

Rob gave me a tour. The house was a large, two-story, wood-framed structure from the '40's and had four bedrooms—one in the basement and three upstairs. There were bathrooms on all floors. I found it curious that the Andersons had brand new wall-to-wall carpet throughout the house but all the furniture was old—well maintained but old. White crocheted doilies covered most flat surfaces—even the dining room table had doily placemats. The house looked like a dandelion field had blown up.

"What's with all the doilies?" I whispered to Rob.

"It's Mom's hobby," he whispered back.

I guess crocheting doilies was a lot healthier for a person than popping Valium or drinking vodka on the sly, I thought philosophically, then followed Rob outside. The front yard was neat with trimmed hedges but the back yard!—to my L.A. eyes it looked like a park with bushes, tall trees, and a garden plot. Rob was explaining that the trees were cottonwoods and the bushes were lilacs when his dad, Marvin, drove up in, what else, a Buick. Seeing Marvin, I knew what Rob would look like in thirty-five years. Add a few wrinkles, a few pounds, some gray hair and glasses, and Rob was a Marvin clone. I also learned where Rob learned his social skills.

"Welcome to the family," was all Marvin said to me as he shook my hand. We followed him inside where he went to the living room, sat in his recliner rocker, opened his newspaper, and effectively disappeared until dinner. Rob took his cue from his father. He went to the living room, sat on the couch, opened a magazine, and the library society was in session.

Alice continued to bustle around the kitchen so I wandered out and asked if I could do anything useful, it seemed the decent thing to do. Alice firmly rejected my offer. "You're our guest tonight. Why don't you just sit and visit with me until the other boys come?" she suggested.

I obliged and asked about the family members I was to meet. I'd obviously hit on her favorite subject. Alice beamed and called out to the living room, "Bobby, bring the photo album, will you?" Rob silently performed his errand and just as silently returned to his magazine. Alice wiped her hands on the dishtowel and sat at the kitchen table to show me her pictures. She located a family portrait that must have been taken at least ten years earlier.

"Now, this is my oldest boy, Tommy," she explained as she pointed to a rather attractive, chubby man. He bore a well-fed resemblance to Rob. "Tommy runs the hardware store with Dad. He has a lovely singing voice. Maybe we can get him to sing tonight. Tommy's married to Nancy." Alice paused as if unsure what to say about Nancy. "You'll meet her," she finished lamely. "Tommy and Nancy have three boys; Eric, Leif, and Steven. Now, this next one is Mikey, he's my second son." Alice pointed to a young, mustached man who looked more like her—shorter, more florid. "He's a banker in Sioux Falls. Just made Executive Vice-President with Citicorp. We're real proud of him. His wife is Marilyn—oh! she's pretty, too. She was a Miss South Dakota." Alice twinkled a sidelong look at me. "You just might put her nose out of joint!"

I winced. The last thing I needed tonight was a beauty competition. In the first place, if I looked like I felt, I'd lose. In the second place, if I won, the unknown sister-in-law would probably murder me.

Alice returned to the portrait. "And this is my third boy, Ricky. He teaches here at SDSU. His wife's name is Christine." Alice paused for a minute, then confided, "She's the only one of my daughters-in-law to not finish college. I don't know why. But she's an arty sort, too, so you'll have lots in common. They don't have any kids yet either but they're young."

Finally, she pointed to a skinny, coltish kid with horn-rimmed glasses and braces. "And that's Bobby, of course, my baby." She smiled fondly. "He came along six years after Ricky and used to tag after his big brother…" she smiled again and shook her head. "He wanted to do everything Ricky did and of course he couldn't because he was so much younger. He couldn't wait until he got as big as his brother so he could tag along." Alice laughed. "And then Bobby grew taller than Ricky. Ricky took after my side of the family, poor boy. He's never liked being the short son."

I stared at the picture, intrigued by this memorial to the devastating changes of adolescence. "When did Rob quit wearing glasses?"

"Oh, college sometime. He's legally blind in one eye and the eye doctor said the bad eye would never get better enough to work with the good eye so he just got rid of the glasses."

I didn't know Rob was legally blind in one eye. I wondered what else he'd neglected to tell me. As I pondered, Alice returned to the sink. "Well, I've got potatoes to peel for supper," she said briskly. "I can't spend any more time on pictures."

By the way, everybody here called the evening meal supper not dinner. Names change, the food's the same.

"Can I at least set the table?" I asked.

"That's nice of you. I'll have Bobby show you where everything is. Bobby! Help Stephanie set the table!"

I was amused and amazed at the alacrity with which Rob responded. I learned later that Alice had been raised in a German community in central South Dakota. Her upbringing manifested itself by a slight accent which I at first thought was a speech impediment; she said "dunt", "kunt", and "shunt" instead of didn't, couldn't, and shouldn't. Apparently, Germans don't ("dunt") resonate through their noses. Alice also would have made one hell of a field marshal. She was incredibly organized and accepted no excuses for failed performance. Alice was opinionated, strong-willed, and when she gave an order or made a "request" (a subsection of order), her husband and sons never questioned her. They did as they were told.

This was to cause much irritation for me. If Rob's mother told him to perform a domestic chore, he accomplished it promptly and cheerfully. If I asked him to do the same task in our home, he always had an excuse handy. In Rob's castle the domestic sphere was mine alone. Unfortunately, it still is.

Rob and I set the table for ten adults (the kids ate in the kitchen) with a damask tablecloth and napkins and doily placemats—Alice's handiwork, of course. I commented to Rob that the doilies were redundant but he said they were a tradition. Then we placed the bone china and the sterling silver. Alice had a complete set for twelve.

"My God, Rob, this stuff is gorgeous!" I said as I placed silverware. "Where'd your folks get it?"

"It was Mom's wedding present from her parents. I guess it was sort of a dowry. This kind of stuff was important back then."

"It's important now. I just can't afford it," I murmured but he ignored me.

"Rob?" I asked tentatively as I folded napkins. "Would you like me to call you Bobby?"

"Absolutely not. I hate it. I chose Rob in L.A. and that's what I want to be called."

He sounded slightly belligerent so I was careful as I asked, "Then why don't you ask your folks to call you Rob?"

"I did but I've been Bobby to them all my life and I guess I'll always be 'little Bobby', the baby of the family."

And he was. The curious thing was that when my tall, handsome, intelligent, take-charge husband was around his family I could see him shrink down to the emotional and intellectual level of a seven-year-old. In an ordinary (i.e., non-family) social situation, Rob had meticulous table manners and was a charming host or guest. When he was with his family he mixed his peas with his mashed potatoes, played with his meat, and generally acted like Dennis the Menace. It was not an attractive transformation.

At six o'clock, Marvin rose from his recliner, rumbled "What time's supper?" and Rob's siblings began to show up.

Ricky and Christine were the first to arrive. Rick was the shortest and stockiest of the boys, and looked the most like Alice. He had curly blond hair, a beard, and sharp gray eyes. He had a doctorate in animal husbandry and taught at South Dakota State University, he informed me. This obviously meant a lot to him because that's the first thing that came out of his mouth as he shook my hand.

Christine was also short and stocky and had red hair and freckles. She and Ricky looked like a pair of gnomes standing on either side of the doorway. Christine, the other "artist" in the family, had a small gallery downtown that sold native paintings and her own pottery.

Rick and Christine lived on a farm just outside of town where Rick was planning to experiment with cattle breeding. His goal was to publish a paper on some aspect of cows and their sex habits. He said he and Chris were also planning to get two riding horses. He offered the use of the horses to Rob and me when he got them. Maybe that was his idea of a wedding present.

Christine gave me a shy hug. "We're so glad you're here. Bobby's been moping around like an old dog."

"I was lonesome, too," I lied as I hugged her back.

"Boy, you must have been to give up such an exciting career. I've seen your beer ad and I rub it in to all my friends that I'm related to such a glamorous person," she confided.

Glamorous? I'd never considered myself glamorous. But, hell, if they were buying it, I'd sell it to 'em—sweetly and modestly, of course.

Alice bustled up (didn't the woman ever walk? She always traveled like a duck on speed). "Oh, you've got the grown-up table finished," she observed as she perfunctorily bussed Christine and Rick. "Maybe you girls wouldn't mind setting the kitchen table for the kids" and she was off again.

Christine and I followed Alice to the kitchen. The men went to the living room to watch TV.

Tom, Nancy, and their three boys arrived then. Tom looked like an older Rob with a keg of beer under his shirt. He was the only son who had gotten seriously out of shape. Nancy had the style of a vigorous sixty-year-old, which would have been terrific except she was in her mid-thirty's. Her hair was heavily sprayed into a helmet and she wore a polyester pantsuit. She smiled at me but the smile seemed out of practice. Her three sons were normal, noisy, rowdy boys. They looked at me blankly, unimpressed and disinterested, and raced off to play with toy guns.

Tom gave me a big, jovial bear hug, commented on how pretty I was and said wasn't it nice to have another pretty woman in the family besides Marilyn (Nancy's mouth thinned out at that). Then he went to the living room with the other men.

Nancy glared after Tom then, in a take-charge voice, she said, "Mother Anderson, let me make the gravy." But when it came to giving orders Nancy was an amateur compared to Alice who said, "I think I have everything under control, Nancy. We won't eat until Mikey and Marilyn get here so why don't you just relax and get to know Stephanie. Or you can help set the kitchen table if you want."

Nancy's mouth thinned again but Big Mama had spoken. Nancy shouldered us out of the way and started to set the table as Christine and I leaned against cupboards, trying to talk and stay out of Alice's way at the same time. Christine immediately asked me about my acting career and I told her it was on hold.

"I just don't know how you could stand to give it up," she said again.

"It's just a job like anything else, Christine, only you're always looking for work. And you get rejected either for the way you look or the way you act. It can wear on the ego after awhile."

"That's hard to believe," Christine protested.

"Well, maybe it's different for somebody like Meryl Streep. I was just a grunt," I shrugged.

Nancy leaned forward and breathed mint into my face. "I don't blame you for marrying Bobby and getting away from all that. I've heard all about those casting couches."

She said 'casting couches' in a stage whisper and looked at Alice meaningfully. I was a little startled by this, as was Alice. Was Nancy implying that I screwed my way into my commercials? I took a good look at her face. Of course she was, the horrible old minty thing. Alarm was dawning on Alice's face. Good, old-fashioned wife and mother that she was, the suggestion that her baby boy had married a less-than-moral woman appalled her. I'd have to nip that train of thought in the bud.

"Nancy, I've heard the casting couch stories, too, but I never had sexual advances made on me. As a matter of fact, I don't know anyone that's happened to. You have to understand, Nancy," I condescended to her, "there're millions of dollars involved and most casting people don't have the time or the power to force unwilling actresses to do anything. There's just too much money at stake."

I paused, a little surprised at myself. Why in the world was I defending the Industry? I knew harassment occurred. I just wasn't going to give Nancy the satisfaction of admitting it.

Nancy sniffed. "Well, I've read where that sort of thing happens all the time."

"Maybe you should quit reading the *National Enquirer*," I replied shortly and Nancy and I glared at each other. Obviously, we were never going to be buddies. Before any other missiles could be launched, Nancy's three sons started running through the kitchen, screaming and pretending to shoot each other. Nancy left the battlefield to chase them into the backyard.

Christine smiled at me apologetically. "Sometimes, Nancy can get a little...self-righteous. We don't pay much attention to her."

"Nancy's real involved with the church," Alice observed neutrally.

"What denomination does she belong to?" I asked. I intended to avoid it like the plague.

"Oh, she's Lutheran, like us, but she's really...serious about it," said Alice.

"What Alice means is that Nancy uses the church to beat up other people," said Chris and Alice didn't contradict her. "Really, her nose is just out of joint because Tom said you were pretty," Christine went on. "Tom's been saying the same thing about Marilyn for years."

"But Nancy doesn't object when he compliments Marilyn?" I asked.

"She hates it! And she hates Marilyn!" Christine giggled. Alice tsked and shook her head. "Nancy'll be after Marilyn the minute she walks in the door," Christine added, "unless she decides to keep you on the hot seat."

Great, I groaned to myself. A new family tradition—cat fights with dinner. And I knew I had to battle this by myself because my husband was glued to the TV with the other monkeys, seeing, hearing, and saying nothing. The pain behind my eyes jabbed again.

Mike and Marilyn finally showed up. Mike was built on the same blocky lines as Rick but was a little taller and much more stylish. The banker brother from Sioux Falls had blown-dry hair, a carefully trimmed moustache, and wore a Brooks Brothers suit with highly polished loafers. His wife, Marilyn, the ex-Miss South Dakota, carried herself proudly. As is true with most beauty pageant winners I've met (they tend to gravitate to La-La-Land), she was attractive and well turned out, a real country club type. Polyester had never touched her body. Marilyn also had that beauty pageant attitude; you know, all teeth and flattery. Personally, I've always found that kind of charm a little smarmy but as a sister-in-law Marilyn was a hell of a lot better than Nancy. We bared teeth at each other in professional smiles and shook hands.

Mike and Marilyn had two children: Ryan, 9, and Tiffany, 8. They both looked like Marilyn; blond, blue-eyed, and well pressed. They ran outside to play with the other junior Andersons.

With the whole clan assembled it was time to mash the potatoes, carve the roast, ferry the food to the table, and get everybody sat down. As guest of honor and only brunette, I was placed on Marvin's right, across from Rob, and next to Tom. Nancy sat on the other side of Tom so we wouldn't have to look at each other or, hopefully, converse. Alice sat in the chair closest to the kitchen so she could run and fetch. She called it the jump seat.

Marvin suggested that, as the new member of the family, I say grace. I tried to demur because I didn't know what Lutherans said but I was urged on by everyone. There didn't seem to be any graceful way out so I dredged up my childhood prayer "Bless us oh Lord, and these thy gifts" which clearly labeled me as a mackerel snapper. I finished the prayer by myself and looked up to see Nancy leaning in front of Tom to glare at me. Once she'd made sure I'd noted her disapproval she leaned back and hissed triumphantly in Tom's ear "Catholic!" in the same tone she'd probably said "unclean" toward lepers in a past life. I looked at Rob and raised an eyebrow. He just shook his head slightly and looked down at his plate, which left me a little miffed. Where was the white knight that came to my aid against drunks and burglars? Rob was dumb as a post and just as useless. Alice broke the silence.

"That was a lovely blessing, Stephanie. Everybody start passing something." She started the platter of roast beef.

The meal looked like a Norman Rockwell feast. Besides the roast, we had mashed potatoes topped with what looked like a cup of melted butter, biscuits, thick rich gravy, squash, and steamed green beans. This was the sort of dinner I'd tried earlier to prepare for Rob and had failed at, dismally. Alice's meal was wonderful—with the exception of the green beans. Midwestern cooks boil all vegetables to a grayish-greenish puree. You can tell what it was supposed to be by the little bits and pieces that hadn't been boiled to death. I'm told this cooking process was dictated by problems with home-canning, but you'd get more nutrition by drinking the water the poor little bits were boiled in than eating the bits themselves…more taste, too.

One dish I'd never seen before as part of dinner was Jell-O with crushed pineapple and miniature marshmallows. I'd always thought of Jell-O as dessert but here it was a side dish. The official dessert was an enormous chocolate cake. Alice had made it herself from scratch. I'd thought all cakes came from a box.

The conversation was dominated by the women with a few shrieks from the kids in the kitchen. The men quietly packed away huge amounts of food and only spoke to ask someone to "pass the potatoes please". Mike stopped chewing long enough to ask me about my trip but that was the only aberration.

Maintaining my composure and providing small talk with this roomful of strangers was becoming difficult. Fortunately, Nancy decided to attack Marilyn since I was out of her line of sight. Tom didn't pay any attention to me either because he was busy shoveling food in his face. Alice spent her time jumping up to refill bowls for the men and trying to head Nancy off at the pass. Christine would catch my glance, roll her eyes, and try to engage Marilyn in conversation about her children. I pushed my food around my plate and wished my headache away. If I hadn't been so tired maybe I could have been amused at this display of insular family bickering, but I just wanted to go to bed.

After dessert, the men retired to belch in front of the TV and we women cleaned up. So far, the women had been in charge of meal preparation, dinner entertainment, and cleanup. The men were in charge of sitting on their dead butts. My headache got worse.

Alice washed, I dried, Christine put things away, and Nancy sat in a corner. She didn't say anything through the dishwashing period. Whatever had fueled her had given up the ghost for which I was sincerely grateful. As a matter of fact, she looked as tired and miserable as I felt.

We completed our work and joined the men in the living room. The children were spread out on any available flat surface so I took that as my cue to excuse myself.

"I'm sorry to be such a party-pooper but I'm exhausted. I hope you don't mind but I think I'll go to bed," I said to the room in general.

Alice became very solicitous and apologetic for not thinking sooner that I might be tired. She asked if she could get me anything and I said "no, of course not. It's been very nice meeting all of you" and I staggered off. Rob called after me asking if I wanted him to join me but I told him to stay and have a good time. The last thing I wanted at that point was a member of the Anderson family bothering me.

I'd almost made it down the basement steps when Alice called out helpfully, "I'll come down and throw the cat out for you."

Throw Pudgy out? Over my dead body. "That's okay, Alice. She always sleeps with me," I called back. "I'll just lock her up in the bedroom."

"She sleeps with you?" Alice sounded horrified. "Is that healthy?"

"Hasn't hurt me so far," I yelled.

"Well, I don't know. We've never had an animal that..."

"Goodnight, Alice. Don't worry about a thing. We'll be just fine," I said through clenched teeth and closed the door.

Pudgy was asleep on the foot of the bed. I picked her up and hugged her fiercely. She meeped, struggled out of my arms, and crankily settled herself back on the bed. She seemed to have the right idea so I crawled under the covers, fully clothed, and fell into an exhausted stupor.

Rob woke me up an hour later when he opened the door and turned on the light. I struggled awake and Pudgy scurried under the bed.

"Well," Rob said brightly, "what'd you think of the family?"

"They seem okay," I yawned. "Except for Nancy."

"Aw, don't pay any attention to Nancy. She's mean to everybody."

"Why in the world do you put up with her?"

Rob said simply, "She's family."

My headache came back abruptly. I staggered off to the bathroom and popped four aspirins. When I returned Rob was undressed and in bed. I stripped down to my underwear and joined him. He threw his arm over me, grabbed my breast, nuzzled my ear, and whispered, "Isn't it great to be here together? And we're finally alone."

Six hours ago I'd been pleased to see this bozo. Since then, I'd been subjected to an evening of playing Christian to a houseful of lions. Not only was I not pleased to be here I had a splitting headache! Did he seriously think I was going to have sex with him? With his whole family upstairs probably listening in?

I whispered back fiercely, "Don't you dare try anything."

What a difference six hours makes. I guess the honeymoon was over.

Beethoven's Fifth was drifting downstairs as I fell asleep. Rob told me later it's called the Death Symphony. Figures.

chapter 7

I woke up about 7:00 the next morning in a better frame of mind. It's amazing what nine hours of sleep can do for you. I rolled over, ready to apologize to Rob, but the face on the pllow next to mine had fuzzy ears, whiskers, and tuna breath. Rob wasn't in the bathroom either, so I put on a robe and wandered upstairs. Marvin, Alice, and Rob were sitting around the table, eating toast and cereal, and sharing parts of the paper. *Winchester Cathedral* was playing on the radio. I hesitated, not wanting to intrude, but Alice saw my face hanging in the doorway and immediately jumped up. "Good morning, Stephanie. I've got juice in the refrigerator and I'll make you some toast. We have to put some meat on those bones," she declared.

I thought I needed to take off five pounds. "I normally just have coffee in the morning, Alice," I said as I got a cup from the cupboard. "Sit down and finish your breakfast." She certainly didn't have to wait on me hand and foot; *I* didn't have a penis. But Alice was in motion.

I sat down at the table trying to make eye contact with Rob but he concentrated on the paper and ignored me. Alice's chatter filled the vacuum. "Did you sleep well?" she asked. "We knew you were tired. That's why we let you sleep in."

Sleep in? It was 7:05 in the morning! If this was life in the Midwest I bet Dorothy ran that tornado down and jumped in. I needed to get into a place of my own.

"So, Rob," I said deliberately, "when do I get to check out our apartment?"

Rob gave me a sidelong glance, put down his paper, drained his coffee cup, and stood up. The last time I saw him move that fast someone was dismantling my car. "Gettin' late, gotta go," he muttered and ran across the kitchen to grab his books. "I'll be home around five. We'll talk then," he added before he was out the door.

His quick exit even got Marvin's attention. I flushed in embarrassment. I didn't know if he was leaving because he really had an early class or because he wanted to avoid a scene in front of his parents. I knew I'd been ugly last night but I had hoped he'd be more understanding.

Alice deposited two slices of thickly buttered toast and a small glass of juice in front of me. I looked up at her apologetically and gestured to Rob's profile sailing across the kitchen window outside. "I was just wondering when we'd go to the apartment. I have to call the moving company and give them a delivery address. I was hoping he'd be free later..." I tried to explain.

"Well, he's busy today. He has school, you know," Alice said. "I can give you the address so you can make your call then we'll spend the day together. Doesn't that sound nice?"

Not really but it's not like I had a lot of options. I ate food I didn't want and got ready to spend time with a woman I didn't know. The 'whither thou goest' contract should have some protection clauses built in.

Marvin had left for the store by the time I'd showered and dressed. Alice was finally sitting down to breakfast but she jumped right up to get my new address for me. I called the moving company and repeated the street address, which included a space number. I was a little confused by this but concluded that "space" was the South Dakota term for apartment.

I was preparing to join Alice at the table with a cup of coffee when she abruptly stood, took her dirty dishes in the sink, and started to run water. "I thought I'd take you on a tour of Brookings and the campus today," she announced as she squirted soap. "We just have a few chores to do first. You can do any laundry you have. If you need to press anything, the ironing board is in the laundry room downstairs next to your bedroom. I'll just get these dishes. But finish your coffee, don't let me hurry you."

Yeah, right. Like anyone could sit and enjoy a quiet moment while the blitzkrieg was on.

I took my coffee downstairs, threw in a load of laundry, and puttered around in my bedroom just to hide out for a while. I spent an inordinate amount of time cleaning out Pudgy's box before I reluctantly dragged myself upstairs. Alice assigned me my chores. I was in charge of dusting and vacuuming. I commented that the house looked pretty clean to me but Alice poohpoohed that remark. "It has to be done everyday, you know," she said. "Cleanliness is next to Godliness."

No wonder church memberships are down, I thought to myself, *the people are dying from overwork.* But I managed to avoid saying it. I was a guest, after all.

Alice came to supervise as I desultorily swiped an end table with a pair of Marvin's old jockey shorts. She watched me stir the dust for a few minutes, disapproval and impatience screaming from every pore in her body.

"No, no, no," she finally interrupted. "You're not doing it right." She grabbed the underwear and the Pledge and shouldered me out of the way. "Now, there's a right way to do things," she said and demonstrated. "You have to move the magazines and dust underneath. You have to pick up the furniture and get the feet" and she heaved up an end table to polish the legs and pick invisible toe jam from the feet. Then Alice grabbed all the doilies and handed them to me. "Take these outside and give them a good shake. I only wash them once a month." She started to leave the room muttering under her breath "young women today" and "doing a job well" when she turned to look at me and said, "Your mother died when you were young, didn't she?" I admitted that was true. Alice looked stricken. "Here I've been yelling at you and your mother never had a chance to teach you how to clean! Well, don't you worry. I'll teach you how Bobby is used to having things done. He'll never know he's left home!"

"Oh good," I said weakly. But I was a good girl and didn't argue. It wouldn't kill me to clean for a few days; I'd pay for my room and board, and penance for my nastiness to Rob. I set my jaw and shook the doilies with a vengeance to *In the Mood* by what sounded like chickens. This was the strangest radio station I'd ever listened to.

We finished the housework in time to make lunch for Marvin and Ricky. I must have looked surprised to see Rick because Alice smiled. "Our house is closer than the farm," she explained. "And Ricky likes to look after his folks. He's my best boy that way."

I remembered what Leslie had said about mothers and sons and their strange bond. The way Rick looked at his mother I could almost see an invisible umbilical cord. He interrogated me about what Alice and I talked about, what we did that morning…It was a little chilling. I felt like I'd moved into Bates Motel. But Marvin didn't seem to find anything weird in Rick's possessiveness. Of course, it would have been hard to tell if he had; he was expressionless as he silently ate his sandwich.

Rick drained his glass and turned his attention back to his mother. "You're probably tired, Mom. Stephanie can get me some more milk." He held his glass out to me expectantly.

I'd been ordered around by Alice all morning and I'd had enough. I didn't owe Rick anything and now seemed the time to set some boundaries.

"If you want some milk you'll have to get it yourself," I said evenly.

Marvin stopped chewing and looked up.

Rick flushed. "I was just trying to save work for Mom," he said.

"If you want to save work for your mother you should eat out," I returned coolly.

Alice was flustered by the exchange. She quickly got the milk from the refrigerator and poured Rick a glass. "I don't mind. I like to have my boys around," she explained and patted Rick's shoulder. Marvin smiled slightly and returned to his sandwich.

After lunch Alice shooed the men out the door, did the dishes, and suggested we take a drive. She wanted to show me the best grocery stores, the post office, the Laundromat (unless I wanted to use her machine; "You're welcome anytime, I'll show you how Bobby likes his clothes done"), and the family business. I followed as Alice unlocked her car, a match of Marvin's Buick—only this one had seats that were covered with doilies. "Careful, Stephanie," Alice warned, "don't wrinkle the antimacassars." I carefully rearranged the doily I'd disturbed and Alice slowly drove off.

This was the first chance I'd had to sit back and take in the town I'd impetuously moved to. My first impression was: Everything was so clean. There was no graffiti or garbage in the streets and the houses were well tended. My second impression was: Everything was so green. This was September so the heat of summer had passed but autumn hadn't really started. The trees—and there were a lot of them—still had leaves and all the lawns were mowed, edged, and trimmed.

Alice drove first to the campus of South Dakota State University "so you know where your husband goes everyday" she said roguishly. I saw a large lawn Alice called the campus green surrounded by old, brick, three-story buildings. The tower I'd seen from the interstate when I'd driven in yesterday was a campanile and had been built around the 1900's. Students were sitting under enormous fir trees and on benches. It was peaceful and scholarly; I could imagine a frat boy singing *Sweetheart of Sigma Chi* under the windows of Winona Hall.

My preconceptions were considerably jarred. I'd expected sod houses and Quonset huts. I mean, everybody on the West Coast is so snotty about the Midwest, I figured they knew what they were talking about. Apparently not.

"This was all there was to the college when I went to school here. Back before it became a University," Alice told me.

"You got a college degree?" I asked surprised. "In what?"

"Home Economics," Alice said proudly.

I didn't even know there was such a degree. No wonder Alice took being a wife and mother so seriously. She was a professional.

"It's built up a lot since I graduated," Alice continued. "Of course, there are a lot more students now. I'll drive around to the other side so you can see the new part."

The new part of the University was more in line with what I'd been used to; big new buildings spread across the landscape. The trees were smaller on this side but the grass, once again, was green and neat. Rows of petunias were planted next to sidewalks to provide color.

"It's so clean," I marveled.

Alice's looked interested. "Oh? Isn't it clean in California?"

I thought of the graffiti and garbage littering the streets of L.A. "Not as a general thing," I said. "My neighborhood was nice but most areas can get pretty messy."

"Don't the residents clean it up?" Alice asked, curious.

"The street sweeper goes through once a week but you know how people are…" I petered out as I looked around. How could Alice know how "people" were? "People" weren't like that here.

Alice drove me down Main Street to the family hardware store. Marvin and Tom were busy with customers so we didn't stay long.

Alice told me if I needed anything family members got a discount. I carefully filed that information away. Then we walked down the street to Christine's 'gallery'. I don't know anything about pottery and was not particularly curious. Christine was busy framing a poster for a customer so we didn't stay long there, either.

Alice showed me the town library, helped me apply for a card, and then drove aimlessly. She seemed to feel the need to entertain me but didn't quite know how to do it. I just wanted to take a nap. I think both of us were getting a little stressed out from being nice to each other.

I was relieved when Alice decided she had to go home and start supper. Of course, since I was now 'family' and no longer a 'guest' I was expected to help. The idea of a nap was ridiculed. "You're a young woman," Alice scoffed. "You don't need naps. Let me show you Bobby's favorite meatloaf recipe."

There was no way out of it. Man, I had to get into a place of my own. Soon.

I couldn't bring up the subject until supper was eaten and the dishes were washed. Alice kept me busy and Rob avoided me. I finally waylaid him as he headed toward the living room and that damn TV set. "Rob," I hissed, "don't you think I should at least see our apartment?"

He just looked stubborn until his mother said, "Bobby, you can't avoid the subject forever. You better show Stephanie what she's in for."

The way everybody kept talking about the apartment was making me nervous. Rob sighed and reluctantly agreed. With his mother, of course, not me.

Rob packed me into his Buick and we took off. I yattered about the day I'd spent with his mother to make conversation but he was silent. I thought he was still pouting about last night, the big baby, so I sat back, crossed my arms on my chest, and stuck my lip out. Two could play the pouting game.

Rob pulled into an alley, bounced past a short row of mobile homes, and stopped at the end of the line. He turned off the ignition, pointed at the last trailer, turned to me and said quietly, "This is it."

I looked at the trailer incredulously, looked at Rob who didn't blink, and looked back at my future 'home'. That poor old tin can had seen hard usage. It was dented, scuffed, and in need of a wash. It sat precariously on blocks and ripped sheets of plastic hung off the windows. I was speechless.

"Maybe we better go inside," Rob said finally.

We got out of the car, walked around the side of the trailer, trudged up some rickety steps that stopped about a foot below the doorsill, unlocked the door, which had a loose hinge, and climbed inside.

The trailer was designed so the exterior door opened directly into the living room. The kitchen/dining area was to the right, and two bedrooms and a bathroom were down a hall to the left. The floor was covered with dark green shag carpet throughout, except for the kitchen, which had linoleum. The walls were covered with some sort of cheap wood paneling and the ceilings were acoustical tile. There were no drapes or blinds on the windows but that really didn't make much difference because you couldn't see past the plastic anyway. It was horribly, stomach-churningly filthy. A thick coating of grease covered the walls and the ceiling was discolored with cigarette smoke. The kitchen appliances seemed to be a bile-shade of avocado but they were so grease-covered it was quite possible that they'd rotted. My Reeboks stuck to the linoleum.

I went down the hallway and peeked into the bedrooms and bathroom. They weren't grease-covered, which was an improvement, but they reeked of cigarette smoke and the dust made me sneeze. The toilet bowl was obscured by hard water stains and the tub/shower enclosure was curtainless. A tiny closet just off the bathroom contained an old furnace. I went back to Rob who'd stayed in the living room.

"Well?" he said.

"I don't know what to say," I returned honestly. I was numb.

"It was all I could get at the last minute. Enrollment at SDSU is way up," Rob explained.

"Mmmm," I said. I walked to a louvered window, looked at it speculatively, and turned to Rob. "Does it open?"

"Sure," he said and struggled with the crank for a minute. It squeaked open, protesting loudly. "Just needs some oil," Rob said.

I crossed to the kitchen, looked in the refrigerator, and counted the dead bugs in it. I moved to the stove and turned a knob, watched the gas flame up, turned the knob off, and wiped my hand on my pants.

"Well?" Rob challenged. "Aren't you going to say anything?"

I gazed around and asked, "How much they paying us to live here?"

"Very funny. Let me tell you, it's only costing me $250.00 a month, plus utilities, and I didn't even have to pay a security deposit!" he finished triumphantly.

"You got robbed."

"Okay, Stevie, you've been mad ever since you got here. Now you have a reason. Go ahead, let me have it."

"I haven't been mad ever since I got here. You've been a pig ever since I drove in," I retorted. "But we can argue about that later. Let's talk about this trailer!"

"It was the only thing in my price range," Rob said stubbornly.

"How about my price range?"

"I'm not going to touch your money. And I told you before, it's just temporary."

"Temporary?!" I yelled, "A school year is not temporary! It's a long time!" I took a deep breath to calm myself. "Rob, I have furniture coming. How can I put it here?"

"Well…you can clean it up a little," Rob said reasonably.

This set me off again. "*I* can clean it up? When did you turn into a cripple?"

"Listen, I have classes all week and I have a seminar this weekend. I'll help when I can but I don't have much free time. I'm sorry but I don't have time to clean and you do."

We glared at each other. We'd been alone together twice in two days and we'd had two fights. Apparently, our marriage had a few bugs in it. But then again, so did our "home".

At least we were free to have a knockdown drag-out which seemed to be what the situation called for. I screeched and Rob roared which I found interesting in the detached, observing part of my mind. Rob had never yelled at me before. But, as I'd learned much earlier in my development, the best defense was a spirited offense so, boy, was I offensive. After a day of being nice to Alice it felt good to finally cut loose and throw a tantrum. I stomped around the trailer, raising dust and waving my arms, and Rob provided his baritone thunder as counterpoint to my shrill denouncements. We had quite a bloodthirsty duet.

"Thank you so much for your consideration regarding my money," I spat. "Too bad you're not equally considerate about back-breaking labor. You're willing to have me turn into a cleaning drudge so you can save a few dollars!"

"All you have to do is wash a couple of floors and a few appliances," Rob said slightingly as I stomped around then added a qualifier as dust billowed. "And maybe vacuum. I don't expect you to be a cleaning woman. But this isn't the big city and I can't afford the princess act so get over it."

"Princess act!" I gasped in outrage. "I've worked for everything I ever got!"

"You inherited everything you ever got!" Rob hollered.

"Well," I spluttered, "even if I did it's mine to do with as I like. And I'm not turning it over to you or saving it for your personal disposal!"

"I'm trying to save your damn money!"

"Right. By forcing me into hard labor."

We'd gotten into a circular pattern here. Since I didn't seem to be doing any significant damage I changed tactics. "And another thing, I'm not your mother. I don't take orders and I won't jump just because you say I should!"

Rob put his fists on his hips. "You know, you've done nothing but sneer at my family ever since you got here!"

"I have not 'sneered' at your family!"

"How about those cracks you made about Nancy?"

"How about those cracks she made at me?"

"Oh, that's just the way she is."

"Well, this is just the way I am!"

We yelled at each other for another ten minutes before we stopped, panting slightly, and looked at each other haggardly. I finally said what had been on my mind for two weeks.

"Do you want to just forget this?" I asked. "I can always go back to Los Angeles. It'll be embarrassing but...well, we did rush into this. It wasn't smart."

"No, I don't want you to go back to L.A.," Rob said impatiently. "I'm serious about this marriage and want it to work. Don't you?"

"Rob, I didn't drive across country for the scenery," I retorted snidely. "But I'm tired, your mother's been running me ragged all day, and you've done nothing but pout at me. If you want this marriage to work you've got one hell of a way of showing it!"

Rob considered my accusation for a moment then said, "I'm sorry if I seemed to be pouting but it really bothered me last night when you didn't want me to touch you."

"I didn't want you to touch me because you took your horrible sister-in-law's side. And I was tired. I'd forgiven and forgotten the whole thing until you pouted at me this morning."

"Well…you hurt my feelings," Rob mumbled.

"Yeah, well, you hurt mine, too."

"I guess. I'm sorry." Rob was still mumbling but he was starting to look contrite.

"I'm sorry, too," I mumbled back. I forgave him; I was too tired not to. We hugged and kissed. I shed a few tears against Rob's manly chest. Normally, that clinging behavior is against my principles but it'd been a long five days.

"Things'll get better after we get on our own," Rob said comfortingly.

I sniffed and looked around. "Sure," I said bleakly.

Rob followed my gaze and grimaced. "I guess I didn't want to admit how bad it was. I was just glad I could find something. I like the folks and all but I'm too old to go back to being a baby again."

"Then how come you wanted us to live in your parents' basement?"

"That was Mom's idea; she was always standing around listening to me talk to you. I had to pretend to like the idea or I'd have hurt her feelings. But, my God, she's always telling me what to do and asking me if I want something. I can't get a minute's peace."

"You didn't seem to object to being spoiled."

"I'd rather you do it than Mom." Rob ducked when I pretended to take a swing at his arm.

I wasn't ready to face Rob's folks right then so I offered to buy my husband a beer. He introduced me to Jim's Tap downtown and as we drank our Budweisers I diffidently suggested that I pay half the rent on a decent apartment.

"Absolutely not," Rob said firmly. "I'm not taking a dime. This is what I can afford so this is what I'll get. Besides, didn't you hear me say there was nothing available? If you don't like the trailer we live with the folks. Those are the only options right now."

I had to admit that I had no respect for a man who expected me to support him; I just never thought it would backfire on me like this. I frowned unhappily so Rob added, "If you can stand the parents another week I can help clean then. We'll just stall the movers."

The thought of cleaning up that awful trailer was almost too daunting to face but I couldn't stand too many more days being ordered around by Alice. Besides, that 'Princess' crack rankled. I made my decision. "Finish up that beer, Prince Charming," I ordered. "The Princess here has to get up early and go to work."

I was out of the shower, dressed, and pouring coffee for myself by 7:00 the next morning. I had talked myself into a state of steely determination. If I wanted out from under my mother-in-law's thumb I'd have to make a place for myself. Besides, my furniture was coming. If necessary, I would work twenty-four hours a day until that damned trailer was habitable. The Andersons were in the middle of breakfast and seemed surprised to see me alert so early. Marvin was so surprised he almost said something.

"I have a lot of work to do on the trailer," I said by way of explanation. "No, Alice, don't get up. I can get my own toast."

"You'll need something more substantial than toast before we get going," Alice said. My ears twitched at the word "we" and I glanced at her. "I'm cleaning with you," she announced.

I quietly rejected her offer. The trailer was my problem, not hers. Alice had done more than enough by providing a temporary sanctuary for Pudgy and me. I didn't feel right accepting any more favors from her.

"But that's what families are for," Alice argued, puzzled at my attitude. She settled back in her chair to finish her coffee and pointed to a cardboard box by the sink. "I packed some cleaning supplies and rags. We can get anything we're missing from the store on our way over."

Not being a complete fool I quit arguing. I checked out the box of cleaning supplies. There was every cleaning product known to woman in that box. "Remind me to get some pumice stone, too," Alice said. She said it was for the toilet.

The only items missing were buckets, brooms, and gloves. The buckets and brooms were in the garage but Alice scoffed at the idea of rubber gloves. She proudly held out her crevassed, chip-nailed, work-worn hands for my inspection.

"I'm getting gloves," I said.

By 8:00 we were breakfasted, shopped, and at the trailer, ready for work. It looked even worse in the cold light of morning. I think it even smelled worse.

"Oh Lord," I breathed prayerfully. "Any suggestions where we should start?"

"My father always said 'Plow here, plow there, plow everywhere, it's all got to be plowed'," Alice said philosophically. "Let's start with the ceilings and work our way down."

Alice poured ammonia in a bucket of warm water, handed me a push broom, and sent me to start on the bedroom ceilings while she tackled the insides of the kitchen appliances. In fifteen minutes I had scummy water running through my hair, my clothes, and on the carpet.

"Will this stuff wreck the carpet?" I called to Alice.

"Nothing can ruin this carpet," Alice called back.

"How about my eyes?" I sputtered.

"Close your eyes," Alice advised which seemed counterproductive. How was I supposed to see what I was doing? But I did my best. I peeked and pushed, peeked and pushed, peeked and pushed. All I got was sore arms.

"This isn't working," I yelled to Alice. She came back to the bedroom, inspected my lack of progress, tsked, and said, "It always worked in the henhouse back home."

"I don't think your chickens smoked," I said.

"No, that's true, they didn't," Alice agreed. After a lengthy consultation, we took a break, went back to the house for a ladder, and started in again.

I think I paid for every sin I'd ever committed that day because I was in Hell. I have never been so dirty in my life. Scummy, greasy water worked into my pores as I scrubbed ceilings and walls with a brush and wiped them down with a rag. I finally gave up on the gloves and took the damn things off. They hadn't protected my hands at all. As a matter of fact, they served as holding tanks that pickled my hands and dumped dirty water on my face every time I lifted my arms.

Alice worked like a machine. We took short breaks for sandwiches and cans of soda then toiled until 5:00 when Alice announced she had to go home to make supper. I looked at her incredulously.

"After a day like this you want to cook?" I asked. "It's Saturday, let me take you out to dinner somewhere." I took in her appearance and my own disheveled self. "After we get cleaned up," I amended.

"No, dear," Alice said as she emptied her bucket in the sink. "I won't let you waste your money like that."

All the Andersons were out to save me money by killing me, I thought woefully. We drove home to make din, oops, supper.

Alice must have divined from my huddled-up crouch in the car that I was exhausted so she sent me to shower while she started frying pork chops. I sighed at the thought of fried food. I could feel my face breaking out already.

Rob took pity on me and offered to wash dishes that night which shocked his parents. I smiled and offered him my rubber gloves. "May they work better for you than they did for me," I intoned derisively.

Pudgy was starting to look like a Chiapet from spending so much time in the basement so I put her on her leash and took her outside for a drag. I was tired but not sleepy and some porch setting sounded like a pleasantly Midwestern thing to try.

Even though it was September I only needed a sweatshirt. And I observed...not much: Two pedestrians, some bike riders, and a few cars. The custom was, if you made eye contact with someone, even if you didn't know them from Adam, you waved. It startled me at first but after awhile I got the trick of the right-handed wrist flick. Pudgy was trying to strangle herself on her leash so I took a chance and released her. I was watching her chase bugs when Rob joined me on the porch.

"Hard day?" he asked as he massaged my shoulders.

"Yeah," I admitted. "How was your seminar?"

"Boring. I can help tomorrow."

"That'd be nice."

Rob sat down next to me and we watched the Mighty Bug Hunter leap high to snag a moth. We smiled at each other and listened to the streetlight buzz.

Rob finally broke the silence. "Did Mom drive you nuts today?" he asked.

"Are you kidding? She saved my life," I returned. "That woman is a dynamo."

Rob shrugged. "She grew up on a farm."

"Did they use her instead of a tractor? Honest to God, she worked me into the ground."

"She's used to it."

"Yeah, well, remind me not to get used to it."

"This is a one-time deal, Stevie." Rob put his arm around me and gave me a quick squeeze.

I smiled and leaned against him. "I can't believe how quiet it is here," I commented into the dusk.

"The neighborhood used to be full of kids but we all grew up and went away," Rob said.

I looked at him. "You sound sad."

Rob stretched. "Not really. Just remembering. You ready to go in? I want to get in a few hours of study."

"Not just yet. I think I'll just sit here awhile," I said. Rob went inside and I sprawled comfortably on the step. One more car went by, the people and I waved at each other, and Pudgy got another bug. After the day I'd just put in there was something to be said for peace and quiet.

chapter 8

Rob woke me up with a kiss the next morning. I opened one eye and croaked, "What time is it?"

"It's 7:30. Time to get up."

"Geez, don't you people even take Sunday off?" I moaned.

"We have to go to church," Rob said patiently.

"Church? Oh Christ."

"Exactly. Better get up. Mom hates to be late."

I tried to move but found myself locked in a fetal position. "I think I broke myself," I said in anguish as I slowly straightened out stiff muscles.

"You better get some coffee," Rob advised and grabbed a pair of clean underwear from a scarred dresser. "I'll be out of the shower in fifteen minutes."

"I'm not going to church," I said to his retreating back but he ignored me. I decided to get out of bed anyway. I had to pee.

I tried to come up with some arguments against church attendance as I hauled myself up the basement stairs. Marvin and Alice seemed faintly concerned when I lurched through the doorway but I didn't pay any attention to them. I made a beeline to the coffee pot and wrapped one red, cracked claw around a cup. "I don't know why I even bother drinking this stuff," I muttered to myself. "I should just hook up an IV and save a lot of time and electricity."

Alice broke into my reverie by saying, "Church is at ten, Stephanie, but we like to get there early. You can be ready to leave by nine-thirty, can't you?"

I tried to tell her I wasn't going at all but I was having trouble focusing my eyes. I'd need more coffee to be in any condition to argue. Alice mistook my silence. "Oh, I forgot. Maybe you'd prefer to go to the Catholic Church. I think their service starts around the same time. We can drop you off on the way. We'll just have to leave a little earlier."

I hadn't been to the Catholic Church since my parents' funeral. I'd held a grudge against God. Silly really, God hadn't been driving drunk. Oh, I guess it wouldn't kill me to be a Lutheran for a day. It'd be like cleaning the trailer, a one-time deal. Besides, I'd have more time to wake up.

A hot shower loosened me up to the point that I dismissed the possibility of polio. I fixed my hair and makeup and put on slacks and a sweater. By nine-thirty I was ready.

Alice eyed my slacks with disapproval when I appeared topside. "I think a nice skirt would be more appropriate, don't you?" she asked with an obvious attempt to control her impatience.

I was about to argue when I noticed Rob making "go" gestures with his head. He seemed so frantic I was afraid he'd dislocate something so I obliged him by changing into a skirt. It only took five minutes but it was five minutes past nine-thirty! I was hustled into Marvin's Buick—no doilies to mess up—and we were off.

The Lutheran church was at the very end of Main Street. Marvin drove carefully down Main, stopping for yellow lights and looking both ways before proceeding on green. The church was a large monolithic building with a facade at least three stories high. A huge mural of Christ with His arms outstretched to welcome the driving population was painted on it. I commented favorably on the mural and Alice nodded then said, "We all think it looks like Jesus is directing traffic. But don't tell anyone." The Andersons laughed quietly.

The four of us parked in a pew and prepared to thank God for whatever we felt appropriate—in my case, rest. I think Rob thanked God that I snoozed through most of the sermon. From what little I heard I wanted to debate the main points. But as Rob whispered, the church was not a democracy and argument from me was not wanted or required. I enjoyed the music, though. The choir was wonderful.

The Lutherans had coffee after the service and our branch of the Andersons ran into Tom, Nancy, and their boys while juggling our cookies and cups. Nancy superciliously commented, "I'm surprised you're not at the Catholic Church." I retorted that I was equally surprised, refusing to give her an opening. She took another tack and inquired as to how I spent Saturday, her tone implying that I sat around eating bonbons and painting my toenails. I said that Alice and I had cleaned and cleaned and cleaned.

"I'm glad you didn't expect me to help," Nancy sniffed.

I assured her that I was equally glad not to have her. We smiled nasty-nice smiles at each other and retired to our corners. Rob snagged my hand and led me away to mingle.

"You handled that well," he whispered to me.

"Thank you. I'm getting pretty good at this slash and run approach to family relations," I whispered back and smiled at Chris as she approached with Rick.

"Mom tells me the family dinner will be put off today until we get your trailer stabilized on its blocks and the plastic on the windows," Rick reported. My heart sank. Another family dinner? We'd just had one. I didn't have the strength for cleaning and Anderson socializing, too. I tried to beg off saying that I was too tired and Alice probably was, too, but Rick waved my objections aside.

"We like to have Sunday dinner together. Our folks taught us to stick together," he said. "If Mom doesn't object I don't see why you should. We're helping you, after all."

Chris jumped in to make peace. "This is a bonding ritual for the men," she said to me. "They'll get out their tools, make a lot of noise, then we'll feed 'em. And, knowing Alice, she'll have the food under control. Our job will be to provide moral support and admiration."

The clan got into work clothes and met in Marvin's garage. The men gathered their tools and left for the trailer. Alice ordered Chris and me around for about an hour, then excused us after the ham was in the oven. Chris and I drove over to the trailer in my Miata to check on the men's progress. It was warm and sunny, a day made for hooky, so I put the top down and we took an extensive detour.

"Put on your shades," I instructed Chris as I put on my sunglasses, "we're going California cruising."

We got a lot of stares and three boys in a pickup followed us for about a block, whistling and hooting, until I downshifted and left them in the dust. "Man, I love this car," I said with satisfaction.

"It's nice now," Chris agreed, "but wait'll winter hits. Does it have a plug-in?"

"A plug-in?" I asked, puzzled. "No, it runs on gas."

"No, I mean…oh, never mind," Chris said. "You'll find out."

I was mystified but let the matter drop.

As Chris had predicted, Marvin, Tom, Rick, and Rob made a lot of noise, discussed angles and shims knowledgeably, and got almost nothing done. But boy, were they were happy. I suggested a little Miller time might be in order.

Tom's face lit up. "You have some beer?" he asked.

"No, but I can go get some," I said. There was a pause as all the South Dakotans looked at me.

"Where?" Rick asked.

"The grocery store, I guess," I said.

"They won't sell you any beer on Sunday," Chris explained.

"Okay, then," I temporized, "there must be a liquor store around here someplace. Just tell me where and I'll go."

They were all grinning at my by then. Tom punched Rob in the arm. "You can sure tell she's from out-of-town. Haven't you explained Blue Laws to her yet?" he snickered.

"Blue Laws?" I repeated.

Rob explained. There was one liquor store and it was owned by the city, hence the name Municipal Liquor Store, and it wasn't open on Sunday. No bars were open and grocery stores didn't sell beer on Sunday. If you wanted to drink on the Lord's Day, a practice generally frowned on, you planned ahead.

"I've never heard of that," I admitted, amused.

Rick chose to take offense. "I haven't noticed that having a liquor store open at all hours on every corner ever did any town any good. You'll just have to get used to it," he said snottily.

Rick and I seemed to rub each other all the wrong ways. I started to explain that I hadn't meant to sound critical but Chris instantly jumped in. "Oh, it's all right. You're new around here. Just be glad Nancy didn't hear you suggest profaning the Sabbath. Although," Chris said aside, "between you, me, and the fencepost, I think she drinks pretty heavily when no one's around. But don't breathe a word to of this to Marvin and Alice. They'd just die."

"Nothing worse than a reformed sinner, huh, especially one that hasn't reformed," I said and tucked the bit of information away. So her slump the other night hadn't been hypoglycemia. Not that I'd ever take advantage of gossip, of course, but it's always nice to have some ammunition. Just in case.

Alice drove up in her Buick with a rented carpet cleaner in the trunk and we all got to work. The men blocked up the trailer and covered the windows with plastic. We women ran the carpet cleaner over the shag rug four times. When the water started running clear instead of brown we quit. The trailer was as clean as it was going to get.

We all trooped back to the homestead for a sober and sane Sunday dinner. After the dishes were done and everyone left I was allowed to go downstairs, all by myself, and read a book. It was the first real time to myself I'd had since I'd arrived and I wallowed in it. I was so mellow with good feeling I was affectionate with Rob when he finished studying and joined me in bed. It had been weeks since our last cuddle. It seemed like a year.

"My folks really like you," he said when he was wrapped around me.

"They don't know me well enough to like me."

"You're family. They have to like you. But they'd like you even if you weren't."

Again with the happy family mantra. They were his family, not mine. But Rob's breath was warm on my neck and his hand was cupped on my breast so I didn't start an argument. As a matter of fact, Rob's penis looming on my thighs took my mind off his family completely. I excused myself, snuck off to the bathroom to install my gasket, and returned with the Kleenex box.

"What's that for?" Rob asked. He was lying naked on the bed, arms folded behind his head, flaunting himself.

"We can't leave stains on your mother's sheets," I explained and tossed the box to him.

"Mom raised four boys. She's seen cum stains before."

"Yeah, well, those were solo efforts. I'm involved now." I pulled my T-shirt over my head.

"When did you get shy?" Rob grinned and reached for me.

"I'm not shy. Just remember the Kleenex."

Sex on a squeaky old bed in your mother-in-law's basement is a novel experience. Trying to be quiet made us giggle; trying to keep from giggling made us giggle harder and the bed squeaked more. I wonder if Alice heard us. Hell, I wonder if the neighbors heard us.

My furniture was en route, my guest status was almost over, and I was well and truly laid. Monday morning I did my daily doily flailing with clenched teeth but I did it. Rob was afraid that I wouldn't have any molars left but I told him not to worry, the end was near. I could endure anything.

Of course, two days later Alice and I almost had the blowup Rob feared. She informed me over breakfast that I had to make myself ready for lunch at the church. Being ordered to church twice in one week? And me not even a Lutheran? This was too much. I locked eyes with her and took a deep breath to tell her off when the phone rang. It was the driver of the moving van calling for directions to Dogpatch. My furniture would be delivered tomorrow.

Alice and I both sagged with relief. You know, I think she was just as sick of me as I was of her. So I didn't argue about the luncheon. I could be pleasant for one more day. I even put on a "nice skirt". Alice collected her keys and purse, handed me a covered bowl, and stood in the middle of the kitchen, taking inventory. "Let's see: Stove's off, salad's ready, men's lunch is in the fridge, what have I forgotten? Oh! Stephanie, maybe you should throw the cat out." She looked at me hopefully.

Keeping Pudgy in the basement was the only battle Alice hadn't won and she wouldn't this time either. I looked her right in the eye and smiled defiantly. She dropped the subject. She must have figured me and my cat would be gone soon enough. It wasn't worth hassling at this point.

I was glad I hadn't raised a stink about going to church because the service turned out to be a wedding shower for me. Approximately thirty ladies in polyester dresses and freshly permed hair had brought cakes and salads. I saw Jell-O salads, fruit salads, vegetable salads—and I swear they all contained miniature marshmallows. This town must have cornered the market in marshmallows or nobody had teeth because I've never seen so many of the little buggers before or since. Looking at the geriatric crowd in front of me, I opted for the 'no teeth' theory.

Alice steered me around the room making introductions. The women were all either retired or married to well-to-do men. I finally got it through my head that this was a work day and all the younger women would be at...well, work. The only woman who was remotely close to my age was my sister-in-law, Nancy, and I could have lived without her.

I wouldn't remember anybody's name, of course, but the ladies expected that. "There're too many of us, dear," a gray-haired charmer soothed as she patted my hand. "It'll take awhile to remember all the names. But we know all about you. We're thrilled to have a movie star in town. And we're glad to have you as a member of our church." She moved on to make way for the next lady.

Movie star? Member of the church? My smile became slightly fixed.

I was gushed over, kissed, flattered, and patted. The good ladies had hidden gifts in the next room and I got to open them after we'd eaten marshmallows. I received mostly kitchen equipment. I got can openers, mixing bowls, casserole dishes, spatulas, and a few things that had to be explained to me like jar lid openers and turkey lifters. I got hand-made potholders and home-embroidered dishtowels. Now, I never learned to sew or do crafts but even I could tell that these ladies did fine work. I even got my own set of place mat doilies from Alice. None of the gifts was expensive but everything was useful.

For my part, I gushed, I exclaimed, I laughed. I did my damnedest to show those good-hearted women how much I appreciated their efforts on my behalf. I didn't plan on using any of the kitchen equipment—that's why God made restaurants—but I sure wasn't going to let them know that. It wasn't tough; I'm an actress, after all.

I was called on to make a speech. I stood up and gave the ladies my best smile. "Well, this was quite a surprise," I began and the ladies laughed companionably. "I just want to thank you for the gifts and the lovely lunch. I'm a stranger here and you've certainly made me feel welcome. I appreciate everything you've done to make me feel at home. And I know Rob will appreciate the kitchen equipment" (I didn't say that he'd probably be the one to use it). "I don't really have anything more to say. Just...thank you for everything." I spread my hands helplessly and smiled again. The ladies patted their hands together and laughed again. I had been showered.

Alice and I loaded the presents in the Buick as the other women cleaned up. As guest of honor, I was not expected to wash dishes or put away folding chairs. That many women made short work of the cleanup and soon Alice and I were on our way after waving goodbye.

Jesus pointed us left to the trailer to drop off the loot. After we stowed things in the kitchen drawers I looked around. The ceilings and walls were as clean as they could be without sandblasting. Taken as a whole they didn't look bad. The kitchen and bathroom were spotless. Alice had been right about the pumice stone working on the toilet. It was white. I owed Alice big time; I'd still be up to my elbows in slimy water if it hadn't been for her and I didn't know how to thank her. I'd like to get to know her better. But how? I'd have to knock her over the head to get her to sit down. My Irish background gave me an idea. "Alice, I should be out from underfoot tomorrow. What do you say we celebrate? If I buy a six-pack of beer on the way home, would you have one with me?"

"I have to make supper," she demurred.

"We have lots of time to make supper. C'mon, Alice, we need a celebration and I hate to drink alone."

"Well...all right! I will!" Alice said daringly.

I made a slight detour to buy a six-pack and, since it was a lovely autumn day, I suggested we drink our beers in the backyard. Alice was shocked. "What if the neighbors saw us?" she asked.

"Who cares?" I riposted. But Alice cared. In her age and socio-economic group having a beer outside and in the middle of the day was something one just didn't do. The road to perdition was slippery and one beer could make you slide. That's why God made neighbors; to make sure you didn't take that first step. We sat in the kitchen.

After half a beer I asked Alice to tell me about her family. I didn't need to ask twice. She bustled off—after half a beer her bustle listed a little to the right but it was still there. Nothing slowed that woman down, not hard work, booze, nothing!—to get another photo album. She took a healthy swig of beer and opened the album.

"This is my grandfather, Herman Berk," she began. "He came over from Germany in the late 1800's and settled in Hoven, that's about one hundred miles north of Pierre" (pronounced pier, not the French way). "Grandfather Berk worked as a hired hand for a few years then bought his own farm and married a local girl, Gabriella, my grandmother." Here she showed me Herman and Gabriella's solemn wedding picture. Nobody in this family smiled for photographs. "They had three sons: John, Thomas, Herman, Jr.—my father—and two daughters: Katerin and Margret." She turned to another family portrait. They were a clean-scrubbed, unsmiling lot. "My father took over the family farm and…"

"But he was the third son. Doesn't the first son normally inherit the property?" I interrupted.

"The other two boys didn't want it. John and Thomas left for Chicago to work in the meat packing plants. They're both dead now."

"Didn't your father want to check out the city lights?"

"No. He stayed home and farmed with his dad. He met my mother when he was eighteen and they got married right away and started a family. They lived with his parents until my grandfather retired and moved into town."

"I'm surprised your aunts and uncles didn't raise hell when your father got the farm."

"He bought them out. It was the Depression so he got it cheap. I was a baby so I really wasn't aware of how bad times were. But we were lucky, living on the farm. We always had enough to eat. We grew our own vegetables and canned them. We even had our own apple trees. We always had eggs and milk so we were luckier than most." She turned to another family portrait. Still no smiles. "Anyway, my mother and father had four children, two boys and two girls. I was the youngest. The oldest was Phillip."

"Is he a farmer?"

"No, he was killed in World War Two. He was only eighteen years old. He joined the Navy and his ship sank."

"The Navy? From South Dakota?"

"Phillip was a great reader as a boy and I think *Moby Dick* was his favorite book. He decided he had to go to sea." Alice sighed. "My mother said Phillip was the best of us; the smartest, the kindest, the hardest worker. His death just about killed my parents." She was silent.

I didn't know what to do or say except, "I'm sorry."

"It was a long time ago." Alice shook herself and continued, "This is my older sister, Sarah. She got married when she was getting her nursing degree here and now she and her husband live in Minnesota. And this is my brother, Herman. He has the farm now." She made a little moue of distaste.

"You don't like him?"

"Well, he's family," Alice said and closed the album with finality.

"Enough about my family. Tell me about yours. Bobby tells me your mother was Mexican?"

I listened for a slighting inflection when Alice said 'Mexican'. When I didn't hear one I said equitably, "Tex-Mex. Mom's ancestors were from Mexico but her immediate family came from Texas. Can I get you another beer?" I asked. I didn't feel like talking about me.

"If you're having one, dear."

I got us both a beer but Alice wasn't finished prying yet. "And you're Catholic?" she continued.

"I guess, if I'm anything. I went to Mass and all but my parents didn't agree with the Church on the birth control issue. Mom told me to take what the priests said with a grain of salt."

"That's why you're an only child," Alice concluded.

"I guess my parents felt it was more important to take care of one child well than produce a litter to further the cause of Catholicism," I said ironically and took a long pull on my beer.

"And do you see any of your relatives much?" Alice probed.

"The only ones I'm aware of are the Texas branch and they see women as incubators with arms and legs attached so we can cook and scrub between gestations. So I washed my hands of them, got myself educated, and I'm doing all right."

Alice tsked and took a long pull on her beer. "I've heard those Mexican men are like that."

I stared at Alice. Me and my mother's family weren't Mexicans, we were Hispanics or Latinos or whatever but we were all Americans. And I was the only one allowed to trash them. I responded with a glint in my eye and steel in my voice. "It doesn't seem like you Germans are much different," I said. "Look at your situation."

Alice was shocked. "My father encouraged both his daughters to go to college. Did you know that I taught for a year until I had Thomas? Then I had the house and the children to think of so I stayed home. But I'm proud of my degree."

I raised a sardonic eyebrow. "From where I sit your education only served to attract a more educated husband for you. Then you became exactly what my female relatives are, housewives and mothers."

This stumped her for a moment. Also, the beer had her slightly fuddled. "There's something wrong with your argument. I just can't put my finger on it," she said.

I took pity on her and grinned. "Choice. You chose this lifestyle. My cousins and aunts didn't have that choice."

"That's it," Alice brightened. "I chose this." She smiled smugly.

She should have just said thank you and we could have moved on. Now I had to play with her some more. And maybe enlighten her. I said challengingly, "But then again, did you? Weren't you steered in this direction by custom and habit?" She mulled this over and I continued, "You've worked really hard the last few days. I have too. How come we have to make supper? Aren't you tired?"

"Yes, I am..."

"And doesn't it burn you up when Marvin, Rick, and Rob sit down and just expect to be waited on? It does me."

"I never thought about it before."

"Well, think about it. It's time we women threw off the chains of the status quo and started demanding some consideration and help!" I forcefully put my beer on the table and burped. "Excuse me," I said.

Alice looked dazed and put her hand over her heart. "I don't know what Marvin would say."

"Who cares!?" I said cheerfully.

At this point Rob walked into the kitchen. He was surprised to see four beer bottles on the table and his mother a little plotzed. "Mom," he said, "you're drinking?"

"Yes, Stephanie and I had two beers apiece," Alice returned with exaggerated dignity. "And you know what? We earned it."

"I'm not criticizing. I've just never seen you drink beer in the afternoon before, Mom." Rob was clearly at a loss. "So. What time's dinner?"

"Oh, when we get around to it," I said and Alice and I giggled and clinked bottles.

"What's going on here?" Rob asked.

"I'm recruiting your mother into the ranks of feminism," I caroled cheerfully.

"Uh huh. I better call Dad and warn him," Rob said. But he grabbed a beer before he left.

Of course, Alice and I did make supper but we didn't work very hard at it. We put out leftover shower salad and scrambled some eggs. There was no more inflammatory rhetoric because halfway through the meal exhaustion and the beer hit us with a vengeance. Marvin didn't say much—no surprise there—but he watched in bemusement as the heads of his wife and daughter-in-law sank lower towards their plates. He just suggested kindly to Alice, "You're tired, Mother. Maybe you should go to bed. The kids can clean up." Alice toddled off. That's what happens when a bustle gets spiffed; it toddles.

Rob washed the dishes and I dried. I apologized for getting his mother drunk and trying to loosen her up—and maybe enlighten her. Rob washed a dish, then said disapprovingly, "She's happy with her life. She doesn't need you telling her it's stupid. You're just making trouble for her and Dad."

I thought about telling him that his mother was a racist and his father was a pig but I couldn't because I knew it wasn't true. They were just people from a different time and place who didn't know the correct lingo. Besides, I was tired so I accepted his scolding without argument. Rob finally relented. "I guess I should be glad you've put up with everything as long as you have. But it's a good thing we're moving. You better go to bed and rest up. Tomorrow's going to be a long day."

I joined Pudgy in the bedroom while Rob wiped down counters and put the dishes away. The revolution was on hold for lack of energy. But as of tomorrow it'd be just the two of us and life would be like it had been in L.A.—my rules, not Alice's. I was going over the wall.

chapter 9

My furniture was delivered but most of it ended up in the Anderson basement. There was just too much for the trailer. I could fit my couch and one overstuffed chair in the living room but my end tables and extra easy chair had to go. My dining room set was too big for the kitchen space; it would have spilled over into the living area and that was overcrowded as it was. We couldn't even wrap the mattress of my king-size bed through the trailer door. The truck driver was getting testy and I was about to panic when Alice drove up to supervise. She took one look at the situation and suggested I store my extra stuff in her basement. I had no choice but to agree and thank her very much. I had to trade my king-size bed for the squeaky double Rob and I had been using in the Anderson basement and my dining set for a tiny little drop-leaf table and two chairs Alice kept in her garage. At the end of the day Alice had a beautifully furnished apartment in her basement and I had more obligation. Rob came directly to the trailer from class, said, "I told you not bring all this stuff", and busied himself setting up the TV and VCR. The backbreaking work was over. Now my official married life could begin.

"This'll be our first weekend alone together. What do you want to do?" I asked Rob over coffee at our tiny little table in our tiny little kitchen the next morning.

Rob shifted uneasily. "About Saturday, Stevie...Pheasant season opens and I'm going hunting with Dad and my brothers. We'll do something next week."

My jaw dropped and my internal temperature rose. "But we haven't had any time alone together since I got here! I thought Saturday would be my day!"

"It's just one day. You can go visit my mother," Rob placated.

"Like hell I will," I retorted, outraged. "I've had enough of your mother! I moved back here to be with you!"

"You see me all the time," Rob said reasonably.

"Yeah, when you're mouth's full or you're asleep!" I abruptly stood up, almost upsetting the table, and started pacing, trying to control my temper as I wrung my hands. It got loose anyway when I couldn't think of anything reasonable to say and I started yelling. I squawked and waved my arms, which was probably a mistake because the last time I did that I got talked into getting married. And look where that got me.

"Stevie, the Anderson men have always gone pheasant hunting together when the season opened," Rob tried to explain when I stopped for breath. "It's a tradition. I missed last year because I was in L.A. I don't want to miss it this year."

"What about me? Aren't I more important than some stupid tradition? You can go hunting any time! This is our first weekend alone!" I screeched.

"Maybe you could come with us," Rob suggested half-heartedly. "It's not the usual thing, a woman going hunting with us, but maybe Dad wouldn't mind. Do you want to go?"

I stopped pacing and glared at him. Did I want to blow our little feathered friends out of the sky? Not really, it sounded pretty bloodthirsty. On the other hand, I'd get out of the trailer and I'd be with Rob doing something new. Then again, it wouldn't be just Rob, I'd be with his father and brothers, too…

"Well?" asked Rob, impatiently interrupting my reverie. "I have to make sure it's alright with Dad. If it is you'll have to be up and ready to go by five Saturday morning. Can you do that?" Rob looked at me skeptically.

"Five? What do you do, wake the birds up? Doesn't anybody sleep in this godforsaken State?" I spat.

"We hit the fields at six. That's when the pheasants feed," Rob said. Then he flung down a verbal gauntlet: "You sure you want to go? It's really not for women."

"I'll be there," I said grimly.

*****

Saturday morning. 6:00 a.m. Sun's just coming up. It's autumn and it's cold. I shivered in my jacket and regretted wearing only one pair of socks.

Marvin, Tom, Mike, Rick, Rob, and I stood around the cars on the access road to a desiccated cornfield, drinking coffee. The men were dressed in old clothes with the exception of Mike who wore a camouflage suit right out of Abercrombie & Fitch. They were checking their shotguns and discussing the plan for the day. I felt like an Arctic explorer blowing on the hot coffee cup that was warming my gloved hands and stamping my feet. I was blearily watching the anemic sun make its appearance when I heard Rick say, "Bobby, get me some extra shells."

Rob rummaged through the trunk of his Buick and silently handed a box of shells to Rick. I raised an eyebrow at his unquestioning obedience and he flushed.

Marvin said, "Okay, everybody ready to go now?"

"Wait a minute," I said. "What do you want me to do?"

My in-laws had apparently forgotten I was there because they all looked at me blankly. They decided that I was Rob's problem and they turned to him for guidance. That was futile because he was as baffled as they were.

"I don't have a gun for you," Rob started slowly.

"That's okay," I said tartly. "I'm not here to blow some helpless bird up before he's had his coffee. I'm just here to observe the manly art of hunting."

"Why don't you stay here and unpack the lunch?" Rick suggested provocatively.

"I thought we'd settled the maid question," I retorted. "I didn't come along to wait on you. Besides, it's cold in the car."

The men all reacted differently to my response. Rick scowled, Tom ignored me (he was used to ornery women), Marvin smiled faintly, and Mike raised an eyebrow at Rob who looked embarrassed.

"Well," Rob said helplessly and looked to his brethren for help. My judgmental tone had not earned me any friends. The men looked at me narrowly then they turned to each other. Some weird form of communication transpired and they all got wicked grins on their faces.

"Well, if you really want to see pheasant hunting up close, the best view would be down in front. Why don't you walk ahead of us a few hundred feet? You'll be able to see everything there," Rob said.

The other men were hiding smiles at this point but I was so ignorant I didn't see anything wrong with the proposal. "Okay," I said agreeably. "Should I start now?"

"Yeah, you go down that row. We'll follow in about five minutes. Just keep moving forward for the next hour or so. Don't worry, we'll be right behind you," Rob assured me.

I looked at the dried-out, six-foot corn stalks in front of me. "You won't be able to see me once I'm in there. You won't shoot me, will you?" I asked anxiously.

"Absolutely not," Rob promised. "We'll make sure to shoot up in the air. You'll be perfectly safe."

This seemed reasonable but… "What if I get too far in front of you?" I asked. "I don't want to get lost."

"Just follow the corn rows," Rob explained. "When you get to the other side of the field, stop. We'll catch up to you."

"Okay," I said dubiously. "You're sure it's safe?"

"Absolutely," Rob assured me so I disappeared into the rows.

I'd never been in a dried-out cornfield before. The ground was uneven and the leaves on the stalks cut like knives. I was, in effect, wading through an extremely dusty, tall, sharp jungle.

"I think I need a machete," I called back after a few minutes.

"You'll be fine. Just watch your eyes," Rob called back. I didn't think anything about the muffled guffaws I heard behind me.

I struggled through the foliage for about fifteen minutes before I had to stop and take a break. Hunting was hard work! I wiped the sweat off my face and sneezed. All the dust was making my nose run. I dug around in my pockets for a Kleenex. *No wonder I was the only woman along*, I mentally sneered, *only men would possibly get any enjoyment from this*. And speaking of men, I wondered where they were. "Rob," I yelled, "are you back there?"

"You bet," he hollered back. "Just keep moving if you want the best view."

So I staggered on. After another ten minutes of this the coffee I'd drunk earlier had been processed and I had to pee. Of course, there wasn't a bathroom within miles; I hadn't even seen a Port-a-san. I peered around. I couldn't see or hear anyone so it was a good bet that no one could see me either. I figured this was as good a place to pee as any, and, frankly, the corn looked like it could use a little water. I dug out a fresh Kleenex for blotting purposes, moved to a level area about ten feet ahead of me, pulled down my pants, and squatted. Being new to the nature thing I had to grab a cornstalk to keep my balance and clumsily pushed it over. A huge pheasant flapped into the air. I was startled but wasn't in any position to do anything about it because I was busy peeing on my shoe. I was duck waddling down the row when I heard two loud booms behind and over me. The bird flopped out of the air onto the ground in front of me and I peed on my other shoe.

"Got it!" I heard Tom's exultant shout followed by congratulations. I shakily blotted myself.

"Stevie!" Rob shouted, "Did you see where it fell?"

"Yeah," I yelled back and hurriedly pulled up my pants.

"Would you pick it up and carry it to the other side?"

"Sure," I responded and shook off my shoes.

I fought my way over to the pheasant and looked down at it. It was dead, all right. I felt momentarily bad; it had been a beautiful bird. But I'd said I'd carry it and I would. I gingerly picked it up by one foot and struggled on.

Before I made it to the end of the field, two more birds had flown up into the air and had been gunned down. I obligingly picked them up, too, but I didn't think they were pretty anymore. The birds were just heavy, flopping things that kept me from using my hands to protect my face.

I finally got to the end of the row. I dropped those damn pheasants and flopped down next to them, exhausted. By now the sun was up and beating on me. My earlier shivering was just a pleasant memory. I was sweaty, dirty, and ready to go home. I looked bleakly at the cornfield on the other side of the road and stifled an urge to scream. I'd invited myself along and if the men could do this, I'd have to, too. At least I'd have a chance to rest before they caught up to me.

I was rummaging through my pockets, looking for just one more Kleenex for my runny nose, when two hunters emerged from the cornfield I'd regarded so unhappily earlier. They were accompanied by a Golden Labrador retriever with a pheasant in his mouth. They took the pheasant from the dog and praised him before noticing me and my pile of dead fowl.

"You've had a good day," said the first hunter and he smiled approvingly.

"Oh, I didn't shoot these," I hurried to explain. "I just carried them here."

"Who shot them?" asked the second hunter.

"I'm not sure. My husband and some of his relatives are back there." I pointed to the field I'd come out of. "One of them did the shooting. I was walking ahead," I said and smiled. "They told me I'd have the best view if I stayed ahead. They'll be here in a few minutes."

The two hunters looked at me then at each other. They had those big, shiteating, masculine grins on their faces. "My wife would never do that," said hunter #1. "She made me get a dog." He patted the Labrador affectionately. Then both hunters started laughing.

Sometimes I'm a little slow but the light finally dawned: I hadn't been walking ahead for the best view, I'd been flushing birds—and retrieving them. I was on eye level with the dog. His tongue was hanging out and his eyes gleamed. He was probably laughing at me, too.

The Andersons showed up at this point. Rob nodded, pleased, when he saw the pheasants.

"One of those is ours," he told me. "We'll have pheasant for dinner tomorrow." Then he noticed my disheveled appearance. "Are you all right?" He glanced at my muddy feet. "What happened to your shoes?"

"I peed on them," I said evenly.

All seven men looked at me incredulously and then I was engulfed in male amusement. I smiled and nodded along with them. Of course, the smile was grim and my molars were locked together but none of those men noticed that.

One of the stranger hunters wiped his eyes. "Excuse me for asking, little lady, but how'd you come to pee on your shoes?"

"Well, I…um…was doing my business when a pheasant flew up and they shot him. It startled me," I explained and they all went off again.

"I'm glad you all find this so amusing," I commented icily when the guffawing died down enough so I could make myself heard.

"Aww, Stevie, you have to admit it's funny," Rob wheezed. "If you hadn't been so snotty this morning maybe we wouldn't have teased you. And, remember, you were the one who insisted on coming along so don't get on your high horse."

Maybe Rob had a point, perhaps I had been a bit overbearing, but I certainly couldn't admit it. I mustered as much dignity as I could, announced, "I'm going back to the car now," and prepared to plunge back the way I came.

"Hey, would you mind going back about twenty feet down?" Rick asked. "There's probably a lot of birds you can scare up on the way!"

I glared at the combined Andersons but it didn't do any good. They were all laughing helplessly again. I fought my way back through the field and pouted in the car. I got back at them, though; I ate some of their sandwiches. I was hungry. Being an idiot is hard work.

The men were still snickering when they got back to the cars. They'd shot three more birds and felt they'd hunted enough. I'd been preparing the tongue-lashing I was going to give Rob on the way home when Marvin asked if I would ride with him.

"I'd like to show Stephanie my father's old farm," he told Rob. Rob looked at my lower lip and the glint in my eye and agreed hurriedly that the expedition would be nice and weakly volunteered to come along.

"No," said Marvin, "I just want Stephanie."

Me stuck with Marvin? All by myself? Hadn't I had a miserable enough morning? But there didn't seem to be a gracious way out of it. Marvin was waiting so I got in his Buick and we drove off together.

I was expecting a silent drive but Marvin surprised me by talking. He told me about the crops grown in the area, explained the different types of cattle I saw, and generally gave me an overview of the country and the people who lived there. It was interesting and I was happy to just sit and listen after the strenuous morning I'd put in.

It was a beautiful day for a cruise. The sky was blue and Marvin told me the wispy cloud formations were called mare's tails. I was charmed by the lack of smog. My shoes had dried off and didn't even smell too bad.

Marvin drove through a tiny town called Oldham, consisting of a one-block main street, and stopped at a cemetery outside the town limits. He told me this was where his parents were buried. It was quiet except for the sound of a breeze whiffling the grass. A few squirrels were running around. The lawn was trimmed and bouquets dotted some of the graves. If there is such a thing as a cheerful cemetery this was it.

Marvin pulled a few weeds around the headstones of his parents, Samuel and Mary Anderson. He told me they'd been farmers in the area. They'd sold the farm when they retired and moved into Oldham. "Alice and I bought the plots next to them," Marvin said, indicating a bare patch of grass next to Sam and Mary. "One of these days we'll buy the headstones so everything will be all ready for us." He looked remarkably content at the thought.

Death? He'd gotten me out here to talk about death? I'd experienced enough death with my parents to last me a lifetime. If he wanted a nice comfy talk about death he'd picked the wrong person. "Personally, I think the whole subject is depressing," I said shortly. "Why don't you concentrate on living?"

Marvin wasn't offended; he was amused. "We all have to go someday, Stephanie," he said. "It comforts me to know I'll be with my folks. And I like to know things are taken care of. I don't want you kids to have to worry about funeral arrangements or beggar yourselves just to plant Mother and me. You'll all have your own kids to spend your money on."

"It's your money but I think it'd be better spent on a vacation or something that you can enjoy now," I retorted. "If I were you I'd do everything I could to avoid dying. Dead is dead. There's nothing comforting about it."

He studied me. "Stephanie," he said, "I don't know one person who ever got out of this world alive. I suspect I won't be the first. I doubt you will be either. It takes away the fear when you accept that it's part of life and prepare for it. Alice and I have lived our lives so our children will miss us...but not too much. Hopefully, the Lord will be happy to take us in." Marvin had probably spoken more in the last few minutes than he had in the last year and he had to clear his throat and spit. Then he continued, "Don't get me wrong, I don't want to hurry the process but there's no reason to live in fear of it either."

We pulled weeds together silently. After some thought, I confessed slowly, searching for words, "My parents were too young when they died and the drunk who killed them is still on the road. There's all sorts of crazy people and strange diseases floating around...Life is too easy to lose and that scares hell out of me. So I don't think about death much."

Marvin listened silently, pooched out his lower lip, then commented,

"Stephanie, I think it'd take a lot more than death to scare hell out of you." He picked up the weeds and carried them to a nearby compost pile. "Let's go. I want to show you our old farm."

We drove down a gravel road a few miles and pulled into an access road behind a large pick-up. Two men were pointing rifles out the windows.

In a city, if you see a guy with a rifle you automatically assume you've stumbled onto a Richard Speck wannabe and you get the hell out of there. If you have any sense, that is. Marvin pulled up beside the pick-up and said, "Roll down your window, Stephanie."

I looked at him with my mouth open and my eyes wide, just knowing I was about to be shot. This was the reason for our little excursion? To get rid of an unpleasant daughter-in-law? I may have been a bit of a pain in the ass that morning, maybe I'd tried to liberate Alice a little bit, but that was no reason to have me murdered, was it? Oh man, Marvin was probably going to leave me in the compost pile with the other weeds he'd just picked.

Marvin noticed my panicked state and smiled. "They're just hunters," he assured me.

Yeah. Right. And I just fell off a turnip truck. But maybe he'd let me live if I cooperated so I did as he asked.

"Having any luck, boys?" Marvin called across my cringing body.

"Saw a couple deer a few minutes ago but they're gone now," the hunters reported.

Marvin and the hunters discussed deer and pheasant hunting, and the prospects for both. I sat there, dumb and pale, with an accommodating grin on my face. Marvin finally wished them luck, waved, and drove down the road a few hundred feet.

"Now, the field those boys were checking out and this one on the other side were all my dad's property," he said and pointed. I sighed explosively. Marvin peered in my face and asked, "Stephanie, you weren't really scared, were you?"

"Yes, I was," I gasped.

"Why, they were just hunters. They wouldn't have hurt you."

"Hey, I grew up in Los Angeles. People with guns shoot people, not birds."

"That doesn't happen here much," Marvin said calmly. "But if it does," he added grimly, "we make damn sure the murderer never gets a chance to do it again!"

I gathered from this that Marvin was not a Liberal.

Marvin expanded on this political theme as he slowly drove down the gravel road. He opined on capital punishment: "Let me put it to you this way, Stephanie; have you ever heard of an executed murderer killing another person?"

Now that he mentioned it, I hadn't.

Marvin continued. "You take those damn big city Liberals. They feel sorry for the criminals and they think they're showing compassion by letting 'em loose. But I sure as hell don't see them taking responsibility when their pet criminal kills another innocent person. I don't know how they can live with themselves knowing they let murder happen. I don't know how they sleep at night."

Marvin was all red in the face and breathing heavily by now. And he'd said "damn" and "hell" in the last five minutes. Obviously, he felt very strongly about this.

"How do you feel about abortion?" I asked, curious. I was pretty sure of the answer but I thought I'd ask anyway. Normally, political conservatives object to abortion even though they approve of capital punishment. I know it doesn't make sense but it seems to hold true. I steeled myself for another heartfelt "damn" or "hell" or maybe both.

"Not my business," Marvin said. My eyebrows went up. "I don't approve of abortion, what with all the birth control available," Marvin clarified, "but I know accidents happen. The sex urge is powerful. And the woman bears all the responsibility. It's not fair but it's so. That being the case, I think it's up to the woman to decide what she wants to do about it."

"What if you'd gotten someone pregnant?" I asked provocatively.

"I'd never put a woman in the position of having to make a decision like that," Marvin said firmly.

"You don't think abortion's a sin?" I persisted, knowing how church-oriented the Anderson family was.

"I'm not God," Marvin said quietly. "I'll leave the judging up to Him." Then he added, "I can't see making some poor ignorant girl have a baby that she can't support and will raise to be as ignorant and poor as she is. That girl and her baby shouldn't have to spend their lives paying for a mistake. And neither should anyone else. The men involved seem to run off generally and the taxpayer ends up footing the bill. It's bad for everybody."

Curiouser and curiouser. Not even a swear word; just a tone of regret and resignation.

"Some people object to abortion because they claim a potential Beethoven is being lost," I commented, still playing devil's advocate.

Marvin snorted. "That's a lot of hogwash. The only thing that comes out of poverty and ignorance is more poverty and ignorance. Why, I wouldn't let most of those people have a puppy from the pound and the government pays them to have kids. It's hogwash," he repeated, then asked me, "Do you believe abortion's a sin, Stephanie?"

"I never really gave it much thought," I said honestly. "I never had to, thank God." I reflected a minute. "Terminating a pregnancy is a big decision. I guess I don't believe abortion's a sin, I just don't know if I could do it myself. But if I found myself in that predicament I sure wouldn't want somebody telling me that I couldn't." I took a moment to think some more and continued slowly, "The people who want to outlaw abortion seem nuts but I don't think an abortion is as simple as clipping your toenails either. I guess I'm just confused. There must be something wrong with me because I don't totally agree with anyone. You turn on the TV and everything's sex—with no consequences. It's like you're a social misfit if you don't jump into bed with anybody who comes along. I've taken a lot of crap because I wouldn't flop on my back and wave my heels in the air for any man who came along." I pulled myself up short; I better remember who I was talking to.

Marvin snorted again. "I don't think those folks on the TV have the sense God gave goats, most of 'em. You just open your eyes and your mind and make your own decisions. You don't have to believe what they tell you. And," he added, "you don't have to believe what I tell you either." He looked at his watch. "Look at the time. We better get a move on or Mother will think I kidnapped you."

He quit talking and turned the car around. I worried that I might have offended him by my graphic comments on sex but Marvin was just working up to the real reason for our excursion. He cleared his throat and began. "You're probably wondering why I dragged you off." I nodded and Marvin continued, "I figure you've been feeling all alone. I know I would if I were in your shoes. Bobby drags you off to a strange place among strange people—you don't even have a mother to talk to."

Frankly, family had been the biggest problem I'd encountered in my great prairie adventure, with dishpan hands running a close second, but Marvin was so kind and I was so tired and smelly that I listened quietly.

"I'm going to step in for your father and give you some advice," Marvin said. "Don't expect too much from Bobby just now. He's having a hard time getting back into the school routine and his studying is what's important now. I told him he was crazy to get married before he was ready to devote the time to a woman that a marriage needs, but he did it anyway and now you're both suffering for it."

I agreed that our early married life hadn't been quite as smooth as I could have wished.

"Instead of being sharp with Bobby," Marvin advised, "maybe you should try to sweet-talk him a little. You can always catch more flies with honey than vinegar, you know. Try to understand his position a little better. And the rest of the family will try to help out more so you won't feel lonely."

I assured Marvin that I didn't need any more attention from the Andersons; I just needed a little understanding from Rob.

Marvin nodded knowingly. "Sometimes my sons take after their mother a little too much. They're all bullheaded and like to have their own way. My Norwegian influence seems to get lost."

I looked at Marvin in surprise. "You're not German?" I asked.

"Of course not," Marvin snorted. "Anderson isn't a German name. And Norwegians aren't as ornery."

I gazed at Marvin. There were differences among all these blond, blue-eyed types? I shouldn't say they all looked alike to me because that was insensitive and bigoted but…well, they all looked alike to me.

"I know the boys gave you a hard time this morning," Marvin said calmly. "But you remember; Alice and I are on your side. We've watched you jump in and take hold since you moved here. You're a good little worker and you're not afraid to tackle big projects. The first year of marriage is rough enough without taking on a whole new way of life but you're tough and smart. You'll see it through." He paused then said with effort, "We're real happy you're a member of our family."

I misted up and dug through my coat pockets for another Kleenex but between the blotting and snottiness of that morning, I couldn't find one. Marvin noticed my dilemma and pointed to the glove compartment. I got a fresh Kleenex and blew my nose.

"I guess that's enough speeches from me," Marvin said. "I didn't mean to make you cry."

"That's all right, I'm just…tired," I sniffled and gave him a watery smile. "Did you already give this speech to Rob?"

"No, that's his mother's department," Marvin said. "She's always been the one to talk to the boys. Well, here we are. And there's Bobby. Just remember what I said about honey."

He patted my shoulder as I got out of the car and then drove off. Rob presented me with a bouquet of flowers as I wearily climbed into the trailer.

"My brothers and I decided we hadn't been very nice to you this morning so we got together and bought you a peace offering," he explained.

Flowers! Well! "I guess I sort of had it coming. I was a bit of a pain," I mumbled as I accepted the flowers. Admitting error has never been one of my favorite past-times.

"Stevie, you look tired. Why don't you take a bath and relax awhile?" Rob suggested. "I rinsed out the tub for you and the water's hot."

After the morning I'd just put in I was a dusty, smelly little person. A bath was a wonderful idea. I disrobed as I trudged to the bathroom, leaving my clothes and shoes where they landed, and ran water into the tub. Rob followed me, picking up my clothes. He stood in the bathroom door and held out my Reeboks like they were two monochromatic skunks. "What do you want me to do with these?" he asked.

"Burn them," I said and crawled gratefully into the warm water.

Rob offered to scrub my back and even tried to help wash my hair. Of course, being inexperienced he got all wet so he took off his clothes and crawled in the tub with me. I'd recovered enough by this time to return the hair washing favor. Pretty soon our soapy ministrations turned to erotic ones. My bodice rippers had described making love in the bathtub so we decided to give it a try. The people who write about this sort of thing obviously have huge bathtubs. Our bathtub was only five feet long and Rob's 6'3" length didn't fit; he almost broke a toe on the faucet. I also discovered that bathtubs are hard. My tailbone got bruised so I put Rob on the bottom. But that was equally hard on my knees. We decided there was a reason beds were invented so we moved to the bedroom with satisfactory results. I totally forgave Rob for the morning's hazing.

"Maybe we could go to a movie tomorrow?" I suggested in the spirit of compromise during our post-coital glow. "Unless you have to study, of course."

"I promised we'd go to the folks tomorrow and eat Sunday dinner with them. Mom's cooking the pheasants we shot today." When Rob saw the look on my face he hurried to add, "But I'll cancel if you don't want to go. I'll just tell them something came up."

I thought back on my conversation with Marvin. I'd try the honey approach and be agreeable. Besides, I'd never had pheasant before.

"No," I said slowly, "I'll be happy to go. I'm sure dinner will be delicious and it's thoughtful of your family to invite us."

The sun came back up in Rob's eyes. "Next weekend is all yours, Stevie," he promised. "Whatever you want to do, we'll do."

I'd won a concession! We sealed our bargain by making love again. Twice in one afternoon—-maybe fighting wasn't so awful if the making-up was so productive. As I drifted off in a nap, one thought troubled me. If marriage was a compromise, how come it seemed like I was doing all the compromising?

chapter 10

⎯⎯⎯⎯⎯⎯⎯⎯⎯⎯⎯⎯⎯⎯⎯⎯⎯⎯⎯⎯⎯

"Leslie, I just got my phone! God, it's good to hear your voice."

"Stevie? I was about ready to hire a detective to track you down! Well, have you come to your senses now that you see what you're in for? Are you ready to come back?"

"I guess I should have called earlier," I admitted. "And no, I'm not ready to come back." I think I'd called Les to get some sympathy but now I had to pretend everything was great so she couldn't say "I told you so" again. "I've been pretty busy," I said cheerfully.

"So fill me in."

I described my in-laws; the good, the bad, and the ugly, and how they sometimes took turns in each role. I told her about Brookings and how clean it was; I told her about the trailer and how filthy it had been.

"You're living in a trailer?" Leslie asked incredulously.

"Yup, I am now officially tan trash. But at least I won't catch dysentery."

"Why'd you bother with this trailer in the first place?"

So I went into the song and dance about Rob's budget and his pride. I explained that it was the trailer or the in-laws. "It's not that I don't like his parents; it's just that a little family togetherness goes a long way. I don't really fit in. I said 'shit' the other day and Alice almost had an aneurysm. And I had to go to church with them all the time. Clean living is all well and good but these people are a little nuts on the subject. I can't even buy beer on Sunday. They've got something called Blue Laws here. Have you ever heard of them?"

"I'm from Pennsylvania, I think Blue Laws originated there. Or maybe it was Massachusetts," Les said. "It doesn't matter. You don't drink much anyway."

"It's the principle of the thing. I don't like anybody telling me what to do."

After a pause Leslie commented, "Well, sounds like you've had an action-packed week."

"I haven't had time to get bored," I agreed. "Did I tell you I went pheasant hunting last weekend? And I had a good talk with my father-in-law. I didn't even know he could talk. I guess he only does it when Alice isn't around."

"You shot a pheasant?!"

"Well, no, I just walked around," I said, neglecting to add that I'd played retriever, "but I learned how to cook one. You cover it with one can of mushroom soup and one can of celery soup, then bake it for a while. I told Alice I'd probably have fried it and she laughed at me. She said wild birds were too gamey and tough to cook that way; you have to boil them to bits. And you have to watch out for buckshot with kill-it-yourself meat. I almost lost a tooth biting into a thigh."

"Yeah, the stuff in the grocery store doesn't need a warning label," Leslie laughed. "Well, Stevie, I'm glad to hear you're settling in so well."

"Well, it hasn't been all fun and games," I admitted. "I've been here ten days and Rob and I have had three fights. We never fought in Los Angeles."

"You didn't spend enough time together to fight," Leslie pointed out.

"Maybe. But we don't spend any time together here either and we still fight. You know, Les," I said tentatively, "I don't think I know Rob very well. He seems a lot different than when we were in Los Angeles. He's got this whole guy thing going on that I don't understand. It's like what I think doesn't count anymore, he only listens to his brothers. And all the Anderson men have a 'head of the house' ethos that's weird. I thought I left machismo behind in L.A."

"Machismo transcends race, creed, and color but I don't think Rob's got a bad case of it. He's probably adjusting too," Leslie advised. "You don't have any close family; you don't know how miserable being back in the bosom of one can be. And you know a Master's program isn't easy. Especially engineering. Have you talked to Rob about how you feel?"

"We don't talk, we fight," I retorted, then added, "At least the making up is fun."

"The making up is why you married him," Leslie said.

"Yeah, at least that's still good," I said. "So, what's been happening with you?"

I listened to her for about fifteen minutes before I regretfully hung up. I felt lost. See, what I hadn't told Les was—Rob wasn't having trouble adjusting at all. He'd organized our lives to suit himself and seemed perfectly happy.

Not only had I spent the last two Sundays at Anderson Central, it appeared that I would be spending every Sunday with them. We had to share the family pew at the Lutheran Church, and then follow Marvin and Alice and feast until Rob decided that he had to study. We'd go home and he'd head for the second bedroom that he'd set up as "our" office. To save money he'd cut down an old door and set it up on two used filing cabinets as a desk. But he spent $4,000 on a state-of-the-art personal computer. When I questioned the expenditure he misunderstood my objection. "Yeah, we do need a new receiver and I'd like a new CD player, too, but the computer is necessary for school. You can use it for writing letters or playing games." He seemed honestly surprised when I said that he should have consulted me and that we could have used the money to rent better living accommodations next semester. "What's wrong with this? Now that's it's cleaned up it's fine." He'd come home from school, eat, and disappear into "our" office until ten each night and most of the weekend. I knew he had to study and teach but we had so little contact with each other that he seemed surprised to see me when he finally emerged from "our" office, almost like he'd forgotten I was around.

I had coffee with Rob one morning before he left for class and mentioned that I was at loose ends and needed something to do. He was digging through some papers and didn't seem particularly interested.

"Why don't you take a few months off," he said distractedly as he got ready to leave. "You've been working or studying nonstop for years. You deserve a rest."

"What'll I do with my time?" I asked.

"All you really have to do is take care of the trailer," Rob said. "I'll take care of everything else." He kissed the air over my head, grabbed his book bag and jacket, and ran.

Maybe being a housewife wouldn't be such a bad temporary niche. Alice and I had already taken care of the worst of the cleaning crap. It's not a position I'd've sought ordinarily but it's not like I had anything better to do.

What a miserable niche it turned out to be.

In my previous carefree existence I was one of those condescending little snots who, when meeting a housewife, would make some patronizing remark like: "Oh, you don't work. Aren't you lucky you get to stay at home!" I'd follow the asshole comment with a superior smirk. I learned just how "lucky" those women were.

Rob needed caffeine and carbohydrates to get him through his day of classes. Somebody had to make the coffee and prepare something he could stuff in his face—and that somebody was me. At six o'clock in the morning. I volunteered to buy a hypodermic filled with caffeine so he could just give himself his morning fix but Rob smiled, patted my head, and said, "I love your sense of humor." So who was joking?

Breakfast wasn't a problem because I knew how to make coffee and Kellogg's took care of the rest. I didn't even object to making lunch because Oscar Meyer and Mr. Campbell made it easy. Besides, it got Rob home and I was getting desperate for human contact. But dinner approached the surreal. I dug out my cookbook and Alice came through with some of "Bobby's Favorite Recipes", including a few interesting Jell-O concoctions. After some study I decided on fish for our first dinner. The cookbook had a lovely picture of a poached salmon that looked easy to fix and suggested fettuccini alfredo as a nice side dish. Salad would serve as the vegetable; it was nutritious, contrasted color-wise, and I didn't have to cook it. And since we were being good by eating salad we certainly deserved some chocolate cake as a reward. I rubbed my hands with glee. I was going to blow Rob away with this meal. I think I was subconsciously competing with Alice.

I made a list and went shopping.

The only fresh fish I could find at the store was catfish so I plugged that into the recipe. The parmesan cheese available was the canned kind but I figured, what the hell, cheese was cheese. I made a trip to the hardware store to buy a mixer and some cake pans and importantly told Marvin about my dessert plans as he calculated my discount. I fantasized just how it would be. Rob would come home at five to find me, pert, pretty, and ready to present him with a spectacular meal. I conveniently forgot my first attempt at cooking.

Well, I did it again.

Rob came home at five to find me in tears in a messy kitchen. The catfish was not a nice, moist, succulent piece of fillet. Alice told me later that the only way to make catfish edible is to bread and fry hell out of it. The alfredo sauce was curdled and scorched, I didn't know how low "low heat" was supposed to be and I got impatient. The cake was supposed to be idiot proof but I guess Betty Crocker had never run into an idiot of my caliber before. I'd pulled the beaters out of the batter, without thinking, at high speed, and chocolate cake batter was running down my previously pristine walls.

I was mopping up cake batter when Rob walked in. "What happened?" he asked.

"I tried to cook."

"Oh."

Rob made scrambled eggs and toast as I finished swabbing my walls.

I learned to cook, of course, but it took time. Rob helped me since he knew more about it than I did. We sat down together and planned simple little things that even I couldn't screw up. I learned to plan, shop intelligently, and cook. Lucky me.

Why were housewives held in such low esteem? I puzzled to myself. It's not like it's easy. Then I finally figured out it all came down to money. A woman who earns a paycheck has worth because some stranger is paying her to do something. Nobody expects her to keep a spotless home, always have the laundry done, and have nutritious, delicious meals on the table. After all, she works. There are support groups for her, she gets dinner out, she gets society's approval because she makes money.

All bets are off for those of us miserable slobs on the home front. We're tapeworms in the intestine of the world. We don't get money or respect because we don't work.

Bullshit.

I struggled with cooking—cleaning I already knew how to do— and I added laundry to my chores. As Rob said, he was busy studying and teaching and since I didn't have anything to do would I mind...?

Of course I wouldn't. I was trying to be a nice, cooperative team player but I was getting increasingly disenchanted with my assignment. Rob hit the home runs and I carried the water bucket. Oh well, it kept me from stealing hubcaps. I got books from the library and read until my eyes fell out.

I finally asserted myself when Rob announced after supper that he was going to watch football with some of his engineering buddies.

"I've been working real hard. I need a night off. I'm going to go watch the game with some of the guys," he announced casually.

"Rob, I haven't spent any time with you in two weeks!" I protested.

"Sure you have. You're seeing me now, aren't you?"

"This doesn't count and you know it," I spat. From the look on his face he didn't know it and didn't know what to say. "If you need a night off why don't we go to a movie or something? My God, we never do anything together. Are you planning on letting me sit here all by myself?"

"But I told the guys I'd come," he said weakly. "I can't tell them my wife won't let me out of the house."

"Let's see," I said caustically, "do the guys wash your shorts, feed your face…sleep with you? Who do you think should get more of your time?"

"Well," he said slowly, clearly at a loss. Then his eyes brightened. "Maybe you could come, too. The guys probably wouldn't care. I'll bring extra beer."

I remembered my evening at the sports bar with Les. Why did my life seem to revolve around a game I cared nothing about? I was on the verge of a tantrum when I remembered Marvin's advice about honey. It had worked once, maybe it was worth another shot. I guess it wouldn't kill me to watch football. There'd probably be some other women my age that I could talk to. Besides, it was better than sitting around by myself. We bought an extra six-pack of beer and headed for the basement apartment of Gary, one of Rob's Teaching Assistant buddies.

Gary, who was even taller than Rob and weighed maybe twice as much, let us in and Rob introduced me. "This is my wife, Stevie," he said cheerfully. "I couldn't leave her home by herself. I hope it's okay I brought her."

As I shook Gary's hand I peeked around his shoulder and saw

a room full of guys dressed in flannel shirts and jeans. "No other women?" I asked hopefully.

"Rob's the only guy who could snag a girl as pretty as you," Gary said with a smile, his eyes twinkling behind his wire-rimmed glasses.

Oh God. I felt like I had "Ball" tattooed on my forehead and a chain connecting Rob's and my ankles. Rob got a beer, slapped a few backs, exchanged roars of greeting and high-fives, announced to the room that I was his wife, and told me to help myself to a chair. Then he shouldered himself between two men on the couch, and promptly got engrossed in the game. The other guys looked at me with interest until a roar from the TV snagged their attention. I seemed to be on my own.

Gary smiled sympathetically and asked if he could get me a beer. I remembered the state of my thighs, designated myself the driver, and told him I'd get myself a glass of water. He showed me where the glasses were in the cupboard and apologized for the dirty dishes in the sink. "Four guys live here and none of us has much time for cleaning up."

"That's okay," I said. "I think that's why Rob married me."

"I'm sure he had other reasons," said Gary. He was such a sweetheart for such a big bear of a man. He took his role as host seriously and threw one of his buddies out of an overstuffed armchair and carried it over to me. "Where should I put this?" he asked.

"Oh, back here some place," I dithered, embarrassed by the glare I got from the roommate left sprawling on the floor on my behalf. "I don't want to be any trouble."

"No trouble," Gary said and dropped the chair. He got a desk chair from a bedroom and put it next to mine. Then he sat with me making conversation so I wouldn't feel like a complete outcast. Too bad Rob didn't care as much about what happened to me.

I sipped my water as he told me about growing up on a farm on the North Dakota border with three older sisters and one brother. He'd just gotten up to refill my water glass when his attention turned to the TV. He stood frozen for a minute then said, "My God, that's you, isn't it?"

I stood up and peered over the fence of heads, which were turning to stare at me. My beer ad was on TV. I watched myself bouncing around in Hollywood jubilation and short shorts. "Yup, that's me," I affirmed.

All the heads, except Rob's, turned to gape in awe. "Wow, you really were a movie star!" breathed one guy next to Rob. Then he punched

Rob in the arm. "Why didn't you tell us?" he demanded. The other men repeated the chorus.

Rob was embarrassed. "It never came up," he mumbled.

"Geez, you must make a lot of money," said another apprentice engineer with an envious look at Rob. Then his awestruck gaze turned into a leer and he grinned at Rob. "You lucky dog," he said lecherously. All his buddies started to snark and drool, too. It was rather revolting.

Rob looked thunderous so I mumbled that it wasn't all that much but it kept my health insurance current. I was uncomfortable by the testosterone-charged atmosphere so I pooh-poohed my commercial until Gary saved me. He grinned at Rob and said, "Pretty and rich. What in the hell does she see in you?"

"Yeah, yeah, yeah," Rob said with a wry smile. The situation appeared to be salvaged and I relaxed. Then the guy who'd gotten thrown out of his chair said to Rob, "So how come you got a TA position? You've got a rich wife to support you. There're a lot of guys who really need the money."

Rob seemed stunned at the attack. He turned white, then red, then started sputtering that he didn't need money from anybody and could support himself and a wife. He went on in that vein until Gary told the de-chaired-one to sit down and shut up. "Rob earned the job," he said firmly. "You're just mad 'cause you can't even get a date let alone marry a movie star" (Ah man!) "so have a beer and watch the game or go home."

That seemed to end the matter. No one wanted to mess with Gary. But the evening was ruined for Rob. He sat through one more quarter then abruptly stood up and brusquely told me we were going home. I thanked Gary for the chair and the water, then was hustled into my jacket and hurried up the stairs by Rob. We drove home silently and I watched Rob's jaw work under each streetlight we passed. He stalked into the trailer and jerked off his jacket. I followed and sat quietly, waiting for him to speak.

"I don't need any money from anybody. I'm not asking any favors. I do my job. Who the hell does that guy think he is?" he finally burst out agitatedly.

"Gary's right," I soothed, "he's just jealous."

Rob sat forward bouncing on the balls of his feet. He had a lot of anger that he didn't know how to handle. "Have I asked you for one dime?" he demanded.

"No, that's been one of our problems," I returned in what I thought was a reasonable tone but it set Rob off.

"No, I haven't," he said self-righteously. "Not one dime comes from you and it never will. 'Other guys need the job more than me'," he said bitterly, brooded, then added, rather nonsensically, I thought, "Why'd you spend the whole night talking to Gary?"

"Gary talked to me," I retorted icily. "You ignored me."

"I get one night off; I don't want to spend it taking care of you. I thought you could take care of yourself!" Rob returned petulantly.

"I did," I pointed out. "That seems to be what you're mad about."

"Well, it looked like you were flirting with Gary. And drinking water! Nobody drinks water during a game. You could at least have had a beer. And why couldn't you wear more clothes in that ad?" he demanded.

"Let me get this straight. You had a crummy night and it's my fault. Right?" I asked snidely. "Well, I wasn't flirting with Gary. He was a nice guy who didn't want me to sit all by myself. I didn't have any beer because somebody had to drive and I didn't want to spoil your time with the 'guys'. And I got paid to wear that costume in the ad. You certainly didn't object to it in California. And I guess I'm supposed to be sorry that I made money but I'm not. I haven't done anything wrong so you can just get over yourself!" And I gave him my best nasty-nice smile.

Rob didn't say anything but I could see his jaw muscles clenching again. He abruptly stood up, grabbed his jacket, and strode out of the trailer. I heard his car start and pull out then I couldn't hear anything except my thumping heart. I didn't know what to make of his disappearance. How could he walk out like that? We had issues! I couldn't fight all by myself so I turned on the TV and cuddled with Pudgy.

Rob came back in about an hour and sat down next to me. I looked at him cautiously and he smiled ruefully. "Mom said I should apologize," he said.

"You talked to your mother!?"

"I went home for some old notebooks and she was there so...well, yeah."

This sounded lame because he hadn't brought any notebooks in with him. When I asked where the notebooks were he said he left them in his car to take to work.

"Oh," I said, still weirded out that he talked to his mother instead of me. "Well, don't apologize unless you want to."

Rob scratched Pudgy's ears and said, "Yeah, I do. Mom said if I only get one night off I shouldn't spend it with the guys. I should stay with you." He smiled bravely but I could see he was starting to feel trapped.

Was I that awful to be around? My face fell so he hurriedly added, "And I'm sorry about the cracks I made about what you wore and not drinking beer. But, Stevie, this isn't California. You can have a beer or two without getting into an accident. There's not much to hit here. Drinking water is just sort of odd." His apology was turning into a justification. My face flushed with anger so he finished with, "But you can drink water if you want to. And we can figure out how to spend more time together." He seemed at a loss and waited hopefully for some comment from me but all I could think was, *You thick, selfish bastard!* Which didn't seem to be particularly helpful at the moment.

"Maybe we should sleep on it," Rob finally suggested and I agreed. *Honey, honey,* I repeated to myself. By the time we reached the bedroom I was receptive when Rob again apologized for criticizing my costume. "You were sexy as hell," Rob admitted. "I guess I just didn't like it when the guys got…well, you know. I better get used to having the prettiest girl around." The compliment pleased me so we had a genial romp then brushed our teeth, got in our sleep shirts, and cuddled up comfortably. As Rob fell asleep I reflected on the difficult time Rob was having adjusting to married life. Poor guy got himself a peacock and put it in a henhouse. While the plumage was lovely, I think he was finding the squawking hard to live with.

But I was finding neglect hard to live with, too. I knew he was busy and he'd probably try to work with me on a solution—at least as long as I was fun to be around. And I wouldn't be fun to be around as long as I centered my life on him. So. Where did that leave me? I fell asleep without finding an answer.

chapter 11

I still didn't have any answers the next day. Or the day after that. I played housewife because I didn't have anything better to do and pondered. Loneliness became a problem. The only person I had to talk to was Rob and I think I overdid it when he came home for meals. Rob gamely said he enjoyed listening to me yak and he developed the ability to tune me out, absently replying "Yes dear" as he read the paper or a textbook. It was the right answer, of course, so I didn't demand any closer attention and yakked away. The only time he got testy was one Monday morning when I asked where he was going and when he'd be back. He apologized when I explained that I was just trying to plan the meal schedule around him. I think he was finding it hard to have to answer to anyone after he'd been on his own. I could relate.

I was so desperate for company I thought about calling Alice but didn't when I remembered that Rob had run home and told her we were at odds. Besides, I saw her every Sunday. Don't get me wrong; I liked Marvin and Alice but every Sunday…? I did my best not to bitch; at least I was around someone other than Rob one day a week. I actually looked forward to doing the laundry so I could go to the Laundromat and be around people. But I was horribly uncomfortable. I didn't speak to anybody and nobody spoke to me. People looked at me out of the corners of their eyes and whispered when my back was turned. I tried discussing my sense of alienation with Rob.

"I feel like an E.F. Hutton commercial," I complained.

"You're being paranoid," Rob said.

But I knew I wasn't. When I drove anywhere I'd see people literally stop and stare. Groups of women would stop talking as I trundled my little shopping cart down the aisle, and start whispering when I passed. Even the four boys in the next trailer were uncommunicative and sullen when I went over one midnight to charmingly suggest—prefaced with a teeth-clenched smile—that they turn the decibel level of their stereo down.

"I think they're getting the stake ready for me," I muttered darkly as I crawled into bed next to Rob after that little confrontation.

"Who's they?" he asked sleepily.

"Everybody in this town!"

"Relax, you're being…"

"Damn it, I am not being paranoid! These people hate me!" I described all my strange encounters to Rob who was now reluctantly awake. "I just don't understand it," I sighed. "I smile, I'm civil. People will hardly look me in the eye. It's getting so I hate to go out."

Rob thought for a moment. "Well," he said finally, "maybe because it's who you are."

"What? A Mexican?" I asked belligerently. Funny how defensive you get living in Norway West, land of the blue-eyed blonds.

"No," Rob said and explained patiently, "This is a small town. Everybody knows you were an actress in Los Angeles. Hell, they've seen your commercials. And you're very, very pretty…"

"Well, thanks for that," I said, mollified.

"Don't mention it. Another thing, you drive a foreign sports car. I bet people do stare at you. You probably scare them half to death."

That put a different slant on things. I could probably quit worrying about a lynch mob.

"What should I do about the staring?" I asked.

"Ignore it. You'll get to know people; they'll get to know you. The staring will go away in time."

Rob curled around me and immediately went to sleep but I stared into the dark. Well, I'd re-invented a life for myself before, I could do it again. A person can't read or clean bathrooms forever.

I decided to go for a walk and scope out the neighbors. I'd already met the boys next door when I'd charged over to ask them to turn down their stereo. If they were out maybe I could introduce myself as a rational human being and we could become friends. No such luck, they all must have been in class. Everybody had someplace to go but me.

I walked to the mouth of the alley past a closed, shuttered trailer with a beat-up pickup parked outside. I noticed the garbage can between the trailer and the pickup was overflowing with whiskey and beer bottles. This was probably somebody I'd didn't need to get to know.

It was a fine, fall day so I decided to hike down the highway to pick up some salad stuff at the grocery store. I trudged past a park populated by mothers with young children and old men, marveling again at how clean everything was. Everyone who drove by me on the highway waved so I practiced my wrist flip. Those friendly waves from strangers cheered me up considerably. Now if people would just talk to me.

I got to the grocery store and trolled the aisles with my shopping cart, smiling and nodding to anyone who seemed receptive. I recognized two blue-haired ladies from my wedding shower so I braked my cart for a brief chat. I couldn't remember their names but that didn't seem important. They were people and, by God, I would talk to them.

The ladies asked me how I was getting along and I said I was doing just fine. I thanked them again for the gifts and the shower and they said they were happy to do it.

"Bobby grew up with my kids and we were pleased for Alice's sake that he finally settled down," said blue-hair #1.

From her tone it sounded like Rob had been a bit of a wildass. This was hard for me to believe. "Finally settled down?" I asked.

"Well," said blue-hair #2, "Bobby always had big ideas. Going off to California and all. I guess he figured home wasn't so bad after all."

"Well…" I equivocated.

"I hear you were an actress," interrupted blue-hair #1.

"I've seen your commercials," said blue-hair #2. "You'll have to tell us all about Hollywood sometime. It sounds so exciting!"

"We also heard you were Mexican," said blue-hair #1.

Oh boy, here we go, I thought defensively. Then had the good sense to look into the old ladies' faces, which were perfectly open and pleasant. They weren't being ugly; they were just making conversation.

"My ancestors were from Mexico," I affirmed pleasantly.

"Well, isn't that interesting," said blue-hair #2. "We mostly have Norwegians and Swedes around here. We'll have a lot to learn from you."

The old girls beamed at me full of good fellowship. Rob was right, in this land of transplanted Northern Europeans I was a pretty exotic item and people were curious. I don't know if they expected me to drag out a serape and do a hat dance—they'd be disappointed if they did—but I decided I'd do my best to be an ambassador of a foreign culture. Los Angeles culture, to be specific.

"I'm sure we have a lot to teach each other," I said as I started my cart rolling. "Nice talking to you. I'll see you around."

I was feeling pretty good about the encounter. It's not like I'd want the old girls for buddies, we didn't have anything in common and they each had forty years on me, but it was nice to make conversation.

I paid for my items at the checkout counter and practiced my smile on the cashier, a chubby, permed blond in her late-twenties. She seemed sullen until I made a comment about the weather. I'd never appreciated what an icebreaker the weather was. I was looking forward to winter so I'd really have something to talk about.

The cashier thawed at my innocuous comment. "You're Bobby Anderson's wife, aren't you," she stated as she took my money.

"That's right," I said, a little surprised. "How'd you know?"

She shrugged. "You know how small towns are. Everybody knows everybody else's business." She handed me my change and added too casually, "You know, Bobby and I went to a coupla sock hops in high school. I'm Sandy Schultz."

"Nice to meet you," I said noncommittally as I pocketed my change.

"He ever mention me?"

"Afraid not."

"I guess he wouldn't." She busied herself bagging my groceries. "I always thought Bobby was gonna do something special with his life," she said and gave her head an exasperated shake. "He had a job in California and everything. He had it made. I can't believe he came back to this one-horse town. And I really can't believe you came with him!" The smile lines on her face deepened to dissatisfied ditches.

"You don't sound very happy to be here," I said inanely.

"Are you?" Her question was an accusation.

"I don't know yet," I said honestly. "I haven't been here long enough to tell."

"Well, let me tell you about small towns. Be right with you, Mrs. Foster," she replied to an "ahem" behind me. "Let me tell you…uh… what'd you say your name was again?"

I had the feeling she knew my name perfectly well and a lot of other stuff about me besides, but this was her way of cutting me down to size. "Stevie," I replied with a slight smile.

"Yeah, well, let me tell you, there's nothing to do here. And if you do go out and have a drink with the girls, the whole town knows. If you do one little thing..."

"Don't you go filling this girl's head with nonsense, Sandy," Mrs. Foster interrupted. She sounded tired of waiting. I turned to inspect her. Mrs. Foster was a portly, middle-aged woman with a red face and a scarf covering her hair. "You're just put out because you stayed out too late and had a fight with your husband. You just tend to your business here and quit wasting this girl's time with your complaining," she said stoutly. She looked like the sort of person who did everything stoutly.

"See?" Sandy said triumphantly to me. "Everybody knows your business."

"We wouldn't if you didn't yell it out at midnight," Mrs. Foster retorted. "And if you don't like it here, why don't you get Bear to move away?"

Sandy was shocked. "Oh, I couldn't leave my friends. Besides, it's a great place to raise children."

The cognitive dissonance was a little too much for me so I thanked Sandy, grabbed my sack, and went home.

"I met an old girlfriend of yours," I told Rob at dinner that night. He looked at me quizzically so I added helpfully, "Sandy Schultz." Rob still looked blank. "The cashier at the Country Market? She said you went to a few sock hops together."

"Oh! Sandy Strand! Sure, she married Bear Schultz. He works for the local beer distributor. I ran into him at a bar before you got here." He started chewing again; the subject didn't seem to interest him. It interested me.

"C'mon, tell me about this romance," I prodded.

"Some romance," he grunted. "I took her to a sock hop."

"She said sock hops. Plural."

"Really? I don't remember more than the one." Rob raised a leering eyebrow at me. "I remember she was a cheerleader and wore one of those cute short skirts. Nice ass." He checked for my reaction but I ain't stupid, I know when I'm being tormented. I remained calm but interested. He gave up. "Bear told me they have four kids. What's she look like now?" he asked.

"Like she's married to a guy named Bear and has four kids. She got chubby over the years. I can see the cheerleader buried in there, though. She sounded unhappy with her life."

"She was always unhappy about something. It was strange, she could be bitching one minute and all smiles the next. She must have had a real short attention span. Fortunately, she's Bear's problem, not mine."

I was gratified that Rob was actually willing to discuss someone with me. "Do you suppose the bitching bothers him?" I pursued.

"They got married right out of high school. I imagine he's used to it by now. He probably doesn't pay any attention to her."

Rob chewed on his salad and I thought about his last comment. Not paying attention to bitching must be a local custom. Fortunately for Rob, I too have a short attention span so I didn't take offense.

"Oh!" I said as I remembered the bottles in the alley. "When I was walking down the alley to the store I snooped in the garbage can of the first trailer. I couldn't believe the number of empty beer cans and whiskey bottles. I thought just one old man lived there. What's the story?"

Rob was shocked. "Stevie, you shouldn't be digging in people's garbage!"

"I didn't dig in it, I just looked. I'm trying to fit into small town life. Sandy tells me that includes snooping. C'mon, tell me about this guy."

"Well," said Rob as he settled back in his chair, "you know I don't like gossip" (oh please) "but this is pretty common knowledge. Everybody calls him Crazy Eddy and he's lived there ever since I was a kid. He works sweeping out a few bars downtown. I guess you could call him the town drunk. He's harmless enough as long as you leave him alone. He goes to work after the bars close and sleeps during the day. He pretty much stays to himself."

"Nice neighbor to have," I said ironically.

Rob shrugged. "He won't tolerate any interference. When I was a kid some of the ladies in a local church group decided to clean him up. It didn't go over very well. Crazy Eddie put up with the first visit I guess because he was so surprised, but the second time a contingent of women showed up he met them at the door with his shotgun and threatened to pepper them with rock salt if they didn't leave him alone. He called them a bunch of do-gooder, interfering old heifers and told them to mind their own business and he'd mind his." Rob laughed. "The story was all over town. And the good ladies have left him alone ever since. I'd advise you to stay away from his garbage cans. He still has the shotgun and isn't afraid to use it. You'll probably hear it on Halloween. Every year the kids go there to torment him and every year he shoots at them."

"It's lucky he hasn't killed anyone yet!" I said, a little put off by the thought of a shotgun-wielding crazy man living three doors down.

"It's just rock salt. It stings; it won't kill you."

"Are you sure?"

Rob grinned. "Believe me; I know. Just stay out of his garbage cans. Remember the church ladies and leave him alone." I was inclined to argue so Rob sighed. "Listen, he doesn't ask anything of anyone. He's not on the county. He earns enough for gas and booze and that seems to be enough for him. He's an old man and has a right to privacy. If you leave him alone I guarantee he won't bother you so get that worried look off your face. At least he's quiet."

Good point. The college kids next door drove everybody nuts with their stereo and they were considered perfectly normal. I guessed I could live with a quiet crazy person.

After another quiet week I still had way too much time on my hands so I decided I'd try to get a job. I already had my Master's, for God's sake; there must be something I could do. I dug out my resume and ran into "our" office to update it on Rob's computer. Unfortunately, my computer skills weren't very advanced and I got as far as turning the damn thing on before I ran into difficulty. I was almost weeping with frustration when Rob came home for dinner.

"I can't get this stupid thing to work," I hissed through my teeth when Rob peeked in the doorway after I yelled that I was in the office. "You're going to have a $4,000 planter in a minute."

Rob smiled a smug, superior smile as he replaced me at the desk until he saw my resume. He frowned but showed me how call up the program I needed. Then I had to put my resume aside to do my housewifery. Rob still didn't say anything about my project; he just looked slightly disturbed. We ate dinner in silence; Rob seemed to have something on his mind and I didn't want to disturb his thought process so I watched the news on TV. Then I cleared and started washing dishes. I knew something major was bothering Rob when he offered to dry. Normally, he tried to get out of helping by arguing that air-drying was more sanitary. I worked quietly letting him get his thoughts together. One thing I'd learned was he wouldn't be rushed. He'd say what he had to say in his own good time and any prodding on my part just irritated him.

"About this resume, Stevie," he began, "why are you putting it together?"

"To go job-hunting, of course," I said.

"Oh," he said and put a glass in the cupboard. "Why do you want a job anyway?"

"Why? Because I'm bored and I want money."

"Hmmm," he said as he massaged a plate. "Couldn't you do volunteer work or something?"

Visions of afternoons with the church ladies danced before me. "No," I said, looking at him narrowly. "Why?"

"Well…" Rob hesitated, took a deep breath, and said, "People will think I can't support you."

"You're can't, Rob, you're a student," I said reasonably.

"We've talked about this, Stevie. If we stay within my budget we can swing it. If necessary I can get a part-time job…"

I had entered the Twilight Zone. Crazy Eddie wasn't the only lunatic in our trailer park.

"Great," I interrupted, "I'd never see you at all. And what am I supposed to do in the meantime? Take up crocheting?"

I bitterly remembered how 'cute' I'd thought Rob's insistence on total financial responsibility was in California. Well, it wasn't 'cute' anymore; it was ridiculous. I wasn't going to live my life cooped up because Rob got a little heat from one colleague about my earning capability. But Rob was looking ornery so I choked back my irritation and got out my mental dance shoes to talk him around. And I'd do it without screeching and waving my arms around. I put my hands back in the dishwater; I wouldn't be so inclined to wave them over my ears if they were wet. I washed a few more dishes and waited for Rob to respond.

Rob polished a fork and struggled to articulate his feelings. Being the strong, silent type has its drawbacks. "You had a great life for yourself. You had an exciting career, a nice place to live; you had it all. I'm as sorry as I can be that I took you away from your home and don't have anything as nice to offer you yet. But I'm not going to make it worse by asking you to work," he finally said. "Dad gave me hell because we got married before I was out of school. And he's right, we should have waited; but I love you and didn't think you'd sit around for two years in California waiting for me. So please; let me do my best to take care of you."

He stood Promethean, proud, self-sacrificing, and noble. I couldn't stand it.

"What a crock," I said. "Rob, you didn't drag me back here by my hair. I made the choice myself. I'm your wife not your adopted idiot child." Rob looked a little startled at my response but it was getting deep in here and my bullshit threshold is pretty low. I added, "I appreciate your desire to protect and take care of me but you're not in a financial position to do it." I remembered Marvin's advice about honey and glanced calculatingly at my Fly. I'd stick to one grievance—being left alone all the time—and leave the money matters for later.

I began again, "Rob...sweetheart," (endearments were foreign to me but it seemed worth a shot) "you know I'm new here and I don't know anybody..."

The Fly was rubbing another dish restively. Not a good sign. "You've met the family," he pointed out.

"Yes, and they've been lovely to me," I agreed, "but I guess what I'm trying to say...I don't have any friends yet, other than you, of course... and, well, I know you're busy so I need to meet people my age." I smiled beguilingly at him. I was rather proud of myself. I'd managed to communicate without screeching.

Rob pondered. "But, Stevie," he said, "I give you as much time as I can."

I felt an impatient screech rising and firmly pushed it down. "I know you do," I said. "And I appreciate the time you spend with me..."

"I don't know why you can't get a hobby or find some way to entertain yourself," Rob interrupted crossly. "I can't devote every minute to you."

That screech was billowing up again. *Back*, I commanded it. "I know that," I said smiling manically, trying not to think of the butcher knife on the counter. "That's why I want a job."

"And who's going to do the work around here?" Rob continued. "I don't have time."

So that was the problem! He'd gotten used to his cushy little life and didn't want to give it up. Well, I didn't like cleaning any better than he did. Enough honey. It was time to break out the swatter.

"You want to know what my problem is? My problem," I bit off the words, "is that I married a selfish pig who dragged me to the outback, uses me as a servant and a pump, and whines when I want out of the kitchen."

Well, at least I got the "discussion" going. We stood at the kitchen sink, hissing accusations and recriminations at each other.

I told Rob I was used, misused, and abused. He was selfish and inconsiderate. He owed me more.

Turns out Rob felt the same way about me. I was immature and demanding. I showed no understanding of the stresses he was dealing with.

No wonder the fairy tales stop at the wedding. What comes after is too fraught with drama for a children's story.

We both started listening to each other eventually. We admitted we were both right and we were both wrong. We promised to try harder and show more consideration and support for each other. We patched things up. After all, we were stuck with each other...for the moment.

"You've had a problem about money ever since we got together," I said, making a sincere effort to understand and be understood. "I agree we shouldn't dip into my principal, I wouldn't do that myself, but I have money from residuals piling up in a savings account that you won't touch." Rob started to speak but I forestalled him with an upraised hand. "Let me finish. I don't feel any better about not contributing here than you did in California so here's what I'm proposing. You pay your own tuition and fees. I won't contribute one cent for that. We'll split all the food and utilities if that makes you feel better. But I'll get a job so we can rent something better next year. It makes perfect sense; you get to keep your pride, I get to live like a person. And I won't be bored. Everybody's happy."

He thought hard. "Sounds like we'd be roommates," he objected.

"We'd be partners," I assured him. "And if you want to support me do it in a way we can both live with. Be my friend."

"I suppose you'd expect me to help with the housework," Rob said doubtfully.

"We'll work something out," I soothed him. I didn't want to scare him too badly.

Rob breathed out explosively. "Well…maybe it would work. But good God Almighty, what will everybody say?"

"Who cares? If they have any sense at all they'll say how lucky you are to have such a helpful wife. Besides, Bear's wife works. Remember Sandy?"

"But she has to, they have four kids to support."

"Well, I have to so I don't end up in a straightjacket. Honest to God, Rob, I'm getting cabin fever holed up in this trailer."

We were smiling by this time. I mentally congratulated myself on the successful completion of our discussion. Damn, I was getting good at marriage.

"You're the first roommate I ever had I could neck with," Rob said, getting into the spirit of things. "But if you're making money what do you need me around for?"

"Oh, car maintenance," I said. "And you're the first roommate I ever had who let me use his penis whenever I wanted to."

I jollied him into a good mood and marveled at the Neanderthal I married. Had Rob always been such a 'guy' or had he reverted to type when returned to his natural habitat? I guess I'd never know.

chapter 12

I fed Rob and finished my resume the next morning. I just didn't know who to send it to. I mulled over the problem as I drank coffee. Who did I know that knew University personnel? Well, Rick worked on campus but I got the feeling he wouldn't help me. How about Chris? If she didn't have any names maybe she could ask around for me. She'd be at her little shop at nine or so. It was only 7:30 now. What should I do for an hour and a half?

I looked down at my thighs spread out on the kitchen chair. I didn't want to have to buy a whole new wardrobe—haute couture in Brookings was apparently a selection of polyester pantsuits provided by K-Mart and I preferred natural fibers—so the decision of what to do for an hour was easy.

I got out a leotard and an exercise tape and moved the living room furniture to one side to provide running space—that was the weight training portion of my self-improvement program—and began. I grunted, I strained, I sweat. When I started jumping I thought that stupid trailer would rattle off its blocks but I persevered. I hadn't exercised seriously for two months what with one thing and another, and I paid for the vacation. The cute little instructor on the tape kept caroling, "You're tough, you're strong, you can do it!" I swore back at her in rhythm, "Fuck you, fuck you." Anger is a great motivator; besides, swearing kept me breathing. Pudgy provided moral support by sticking her tail in my face and "meeping" at me encouragingly. After an hour of agony I stretched out and cooled down. I also made myself a promise to get on some sort of schedule before I went completely to hell.

I took a shower, called Chris, and invited her to lunch. We met at a downtown restaurant that facetiously advertised itself as the "Sioux River Yacht Club". I was beginning to discover a sly, self-deprecating sense of humor in this part of the country.

Over a sandwich and iced tea I confided to Chris that I wanted to apply for a teaching job at the University and asked if she knew anybody in the theater department. "I've got a Master's degree; I used to teach acting. Maybe this place could use a drama teacher," I said.

"That's a wonderful idea," Christine enthused. "I don't know if they've ever had a real professional before. I even know the department head! We took a woodworking workshop together." She wrote down his name on my yellow pad, wished me luck, waved away my thanks, and asked me how I was making the adjustment to the Midwest.

"Oh, as well as can be expected, I guess," I said. "Rob had some funny ideas about me working. Can you imagine?" I laughed.

Chris didn't laugh with me. "Yeah," she said slowly. "Rick's been trying to make me give up my shop for a year now. He says his mother never worked, she always put her family first. And his brothers' wives don't work; I think he's afraid they look down on him. Associate Professors don't make much money, you know. But I just don't know what I'd do..." she trailed off, lost in her own thought. She came back to herself and caught me watching interestedly. "It's no big deal. Besides, if I closed up shop he wouldn't have an excuse to spend his lunch hour with his mother."

"Maybe I should send Rob to Alice's. He's happy as long as he's fed," I said ruefully.

"The first year of marriage is pretty much learning to live with each other," Chris comforted me. "You spend a lot of time compromising. It's tough."

"That's what Marvin told me," I said and added after a moment, "I probably wouldn't mind compromising but it seems like the compromise is all on my side. And that's not compromise at all, is it? That's surrender." I brooded on the unsettling thought.

"I think the first anniversary is a celebration that the husband and wife survived," Chris said and made a face.

Was this bitterness I was hearing? "How long have you and Rick been married?" I asked casually.

"Five years," she said flatly. "And let me tell you, it doesn't get much easier." I waited, hoping she'd expand on the theme but she changed the subject. "We're having a few friends over Friday night for drinks. I thought maybe you and Bobby would like to come. It'll be mostly friends of Rick's from the University so you probably won't have much in common with anybody—you know, Ag professors—but maybe you'd have a good time."

Chris smiled at me hopefully. It sounded like she needed some non-Ag types there for herself. Well, I fit the bill. And the thought of meeting somebody—anybody!—under the age of fifty was appealing.

"I'd love to," I said warmly. "I'll have to check with Rob but I'm sure it'll be okay with him. What time should we be there? Can I bring anything?"

"Oh, come around eight," Chris said with relief. "You could bring a dip or something. I know! How about nachos? You must have a good recipe for that."

I didn't but I'd get one. How did anyone entertain before Mexican cuisine came along?

"Oh, by the way," said Chris as we were leaving the restaurant, "don't mention this to the rest of the Anderson boys. I had to invite Alice and Marvin, Rick insisted, but they have square dancing, thank God. We didn't invite the other boys; I'd like to do something without all the Andersons. Besides, the only ones who'd show up would be Tom and Nancy. Marilyn always acts like she's slumming."

I nodded sympathetically and promised to keep my mouth shut. It seemed I wasn't the only one having trouble with this close-knit family crap.

Rob wasn't enthusiastic about the party but agreed to go. He was miffed when I told him Chris didn't want the rest of his brothers to know about it. "Tom and Mike's feelings will be hurt," Rob said.

"Not if they don't know about it," I said shortly. "Honestly, Rob, not every social occasion has to be a family reunion. I'm surprised Chris invited us."

Rob let the subject drop.

I was in a mild tizzy that week. I was going to a party! I called Leslie for a nachos recipe, which is ironic when you think about it: Me, the Aztec princess, calling my WASP friend for Mexican recipes.

"So, what else is new in God's country?" Leslie asked after giving me a recipe.

I reported that I'd roughed out a resume and was applying for a teaching job at the University. "And I've even been talking to people!" I concluded triumphantly.

"That's a big deal?" Leslie asked in disbelief.

"I think it is. I look different, I dress different, I talk different than anyone else here. Everybody is blond, blue-eyed, and chubby. Rob says people are chubby because the climate's so cold, it takes a lot of body fat to keep warm. He says it's pretty obvious I came from a warm State. I get a lot of stares but not a lot of conversation."

"Rob's not fat," Leslie pointed out.

"He wasn't. I'm going to have to put him on a diet, too."

"Boy, do you sound like a little wife. How is Rob anyway? Is marriage all hearts and flowers?"

"It's never been hearts and flowers," I retorted. "It's just complicated."

"I always figured 'happily ever after' was too good to be true," Leslie said. We both sighed then she added cautiously. "You know, Stevie old buddy, you can come back for awhile if it gets to be too much. I have an extra bedroom."

"Thanks, Les, but everyone tells me I'll be okay if I can make it past the first year. And nothing's really bad. I think sometimes I'm just homesick."

"Well, at least Rob's happy."

"Les, I honestly don't think so. We probably should have had a longer courtship period but it's too late now," I said thoughtfully then added, "The sex is still good, though. As matter of fact, it's getting better."

"Great," said Les impatiently, "you spend two hours a week in bed. What do you do the rest of the time?"

"I read a lot," I admitted. "But! I have my first party coming up!"

"Well, I'm thinking good thoughts in your direction," she said. "Call and bitch whenever you feel the need."

"Don't worry, I will."

By the time Rob got home from his staff meeting that Friday I was running around in my bathrobe and hot rollers like a demented woman. The recipe for nachos Les had given me called for refried beans, an unheard of item in Brookings. So I'd gone to the library and found a recipe. Of course my product turned out looking predigested. But then again maybe refried beans always looked predigested. I'd never seen them in their virgin state before. I was trying to bury my beans with chips when Rob walked through the door.

"We have to be at the farm at eight," I said shortly. "Make yourself a sandwich and take a shower. I'm too busy to wait on you right now."

I finally gave up on the nachos, covered them with foil, put them in the oven to keep warm, and finished my toilette. I left my hair long and curly and put in one comb to sweep it up and out of my eyes. I took extra care to make sure my make-up was perfect. I was looking hot but informal in a black leather miniskirt, red turtleneck tunic sweater, short heels, and matching earrings and bracelet. I was ready for my social debut.

I was checking on the nachos when Rob came out of the bedroom, buckling his belt. He was dressed in jeans and a flannel shirt. About the best that could be said for him was that he was clean.

I looked at him in dismay. "Is that what you're going to wear?" I asked as tactfully as possible.

"Sure." Rob was undisturbed.

"But, Rob, this is a party."

"This is what I wear to drink beer." He finally took a good look at me. "God, Stevie, you look great!"

I looked down at myself and looked back at him. "Maybe I'm overdressed. Should I change?"

"No, no, don't take it off." His eyes gleamed as he walked toward me to put his arms around me. "Maybe we could be late."

I pushed him away. "Nope. The nachos are ready to go. I'll just put on some jeans…"

"No, I'll change," Rob said gallantly. "You stay just the way you are."

I smiled to myself as he hurried off, relieved that he was changing. *After all, jeans and a work shirt were too casual for a party,* I thought. A sport coat, at least, was called for.

We drove over to Rick and Chris' farm in the Buick. It was a cool, fall night with lots of stars out. Stars! I'd never seen stars like this in the city. Los Angeles had too many other lights competing and the stars lost out. I smiled with pleasure and fantasized how the evening would be. I could see a fire burning warmly in the stone fireplace of a country home surrounded by a wraparound porch and just stuffed with architectural wonders. I'd wander through a wood-paneled dining room with a glass of wine in my hand, smiling graciously at the tweedy faculty members standing in front of hunting prints. This was going to be so cool. The nachos and Rob's hand were warm on my knee.

When we arrived about ten other cars were parked around an old, white, clapboard house that had a rickety stoop instead of a wraparound porch. My smile wavered but didn't disappear completely until Chris opened the door, dressed in a flannel shirt and blue jeans—almost an exact copy of the outfit I'd talked Rob out of wearing. She looked startled when she saw me in my relative splendor but she recovered quickly.

"C'mon in, you guys. Beer's in the kitchen. Just help yourself," she said and ushered us in.

"I'm overdressed," I babbled, "but I thought, well, it was a party..." I trailed off.

"We're pretty informal around here," Chris said. "Hey, everybody," she shouted gaily over the noise of the other guests, "this is Rick's brother, Bobby, and his wife, Stephanie."

Ten couples, all dressed in the blue jean/flannel uniform and all holding beers, turned to look at us. Conversation died out completely. I don't think our impact would have been any greater if we'd walked in stark naked.

"Hello," I said weakly to the wide eyes and open mouths.

The mouths belonging to the women snapped shut and formed grim lines at my greeting. I noticed them moving closer to their men. *Oh boy*, I thought, hideously embarrassed, *they think I'm a scarlet woman*. With my red sweater and red face I guess they weren't too far off. Rob came to my rescue.

"Stevie looks great, doesn't she," he said to Chris as he proudly put his arm around me.

"She sure does," said Chris ruefully. "It wouldn't hurt any of us to dress up a little more." She took my plate of nachos. "Does this need to be heated up? Let's go to the kitchen." Rob and I followed her out. I was grateful to have the chance to recover my composure.

Chris led us to the back of the old farmhouse and, as I took in the ambiance as unobtrusively as possible, my fantasies disappeared in a disappointing puff. Chris' country house had small boxy rooms. There was no fireplace, there were no charming nooks and crannies, no wide wood molding, no hunting prints, no real charm at all.

I was looking around at the square kitchen, comparing it unfavorably with my trailer when Chris, who'd been unwrapping the nachos, noticed my less-than-flattering appraisal.

"It's not much, is it," she said.

"No, it's fine," I said glibly.

"That's okay, I know it's horrible. It only has one bathroom and sucks up heat like there's no tomorrow. But Rick likes the farm. He has his cattle project, we have room for horses, and I made a pottery shed out of the old chicken house. So there are advantages. I keep hoping the house'll burn down so we can build something new but I don't think we'll be that lucky."

"Why don't you build something new anyway? Just bulldoze this when you're ready to move?"

"Can't afford it. We may not like the house but we still have to pay for it. It's not so bad. I've gotten sort of used to it. I'd prefer living in town but Rick really wants to have access to his research. And you know the Anderson boys; they have to have their own way all the time. It's not worth fighting over." We snickered together knowingly (ignoring Rob, who looked pained) until Chris caught sight of Rick standing in the doorway. She quit laughing and changed the subject abruptly. "These nachos look good."

"I got the recipe from a friend in L.A.," I said quickly. Now was not the time to start dishing the Anderson boys especially after the way Rob had stuck by me—and the way Rick was glaring at Chris. "I had a terrible time finding refried beans. I finally tried making some myself. I hope they taste alright."

"Yeah, we don't have much in that line in Brookings. I'm sure they'll be fine. Besides, nobody here will know the difference. You two grab a beer and I'll introduce you around."

We returned to the living room. The men were too warm and the women too cold. I was catching emotional pneumonia from the temperature extremes. I didn't really understand the resentment of the women. Let me rephrase that: I understood the jealousy because the women were a chubby lot who did little to make themselves attractive. What I didn't understand was the clutching of husbandly arms. I was with Rob, for God's sake, tall, handsome Rob. Why they thought I'd be interested in their balding, pot-bellied little mates was beyond me. And if their husbands paid too much attention to me, well, it wasn't because I encouraged them. I stuck my chin out and carried myself like royalty. Rob stayed close, thank God.

The only outright attack came from a particularly rabbity-looking woman called, rather incongruously I thought, Glory. Chris introduced us to her, she looked me up and down, and said in that false 'I'm telling you this as a friend' tone, "Aren't you uncomfortable wearing a skirt like that? You'll freeze your butt off. And it really isn't appropriate, you know. People will think you're, well…not really respectable."

The room went dead, except for a choked-off laugh from Rick, and ratty Glory looked very pleased with herself. She'd certainly put me in my place, hadn't she? And to tell you the truth, I wasn't quite sure what to do. I wanted to slap her rodenty little face but I didn't want to cause a scene and embarrass Chris. On the other hand, the scene had already been created, hadn't it? I stood there in the center of the room, my legs hanging out of my short shirt, seriously outnumbered, trying to form a response, and wishing I'd never come when Rob spoke up.

"If, in fact, it's true that you can freeze your butt off in a short skirt, Glory, you should try it. You could use a lot less in the butt department. But please don't wear one where I have to see it. Stevie's a beautiful woman with the legs to pull off a skirt like this. If you tried it, it'd look like two hams hanging from a very broad beam." He looked down at me and his wide, mobile mouth curved into the smile that had turned me ga-ga in the first place.

Glory turned white, then red (almost the shade of my sweater) and abruptly left for the kitchen. The rotund man next to her, probably her husband, just looked embarrassed and filled his pipe. Rob and I were left in possession of the field, pleased with our victory.

When we had a minute to ourselves I murmured to Rob admiringly, "For a man who doesn't talk much you sure come through in a pinch."

"I had a feeling some the women might give you a hard time," Rob said calmly. "I had a few insults ready. Don't act so surprised. You need a little backup I can provide it. I can learn things, you know."

My God, he did pay attention sometimes. What a relief. He'd routed the Wicked Witch of the Midwest just for me and I fell in love with him all over again. I surveyed the room. We were at a party, by

God, and I was going to enjoy myself. How much trouble could I get into with Rob at my back? We could handle anything together.

Rob and I mingled and listened to the ongoing conversations though I couldn't contribute much. The talk was mostly about local politics, about which I knew nothing, and animal husbandry about which I knew even less. Rob stuck close and was as proprietorial about me as the women were about their spouses so my lack of animal knowledge didn't bother me.

We joined a group that was discussing the care and feeding of hogs. A gray-bearded, flannel-clad man was pontificating about different breeds—China whites or Poland whites…anyway something whites. I listened and nodded wisely. The man looked at me nodding along and asked, amused, "Do you know anything about pigs?"

"Not the four-legged kind," I returned, deadpan, and the group broke up. I grinned along with everyone, please at my own cleverness. I even had another beer.

Two of the wives, Gail and Connie, cornered me to ask me questions about diet, exercise, and HOLLYWOOD, which I answered as best I could.

"Just ignore Glory. If I was as skinny as you I'd wear a shorter skirt than the one you've got on," Gail said enviously. "If I could afford it," she added.

"How do you keep your weight down?" Connie, a heavy-set, tightly permed, spectacled woman that everybody deferred to, asked.

"Well, I watch what I eat," I said with my fingers crossed then decided to bite the bullet and be honest. "To tell you the truth, I'm putting on a few pounds. I've been really lazy about exercise. I'm just starting to get back into a routine again."

Connie and Gail questioned me closely about my exercise regimen and I explained about my tape collection. "I'm just having a hard time getting motivated," I admitted.

We agreed that group aerobics would be just the thing for all of us—misery loves company, after all—and scheduled our first group groan for the following Monday.

I was flying. I was at a party, I was admired, I was making play dates. And if things starting getting a little rocky I found Rob at my shoulder, helping me over the rough spots. Glory never reappeared. Chris said she and her husband had left early.

Rick wasn't too happy with either Rob or me but managed not to say anything derogatory. I was slightly surprised that he didn't pout at me for getting too much attention. I guess he only objected to having people horn in on his mother's time.

I was euphoric on the ride home and analyzed the party into the ground. I crowed over Rob's squelching of Glory the Rat and repeated verbatim his comment.

"Yeah, I sure told her off," Rob agreed as we let ourselves into the trailer. He helped me off with my coat. I danced around the cramped living room, pleased with my social success.

"And those people laughed at my jokes. Did you hear my bon mot about the pigs? 'Not the four-legged kind'," I cackled. "Pretty good if I do say so myself."

"Yeah, that was funny," said Rob and he helped me off with my sweater. He started on my skirt.

"And two of the women want to start an aerobics class," I said, not distracted from my triumph by Rob's roaming hands.

"That'll be nice," said Rob and shut me up by kissing me.

I broke off the kiss. "Rob, is that skirt really too short?"

"It's just right," said Rob and kissed me again, a very passionate kiss. Seemed Rob really did like that skirt.

"Maybe I won't wear it again," I teased. "It takes forever for me to shave. You know I have pubic hair growing down to my knees. That's a lot of territory to cover."

"It's great territory," murmured Rob and knelt down to investigate the territory closer with his lips.

"Well, you know how lousy I am with a razor," I gasped. I was starting to get a little distracted by sensation. "I always cut myself."

"You'll survive," Rob assured me. He stood up and made like Heathcliff, carrying me into the bedroom.

Afterward, I raised myself to look Rob in the face as he dozed. "I made the right choice following you back here. For awhile there I wasn't sure but I think everything is going to be all right," I said seriously. "I'm finding a place for myself. This is going to work."

"I always knew your place is with me, Stevie, now shut up and go to sleep."

Rob tucked me under his arm and dozed off again. It was quite possible that he was right, I mused before I fell asleep.

chapter 13

I was so gratified with my social success I didn't grumble at all when Rob woke me early the next Sunday so I could attend church and the family dinner. I wanted to thank Chris for the invitation. Of course, I had to do it discreetly. If I wanted to be included in future parties I'd better keep my mouth shut around the un-included Andersons. I cut Chris from the herd at the after-church coffee klatch after Nancy had vented her spleen by insulting us both. It was easy to ignore Nancy's snipes; I'd been to a party and she hadn't. Neener, neener, neener.

"I really appreciated meeting new people," I concluded warmly. "Connie and Gail want to exercise with me. We're meeting at Connie's house for aerobics."

"Connie? Connie who?" Chris asked.

"I don't know. Her husband teaches with Rick," I said.

"Connie Schwartz? You're kidding me! A chunky woman with short curly hair, mid-thirties?"

"That's the one," I said, puzzled at her surprise. "I was talking with her and another blond named Gail about diet and we decided to get together to sweat. Connie's providing the house, I'm bringing the tape."

"Gail Lundquist? She's in on this, too?"

"If that's her last name, yeah." It occurred to me that Chris might like to come along. "We're meeting tomorrow at four if you want to join us," I offered.

"Dr. Schwartz is Rick's big boss. Rick was a little upset with me that I didn't make more of an effort to speak with Mrs. Schwartz. It'd be good for his career if I socialized with the department wives more," Chris said.

"Here's your chance."

"I'd have to close the shop early but I do need the exercise. Rick made a crack about me gaining weight. I think he's mad because I don't look like you in a skirt anymore," Chris confessed. I was a bit flummoxed at this but before I could say anything Chris asked, "Would it take much time? Rick likes me home at 5:00. What would he say if I wasn't there?"

"Who cares?" I said. "You just said he wanted you socializing with the wives. He'll probably be delighted."

Chris was clearly tempted. "You know, I've always wanted to see Connie Schwartz's house. Okay, count me in."

"Great. Just wear something comfortable. Oh, and can you tell me how to get there? Connie gave me the address but street names don't mean anything to me yet."

"I can drive. I'll pick you up at a quarter to."

I mentioned to Rob at breakfast Monday morning that I wouldn't be home until after five that afternoon but he was deep in his paper and just grunted. I was a little nettled at being ignored but let it pass. I had my own affairs to take care of and if he wasn't interested, that was his problem.

I was waiting on the front step in my sweats when Chris drove up in her pick-up. The air was crisp and clear, the sky was blue, and the leaves I could see from the alley were red and gold.

"I just love fall, don't you?" I asked Chris as I climbed into the pick-up.

"It's okay, I guess," she shrugged back. "To me it means winter is just around the corner."

"I'm looking forward to winter, too," I bubbled.

Chris was amused by my enthusiasm. "You've never been through a real winter, have you?"

"Nope, Los Angeles just has two seasons, wet and dry. I really like the changing leaves. I can't wait for the snow."

"You'll be good and sick of snow before winter's over," Chris predicted and put the pickup in gear.

Chris filled me in on Connie and Gail as we drove to Connie's.

155

Connie's husband was Dean of the Ag Department and a real big shot in Rick's world.

"I was surprised they even came to the party," Chris confided. "They don't normally socialize with people as far down the chain as Rick. That's why Rick wasn't too upset when I told him I'd be late without checking with him first."

I stared at her in disbelief. This was 1991, for God's sake; nobody had to get permission from a husband for anything anymore. But I was distracted from my outrage when Chris obliviously continued. Gail's husband had something to do with the Sheep Unit. He was a rung above Rick's level in the Agricultural hierarchy. Both women had Home Economics degrees from good old SDSU. There was an eerie correlation between Ag oriented men and women majoring in the domestic sciences. I guess husbandry of one sort or another was the common bond. Or maybe it was that the women looked like cows. *Now, now, Stevie,* I said to myself, *don't make fun.* At least they were trying to do something about their bovine hindquarters. And I needed a little work in that department myself.

Chris pulled into a driveway two blocks from the campus green. Connie's home was a three-story house, white with forest green trim, separated from the sidewalk by neat hedges. This was the residence of a local bigwig and as we stood on the porch after ringing the bell I woefully compared it to my horrible little trailer on Tobacco Road. Gail was already seated in the living room when Connie let us in. Both women were wearing sweat suits. Gail was in serviceable gray but Connie was magnificent in pink with a bouquet of petunias embroidered on the shirt. When I commented on how pretty the petunias were Connie thanked me, said she'd done the work herself, and showed us around her home. I looked at the huge rooms, expensive furnishings, and new appliances hungrily. There wasn't a shred of plastic on her windows; Connie had drapes. There were tastefully painted ceramics and framed needlepoint squares on the walls—her own work, of course. As I oohed and aahed I felt poor, shabby, and outclassed. Chris followed timidly and didn't say a word.

We finally returned to the family room. I inserted the exercise tape and stripped off my sweats to the tights and leotard underneath. I managed to look pretty damn good in spite of my brief aerobic vacation.

Connie may be local royalty but I was thin and in the world of women, that gave me an edge.

"In six months you'll all be wearing leotards just like mine," I graciously assured the women when I noticed their eyes had bugged out at my outfit.

I gave them some instruction about aerobics since this was a new discipline for them. I told them about stretching out, warming up, cooling down, and breathing. "Above all, listen to your bodies," I lectured. "We don't want any heart attacks or muscle strains."

I'd chosen a 40-minute tape as today's selection, which was probably stupid. I was used to it, more or less, so I got my heart rate elevated and worked up a good sweat but my colleagues suffered. They huffed, they puffed, they groaned, they sweat buckets, but dammitall, they didn't quit. They didn't talk much either. They needed their air for breathing. Connie broke silence only once when her two pre-pubescent boys sat on the sofa and giggled at us.

"You kids go play outside," she gasped, red-faced and snarly. The kids left in a hurry.

When the forty minutes ended we flopped down with glasses of water to re-hydrate and talk.

"Everybody ready for Hobo Day?" Chris asked diffidently.

Connie and Gail nodded but I had no idea what they were talking about. "Hobo Day?" I repeated.

Connie made a wry face. "It's the largest organized drunk in South Dakota," she said and the others laughed.

Oh! It was a celebration of some sort but…what were they celebrating? I was sitting in a room full of agricultural wives so I made an educated guess. "Is it a harvest festival of some sort?" I asked.

The three women broke up. I'd have liked to join in but I still didn't know what was going on. Gail finally noticed my lost look and took pity on me.

"Hobo Day is the University Homecoming," she explained kindly. "Everybody dresses up, or down I guess, as bums. Everybody drinks, there's a football game, and everybody drinks some more. It's normally pretty harmless alcoholic fun but things have been getting out of hand the last few years. There's been some pretty serious vandalism. Maybe it won't be too bad this year."

"Bums," I mused. "Where I went to school they had homecoming kings and queens. Why bums?"

"SDSU is a land grant college," Connie said, wiping her face with a towel. "We got all the poor students. And during the Depression money was really scarce. So instead of spending money nobody had on evening gowns and tuxedos, the students dressed as hoboes. I guess they figured when you're poor you might as well laugh at yourself. You know, beat everyone else to the punch. And we've never changed. This is our joke on ourselves and we like it. The other South Dakota colleges have normal homecomings so this is something special. I've got four alumni coming to stay so I have to clean and organize food." I looked at Connie's spotless house and wondered what in the world she had to clean.

"Rick has friends coming, too," said Chris. "How about you, Stevie? Rob invite anybody?"

"I guess not," I said. "This is the first I've heard of any of this."

"Isn't that just like a man," tsked Gail. "There'll be lots of parties so you'll have a good time. Lord, it's only two weeks away!"

Connie looked at her watch. "And I've got supper to get on the table."

We broke up after agreeing to meet three times a week. I congratulated myself again on making an effort to make friends. At least I found out what was going on in my new world. Who knows when Rob would have gotten around to mentioning what sounded like the social event of the season? Hobo Day sounded a whole lot more fun than church. And I wanted to be a participant, not an outsider.

When Chris dropped me off at the trailer I was met by a scowling Rob. "Where have you been?" he demanded. "Do you know what time it is?"

This from the man who never told me where he was going or what he was doing. At least not in the detail I wanted. "I'm going to study," he'd say, exasperated, when I grilled him. The whats, with whoms, wheres, and estimated time of arrival home were apparently none of my business. "God, Stevie, do I have to account for every minute I'm not with you? You're not my mother, you know," he'd say. I'd retort that I'd just been making conversation. We'd argue, he'd walk out, I'd pout, then we'd make up in bed. Well, the shoe was on the other foot now and I'd make sure it pinched.

"God, Rob, I was just exercising with the girls. Do I have to account for every minute I'm not with you? You're not my mother, you know," I mimicked him. He had the grace to blush. "I told you where I'd be this morning but you weren't listening. As usual," I added. That's me all over; I can't just make a point, I have to beat it into the ground. And I got the predictable result, a pissed off husband.

"I was listening. I guess I just forgot," Rob defended himself.

"Uh huh," I said skeptically.

"I was worried about you," he insisted.

"Right. You just want food."

"Well, I am hungry," he admitted.

"Honestly, Rob, there's food in the refrigerator. All you had to do was open the door. You know how to cook, you taught me."

"I like it better when you make it," he grinned boyishly.

I remembered what Chris had said about being available for Rick and I remembered the outrage I'd felt. "Have you always been such a chauvinist," I asked coldly, "or have you been taking lessons from Rick?"

"Hey, it was just a joke," he said impatiently.

"Well, I didn't think it was funny."

We glared at each other. Funny how things that were cute and endearing when you're just living together become red flags when you're married. Wedding vows seem to turn language and inflection upside down. Or maybe expectations change. Whatever. Now, I was pissed, too. I'd put up with the hunting trips, Rob's eternal family, his taking me for granted…I could out-pout Rob any day and, by God, I was in just the mood to prove it. I went to the kitchen and savagely pulled food out of the refrigerator.

Rob broke the silence first. "You could have left a note or something about where you were. I was worried."

"You weren't worried, you were hungry," I retorted. "And I'd already told you where I was going to be."

"I was more worried than hungry," Rob argued, "and I don't think you said anything this morning. You're always accusing me of being a pig. Well, this was a piggy thing to do."

"You're a pig a lot more often than I am. This was my first shot at the bacon title," I countered in a high screechy voice. "And I did tell you my plans this morning. If you refuse to listen to me you can damn well starve to death."

My eyes felt like they were starting out of my head and the veins in my temples were throbbing. I don't think I was particularly attractive at that point. Rob's attempt to out-argue me was clearly not working so he drew back.

"I'll try to be more considerate," he said with effort.

"Then I will, too," I hissed.

"Is this settled then?"

I nodded tightly.

"Good." He grinned. "So. When's dinner?"

He was incorrigible. I burst out laughing. Thirty seconds ago I was ready to murder him for the same comment. Perhaps context is everything? I'd have to give this some thought. But first I made dinner.

"Who were you working out with?" Rob asked over broiled fish and salad. Making conversation over dinner—he must really be trying to make peace.

"Chris and two women I met at her party," I said and reported with whom and where.

The names didn't mean anything to him but he remembered the general look of Chris and Rick's party guests. "Those women could use it," he said. "You think they'll stay the course?"

"I hope so. They're nice women and I need friends. Oh! They brought up the subject of Hobo Day."

"Oh yeah. Remind me to buy a couple cases of beer. We might have some guys coming over."

My eyebrows climbed and I asked ironically, "When were you planning on telling me about this regional holiday and these potential guests?"

"I thought you knew."

"I do now."

"Well, that's all right then."

I just looked at him. How do you argue with logic like that? And men claim women don't think coherently.

"Oh, and Stevie," Rob continued after he'd chewed some salad, "the Engineering Department is in charge of driving one of the beauty queens and we need a convertible. I told them you probably wouldn't mind if we used your Miata."

"Beauty queens? Connie said everybody dresses like bums."

"Sure. Weary Willie and Dirty Lil have been taken care of. I'm talking about the queens. You know, the Pork Queen, the Dairy Queen, the Hereford Queen…"

He must be putting me on. My eyes narrowed and my lip curled. Of course he was. God, I was so gullible. I started to laugh. "Boy, Rob, you really had me going there for a minute," I chuckled. He looked at me blankly. "You're joking, aren't you?" I demanded. He shook his head. "C'mon Rob, no woman in her right mind is going to want to be a Pork Queen," I scoffed.

"No, no, it's true. They're pageant winners. It's an honor," he protested.

"Oh," I said, momentarily shorted out by culture shock. "Well, I guess I could drive a…queen down the street. Which queen did you get?"

"The Hereford Queen."

"The Hereford Queen," I repeated, then I giggled. I couldn't help it. "I'm sorry, I'm more than happy to drive the Hereford Queen…" and the title set me off again. I'd have to control myself so I wouldn't hurt Miss Hereford's feelings.

Rob laughed with me, thank God, then sobered. "See, Stevie, the thing is…the guys want me to drive."

"You can drive. But the cattle queen will be sitting on the back and that still leaves one seat. I'll ride with you."

"No…see…the guys…well, they've seen you."

I didn't understand Rob's reticence. "So? I don't have a harelip. I won't shame them. From what I've seen I've got it all over most of the local talent in the looks department."

Rob squirmed. "That's the problem," he said.

I stared at him. "I don't get it."

"I know. Stevie, you laugh at these titles but this is maybe one of the best moments some of these girls will ever have. And, well, they should have their moment."

Oho! "You're afraid I'll steal her thunder," I concluded.

"Well, not just me, but yes."

"So you want my car, not me," I clarified.

"That's about the size of it."

The explanation was sweet, and flattering to me in a backhanded way. The only problem was—I wanted to play, too; once a showwoman, always a showwoman. I toyed with my salad for awhile before suggesting, "How about…if I dress as a bum? Can I go along then?"

Rob agreed that my bum idea was a reasonable compromise and that his Engineering buddies would probably go along with it. He decided to dress down with me.

So I had my own grocery lists to ponder and a date for Homecoming!

Hobo Weekend started on Thursday night for the boys next door. They kept us awake through most of it but Rob said to leave them alone; they were just blowing off steam. They must have had fun; they broke one window.

Rob and I went to four parties on Friday but didn't stay long at any of them. We had to get up early to wash and wax the Miata for the heifer queen, you know.

"Don't call her that," Rob ordered.

"I won't," I promised. At least not to her face I wouldn't.

We got into our costumes. I'd cadged some of Marvin's old clothes from Alice, rubbed them in the dirt, and tore them in strategic places. "It's too bad I didn't know about this earlier," I sighed as I ripped. "I'd have gotten Leslie to buy a wardrobe from some street person in L.A. Realism, you know?" I dirtied my face with make-up and tucked my hair under a cap. "No way am I going to take attention away from the cattle princess," I commented when I saw myself in the mirror. "Nobody'll even know I'm a girl."

"You look fine, Stevie, and don't call her the cattle princess. You promised to behave yourself, remember? Then let's go."

It was a perfect fall day when Rob and I drove our dirty selves over to the parade staging grounds in my shining Miata. My buddy, Gary, passed around beers as we waited. I'd never seen anybody drink outside since I'd been in Brookings. "What happened to the Blue Laws?" I whispered to Rob.

"All bets are off today," Rob said.

Miss Hereford was waiting with the boys, drinking her own beer. She was a pretty blond girl, not more than eighteen. She was tall—at least compared to me, hell, everybody here was tall compared to me—

and slightly plump. She wore cowboy boots, jeans, a western shirt, and had a cowboy hat perched on the back of her long hair. A satin banner stating her title strained across her ample bosom. I frowningly compared her chest with mine and whispered into my shirt, "Aren't you two ashamed of yourselves?"

Miss Hereford looked relieved at my costume. I looked like the Artful Dodger. No way would I outshine her.

"I heard you were a movie star," she said in a disbelieving, breathy little voice.

Again with the movie star bit. I went into my usual explanation. I was getting pretty good at it by now. "I'm not a movie star," I corrected. "I just shot a few commercials."

She looked unconvinced so I let it drop. I took the time to wander down the line of high school marching bands, floats, the Bummobile (an old Model T for Weary Willie and Dirty Lil), and stunt cars. A stunt car is an old car or pickup (basically anything with four wheels that could still make it down the parade route) decorated with toilets, hammocks, outhouses, and drunken students. Some of the stunt cars were so tall they got caught in power lines and so rickety they lost some of their plumbing decorations as they meandered down the road. I'd never seen anything like them before and I took the time to inspect and admire the tallest stunt car. I even had a beer with some of the "bums"—just to be sociable. The sun was warm, the air was clear, and a party mood permeated. If Norman Rockwell had painted a Midwestern homecoming this probably would have been it. Maybe he would have left out the beer.

I spotted more convertibles complete with beauty queens. Sure enough, there was a Pork Queen and a Dairy Queen.

"What, no Miss Chicken?" I asked Rob and cackled.

"There's a Poultry Queen. And if you make any cracks I'm taking you home," Rob threatened.

It was quite a parade. People were lined up four deep along the three-mile parade route. The entire population of South Dakota must have come to watch.

"All these people," I marveled to Rob. "It feels like home!"

"Not quite, no gunshots," Rob said.

I thought about Crazy Eddie and his rock salt but I kept my mouth shut. I hadn't heard any shots from his part of Dogpatch yet. Halloween was his holiday and that was two weeks off.

Rob and I drove our bovine princess slowly down the route. She was having a high old time, waving, smiling, and throwing candy. The only time we chauffeurs had occasion to wave was when we saw the Anderson clan together in the crowd. Tom, Chris, Rick, Alice, and Marvin all waved and smiled at us but not too enthusiastically. They were South Dakotans, after all, and didn't want to draw too much attention to themselves. Nancy just looked disgusted and disdainful at our get-up.

"You know," I commented to Rob, "someday Nancy's face is going to freeze with that frown."

"It already has," he growled back.

We had another beer with the engineering 'boys' and Miss Hereford after the parade, then it was time to clean up and go to the football game. Rob even bought me a blue and gold chrysanthemum corsage that was so big I felt like I had a bush on my chest. I peeked around it to peer at myself in a mirror and grinned with delight. It was so kitschy it was neat.

The football game was the usual incomprehensible action but I yelled when everyone else did and pretended I knew what was going on. South Dakota State University's team was called the Jackrabbits. They lost.

"Jackrabbits?" I asked incredulously. "Your team's named after a bunny? What a wuss name. No wonder they lost."

"Jackrabbits are not bunnies," Rob corrected patiently.

"What's the difference?"

"About ten pounds and legs like a kangaroo."

I looked at the lopsided score. "Sure played like bunnies," I commented.

"Have another beer."

And that's basically what Rob and I did for the rest of that lost Saturday. We had a beer with the boys next door just to be neighborly and headed off to other parties, some in bars, some in houses. Normally, I'm not much of a drinker; two glasses of wine get me silly, but when in Rome, drink until you puke. I lost track of time and place after my fifth beer. I remember being in a bar that was so crowded a passed-out coed was lifted overhead and deposited on the sidewalk outside. And I knew it was evening when the beverage of choice changed to mixed drinks. I have never attended a bacchanal of the proportion of Hobo Day before. I don't remember what time Rob and I got home but I do remember driving the porcelain bus most of the night. Fortunately, Rob could hold his liquor better than me. I don't know what we would have done if he'd gotten sick, too. A one-toilet house can be a real drawback.

I had a monstrous hangover Sunday morning. "Why did I do that to myself?" I croaked as I swallowed aspirin with a Diet-Pepsi. The smell of coffee turned my stomach.

Rob didn't look much better. "Thank God it's only once a year," he mumbled and looked at me strangely. "I've never seen you drink like that before."

"That's because I never have," I admitted. "I must have had a really good time to feel this bad."

"I guess so." Rob was still watching me like I was some strange woman he'd picked up the night before and wished had gone home much, much earlier.

I didn't care. I'd just been trying to fit in and now I was being punished for my lack of moderation. "I can't remember much of last night. I think I'll join AA."

"You and everybody else in town," Rob snorted and helped himself to the aspirin.

We were so miserable we skipped church. Our hangovers were penance enough. Rob went to the family Sunday dinner but I skipped it. I was sick. Rob reported that Nancy was quite snide about the missing sinners but since Nancy, Tom, Rick, and Rob were the only siblings to show up I didn't take it personally. I was too sick to take anything personally.

The Blue Laws went back into effect after Hobo Day and people went back to work. There'd been a few injuries but nobody was killed, and not much property had been damaged. Which is surprising when you thought of how much booze had been consumed.

"People work hard, then they play hard," Rob explained. "We had some trouble a few years back but the troublemakers were expelled. There's no incentive to be an asshole here."

I found out later that everything wasn't as cozy and Never-Never Landish as Rob described. Turns out Brookings had the largest AA chapter in the country. Maybe the fact that it was the only one in this part of the State accounted for the numbers but it proved to me that everything here wasn't sweetness and light.

Well, I'd wanted to see new places and experience new things and that's what I was doing. I just hoped my liver survived.

chapter 14

Two weeks into November I could hardly remember what life had been like before the Great Pre-Winter Depression. Once there'd been green grass; there might even have been a chirping bird or two if it didn't get blasted out of the sky and eaten. No more. What used to be blue and green was now gray and brown. The crops had all been harvested and plowed under. The stubble that was left had a dark-gray leaden look that was matched by the overcast sky; the landscape could have come out of a Stephen King novel. Actually, it looked a lot like L.A. without the traffic.

My world had turned monochromatic and my mood reflected it. "No wonder Northern Europeans are so pale," I grumped after a succession of dull, sunless days. "I'm losing my tan."

"This is nothing. Wait until winter hits," Rob said.

"It gets worse?" I asked, dismayed. "I'm already living in an Ingmar Bergman film."

Pudgy was even affected by the atmosphere. She seemed to be sleeping all the time, which isn't like her. Normally, she's into everything and commenting on it. I got so concerned I took her to a veterinarian, a no-nonsense, middle-aged man who kept feed sacks in his office. I outlined Pudgy's symptoms as the vet checked her over. Then he asked how old she was.

"About twelve and a half," I told him.

He shook his head. "Your cat's old, that's all," he said simply. "She could last another year or so but I wouldn't count on it."

Old? Pudgy? The only stable thing I'd had in my life since I was sixteen? "But I've heard of cats living for twenty years," I quavered.

The vet took a look at my stricken face and figured out that he wasn't talking to a farmer about a cash crop; this was a beloved pet.

"Anything over eight is old for a cat," he said more kindly. "Your kitty just got old. There's nothing anybody can do about it." My quivering chin seemed to unnerve him so he added, "Tell you what, young lady, I'll give you some vitamins. Maybe that'll perk her up."

I took Pudgy home, stuffed a pill in her, and went to the park to sit in the swings and shiver in the cold as the wind wheezed through the naked trees. Depressing as it sounds it was still better than sitting in the trailer collecting dust. I had lots to feel sorry for myself about.

At the end of October I'd interviewed the head of the Speech/Theater Department—or maybe he'd interviewed me. Whatever. He was very nice, very complimentary, and had nothing to offer me.

"I've seen your TV commercials," Dr. Torgeson commented as I seated myself in his office.

"Oh well, it's money," I said, smiling slightly.

"And your resume here," Dr. Torgeson added quickly, "it's quite impressive."

I expanded on my background, both professional and educational. Dr. Torgeson listened closely then told me he would love to have someone with my credentials on the staff. "We've never had a professional teach here," he confided and I smiled, encouraged. "Unfortunately," he continued, "this is the middle of the year and we're fully staffed, of course."

I had an argument prepared. "I'd be willing to work part-time," I offered.

"That's commendable but we don't have the budget for even a part-time instructor. I'm sure you understand…"

Of course I did. I knew I couldn't just walk in, offer them my superb self, and expect to get a teaching job in the middle of the year. Oh, I'd signed a contract with a flourish in my daydreams as I made Rob's lunch—hope springs eternal, after all—but this was reality.

Dr. Torgeson distracted me by asking about the acting business. I gladly told him some of my experiences on commercial shoots to hide my disappointment. He listened, fascinated. Hollywood sure has a hold on people.

When I finally stood to leave Dr. Torgeson shook my hand, assuring me if anything came up he'd be in touch, and I disconsolately went home. Long gray days of cleaning the toilet stretched in front of me.

Rob was sanguine when I reported my lack of success. "Maybe next year," he said, offhand. "Why don't you take some time off and enjoy yourself? Let me take care of you."

There had been a time when the thought of being 'taken care of' had appeal—three short months ago to be exact—until I found out just what the phrase meant. According to Rob (and his family) the cooking and cleaning I did was the least I could do since Rob was the breadwinner as well as being a full-time student. Nancy told me I should thank my lucky stars I didn't have to 'work', do what I was told, and keep my mouth shut. Rob was 'taking care of me' without touching a penny of my money, which was considered admirable. Of course, living off him made me a spoiled princess and therefore subject to criticism.

I was in a no-win situation. I'd earned an MFA to become custodian of the toilet. Not only was I cleaning it, I was fixing it which ironically meant I had to improve my cooking skills. I'd gotten so tired of unclogging the toilet after Rob's monstrous B.M.s I'd starting forcing bran muffins down him to keep the amount of his waste to flushable proportions. Being 'taken care of' meant I had to become a dietician, a chef, and a plumber. The circle of life had taken on a whole new meaning for me.

Marriage; it's a fine institution if you like institutions, I sneered to myself. Okay, it's an old joke but, as with all jokes, there was some truth to it. Why in hell does anybody get married? I pondered as I channel surfed in my search for truth. According to the talk shows I was looking for a father figure. That concept made me uncomfortable because I enjoyed sex with my husband (when we got around to it) and I hated to think our relationship was incestuous. I'd never even dreamed of my father in the nude so I dismissed that idea.

I also discounted the idea that I married Rob for a familial bond. I had as little in common with the Andersons as I did with the Morales and as little desire to see them. How the hell did I manage to save myself from my own relatives only to be surrounded by Rob's? I'd spent just about every Sunday of our married life with his parents and I'd had enough.

Maybe it just came down to sex. But you could have a sex life without getting married; people do it all the time. And my sex life had dried up after Hobo Day. Rob said he was under pressure with studying and teaching and he was tired all the time. I had the uncomfortable feeling his lack of libido had more to do with me puking my guts out after my mammoth homecoming drunk. It's hard to think of someone as a sexual object when you've seen her with the dry heaves. Whatever the reason, I was growing shut again.

So where did this leave me? Shivering all by myself on a swing. *Might as well go home and do some chores*, I sighed and trudged off.

When I let myself into the trailer there was a bouquet of flowers on the kitchen table along with a pizza. This was puzzling because Rob seldom 'wasted' his money on flowers. He had to be in some pretty major trouble before he'd part with a dime on something so frivolous. I heard him rattling around in the bathroom as I read the accompanying card.

> "Dear Stevie,
> Just because I love you.
> Rob"

Rob came out to the kitchen as I placed the card next to the bouquet.

"Flowers and pizza. Have you done something that I should know about?" I asked.

"You've been looking a little blue lately" (Blue? I'd turned into a Smurf!) "and I hoped this would cheer you up a little," Rob said.

I lost a few shades of indigo at that. Sure, marriage is uncorking toilets and washing skid-marked skivvies. Sometimes it's also sharing moods with someone who buys you flowers hoping the gesture will help. And the gesture helps. It really does.

*****

Rob and I were having another quiet evening at home, him studying and me stuffing pills down Pudgy, when the subject of Thanksgiving came up.

"I've got four days off. Would you like to go to Minneapolis?" Rob asked casually.

I stared at him with my mouth open. Would I like to go to a city?

This was like asking a soul who'd spent some time in Purgatory if she'd like a short trip to Heaven. "Oh, Rob, I'd love it!" I said in relief.

"There's only one problem," Rob said. "Mom's brother and his family are coming for Thanksgiving dinner and Mom wants you to meet them. But we could take off after dinner on Thursday. That'd give us all of Friday and Saturday in the city and we'd come home on Sunday."

So, this trip to Minneapolis was probably a bribe to get me over to the Anderson's for yet another dinner without a big fight. Nothing's free in this world. But if all it took was one more family affair to buy a trip anywhere, I'd do it. It's not like I had anywhere else to go on Thanksgiving anyway.

I called Alice and offered to make a pecan pie for dessert. I'd been watching cooking shows on TV and I was confident I could pull off a pie without too much trouble.

I arranged for Connie to feed Pudgy and stuff vitamins down her, planned what wardrobe to take, and packed. Rob was pleased with my mood change. I was, too. Depression is like a diaper; it's bearable for a while but pretty soon it stinks and it's time for a change.

I was in the bathroom putting on my make-up Thanksgiving morning with an audience of a cat and a husband. The cat because she got her ears scratched, the husband—I don't know why he hung around.

"Don't you get bored watching me put on make-up?" I asked Rob.

"I like to watch the faces you make," he said as he lounged in the doorway.

"I don't make faces," I mumbled as I grimaced putting on my mascara. "Didn't you ever watch your mother get ready?"

"She only uses lipstick. There wasn't much to watch. And the result wasn't as good."

I smiled at the compliment and Rob patted my butt appreciatively. Maybe Minneapolis was going to be fun.

We loaded up the trunk of the Miata with a suit bag and I made sure the toilet wasn't running and the stove was off before turning to Pudgy. "I'll be back on Sunday so be good for Connie, okay? Take your pills and don't dump on the floor." I gave her a quick kiss. I didn't feel too guilty about leaving Pudge. She was starting to act like her old self after the vitamin regimen. I blessed the horse doctor for prescribing for her and cursed him for scaring me so bad. My cat was getting old but she was far from dead.

I put my pecan pie in my lap—it hadn't turned out too bad, if I did say so myself—and we took off. We were the last to arrive at the Andersons'. The whole family was there, including Alice's brother Herman Berk, his wife Ethel, and their two adult sons, Milo and Ronald.

Rob had told me there'd probably be tension and told me why in his own unhurried way. I knew some of it already so I threw in helpful comments. It kept him on track.

"There were four kids in Mom's family. Uncle Phillip who died, Herman who you'll meet today, Sarah who lives in Minnesota with her husband, and Mom," he began.

"I know," I interrupted.

"How?"

"Your mother told me." I looked around to see Rob gazing at me in silent surprise. "What?" I asked. "I talk to your mother—probably more than you do. Anyway, what's the problem between Alice and Herman?"

Rob continued. "Herman had just gotten out of the Army when Grandpa Berk keeled over from a heart attack right in the middle of harvest. Mom and Dad were starting the hardware store and Mom was pregnant with Tom so she wasn't in much position to help. And Aunt Sarah was too far away. Herman wanted to take over but Grandma Theresa wasn't interested in taking orders from him. I guess there was a lot of fighting going on. Then he married Ethel, the old-maid daughter of the farmer next to him. He was already planning ahead. He always said Ethel wasn't pretty but she was a good worker and came with a section of land."

"Is that why you married me? I'm a good worker?" I grumbled, miffed. "I'm surprised you didn't check my teeth before you married me."

"What makes you think I didn't?"

Rob snickered when I swung at him and deflected me deftly. Rob's new hobby was teasing me. He said he liked to watch the explosions.

"Back to the family problem," I said after I'd composed myself.

"When Herman married Ethel, Grandma wouldn't let him stay in her house so he bought a trailer and he and Ethel lived in that until

Grandma died. Mom tried to run interference and make peace but she just got yelled at from both sides. The real problem between Herman and Mom came when Theresa died. She left everything to Herman but the will was written during her last illness and she was a little nuts. I heard there was some talk about contesting the will but nothing happened. I do remember Herman yelling at Mom one Thanksgiving that he'd taken care of Gramma until she died and he'd run the farm all those years so it was his. Besides, both Mom and Sarah had gotten silver and china when they were married and he'd never gotten anything. Mom and Sarah were just women anyway and had men to take care of them so they weren't going to get "his" property."

"That's ridiculous. Your mom and aunt should've sued. I would've."

"Well, Herman did take care of Grandma and Mom always felt guilty about that. There's not much she could have done anyway; she had her own family to take care of and couldn't spend a lot of time driving back and forth. Hoven's about three hours away so that's a lot of driving."

"But still..."

"One thing my folks believe firmly in is: You don't take your family to law," Rob said. "Mom got the photo album which is what she really wanted. But Herman got the farm, which really isn't fair. So there's some resentment between Herman and Mom. They only get together once a year for Thanksgiving."

"Why do they get together at all?"

Rob shrugged. "They're family."

Another All-American concept, the congenial, family Thanksgiving, blown to bits. Well, we wouldn't have to stay long. Just eat, help with dishes, and hit the road. I smiled in anticipation of the next few days. Minneapolis was calling to me. It said: Come, Stevie, relax, enjoy, shop.

The scene at the Andersons was peaceful when we entered. The dining room table had been extended into the living room to seat fourteen adults and had taken up so much room the men had to hunch their chairs close to the TV. They looked like aging boy scouts around a campfire. The uncle and cousins had big, red faces and bald heads over fat, flannel-clad stomachs.

I asked Rob as we took off our coats, "Don't your cousins have wives?"

"Look at them," he said. "Who'd have 'em?"

Alice, already looking a little wild-eyed, came out of the kitchen with Aunt Ethel when Rob started introducing me to the Berks. Ethel was wearing a brightly colored polyester muumuu. Now, I've seen big women, I'm related to some, and I know it takes a lot of rice and beans to get that way. Potatoes were the local starch instead of beans but the result was the same—Ethel carried a lot of taters in her sack dress. She had dull, suspicious eyes, a characteristic she shared with her sons. From where I stood being a good worker seemed to be the only thing she had going for her. I hoped she liked doing dishes.

"Stephanie," said Rob taking my attention away from Ethel's physical attributes, "this is my Uncle Herman, Aunt Ethel, and cousins, Milo and Ronald."

I smiled at the Berks and offered my hand. They looked at my hand and grunted. I didn't get offended. As a matter of fact, I was glad in a way. If they wouldn't shake my hand, they sure wouldn't try to hug me. I dropped my hand but kept my smile.

Ethel returned an unpracticed smile that puckered up her face like a big anus. "Pleased to meet you," she farted from the pucker.

"Happy Thanksgiving," I said neutrally and turned to Alice. "I brought a pecan pie."

Alice inspected my pie with a critical eye. "It looks good," she judged approvingly. "Take it into the kitchen. That's where the other girls are. I have to check the table."

I hurried off. I was developing my own version of the housewife bustle. I left Rob wedging room for his chair in the TV circle.

The other 'girls' were draped around the kitchen counters—and each of them had a glass of wine. Chris lifted her glass in greeting. "Want some?" she asked.

When I nodded she poured that last of the bottle into a Flintstones glass that I'm pretty sure was once a jelly jar. Nothing went to waste in Alice's house; not Marvin's underwear, not jelly jars. Chris noticed my smile and said, "Alice doesn't have any wine goblets, you know, and she doesn't want us to take the water glasses off the table. So you take what you can get."

"I'm surprised she even has the wine," I said.

"I brought this for us 'daughters'," chimed in Marilyn. She made a quote sign with her fingers and took a sip.

Nancy, the resident disapprover, even had a jelly jar. I toasted the other 'daughters' with 'Wilma'. "Happy Thanksgiving," I said. "I wish I'd known we could have wine. I'd have brought a bottle myself."

"That's okay, I have two more out in the car." Marilyn said. "This is your first Berk dinner, isn't it? You'll see why I brought plenty of tranquilizer."

Alice and Ethel hove into view at this point and the usual amount of bickering started. The only difference was the fighting was done by teams instead of one-on-one, and I was on the home team instead of being 'it'. I bet the original Thanksgiving was set up the same way, Pilgrims versus Indians cooking a funny-looking bird and making points off each other. I sipped white wine from my jelly jar and imagined the first kitchen fracas between Pocahontas and Priscilla.

Priscilla: (after seeing Pocahontas' creamed corn casserole)
              We feed corn to cattle where I come from.
Pocahontas: So do we.

(Glares all around)

I imagine the first still was invented shortly after that.

Ethel was pretty seriously outnumbered so she tried to cut me from the pack early on, probably thinking I was an easy target because I was new. She looked at my pecan pie incredulously. "Pecan pie? We always have pumpkin pie."

"Oh Ethel, nobody likes pumpkin pie anyway," Alice said to her then turned to beam at me. "Stephanie has family in Texas, you know, and pecan pie is a tradition there."

Score one for the home team. Alice was a great guard but Ethel wasn't ready to give up. She looked at me dubiously and said, "I thought she was a Mexican."

Her tone left little doubt as to how she felt about Mexicans. Alice looked ready to deflect again but I handled that particular ball myself. "Yes, I am," I said smoothly and my eyes glittered. "But you remember that little place called the Alamo? When us dirty Mexicans beat those German butts we took their pecan pie as war reparations. It was only thing worth taking. Oh! You're probably German, aren't you, Ethel. Well, eat hearty."

Ethel took a time out and all the daughters-in-law went to the garage where we opened another bottle of Marilyn's wine.

"I wish I could think that fast," Marilyn snickered into her Bam-Bam glass. "I just get so mad I can't think at all."

I just smiled smugly.

"The Berks are such awful people," Nancy threw in. "Far be from me to criticize" (HA!) "someone's wardrobe but that dress Ethel's wearing…"

"I guess when Omar the Tentmaker's your tailor you don't have a lot of choices," Chris commented. "Besides, I don't think Herman would part with a penny for a new dress."

"Pretty tight, huh?" I asked.

"Tight! He pinches a penny until it screams. That's one of the reasons Alice always has them for Thanksgiving. They won't feed all of us. Costs too much."

"The free meal in the only reason Herman comes," Nancy said scathingly.

We all snickered into our wine and shivered in the cold.

"Say, isn't this backwards?" I asked. "Aren't the men supposed to be sneaking off to drink while the women work?"

"They're too busy watching football," Marilyn drawled.

We all helped ourselves to a touch more wine.

"Alice says you're leaving for Minneapolis tonight," Chris said to me enviously. "Sounds like fun. I'd like to take a few days off but Rick needs the time to catch up on some work."

"Rob and I need to have some fun together," I admitted. "Maybe being back in a city will get us out of the rut we've gotten into."

The three women pricked up their ears. "Problems?" Marilyn asked.

"I don't know. I guess it's just the adjustment process everybody has to go through when they get married. It's just…well, you know, Rob's busy all the time with school, we never talk anymore," I said casually. I didn't want to tell them that he hadn't touched me in any satisfying way since Hobo Day. Alice's garage didn't seem the appropriate place to make sexual confessions.

"Bobby's under a lot of pressure, you know," Chris said. "The

Master's program he's in is very competitive. He'll probably relax after the semester's over."

"I think you should consider yourself lucky he has any time for you at all," Nancy declared. "Bobby has enough to take care of without having to entertain you. 'He doesn't talk to you'," she mimicked. "Honestly! You'll have plenty of time for talk later."

"Stephanie isn't jumping all over Bobby," Chris interposed. "She's just saying she's having a little trouble adjusting. It's perfectly normal."

"You young women expect too much," Nancy shot back at Chris. "Rick told Tom that you've started whining about things, too. Now, I could understand if that sort of remark came from Stephanie's husband. She seems to think the universe revolves around her."

"Rick said that to Tom?" Chris asked, looking hurt.

"Hold it, hold it," Marilyn interrupted. "You're getting a little out of line here, Nancy."

"And you, Marilyn," Nancy rounded on her, "you're just as bad as she is. You think you're special just because you won a beauty pageant. I've got a good notion to give you a piece of my mind!"

"Don't bother. You couldn't spare it," Marilyn retorted.

Our independent states were fighting among themselves, obviously the wine talking. I was afraid jelly glasses would start flying. We needed to regain our solidarity before serious blood was drawn. Besides, I was cold. "Maybe we should go inside and help Alice," I suggested. "She's in there with Ethel all by herself."

An uneasy truce returned at the thought of the common enemy. Maybe that's why Alice invited the Berks every year. It strengthened the immediate family bond—what there was of one.

The women got dinner on the table without further bloodshed. Alice had roasted a huge stuffed turkey and a ham. She'd made the usual boiled bits of greenish gray vegetables, crescent rolls, mashed potatoes and gravy, cranberry sauce, and the inevitable Jell-O mold. She needed all our help to carry things around, which we did with some silly snickering. Nancy so was tipsy she almost dropped the mashed potatoes and giggled when Chris saved them.

"Nancy hasn't had that much wine," I murmured to Marilyn.

"She probably had a couple of shots before she came," Marilyn murmured back.

We pried the men away from the TV and sat. I was placed between

Cousin Milo and Rob with Herman and Ronald directly across from me. The only words the Berk men gave up willingly were the prayer. Then they stuffed food in their mouths and conversation had to be pried from them.

I tried to initiate some sparkling repartee with Milo since he was gobbling next to me. "Do you enjoy farming?" I asked.

Milo looked at me with such fright that I thought he'd choke. Then he blushed, said, "Yep" and went back to shoveling food in his mouth.

"Just let him eat," Rob whispered to me.

Since the Berk men were concentrating on their plates I took the time to observe them more closely. I'd mentioned that they were stout and bald but now I noticed what astonishingly blue eyes they had. Maybe the eyes were such a surprise because the faces were so ruddy—up to the eyebrows anyway. Their bald heads were pure white. I had to smile; the red, white, and blue effect was sort of patriotic. They had their flannel shirtsleeves rolled above the elbow and their forearms and hands were very red, strong-looking, and very thick. The fingernails were clean.

After the turkey was demolished, the men leaned back in their chairs while we women bussed the table and delivered coffee cups and pie. I was waiting for some comment with reference to the pumpkin versus pecan debate but as far as the men were concerned (and I include my loving husband) if it was edible, it was acceptable. My pie disappeared without comment.

Then we all sat back with our coffee for conversation. The kids were fighting in the kitchen but Marilyn ignored hers and Nancy was too looped to referee. She sat with a glazed look in her eye. Tom propped her up periodically when she tipped over.

Herman said his first words to me. "I hear you're in the movies," he said laconically.

I unconsciously copied his curt style. "I shot some commercials."

"Any money in that?"

"Some."

He looked me over. His sons were also checking me out...but avoiding eye contact. Herman gave his summation to Rob. "Well, she's pretty," he concluded. "She a good worker?"

"Very good," Rob said.

"That's all right then." Herman sucked his teeth and made a decision.

"Think I'll go watch some TV." He pushed himself away from the table and walked over to the circle of chairs in the living room. Every one of those wretched men followed him, leaving the women with K.P.

Talk was at a minimum as we put away, washed, and wiped. Nancy disappeared early to take a nap. Alice and Ethel kept the conversational ball rolling primarily with discussions of church activities. Ethel was also a Lutheran and there was a feeling of "my church can beat up your church" in the air. Things got a little heated over which church threw the best pot luck supper; Ethel's mouth pursed up and Alice's chin was starting to quiver when Chris tactfully changed the subject, asking after Ethel's health. That started a dissertation on Ethel's female complaints. The afternoon was wearing on so I took Alice aside.

"I hate to eat and run," I said, "but Rob and I need to leave for Minneapolis; it gets dark so early."

Alice patted my arm. "Why don't you see how the football game's coming along?"

I went into the living room where every one of those damn men was asleep and snoring gently. Even Rob had his head tipped back. I wanted to give him a little shake but I would have had to step over Ronald and Herman and I didn't want to wake them up. I went back to the kitchen. "They're all asleep," I reported glumly to Alice.

"Well, best let Bobby sleep for awhile. It's a long drive to Minneapolis," Alice advised and turned back to Ethel who had moved from her innards to her feet.

Chris, Marilyn, and I exchanged a look, grabbed our jelly jars and coats, and retreated to the garage. We cackled and snorted over our wine. We probably looked like the opening act of *MacBeth*.

Marilyn got a particularly wicked look on her face. "I brought a pack of cigarettes," she said conspiratorially. "You guys want one?"

Chris declined the offer but I accepted even though I don't normally smoke. We dug a milk carton out of the garbage for an ashtray and lit up. I haven't felt so depraved in years.

"Won't Alice object?" I asked as I puffed inexpertly, making sure not to inhale.

"We're in the garage, for God's sake. It's not like we're in the house," Marilyn replied. So we drank and smoked contentedly.

"Explain the suntan to me," I asked the others after a moment. "You know, on Herman and the boys." (The 'boys' were in their thirties but that's what everybody called them.) "The white scalps and red faces?"

"Oh! We call that a farmer tan," Chris explained. "Farmers always wear their caps in the fields so their heads don't get sunburned. You wouldn't notice it so much on people who have hair."

Her matter-of-factness about the lack of hair stuck me funny and I started to giggle. I don't think Chris and Marilyn knew what I was laughing about but they started to giggle, too. We tried to stifle our giggles but that just made things worse, like in church. Our giggles became helpless guffaws. We must have made a lot of noise because Alice stuck her head into the garage to shush us. Marilyn and I hid our cigarettes behind our backs.

"You girls be quiet or you'll wake the men," Alice scolded.

"God forbid," Marilyn muttered rebelliously but she made sure Alice didn't hear her.

Alice sniffed and frowned. "Are you girls smoking out here?"

Marilyn and I looked embarrassed and admitted that we were.

"Well, don't let the little kids see you," Alice said. "I don't want them starting that filthy habit." She paused and looked us over. "I think you girls better come inside before you get into trouble."

I was happy to put my cigarette out. I'd inadvertently gulped down some smoke when Alice popped her head through the door and it was starting to make me sick. And it was a little ridiculous, grown women acting like teenagers sneaking puffs in the school bathroom.

Ethel was still droning on when we got back to the kitchen. But you can listen to anything if you've got a full Flintstones glass. I was starting to get giggly again when Ethel fixed Chris with her eye and demanded, "When are you going to have kids?"

Chris blushed and stammered, "I don't really know."

Then it was my turn. "And you, Stephanie, is it? When are you and Bobby going to start a family?"

Ethel's tone was accusatory which ticked me off. Who was she to interrogate me? I was feeling a little manic anyway so I glibly replied, "Oh, I don't know. Right now we haven't got any room for a kid. Maybe we could keep it in Alice's garage. And diapers sound like a drag. How long does it take a baby to learn to use a litter box anyway?" I smiled brightly at Ethel, who looked like I'd uttered blasphemy, the old buffalo.

But Marilyn, Chris, and even Alice laughed. It was a joke after all, maybe in questionable taste, but a joke.

Our hilarity woke up the sleeping men and Rob came out to investigate. I took advantage of the moment to suggest we hit the road.

We were putting on our coats and making our goodbyes when Alice handed me a brown paper sack. "It's just a little lunch for when you get hungry later," she explained. "Most of the restaurants will be closed today and they're so expensive. I don't want you to have to waste money on food."

Rob volunteered to drive and I didn't object one bit. I'd done my hausfrau duty while Rob snoozed so I felt justified in slacking off. Besides, Rob pointed out that I'd been drinking, again, and wasn't in any condition to be behind the wheel.

"God, Stevie, have you been smoking?" he asked distastefully as I crawled into my bucket seat. "You stink."

"I had half a cigarette, okay?" I retorted. "It's not that big a deal."

This was not the way I'd envisioned our trip starting out so I curled up and slept through the four-hour trip. Sometimes Rob was such a pain.

chapter 15

Rob shook me as we approached Minneapolis. I woke to A City! It may have been a lot smaller than L.A. but it still had lights, tall buildings, theaters, museums, and restaurants! I was back in Oz.

We silently pulled up in front of the Radisson Hotel and a bellman took our luggage. I wasn't sure what to do with Alice's brown paper sack. I was tempted to leave it in the car; it's hard to pull off a Princess Grace act carrying a sack lunch though a hotel lobby. On the other hand, it'd been four hours since I'd last stuffed my face. I firmly tucked the sack under my arm and regally carried it up to the room. I was poised and gracious as the bellman hung up the suit bag, pointed out the hotel features, received his tip—which I gave him—and left. Then I put down the sack so I could jump gleefully on the king-sized bed and bounce around. I scurried to the bathroom; the toilet paper was folded in a triangular point, the towels were thick, and the stealables (generic term for shampoo, conditioner, shower cap) were satisfactory.

"We even have a shoe polisher!" I crowed and finished my inspection by hurrying to open the drapes. My view was a carpet of lights in the dark night. "I'm back in civilization," I sighed contentedly.

"You never left it," Rob said shortly and turned on the TV. He seemed to be pouting about something and he'd four hours to brood. Well, I wasn't about to let him dampen my sense of liberation. I was on vacation!

My attention returned to the brown paper bag. "I'm hungry. You want something?" I asked Rob as I opened the bag of turkey sandwiches, carrot sticks, and leftover pie. I didn't wait for an answer. I ran down the hall for a diet soda to wash my picnic down.

Rob joined me on the bed and helped himself to a sandwich.

"Boy, that Berk family is something," I said conversationally as I munched. "Good thing Marilyn brought the wine. I don't think I'd have made it if we hadn't gone to the garage to drink."

"I didn't know you were such a lush," said Rob with a raised eyebrow.

"Lush? We each three glasses of wine over the whole afternoon. That does not make a lush, Rob," I returned, annoyed.

"Good thing you quit before you got sick. I'd hate to have had you throwing up all over everything again. And now cigarettes!" Rob said disgustedly.

"I had half a cigarette!" I protested. "And I don't spend my social occasions throwing up! It happened once and nobody saw me but you." I was getting tired of defending myself and turned the table. "And now that I think on it you were the one who kept handing me beers last month. These are your customs, not mine. The last time I refused a beer you yelled at me so make up your mind what you want."

My argument went right over Rob's head. "And another thing," he continued without much of a pause, "I thought it was pretty tacky of you to leave Mom alone with Ethel all afternoon."

I stared at Rob with disbelief. "If you didn't want your mother to be alone with Ethel you should have gotten off your dead butt and helped in the kitchen. But noooo, you just watched TV!" I retorted. "I baked a pie, served dinner, and cleaned up afterward. Tell me, how was the football game?"

I was so pissed I inhaled a mouthful of carrot. I had to take a short break; it's tough to fight when you need the Heimlich maneuver. After I'd coughed up my carrot we agreed to have this discussion when we got back to Brookings. As Rob pointed out sarcastically, we could always fight at home. We moodily watched TV.

Sometimes I think it's too bad TV was ever invented, particularly in this sort of situation. Maybe if we'd had a knockdown, drag-out fight then we'd have saved ourselves a lot of trouble later on. As a rookie married person, what I didn't know was a) it's okay to fight and b) you can fight without doing permanent damage to each other and the marriage. That's something you have to learn.

After an hour of extreme civility, Rob and I put our picnic away and got ready to sleep.

"It was nice of your mother to pack the sandwiches, wasn't it?" I said, trying to make peace.

"Yes, it was. I hope you remembered to thank her."

"I did," I said sweetly. "Did you?"

We got on our respective sides of the bed and stayed there. Rob started snoring almost immediately. Nothing stops him from getting his eight hours. But I'd had a four-hour nap. I rolled around for a while—being careful not to touch Rob, of course. To hell with him, I finally decided. I'd spent three months trying to please this impossible son-of-a-bitch and all I'd gotten in return was guilt-tripping, whining, and faultfinding. If Rob wanted to pout for the next few days he could do it by himself. I was going to do my best to enjoy myself this weekend. I finally fell asleep.

I woke up next morning to the sight of a fully dressed Rob holding out a cup of coffee. I struggled up on my elbows and focused my eyes.

"I went downstairs for some good coffee," he explained.

"Thank you," I mumbled, rubbing my eyes. "How long have you been up?"

"About an hour. I didn't turn on the TV or anything. I knew you were tired."

I looked at the bedside clock. Eight o'clock. I sipped the coffee and eyed Rob warily.

"So, what do you want to do today?" he asked.

"I thought I'd do some Christmas shopping and I'd like to get a decent winter coat."

"I'll go with you."

This was unexpected. Rob was practically wagging his tail. Perhaps he'd seen the error of his ways. Or was he just softening me up for the next round? It was too early in the morning to get my mind wrapped around this. My perplexity must have showed on my face because Rob held up his hands in surrender and grinned.

"Let's call a truce, okay? We don't want to waste the weekend."

It wasn't an apology but it was better than nothing. Besides, I'd already reached the same conclusion last night. "Okay," I agreed and we shook hands on the deal.

We were very polite and considerate to each other over breakfast. It was like a blind date but at least we weren't at each other's throats. We started shopping at Dayton's and I fondled the merchandise. "Designer labels," I murmured thankfully.

Rob snorted. "You could get the same thing in Brookings for a third of the price."

"Not unless I wanted it in polyester," I retorted and gasped over an off-white cashmere tunic sweater.

Rob looked at the tag. "Stevie, that's $250! You can't spend $250 on a damned sweater!"

"Yes I can," I crooned as I caressed the cashmere.

"But we need a new stereo receiver!"

"I don't want a new receiver. I want a sweater," I said.

"Stevie, I absolutely forbid you to waste money like that."

"You do, do you?" I flagged down a salesclerk and handed her my credit card. "I'll take this." I turned back to Rob. "Anything else you want to forbid me to do?"

Rob had sense enough to shut up. The truce slammed back in force.

I bought myself a three-quarter-length coat, some snow boots, and splurged on a new wool suit with a double-breasted jacket and a short, slim skirt. I bought leotards for my exercise buddies' Christmas presents and a set of wine glasses for Alice. Rob blanched at each purchase but he only objected once more. "Mom doesn't need wine glasses," he said.

"Yes, she does," I said right back. "She can save the Flintstones for breakfast."

My credit card was warm by the time I got done. I hadn't touched a dime of my accrued residuals in four months and it was time to spend money before my bank account spontaneously combusted.

We returned to the hotel with my loot. On the way Rob said, "I budgeted in one nice meal for the weekend," he said. "And maybe you'd like to go to a play or something?"

Of course I would. I'd heard of the Guthrie Theater so I got on the phone and put two tickets on my credit card. Rob said nothing.

I put on my new suit and preened in front of the mirror, pleased with my reflection.

"Aren't you supposed to wear a blouse under that jacket?" Rob asked.

"I could," I agreed, "but it's 'in' now to wear a lacy bra and keep the jacket buttoned. I like the look, don't you? It's supposed to be sexy."

Rob looked dubious but didn't say anything. We drove to the old warehouse district of Minneapolis, which had been rehabbed into yuppie heaven, and found a French restaurant. Rob hadn't said much all the way from the hotel so I knew he was displeased about something, which made me nervous. I tend to natter when I'm nervous and Rob seemed bored with my pointless small talk so we were on a collision course. As we were led to our table and handed menus I yakked. Rob looked long-suffering which made me more nervous so I yakked even more. Rob finally sighed loudly, looked at his watch, and sent a patient, martyred look in my direction. I'd have preferred being slapped. His look acted like Kaopectate on my verbal diarrhea. I dried up, ordered a second glass of wine, and ate my dinner in silence.

"Are we going to spend this weekend being polite to each other?" I asked him over dessert.

"Now what's wrong?" Rob asked, bewildered.

"We can't have any fun if we're walking on eggshells around each other," I said impatiently. "Can't we just act normal?"

"Isn't polite normal?"

"C'mon Rob, you know what I mean."

Rob shook his head. "Stevie, I sometimes think words don't mean the same to you as they do to me."

He might just have something. "You're very literal," I said ruefully. "You hear what people say but ignore how they say it. I listen more to the way things are said instead of the actual words."

Rob looked confused. "Huh?" he asked.

"I hear inflections and you hear words. Like when somebody says 'Nice job.' You take the comment at face value as a good thing. But a simple phrase like that can be complimentary or sarcastic. The inflection changes the meaning," I explained.

Rob looked skeptical. "Sometimes people mean exactly what they say."

"Yeah, but sometimes they don't," I countered. "Do you suppose this is a man/woman thing or just a problem you and I have?"

"I think you think too much," Rob said. "Are you ready to go?"

We drove to the Guthrie. After the play I sighed, "You know, when

I see a company like that I think I made the wrong decision about leaving acting."

"You didn't," Rob said. "You're just saying you miss it to make me feel bad. If you had to act you'd hate it."

After a stunned moment I said shortly, "I'm pretty sure you don't know or care about what I think or want so don't try to tell me about me."

We had another frigid night.

We spent Saturday playing tourist. We went over to St. Paul and inspected the James Hill mansion. I crawled down the bank of the Mississippi to dip my fingers. We stopped at the Whitney Hotel for a cup of coffee. We went to the top of the Foshay Tower and gazed at the view. I playfully pretended to throw a cap in the air, ala Mary Tyler Moore, looking at Rob for approval and appreciation. Rob hissed at me to quit making a spectacle of myself, people were looking at me. I was squelched for the rest of the day.

We didn't try to make love that night either. Rob didn't bring me coffee the next morning. We packed up and left for Brookings right after a constrained breakfast.

My much-anticipated weekend to The City for sexual renewal and marital harmony was a bust. Maybe Rob and I needed to put a little space between us—but we already had a chasm looming that I didn't know how to cross. Maybe I needed to be alone to analyze the situation. Maybe...I didn't know what either of us needed. My new winter coat couldn't warm me against the frost in Rob's attitude.

*****

We spent the first two weeks of December being polite to each other—whenever Rob was around, of course. He had finals so he spent most of his time either at class or with various study groups. He came home to grab a quick dinner and to get the towels wet.

I was just as happy to have him gone. There's only so much nice I have in me and I'd been running on fumes since Thanksgiving.

I took the time to send out Christmas cards to what few friends I had. There were ten cards left from a box of twenty so I even sent one to my old agent, Heather. She'd probably burn it but I could afford to waste a stamp.

I wrapped a few presents and bought a little tree all by myself. I sang carols to Pudgy and met with my exercise buddies three days a week to keep the holiday food at bay.

I got my first real taste of winter. It was cold outside. Connie gave me hot chocolate when I went to her house and assured me that this was just the tip of the iceberg—no pun intended. I started mindlessly driving around town, just to get out of the trailer, and discovered that the Miata is not a cold-weather car; that prairie wind howled and rattled through the canvas top and the heater didn't work all that well. I remembered back when I first moved to Brookings how people had looked askance at my little ragtop. I'd thought they were jealous. Had I known anything about a Midwestern winter, I'd have known their regard was horror. But aimlessly driving a refrigerator was better than sitting in the trailer all the time.

Pudgy and I were watching *How the Grinch Stole Christmas* for the fifth time when I got a call from Leslie. Before I got a chance to yowl forlornly she told me she'd met a man. She thought maybe this was the one but she wasn't sure, etc., etc., etc. His name was Peter, he was from Boston, and he was a lawyer. She bubbled on for about twenty minutes and I did my best to squeal, exclaim, and congratulate her. I guess I didn't do a very good job because she stopped abruptly and said, "You sound kind of down, Stevie. Anything wrong?"

"I think I'm catching a bug," I lied. "You have no idea how cold it is here."

"Sure I do. I'm from Philadelphia, remember?"

"I guess it takes getting used to," I said, trying to get some enthusiasm for life back in my voice. I told her about the trip to Minneapolis and pretended it had been wonderful. I told her about my new clothes and how pleased I was with them.

Les said abruptly, "You haven't said anything about Rob. How is he?"

"Fine, I guess. He's studying for finals so I haven't seen much of him," I evaded.

Reassured, Leslie returned to the subject of Peter.

"Okay, old married lady, any advice on how to protect yourself in the bathroom while living with a man," (bathroom? living? this was farther along than I'd have thought. When was the last time I'd spoken to Leslie?) "besides the obvious: you know, making sure the toilet seat's down?"

It was time for me to act happy. "Make sure you have two bathrooms," I said promptly. "But if you only have one, always pee first. Rob farts when he pees and he does it right in my air space so I have to sit in the miasma. It's worst when he's been eating his mother's baked beans; he does fart arias. I swear I heard him do the opening of *Carmen* the other day."

Leslie howled. "Stevie," she giggled before hanging up, "you always make me laugh."

That's me, a laugh riot.

I sat in the chair feeling very sorry for myself. I was a stranger in a strange land and it was Christmas, which made it even lonelier. Pudgy jumped on the back of the chair and licked my ear, then she jumped in my lap. "Ah, Pudge, thank God I have you," I sniffled and hugged her.

Well, things finally blew up, they had to, and what finally triggered the blow was a good thing. I was moping around listening to the wind rattle the trailer when the phone rang. It was Dr. Torgeson from the Speech Department requesting a meeting as soon as possible. The only thing on my agenda was cleaning so I got dressed up in my new suit for a one o'clock appointment.

"The staff has discussed your qualifications and the current budget and we've agreed we should find a spot for you," Dr. Torgeson informed me after I sat down. "I can put you in the Resident Artist category. It's only a part-time position," he qualified, "but we'd like to take advantage of your professional experience and credentials. What do you think?"

What did I think? I thought it was great! We agreed that I would teach two acting classes, meeting on Tuesdays and Thursdays, and that I would assist in directing one of the plays starting next semester.

I hugged myself euphorically as I walked to my car. The pay wasn't much but it would give me something to do and somewhere to go two days a week. I giggled in relief and delight. I wanted to share my good news with someone…but who? Rob had mentioned that he'd probably be going out for a beer with some classmates after his last test and Pudgy wouldn't understand the importance of my news. Fortunately, the exercise group was meeting that afternoon. Chris, Connie, and Gail were happy for me and insisted a celebration was in order. We were quite a sight at Happy Hour, four smelly women in sweats making toasts over a pitcher of beer.

"What did Bobby say when you told him about the job?" Gail asked.

"He doesn't know yet," I said. "Maybe he'll be home by now so I can tell him."

"You two have a lot to celebrate," Connie smiled.

I was full of cheer and beer. Connie was right; we should celebrate. On the way home I took a detour to the Municipal Liquor Store and picked up a bottle of cabernet.

Rob was sitting in the living room with his arms crossed on his chest when I sailed in, waving my bottle. "Where have you been?" he asked, eyes narrowed.

"Exercising," I said, surprised at his tone. "You said you were going out with your buddies so don't get pissed that I didn't sit around waiting for you." I changed gears. "Boy, Rob, have I got some news for you!" I waved my bottle triumphantly under his nose.

"It smells like you'd had enough booze. You could probably use food more than alcohol," he said slightingly. "And since when do you drink beer while you exercise?"

"We split a pitcher after we worked out, of course," I said shortly, my eyes narrowing to slits to match Rob's. "What's the matter? All your friends have homes to go to and you feel picked on because you had to come back here? You don't have to stay on my account." I put the wine bottle on the TV and shrugged off my coat. "You know, Rob, I was in a good mood before I walked in that door. Thanks for spoiling it for me."

"Could we, for once, spend an evening without discussing your internal temperature?" Rob retorted. "I'm tired and I could do without the whining."

"Whining?" I repeated and turned to glare at him. "I don't think I've been whining at all but if I have, well, it's about my turn. I've been listening to you bellyache for the last four months!" I tauntingly mimicked him, "'Oh, Stevie, don't talk to me, don't expect me to even notice you're here, I've got to study, I can't be distracted, I need my dinner on the table when and if I decide to show up!'" I grabbed the wine bottle and took it into the kitchen. "I ought to break this bottle over your head, you miserable son-of-a-bitch," I snarled as I plunked it on the counter. Then I tried to walk to the bedroom.

"Well, at least it'd keep you from drinking it," Rob snarled back, getting in my face. "Jesus Christ, the only thing you've learned since we got married is how to get drunk. And don't you call me a son-of-a-bitch. My mother is a wonderful woman. And since we're talking about her, Rick told me she was upset by your anti-German comments at Thanksgiving. Everybody has to be so sensitive about your ancestry but you feel free to say any insulting thing that comes into your head. Who's the bigot here anyway?"

I was blindsided by Rob's accusations. I thought they were so unfair, so stupid, so...so...I was beyond words. I was tired of the boredom and the loneliness of my life. I was frustrated with the misunderstandings and constant tension. The beer I'd drunk destroyed what little self-control I had left and Rob's angry face crowding me was a provocation. I completely lost it and swung a fist at his head. Good thing I'd put the wine bottle down or we'd really have had a mess to clean up—not to mention a possible concussion for Rob. My punch didn't do much good. I had no experience with boxing and Rob, after a moment of amazement, countered my wild blows very effectively. His arms were a lot longer than mine so he all he had to do to hold me off was put a hand on my chest. I couldn't reach past his biceps so I tried kicking. He just moved his legs out of the way but I wouldn't quit. I must have looked pretty silly flailing and kicking because Rob started to laugh. That chilled me down and made me kind of crazy.

My fists may have been ineffectual but I came equipped with a set of knives on my fingertips and I wanted blood. I wanted to wipe that grin off Rob's face. I wanted to hurt him. I took deadly aim and clawed at Rob's face. He jerked his head back in time to keep from being blinded but my nails dug into his neck. He tried to grab my hands.

"Stop it," he ordered in a shocked voice. But I'd found a way to hurt him and I intended to do a lot more damage. I circled him, fingers poised, waiting for an opportunity to strike again.

I found an opening and leapt. Rob grabbed me and wrestled me to the couch, pinning my arms. So I started kicking again. He finally pinned my arms and legs with his body. The only free weapon I had was my mouth so I tried biting him. I was gasping and keening in the back of my throat. I managed to get an arm loose and tried clawing again.

That's when Rob hit me. He landed three body blows to my ribs. Even crazy as I was I could feel him pull the punches. Good thing he did, too. He'd have broken my ribs.

191

"Stop it, Stevie! For God's sake, stop it!" he said desperately and shook me.

My vision cleared and I stared up at him. Then I started to cry—which isn't easy when you have 190 pounds resting on your chest.

"Are you finished?" Rob asked. "Can I get off you now?"

I nodded and we both wearily sat up on the couch, drained. It takes a lot of energy to fight like that. No wonder professional boxers train for years.

"Did I hurt you?" Rob finally asked. "I tried not to but you wouldn't stop. I just wanted you to stop!"

"You didn't break anything," I said and winced. "I'll be bruised but that's it. How's your neck?"

He touched his neck and stared at his bloody fingers in disbelief.

There was a knock on the trailer door. "Who the hell could that be?" Rob muttered but he rose to answer it.

Two of the boys from next door stood outside, looking frightened but determined. "Is everything all right here?" asked one of the boys.

"Yeah, everything's fine," Rob answered tersely.

"How about your wife?"

"She's fine."

There was a slight pause then the other boy said to Rob, "I'd like to hear that from her."

Bless his ghetto-blasting heart, he wanted to make sure I was still in one piece. I guess he hadn't noticed Rob's neck. I went to the door, wiping my eyes. "I'm fine. We've just been having a fight," I explained.

"We heard," the first boy said uncomfortably. "Well, as long as everything's okay, we'll just go…" and they backed away.

"Great, now people are going to think I'm a wife-beater," said Rob as he closed the door, then turned pale. "I am. Stevie, I'm sorry. I just didn't know how to make you stop."

He looked defeated with blood clotting on his collar. And I felt ashamed. "You're not a wife-beater, Rob," I said tiredly. "I started it. It isn't fair to attack you and not expect you to fight back. To tell you the truth, I probably wouldn't have any respect for you if you didn't." I sat down and winced again. "My mistake was fighting someone who's half again as big as me. The next time I decide to hit somebody remind me to pick on someone my own size."

My attempt at levity fell flat. Rob sat next to me on the couch but we didn't look at each other.

"Well, do you want a divorce?" Rob asked finally.

"I don't know. Do you?"

"I asked you first."

I was silent. Tears were running down my face. I went to the bathroom and returned with the tissue box. Rob's neck wasn't dripping blood anymore but he could probably use a Kleenex, too. We wiped and dabbed gingerly.

"Why do we fight all the time, Stevie?" Rob asked sadly. "We never did in Los Angeles."

I blew my nose. "You weren't so unreasonable in Los Angeles. And we may not have had much free time but when we had some we spent it together. Here, the only function I serve in your life is to cook and clean. You're never here but you expect me to sit around waiting for you. We don't even make love anymore. I know I've got to lose five pounds but I don't think I'm that unattractive..."

"Stevie, you're beautiful."

"Well, I feel ugly. I can't do anything without getting scolded anymore. I'm beginning to think you're ashamed of me."

"If you'll let me explain..."

"You'll get your turn in a minute. Let me see, I had a whole list of your crimes and now I can't seem to think of them." I shrugged. "I guess that's about it. I was just lonely before I ran into you. Now I feel misused, abused, ugly, and lonely. You should have married somebody from around here. They'd have fit in better and you'd be happier." I wiped my nose and eyes. "Okay, your turn."

Rob took a deep breath then began, "First of all I'm not ashamed of you, far from it. And as for not fitting in, you fit in better than I do. People like you. Everybody's seen you on TV, you're pretty and lively, they can't understand what you're doing with me. To tell you the truth, I don't either. You walk into a room and it lights up. I just take up space. And everybody seems to think I'm ignoring you. Did you know the minister tracked me down and gave me hell because he saw you driving around town? He thinks it's because you're miserable. I didn't even know you were cruising. Even my dad's on me to pay more attention to you. And Gary, you know, we went to his place? He thinks I should drop some courses if that would make you happy. Dammit, this Master's degree is important to me. Being a Teaching Assistant is an honor and it pays for my courses. But it means I don't have any spare time! Nobody seems to understand that."

I just looked at him. "So this a popularity contest and you think you're losing?"

"I don't know. I guess so. And another thing; everybody thinks you're supporting me. Stevie, I've always paid my own way. Now people think I'm your pet. And I'm too big to compete with Pudgy."

A crack about a litter box the size of the kitchen was on the tip of my tongue but I decided now was not the time for bathroom humor.

"Rick says you drink too much," Rob continued. "He told me he hates to have Chris be around you. He says Chris is hanging out in bars with you instead of being at home where she belongs. He says it's my fault, that I give you too much freedom. He says I should put you on a schedule and stick to it. He says that's what he did with Chris and it made a huge difference in their relationship." I was flabbergasted by that pronouncement. But Rob was still speaking. "Stevie, I know the schedule idea is stupid but you never really drank much until you came here. So that must be my fault, too. I feel like I've ruined your life."

"Do you think I drink too much?" I asked. "Honestly, the only time I overdid it was on Hobo Day. It's just been a couple of beers here and there since. That's not so bad, is it?"

"Not really. But Rick pointed out that we never had wine at the family dinners until you came."

"But Marilyn brought the wine, not me," I protested.

"That's true, isn't it?" Rob stopped, puzzled. "But Rick's my brother; why would he say something like that if he didn't think it was true?"

"I don't know," I said. "Just out of curiosity when do you and Rick meet to discuss your love lives?"

"Oh, when Mom has a church meeting we get together for lunch," Rob said and ducked his head. "I didn't tell you because he's usually pretty critical. I didn't want to hurt your feelings."

"And this doesn't strike you as odd?" I asked.

"I never really gave it much thought," Rob admitted. "Anyway, according to Dad I don't spend enough time with you. The entire Engineering Department thinks you're too good for me. My brother thinks you wear the pants in our family and that I'm a wimp. Everybody's got an opinion on what I'm doing wrong with my wife. And I don't have time to do anything about it."

Rob seemed to have broken the verbal logjam. I didn't interrupt; I just tried to take mental notes if a response was required. Rob got up to pace in front of the couch. He scrubbed his hair furiously as he paced.

"I thought you'd like the trip to Minneapolis. Stevie, I had finals coming up and I could have used to the time to grade papers and get caught up but I wanted to make you happy. But all you did was make snide comments, flaunt your money, and make me feel small."

Oh. So that's how he saw that weekend.

Rob stopped pacing, sat on the couch, and looked at me in frustration. "I'm trying to do right by you but I don't see why your life so much more important that mine. At least tell me where you were this afternoon so when one of your fans buttonholes me I can defend myself."

"The exercise group went out for a beer after our session to celebrate," I said absently, trying to assimilate everything Rob had said.

"Oh yeah, the wine," Rob said bitterly. "What are you celebrating? Did you finally decide to go back to California?"

I blinked. "Dr. Torgeson called today and offered me a part-time teaching position. I start in January."

Rob dropped his head back on the couch in defeat. "Great. Now you'll be a teacher and I'll just be a lowly grad student. Castrate me now and get it over with. And Rick's going to be really pissed. He worked for years to get a job at the University. Only you could just walk into town and get a professorship."

When had Rob turned into such a drama king and where had he learned it?

"I'm just a resident artist, Rob, I don't even get benefits," I said impatiently. "I think we're on the same level socially—below Rick. That should keep him happy. And you too. At least I'll have something to do so I won't be wasting gas and giving the good people of Brookings something to talk about."

"Oh, sorry" he said and sighed. "I guess your fans are right. I am an asshole."

"Not completely."

"No, I am. I hit you. I still can't believe I did that. I've never raised a hand to a woman in my life."

I looked at Rob's neck again. "Well, I've never clawed anybody before so we're even."

But Rob wasn't listening to me. "I wouldn't blame you if you did leave me. It'd probably be better for you." He sighed again. "Stevie, every time I come home and you're not here I think, 'this is it. She's not coming home anymore'. I'm not hungry; I'm scared. And then I make it worse by yelling at you. Maybe I'm just trying to make it my choice. I don't know. I'm not good at this introspection stuff."

"I'm glad you finally told me what's on your mind," I said honestly. "We should have had this talk a long time ago."

"I would have had to admit that I can't take care of everything when I told you I would," Rob said and added softly, "I feel like a loser."

"You're not a loser," I assured him, "you're just overwhelmed. And I can help now that I know what's going on. Rob, you just can't shut me out when you have a problem. Talk to me."

"I just did. Any ideas?"

What a relief it was to finally hear his viewpoint. I could work on solutions now that I knew what the problems were. I frowned in concentration and flipped through my mental notes. "First, I liked the trip to Minneapolis; I thought you were being mean about the sweater… and about acting…and about your mother and, well, you get the idea. That was just miscommunication. About interference from your dad and brother…well, maybe we shouldn't see so much of them. While I appreciate your father's support it's not his place to nag you, that's my job. And Chris is not hanging out in bars; she's sweating with some very respectable faculty wives because your brother made some nasty cracks about her weight. I'm pretty sure she's more miserable than me so don't listen to Rick about marriage strategy. About the pocket protector crowd…quit listening to them. You've got to quit caring so much about what other people think. And about our personality differences, if it makes you feel any better I'll buy you a joke book so you too can sparkle at parties." I made a mental overview of my speech. I seemed to have touched on all points. "I think this fight is the best thing that could've happened," I concluded. "At least we got the problems out in the open and can work on them. But next time, let's just yell at each other, okay? I won't throw punches if you don't."

"Stevie, I promise I will never lay a hand on you again," Rob said solemnly but he was looking less squashed than he had earlier. Maybe he felt like a huge burden had been lifted, too.

"You don't have to go that far," I objected wryly. "I can think of times I want you to lay a hand on me." The fight was over but I still had nervous energy to expend. "You up for a reconciliation? Unless you want dinner instead."

Rob agreed that we needed physical contact more than food so we took the box of Kleenex with us into the bedroom. It had been so long since we'd made love we were clumsy and awkward. We had to be particularly careful to avoid each other's wounds. It wasn't as satisfying as it used to be but it was better than brawling. Afterwards, we lay in each other's arms, exhausted.

"Where's Pudgy?" I asked suddenly.

"I don't know," Rob said drowsily. "She slipped out when I got home."

"I've got to find her," I said and threw on a bathrobe.

"She's a cat. She'll be fine. Come back to bed," Rob protested.

"She's never been in this kind of cold!" I stepped into my slippers, threw my coat over my bathrobe, and went outside to call for her. Pudgy came running at the sound of my voice and I gathered her up in my arms. "I'm so sorry," I crooned. "I forgot all about you."

I looked up from her to see the boys next door outlined in the window of their trailer.

"Fight's over, boys," I called to them. "No serious damage done. But thanks for checking."

Their faces disappeared. I didn't feel too bad about disturbing their peace; God knows I'd put up with their stupid stereo often enough. I went inside to warm my cold feet against Rob's warm thighs and snickered when he yelled. My cold feet were small punishment to inflict for the evening I'd put in.

Rob fell asleep but I lay thinking as I listened to him snore. I'd learned something tonight. I'd never suspected Rob's lack of self-esteem; I'd thought only women suffered from that. How strange to think that men were people, too. And it was time to set some boundaries with the Andersons—for my own protection. Especially Rick. But I did owe Alice an apology about the anti-German cracks. I may have felt provoked but that was no excuse for racial slurs. If I didn't like bigotry, I shouldn't act like a bigot.

chapter 16

I was bruised mentally and physically after the big fight but I was lucky; a sweater covered my bruises. Rob had to wear a band-aid to cover his scratches. I don't what he told people. Maybe he said he had hickies; maybe he said he was married to a vampire; maybe he didn't say anything. I hope not; I was embarrassed. They say you only hurt the one you love—probably because only the one you love can get under your skin like that—but there had to be a better way to start a dialogue. Somebody was going to get hurt if we got into another fistfight and, considering our respective sizes and levels of expertise, I was pretty sure it was going to be me.

Our fragile peace put sex back in our relationship. It wasn't as easy and spontaneous as it had been, but at least we were back together.

Oh! And Pudgy got frostbite on the tip of one ear and it fell off. I really felt bad about that.

Well, I couldn't change Pudgy's ear or Rob's scratches so I forgot about them and tried to get into the Christmas spirit. There still wasn't much snow but all the stores were decorated and the Main Street merchants had put up lights. Beverly Hills didn't have anything to worry about but I liked the folksy display. Rob strung some lights on the trailer and we bellowed a few carols together. I made sugar cookies from an old Berk family recipe that I got from Alice. Rob insisted on helping; he liked to cut the shapes and eat the raw dough. Being an engineer, he was very careful to get maximum amount of shapes out of each sheet of dough. Rob took his job seriously and his concentration was total. I'd hire him to build a sewer.

I even made fudge. I was making Christmas for Rob as penance for my past fractiousness. Except when he was grading papers Rob spent most of his time with me without complaint. Maybe he was paying penance, too. Or maybe he was shoring up points for the next term. We spent an evening together wrapping presents, then plugged in the tree, and huddled in front of the blinking lights.

"It's nice, isn't it?" Rob murmured and put a tentative hand around my shoulder.

"Yeah," I murmured back and just as hesitantly moved into his armpit. "I just wish we had a fireplace."

"Don't worry, Santa will find you," Rob said. He kissed my forehead and I snuggled into his neck. For a moment we were both afraid to move. Then I sighed deeply and relaxed. Rob did too. We stayed close when we moved to the couch and watched *It's a Wonderful Life* on TV— which has to be one of the most depressing movies I've ever seen but it put things in perspective. I could have had a whole town of goofballs strapped on my back instead of a few marital problems.

I still had to buy a present for Leslie and time was running out. I decided to visit Chris' shop. Les just loved artsy-craftsy stuff and Chris had a large selection of pots to pick from—maybe I'd even get a discount. I had an ulterior motive for wanting to see Chris. I remembered that during The Fight Rob had said something about Rick telling him I was a bad influence and he didn't like Chris hanging out with me. I wanted to find out what dirt Rick was spreading.

Chris seemed a little distracted. She helped me select a small, tasteful pot and we wrapped it for mailing. She was quiet so I filled the silence with talk about my cookie baking and trailer trimming. I told her I was busy getting my teaching plans organized. I even told her about The Fight but I put a humorous spin on it. "Poor Pudge won't even go outside anymore. She doesn't trust me. She must think I'm going to start another fistfight and she can't afford to lose any more of her ears," I concluded and admired the wrapping job we'd done.

"Did the fight help?" Chris asked.

"Well, it broke the tension," I admitted. "I don't know if it did any good. I'll let you know in fifty years if I hang around that long."

"Maybe I won't be around in fifty years," Chris said darkly.

Ahh! The opening I'd been waiting for. "Chris," I said slowly, sticking a mailing label on my package and taking care not to look at her, "Rob told me Rick said I was causing a problem between you two. Am I?" I looked her full in the face and was shocked by what I saw. Chris had tears in her eyes and her chin was quivering badly.

"Let me lock up and we'll go in the back room," she said.

Chris closed the shop and I followed her to the back, mystified. We sat on a crate and Chris twisted her hands together as tears slowly rolled down her cheeks and dripped on her sweater.

"Rick says I've gotten too mouthy ever since you came," she admitted. "I mentioned that I like the way you stand up for yourself." She dripped some more and I dug a Kleenex out of my purse. She blew her nose and added vehemently, "That made him mad so I told him I was tired of doing what he wants to do all the time. And I told him I wanted to be treated with a little respect." Chris pounded her fist on her knee and she angrily wiped her eyes.

Sounded like a perfectly normal desire to me and I told her so.

"We always have to spend holidays and Sundays with Rick's family," Chris continued. Gee, where had I heard that before? "Stephanie, my family lives sixty miles away and I never get to see them. It's always his family, his friends. And he doesn't like me having the shop. He's really putting pressure on me to close it." She paused to mop up more tears then continued. "Do you know, if I want to vote for a Democrat I have to lie and tell Rick I voted Republican? He won't listen to a word I say unless I'm agreeing with him and I'm sick of it!"

If Rick was where Rob was getting his ideas about marital relations it was a miracle we'd managed to last as long as we had without going a few rounds.

"We can never even discuss anything," Chris was saying. "Rick just walks out on me when I try. How'd you get Bobby to talk to you?"

I half-smiled at her. "I took a swing at him."

Chris smiled back wistfully. "I wish I could do that but I wasn't raised that way. You're lucky you have your temperament. I'm like a cow; I just turn my back to the wind and take it."

Lucky me, I thought wryly, I'm capable of beating up people. "How about counseling? Have you tried that?" I asked.

"Rick won't go. He's perfectly happy. Or he would be, he says, if I'd quit hanging around with you and getting funny ideas." She sighed.

Chris could see from the helpless look on my face that I didn't know what to say.

"He said my family gave me funny ideas, too. That's why he doesn't want me to see them. I think he doesn't want me to see them because they're not very educated and don't have a lot of money. Sometimes I think the only reason he married me is because I'm the only woman dumb enough to put up with him," she said and set her chin. "If I had any sense at all I'd leave him. And I would but..."

She trailed off so I prompted her. "But?"

She shrugged helplessly. "I'm pregnant," she confessed.

I looked at poor woebegone Chris, seeking any outward signs of pregnancy. She didn't look any different than usual in her baggy sweater except that her chubby face was dripping tears. "Are you sure?"

She nodded. "I told Rick a year ago I wanted to start a baby but he said we weren't in a financial position to have one right now and we'd have to wait a few years. So I'm scared to tell him and, oh God, I don't know what to do!"

Chris was sobbing at this point. I just sat on my crate like a lump; I didn't know what to do either. I'm not a great hugger of people but that seemed to be what the situation called for so I gingerly put my arm around her. I must have done it right because Chris threw her arms around me and cried into my neck. I patted her back inexpertly until she got control of herself.

"I'm sorry," she sniffed and wiped her nose on her sleeve. "I'm making a fool of myself."

"No, no," I soothed, "you're understandably upset." I patted some more and tried to think of something helpful. I remembered Marvin's reasonable attitude toward abortion. "You can't be very far along. Could you like...terminate it?"

Chris looked shocked. "I could never do that! Well, maybe if I were an unwed mother or something tragic like that...but I couldn't do that to my own baby." She covered her abdomen protectively then looked at me like I was going to drag her off by her hair and scrape her out until I apologized for even suggesting such a thing.

We both sat glumly until a horrible thought struck me. "Just out of curiosity, what kind of birth control were you using?"

"A diaphragm."

Oh Lord. I thought of my gasket sitting in it's little box at home in the bathroom. I knew they failed every now and again but I'd never known anybody it'd ever happened to. I shook myself; I'd worry about that later. Chris was looking at me hopefully like I had answers to her problems.

"Okay," I said to Chris, trying to organize my scattered thoughts. "About your family…go see them on your own. He can't really stop you, can he? About the shop…well, just ignore him. And about the baby… you have to tell him. How can he be mad? It's not like you got pregnant by yourself. He'll probably be happy when he finds out. Maybe he'll appreciate the money you bring in from the shop with an extra mouth to feed. Put it to him that way. You'll have answers to all his objections."

"He won't listen because they won't be his answers. He's a professor, you know. He's got the answers to everything," Chris sniffled resentfully.

"He's a professor of cows," I pointed out.

"Tells you what he thinks of me," Chris retorted.

We both sat there, gloomily. Chris finally blew her nose one last time and stood up. "I know there's nothing you can do. I just had to talk to somebody."

"Sure," I told Chris in relief, "I'm behind you whatever you decide." She still looked so miserable and scared that I made an unwilling, squinch-eyed offer. "Would you like me with you when you tell Rick about the baby?"

Chris smiled at me gratefully and said, "No, he hates you." She dabbed at her eyes, glanced at her watch and gasped. "I have to go. I have to get my shopping done or I won't have dinner ready." She hurried me to the front of the shop.

"Uh, Stephanie," Chris hesitated as she locked up again behind us, "you won't tell anyone about this, will you?"

"Absolutely not," I promised.

"Not even Bobby?"

"Not even Rob. But if you need to talk, call me."

Rob was in the kitchen reading the paper when I got home. I showed him the wrapped package and described the pot to him.

"How's Chris?" Rob asked.

"Oh, she's fine," I said lightly and started washing lettuce for salad before I announced, "I think I'm going on the Pill. I've been reading statistics, the gasket has only an 85% prevention rate."

Rob shrugged and turned a page. "Whatever you think is best. We don't have the time or money for children right now."

I gazed at Rob affectionately. He was a Neanderthal, and I may have thought of leaving him periodically, but he could have been a lot worse. I got the good brother.

*****

The next day Rob called his professors and found out he'd aced all his courses. He was relieved but I was jubilant. "I'm married to a genius!" I crowed.

"Not a genius," he said modestly, "but close."

The only thing missing for a perfect Currier & Ives Christmas was snow, and that minor imperfection was corrected shortly. Big fluffy flakes started to drift down in a gentle breeze that was a pleasant change from the usual prairie gale. I ran outside to watch them waft down through the glow of the streetlights. The falling snow muffled most sound. Rob came outside to watch me try to catch snowflakes on my tongue. "I've read about catching flakes but I've never done it before," I said into the dusk. "I love snow."

"I'll check back with you in March. Wait'll you've had three months of blizzards," Rob grinned at me.

"Oh, Rob, you like it, too. Admit it."

He looked at my flushed cheeks and sparkling eyes.

"I love you in snow," he said and kissed me. We locked together, catching snow on our eyelashes and hair. Well, one thing led to another and we went back inside to enjoy each other. Love had triumphed and we were wearing out parts of our anatomy again.

We were napping together when Alice called. Rob's face was a study when he hung up.

"I guess we're on our own for Christmas this year," he said in response to my inquiring look. "Mom said Chris just told her that she was going to spend Christmas day with her family this year. Then Marilyn called and said she was flying down to Arizona on Christmas day to see her parents. So Mom called Sarah in Minnesota and got herself invited there for Christmas. We'll spend Christmas Eve with Mom and Dad but we're on our own for the day."

"Something wrong with that?" I asked, remembering the uncomfortable Thanksgiving.

"No, it just doesn't sound like Mom, especially with Christmas so close. Why the sudden change?"

I didn't really care. I was just hoping we wouldn't end up in some sort of snarl. It was Christmas; it would be nice to get through a simple holiday without a major trauma.

Alice called me to discuss Christmas Eve plans and to apologize for leaving town on such short notice. "Chris felt she should spend time with her family. And Marilyn's parents wanted the grandkids. I hope you and Bobby aren't disappointed. What will you do all by yourselves?"

"We'll be just fine, Alice, don't you worry about us," I promptly answered, still surprised at Chris' initiative. "Rob tells me you're going to Minnesota. You just go and have a good time."

"Yes," sighed Alice. "My sister Sarah'll have her whole family there." She sounded so despondent I made another one of my unwilling, insincere, squinch-eyed offers.

"You're welcome to spend the day with us if you'd like," I said with my eyes shut, fingers crossed, and breath held.

"No," said Alice. "That's sweet of you but we've already made arrangements with Sarah and Junior."

"Junior!?" I asked.

"Sarah's husband. He was a Junior and we've always just called him that even though Senior is dead," Alice explained.

"What a way to go through life," I murmured.

"It could have been worse, Stephanie. He had an Uncle Fat."

"Good God. What was his real name?"

"I don't remember. We all just called him Fat."

"Was he?"

"Was he what?"

Who's on second? I don't know. Third base! Alice and I were doing a vaudeville routine. "Was he fat?" I asked patiently.

"Oh my, yes. That's why he got the name." Alice paused then sighed. "It just won't be the same."

"What won't?" I was still befuddled by Junior and Fat.

"Christmas. I love having Christmas together. I don't know why things have to change." She sighed again.

"Well, Alice, life is change," I said as reasonably as possible.

"I know. It just doesn't seem fair. The wife always seems to get her way. Her family comes first."

I had sense enough not to point out that this was probably the first time in recorded Anderson history a daughter-in-law had revolted. Maybe, if I was tactful, I could make Alice see that she was being a little selfish. "Alice, you'll have everybody on Christmas Eve. Don't you think the other families would like to see their children and grandchildren on Christmas? Maybe next year you could have Christmas Day."

"But then I won't get Christmas Eve!" she wailed.

This was ridiculous. My patience, not my long suit at any time, was just about gone. "Your sons have other responsibilities now," I said shortly. "If it makes you feel any better there's even a biblical reference about cleaving unto your spouse and forsaking all others."

"Don't you go quoting the Bible at me, young lady. I'm pretty sure I'm a lot more familiar with it than you are," Alice snapped. "And I'm certain that doesn't mean you should forsake your own parents!"

I was pretty sure it did. Those ancient Jews probably had a lot of experience with in-law problems but I managed to swallow that comment.

"I guess I'll have to accommodate all you girls now," she continued waspishly. "I suppose you'll want a piñata. I don't know your traditions so you'll have to give me orders."

"My parents just had a tree in our house," I said just as waspishly. "But if you want a piñata go ahead—although where you'll find one around here at this late date is beyond me."

The conversation ended coolly. Christmas Eve was starting to sound like a repeat performance of Thanksgiving with no Berks to gang up on; the fighting would all be in-house. Poor Rob; he was just healing.

We drove to the Anderson homestead Christmas Eve. Alice's lighted tree beamed at us from the picture window and we could see Nancy's boys racing around it inside. The manger scene on the lawn was lighted and I smelled turkey as I walked through the front door. Rob took our coats and hung them up, put our presents under the tree (I'd gotten Rob's siblings cheese packages from the Dairy Unit of the University; the Andersons could die of cholesterol poisoning for all I cared), and I presented Alice with a Jell-O mold. The house was warm, the food smelled good, people were smiling, and snow was drifting down outside. It was the perfect lead-in to a horror movie.

The women trooped into the kitchen. Oddly enough, the men followed us. There's no football on Christmas Eve so I guess they

205

decided to watch us work instead. It was the closest thing to broken field running they were going to get.

I'd just tripped over Marvin's feet when Marilyn whispered in my ear, "I've got wine in the garage. Grab a glass and we'll take a sanity break. I'll go get Chris." Marilyn whispered to Chris whose eyes lit up. Marilyn held up three fingers to me and grinned. I was a little surprised that Chris wanted wine but she knew what she was doing…I hoped. One glass of wine wouldn't do any damage to the fetus and it wasn't my place to tell her how to run her life.

Alice watched me get the jelly glasses and the three of us start out for our coats. She looked over her bifocals at us and put her hands on her hips. "You girls better have your wine in here. It's getting too cold to stay out in the garage." We stopped in our tracks, grinning shamefacedly. "There's a biblical precedent for celebrating with wine, isn't there, Stephanie?" Alice continued. I couldn't quite read the look she gave me; conspiratorial, resentful, amused, all of the above. Was this an olive branch? I smiled at her uncertainly. "Jesus didn't turn water into 7-Up at the wedding of Cana, he turned it into wine," she added. "If it's good enough for Jesus, it's good enough for me. As a matter of fact, I'll have some wine myself. Stephanie, you better get me a glass, too."

Marilyn retrieved two bottles from her car and ceremoniously poured four glasses of wine. There hadn't been a peep out of the men until Marvin spoke up. "Well, I guess if a glass of wine won't hurt Mother it probably won't hurt me, either. Besides," he smiled roguishly as he got a jelly glass, "I'd hate to go against the Bible."

The boys followed Marvin's lead by grabbing glasses, and Marilyn broke into the second bottle. We toasted solemnly, wished each other a Merry Christmas, but were interrupted by Rick before we could drink.

"You shouldn't have that," he said to Chris.

"I can do whatever I want," said Chris defiantly but looking nervous as hell.

Alice looked surprised at Rick's tone. "If I say she can drink in the house it should be enough for you, dear," she said to him. "This is my house."

Rick looked at Chris again. "Do you want to tell them or should I?"

"I don't care," Chris said sullenly. "It's your family. You tell them."

Rick addressed the rest of us. "I didn't want to tell you all like this but I don't seem to have much choice. Chris is pregnant." He turned to glare at her and she stared into her glass. Their disharmony ruined what should have been a happy announcement.

"That's why I don't want her getting drunk," Rick continued and turned his glare to me.

What was I supposed to say? I looked to Rob for guidance, hoping he'd help me out but he just stared at his hands. He'd told me after our fight that he wouldn't take sides with me or his family and at the time it'd sounded reasonable. Right now it seemed totally chickenshit. I was still trying to form a response when Chris spoke up.

"I asked the doctor and he said one or two glasses of wine a week wouldn't hurt the baby and would probably help me," she said tremulously to Rick. "Since it's my body I'll make the decisions about what's right for me."

Rick sent a blast of his anger back at Chris. "It's my baby and you'll do what I say!"

Alice jumped in. "Isn't that wonderful? Marvin, we're going to have another grandchild! This does call for a celebration. And it's the best Christmas present you could have given me," she said to Rick then turned her attention to Chris. "But maybe Ricky's right, dear." She tried to take the glass from Chris' hand. "Maybe for the baby's sake you shouldn't have alcohol right now."

Chris clutched her glass tighter and said through her teeth to Alice, "I've decided to have a glass of wine." She upended Fred. "That was good," she said and held her glass out to me, "I think I'll have one more so we can all toast. Stephanie, would you pour it?"

All eyes were fastened on me. Oh man, how do I get in these things? "The doctor said it was all right?" I hedged.

"He said one or two a week would be okay. This'll be my second for the week."

Chris and I locked eyes for a minute and I read a plea for support in hers. I surveyed the assembled family. Nobody seemed particularly bothered except for Rick. His dislike and anger radiated at me, which made my decision easy. Might as well back Chris up. What could Rick do to me; beat me up? I'd brain him with the wine bottle. The almost empty bottle gave me an idea. I poured Chris a tiny bit of wine.

"Why not," I said gaily, "let's everybody have another glass and toast the new baby."

A general toast accomplished two things: it might calm this volatile situation and would empty the second bottle so there'd be nothing left to fight over. It was pretty clever solution if I do say so myself.

We got through dinner without any other blowups although Rick studiously avoided talking to me, which didn't hurt my feelings one bit. For once I didn't resist going to church. I was pretty sure nobody would fight there.

But we had to open presents first. Alice gave Rob and me an afghan that she'd made herself, sort of a doily on a large scale. She'd even made it in earth tones so it wouldn't clash with the couch.

Alice seemed to appreciate the wine glasses I'd gotten her. "It's too bad we didn't have them earlier," she observed.

"Something to drink out of," Rick sniped. "Figures."

Apparently we back on war footing. Time to make nice with the Lutherans.

The Christmas Eve service was charming, although a bit long; towards the end snoring accompanied the choir. I didn't find anything to debate in the sermon; it was basically a good news discussion and even I couldn't find fault with that. The high point of the evening for me was the rendition of *O Holy Night*. A chubby little blue-haired lady (I couldn't remember her name but I think she gave me potholders at my shower) stood up in the middle of it. Boy, was I surprised when a soaring, lyric soprano came from her wrinkled little lips in an obbligato. It was so beautiful it brought tears to my eyes.

Rob and I joined the Anderson caravan to admire the home lighting displays then went back to the trailer, exhausted. Christmas with family can be just as crappy as Christmas all by yourself. Those Hallmark commercials lie.

"Boy, Chris and Rick are in a world of trouble. This pregnancy was an accident, you know," I commented as I got into bed.

Rob sat on the bed and took off his shoes and socks. "Stevie, did you tell Chris to get an abortion?"

"Absolutely not!" I said, shocked. "Well, I asked if she'd considered termination as an option because she seemed so scared and unhappy but that's it."

Rob took off his pants. "Well, apparently she told Rick you tried to talk her into it. He's furious."

"Rob, I swear, that's not what happened."

Rob hung up his pants. "I wish you'd stay out of it," he said. "Rick also told me you put Chris up to going to her parents for Christmas."

"I did not!"

"Well, he said she'd never have come up with the idea on her own."

I thought back to the conversation Chris and I had had. "All I said was that I'd support her in whatever she decided to do. I didn't get specific."

Rob shook his head and climbed into bed. "Listen, they were just fine together before Chris started acting up. It's probably just hormones anyway."

I raised myself on an elbow and looked at Rob in astonishment. "That's the most sexist thing I've ever heard," I declared. "Things weren't fine and it's not just hormones."

"Okay, whatever you say." Rob pulled me down and arranged me on his chest. "You stay out of it. It's not your business."

I agreed to keep a low profile. Since Chris was misrepresenting my suggestions I had nothing to gain but trouble.

We had our private Christmas the next day and opened our presents to each other. I'd gotten Rob some sweaters and slacks. Those eternal flannel shirts and jeans had to go.

Rob looked at his presents and raised an eyebrow at me. "Trying to change my image?"

"Well, you needed something nice," I said quickly. "You're not mad are you?"

"I've just never had anybody buy me clothes before except Mom. I like your taste better."

He handed me a tiny package wrapped with a big bow. It looked like jewelry, thank God. I'd been expecting a three-year subscription to *Reader's Digest*. Or Ginsu knives.

I opened the package to find a tiny pair of leaf-shaped earrings. "Rob, these are lovely," I said. "How come they're pink and green?"

"It's called Black Hills Gold, all mined from the Homestake Mine in the Hills," Rob lectured. "It's alloyed with silver to get the green color and copper to get the pink. But it's all gold."

Leave it to an engineer to know all about mining and alloys. I inspected the earrings. They were awfully small but surprisingly tasteful. I smiled and nodded approval at Rob. He was learning how to shop for me. That's a valuable skill for any husband. Ho ho ho.

We had hamburgers for Christmas dinner and went to a movie. Finally, all was calm, all was bright.

chapter 17

The first week of Christmas vacation Rob practiced wearing his new clothes and I practiced taking them off. It was a pleasant way to pass the time but after ten days of being cooped up in our little tin trailer we were getting on each other's nerves. We started being polite to each other again; another blow-up seemed inevitable and when it came it involved his family...as usual. It least it was a different brother this time.

Shortly after New Year's I'd staggered out of the bedroom after a nap as Rob was hanging up the phone. He informed me that he had just organized a ski trip in the Black Hills with Mike, Marilyn, and their two screaming brats. "Mike and I'll split the cost of a condo. It'll give us something to do until school starts. Doesn't that sound like fun?" he announced.

I was fuzzy from the nap and had to take a minute to digest this. When the concept filtered through I was not happy and the trip didn't sound fun. "You decided this without even discussing it with me?" I asked, annoyed. "When were you planning on telling me?"

"I just did," Rob said calmly but my appalled expression must have gotten through his thick skull that everything wasn't fine and dandy with the little woman.

"I'm sorry I didn't get your formal okay before I told Mike we'd go," he said. "Now he's expecting us. Anyway, I don't know what you're getting so mad about. We need to get out of this trailer, we're tiptoeing around each other again and that means trouble. You'll like the Black Hills; it's pretty there. And Mike and I didn't ask anybody else. Tom can't leave the store and Mike doesn't think Rick can afford it so you won't have anybody to fight with. Oh, and we're taking Mike's car so don't pack too much. They'll have the kids and everything and there won't be much room."

The nerve of the man. "Tell me, just how far is it to the Black Hills," I asked Rob, my eyes narrowed.

"Oh, about eight hours. We'll take a day to drive out, spend five days skiing, and drive back. And if you're worried about doing all the cooking, don't. Marilyn'll take turns with you. See? It's all taken care of."

Rob's tone and manner left no doubt that, at least for him, it was a done deal and I should be grateful he was 'taking care of me'. Of course, I blew up.

"You expect me to spend eight hours trapped in a car with Mike, Marilyn, and their kids?" I yelled. "Are you crazy? That's not a vacation, that's the first circle of Hell!"

"Well, I'd like to maintain some sort of relationship with at least one of my brothers," Rob said pointedly.

I was so outraged I threw a handy book at him; I missed and dented the cheap wall paneling. He threw it right back so I didn't have to retrieve it but his aim was better. It glanced off my shoulder. It hurt. The violence ended there because he walked out.

I paced, muttered, and waved my arms in the air. I hated the trailer, I hated Rob's family, I hated being married, I hated everything. I was cranky from my nap and the last thing I wanted to do was spend a week with a bunch of Andersons. It's not that I didn't like Marilyn but I'd had enough family crap. I suppose I'd offend everybody if I just refused to go; I wished I had a good excuse at hand.

I was brooding on the problem when the phone rang. My ex-commercial agent, Heather, half-yelled in my ear, "Thank goodness you sent me a Christmas card. I was going crazy trying to find you."

"Heather?" I asked lamely, more than a little surprised. "How are you?"

"I've got a hangover," she said. "Listen, I've had ad agencies asking for you. Can you come out to L.A. in the next couple of days? I want to schedule some interviews for you."

Heather had just handed me the escape hatch I'd been searching for. "I can come out tomorrow," I said without a pause. This was no time to play coy.

"Great. Call me with a number where I can reach you when you get in." Heather hung up as abruptly as she'd called.

This whirlwind proposition left me sort of dazed. And very pleased once I sat down and assimilated it. Someone in The Business remembered me! Boy, I must be hot! And I was going home. To Los Angeles! I wouldn't have to go on the family ski trip!

I started making plans. I needed a babysitter for Pudge. I'd already tapped Connie once and I didn't want to wear out her good nature so I called Gail. Then I called the airlines and booked a flight. My last call was to Leslie who said she was happy that I was coming "home". She insisted that I stay with her.

"I have two bedrooms. It's stupid to rent a hotel room," she said. "Just don't be surprised if Peter spends a lot of time here, too."

"Well, if you're sure you don't mind. I'll rent a car so I won't put you out too much," I said gratefully.

"Oh, Stevie," Leslie said impatiently, "you don't have to rent a car. You can drive me to work and take my car."

I was packing when Rob came home.

"But I don't want to go to Los Angeles," he said petulantly when I'd explained where and why I was going.

"So who asked you?" I said shortly. "You go maintain a relationship with your relatives. I'll be happier in L.A."

Rob and I agreed that maybe we needed a little time apart—I was thinking trial separation but maybe it was best not to open that can of worms just yet. Mike and Marilyn picked Rob up early the next day. "I'm sorry you have to go to the airport by yourself," he said awkwardly, "but we set this time up..."

"It's not a problem," I said. "I've got it handled."

"Yeah, well...take care of yourself," he said and glanced out the door. "Marilyn's really disappointed you're not going."

"You go where the job is," I shrugged, pretending Heather's call hadn't been a Godsend. "Don't break a leg."

"I'll try not to. Say 'hi' to Leslie for me."

"Sure."

Rob jumped when Mike honked the horn impatiently. "Guess I better go. Have fun." Rob gave me an awkward peck on the cheek and left. I couldn't believe how blasé he was about the separation. If he cared so little about me maybe I wouldn't come back at all.

Flying into Los Angeles was literally and figuratively flying back into sunshine. Leslie was waiting for me at the gate when I deplaned and gave me a big hug.

"You've hardly changed at all," she declared.

"Not so you could see," I said, "although it feels like I've been gone a lot longer than four months." We went to the baggage carousel and waited for my luggage. I gawked at the crowds and grinned in delight. "Look at all the people! Black ones, brown ones, white ones, yellow ones…" I exclaimed then noticed Leslie looking at me oddly. "I know, I'm acting like a tourist," I admitted and went back to staring without shame. I wasn't even irritated when I got jostled by a man trying to balance a ratty suitcase and two cardboard boxes. "Leslie, I just got shoved by a Third World member! Isn't it great?"

"First time I've ever heard you get excited about crowds," Leslie said skeptically.

"I'll hate it by tomorrow but right now…" I took a deep breath of stinking humanity. "It's good to be back in L.A.," I said with satisfaction.

We drove to Hermosa Beach in Les' Volvo. My euphoria continued through the stop-and-start traffic on the freeway. "Look, Leslie, a Mercedes-Benz, and Toyotas, and Acuras, and Hondas! Cars, Leslie, all kinds of cars! Do you think there's a chance we'll get shot at?" I asked eagerly.

Leslie took her eyes off the road just long enough to stare at me. "Have you lost your mind?" she asked.

"Probably. Leslie, I want to eat Chinese food, good Chinese food. And pasta. With proscuitto and cream sauce. And burritos. I think I'd sell my soul for a burrito." I was salivating at the thought of all the restaurants I had access to. No more Jell-O for me.

Leslie was looking at me strangely again. Fortunately, traffic had ground to a standstill so she could stare without killing us. "We'll go anyplace you want," she said and paused for a moment. "Are you all right, Stevie?"

She sounded so concerned I grinned at her reassuringly. "Just glad to be home. I'll get over it in a day or two."

We finally got to Leslie's garage and unloaded me and my stuff. As

Leslie unlocked her front door I took a good, long look at the door of my condo. "How are the tenants?" I asked Les, jerking my chin across the hall.

"They're really nice people. He's a lawyer and she's a financial consultant. I try to keep an eye on things so I've gotten to know them. They'd like to buy the place if you ever want to sell."

I frowned. "I don't think I want to sell right now. You never know; I might need it back one of these days."

Leslie eyed me. "By the way, how is Rob?"

"I'm on vacation, Les. I don't even want to think about him." I staggered into her place, dropped my suitcase, and exclaimed, "No paneling!" Then I ran across the living room to look out the window. "There isn't any plastic! Oh, look at the palm trees! Neat!"

Les' only comment was, "If you get all lyrical about graffiti I'm checking you into a hospital."

We dragged my luggage into the spare room and I unpacked. Then we sat down with bottled water to catch up. I got to hear all about Peter, the lawyer. She told me how wonderful Peter was; how kind and gentle, how strong and determined; how handsome he was, what a good friend and mighty lover.

I said wryly, "You sound like me six months ago."

Leslie smiled. "I know. Peter's Jewish so we have religious differences instead of racial but it's pretty much the same thing. He even wants to move back East. It's eerie how much like Rob and you we sound."

"Think about what you're getting yourself into. Think hard," I advised darkly.

She absorbed my bitter comment then asked, "What exactly is going on between you and Rob?"

"Later. So when is this paragon of yours coming over so I can check him out?"

"About seven. He says he wants to take us someplace special so wear something pretty. If you want to take a nap or a shower feel free. You've got time."

I took extra pains with my makeup and dress that evening. I wanted to impress this new boyfriend of Les'.

Peter was everything Leslie said he was from what I could tell at first meeting. He was charming and attractive—not as good-looking as Rob, of course, but definitely streetable. I guess he wanted to impress

Leslie's girlfriend, too, because he took us to Orsini's. That was fine by me. I love Italian food.

Peter was perfectly at home in a four-star restaurant. He knew the wines to order and the best dishes to recommend. I enjoyed myself although after awhile I felt like the training wheels on Leslie and Peter's bike. I bumped along with them trying not to get in the way too much as they held hands, giggled over private jokes, and smooched unobtrusively. I just smiled and ate my veal.

Which I promptly threw up when I got back to Leslie's. One hundred bucks down the toilet. Literally. I don't know why I got sick. Maybe the food was too rich. Maybe I'd eaten too much. Maybe the stress with Rob was throwing my system out of whack. Who knows, who cares. Oh well, I sighed, I wouldn't have to worry about calories. They were floating in front of my face—big pink chunks of veal. *I must learn to chew my food better*, I thought ruefully.

I was embarrassed when I heard a knock on the door and Leslie's voice asking, "Are you all right, Stevie? Peter and I thought we heard something."

Of course they heard something. They heard me barfing my guts out although I was trying to be as quiet as possible. Boy, I bet the visiting, vomiting girlfriend was really impressing Peter.

"I'm okay," I called back. "I guess dinner didn't agree with me. Sorry to disturb you. Go on back to bed. I'll be fine. Tell Peter I don't make a habit of this, okay?"

Leslie left and I crawled into bed. I missed Rob momentarily. If he'd been there he'd have made some smart crack about not being able to take me anywhere, I'd snipe back, and everything would be okay again. And my feet would warm up.

I waved off Leslie's concern the next morning. Peter took her to work and I planned my day as I chewed crackers washed down with 7-Up. Heather had scheduled five interviews for me and I needed to control my gag reflex.

I carefully drove the Volvo through Hermosa Beach and onto the San Diego Freeway. After the Miata it was like steering a barge. I must have looked like a ten-year-old peering anxiously over the steering wheel. And I wasn't used to driving an automatic transmission. I kept paddling around with my left foot looking for the clutch and I almost put myself through the windshield when I accidentally hit the brake. I managed to get to Santa Monica without incident but I almost sobbed in frustration when it came to parallel parking. My difficulties were made worse when some yahoo in a Bronco honked, screamed, and flipped me off when I didn't get out of his way soon enough. I wished he'd parked close to me. I'd have puked on his hood.

I smiled my way through the interviews and felt settled enough to go out for Chinese food that night. Peter treated us to Madame Wu's and I was careful not to eat too much and to avoid alcohol. Peter was solicitous about my digestion. I guess he didn't want to have to listen to any more midnight retching.

The second day of interviews was pretty much the same as the first. I'd drop off my picture, slate my name, smile, and try to make something of a stupid line. Already I was starting to object to being treated as sub-human by casting office personnel. If they were so smart why weren't they doing what I was doing? There was a lot more money being stupid in front of the camera than behind it. And I was beginning to hate L.A. drivers. I was honked at, screeched at, and gesticulated at as I tried conscientiously not to smash into anybody. I found myself muttering, "You go ahead and honk, you son-of-a-bitch. Yeah, I see your finger. If we were in South Dakota I'd pull the shotgun off the back of my pickup and then we'd see how many fingers you'd show me."

Forty-eight hours in Los Angeles and I was talking to myself. Making threats even. Oh dear.

What I needed was a little time by myself for reflection. Unfortunately, that wasn't going to happen anytime soon. Leslie and Peter were being good hosts and entertaining me royally and I was royally tired of being entertained. Peter took us to a French restaurant and, of course, ordered the correct wines and gave a brief dissertation on the history, preparation, and quality of the respective dishes. I listened politely and wished with all my soul that he'd just shut up.

Their happiness was particularly annoying. I was really getting tired of the billing and cooing going on at their end of the table. Couldn't those two keep their hands off each other? We were in a public place, for God's sake.

I wandered over to the local library just to have some time alone. I curled up in a chair with Jane Austen hoping a few hours with a good book would cheer me up. I wasn't the only person in the world to choose the library as a hideout; a bum sat next to me. I tried to be charitable

217

about his smell but when he leered at me and demanded spare change I decided I was safer at Leslie's.

The weekend yawned in front of me as I waited for the verdict on callbacks. God, I didn't want to be impressed by any more fine restaurants. I didn't want to be charmed. I wanted to watch TV. I wanted a burrito.

"I think I'll just stay home if you don't mind," I said to Leslie that night. "Maybe put in some time with the tube. You two go out. Enjoy."

Leslie tried to hide her look of relief. "Well, if you're sure you don't mind…"

"Not at all. You and Peter go have fun."

"Why don't you give Rob a call?" she suggested. "You haven't talked to him since you got here."

"He's probably still skiing," I said shortly. "Go. Have fun. Don't worry about me, I'll be just fine here."

Leslie and Peter must have decided over dinner that I needed a weekend in Santa Barbara because Peter presented the trip as a fait accompli when he got back that evening. Why were men always handing me trips that I didn't want to go on? I politely declined. "You two go ahead," I urged. "To tell you the truth I think I need to sleep in and relax."

"We were hoping we could talk in Santa Barbara," Leslie said hesitantly.

"I need to think first," I said.

I helped Les pack and waved at them from the front step as they left. I spent my weekend reading and doing crossword puzzles. I also met my tenants. I almost bumped into the man when I went outside to fetch the paper.

"I'm Stevie O'Neill," I introduced myself and held out my hand. "I own your condo."

"Nick Morris," my tenant said and shook my hand. "Honey, come and meet our landlady," he called into my old place. "This is Tracy," he said when his wife appeared.

"Please come in," she said graciously. "The coffee's fresh."

I accepted the offer because I wanted to see what they'd done with the place. I tried not to be too obvious as I peered around. They'd decorated with leather, glass, and chrome. It looked great if you like that moderne sort of thing.

"The place looks different," I commented as I sipped the cup of French Roast coffee Tracy handed me.

"Oh, we love it here," she exclaimed. "As a matter of fact, we were hoping you'd be interested in selling."

"Leslie mentioned that," I said. "I'm not ready to sell now but if I change my mind, I'll let you know."

Rats. It had been in the back of my mind that if I needed to leave Rob in a hurry I'd like to come back to my place. Well, it appeared I didn't have an emergency haven; I had tenants…with a lease. I pouted all Sunday about that.

My foul mood continued Monday when I met Heather for lunch.

"Listen, you got three callbacks," she informed me after we were seated. I beamed, pleased, until we were handed menus and she added critically, "You better just have a salad. You've put on weight, haven't you?"

"A little. It's cold in South Dakota," I muttered in self-defense. "I haven't gained that much."

"Aren't you just about finished with this marriage thing?" Heather demanded. "If you want a career in the Business you better get your ass back to where the Business is."

"I know, I know," I said, feeling harassed. Was I finished with the marriage thing? Maybe I should stay in Los Angeles. But how? And where?

Les seemed resigned when I told her about the callbacks. I think she was getting sick of me hanging around all the time, pouting and hogging her car. I didn't blame her. She still objected to me going to a hotel so I insisted on at least renting a sub-compact. It was an automatic so I still paddled with my left foot but I could park the damn thing. That Volvo was too much for me.

After all the interviews and callbacks I got one lousy job.

"I expected more. But it's a hair commercial and you'll be the spokesperson," Heather said philosophically. "This could really lead to something so you quit eating, you hear me?"

I didn't have much appetite anyway. I wondered if Rob thought about me at all. Probably not. I bet his brother had spent the week trying to convince him to dump me and it probably didn't take much convincing. Panic was setting in. The only job I'd gotten would be over in two days and Rob hadn't even tried to call me. I'd manufactured a scenario in my feverish little brain that he didn't even want me to come home. He obviously didn't care about me one little bit. I didn't know where to go or what to do.

It was time to confide in Leslie and Peter so I sat them down and gave them the saga of my fledgling marriage. I described the fistfight—Peter's eyebrows really went up when I told that story. I bitched about the omnipresent Andersons, about Rob agreeing to a ski trip on my behalf without consulting me. I told them about the seemingly constant tension and misunderstandings.

When I finished Leslie was staring at me with her mouth open. "My God, you've been busy the last few months. I thought you might run into…well, a racial thing but that's the only thing you've missed."

"You know, Alice made a little comment about a piñata. And one old aunt made a crack about me being a Mexican," I said, more than willing to add racism to the list of Anderson sins. I omitted my own little indiscretion in that area.

Peter shook his head slowly and said in a lawyerly way, "If you only had two comments in four months, I don't think your ancestry is a big problem. It's just easy ammunition in a family spat. Frankly, the Andersons sound surprisingly benign. I would have expected much worse just because you're an outsider. My father said if in-laws didn't hate you for one thing they'd hate you for another, that's what in-laws do."

I blinked at this bleak little pronouncement but Leslie laughed and squeezed his arm. "We won't have problems like this, will we. I bet I'll be able to wind your family around my little finger."

From the look on Peter's face I doubted Leslie would find Peter's genetic attachments so easy to charm. Peter quickly brought the conversation back to my problems.

"Rick sounds like a classic control freak and a bit of a spoiled brat. What's unusual is his place in the family; I'd expect someone who acted that way to be the baby of the family but he's not, is he?"

"No, Rob is," I said. "But I think Rob was an accident. There's a six-year difference between them."

"That explains it," Peter said judiciously. "Rick was the baby for a long time. I suppose he's still jealous of his brother for being an interloper. And Rob brought another one home. This Rick character must be feeling quite threatened."

"I don't care what he's feeling," I said. "I don't like him and I wish I could stay away from him."

"You're in tough position," Peter said sympathetically. "Sounds like Rob is, too."

"I know," I agreed fervently. "And, honestly, I don't want to get between Rob and his family; I don't think I could if I wanted to. But, jeez, they're driving me nuts!"

Peter switched gears. "Let's talk about the positives of the relationship," he said. "What do you like about Rob?"

I thought for a minute and admitted grudgingly, "Well, the sex is still good—when we get around to it. His schedule has been pretty hectic."

Peter said we needed to have a dialogue and suggested I call Rob, which I absolutely refused to do.

"We had a 'dialogue' after the fight and I guess it didn't do any good. And if Rob cared at all he'd have called me." I sighed. "You know, I thought the worst of our problems were behind us. And I was just getting into winter. All the good stuff was starting. I even got a part-time teaching job but now I don't know if I should even go back. I know I can't stay here" (Leslie looked alarmed at the thought) "but my condo is leased out," I said forlornly. "I'm too fat to get any acting work, my husband doesn't give a crap about me, and I don't know what to do." This last sounded so pathetic even to me that I sighed.

Les and Peter commiserated with me until they went off to bed together. I stared after them enviously. I didn't even have Pudgy to comfort me.

My commercial job replaced Rob as a reason for depression; after the first day of shooting I was ready to either slit my wrists or take up typing. The director seemed to think that I was personally responsible for all the problems on the set. He was particularly irritated with me when a problem with the lighting developed. After the forty-second take he threw his hands up because of a recurring shadow. "Get her out of there and fix those lights," he bawled and stalked off angrily.

The makeup lady clucked sympathetically as she wiped sweat off my face and reapplied base and powder. "Try not to sweat, honey," she whispered. "It smears the makeup and you don't want to make the director any madder than he is."

Like the shadow was my fault? This wasn't a career, it was punishment. I wasn't being paid enough to take this abuse.

I was exhausted and dreading the following day when I dragged myself back to Leslie's. She and Peter were waiting for me looking like co-conspirators. I took a moment to savagely ask myself why Peter even bothered to pay rent on an apartment; he never even saw the place.

"I know I probably shouldn't have," Les said when I looked at them questioningly, "but I called Rob today." I just stood there staring at them. Leslie must have thought I was mad because she hurried on. "Now before you start yelling let me tell you what he said. He told me that he'd just gotten home from his trip and didn't even know you were so unhappy."

I had to sit down at that. How could he not know I was miserable? Was I in this relationship by myself? Was the man stupid or simply trying to drive me insane?

Leslie interrupted my reverie to say, "Rob admitted that there'd been a slight misunderstanding about the ski trip but he'd thought you'd settled it. He's going to call tonight and get things all straightened out. Now, go ahead and yell." She sat back smiling smugly and Peter patted her hand in approval.

I was digesting this tidbit when the phone rang, right on cue. Leslie answered and handed the phone to me. "It's your husband," she said then pulled Peter from the room so I could have some privacy.

I wasn't sure what to say so I asked cautiously, "Rob? Did you have a good time skiing?"

"No, the kids screamed the whole time and everybody fought about chores and money. Rick showed up about three days into it mad because he hadn't been invited. Marilyn absolutely refused to do all the cooking. She called us a bunch of pigs and flew home five days ago. She left the kids with us. It was awful."

I got a warm glow hearing about his miserable ski trip. I felt so good I didn't even say 'I told you so'. I had my own woes to confide. "It's not so good here either. Leslie is sick to death of me and I don't blame her. And the city is dirty and smelly and crowded and everybody thinks I'm fat. The director hates me and I miss my cat," I said tiredly.

Rob asked, "So when are you coming home?"

"I don't know if I should," I blurted. "I don't think you treat me very well."

"If it makes you feel any better Marilyn agrees with you," Rob said, discomfort shading his words. "Before she walked out she told me I should have asked you if you wanted to come before setting the trip up."

"That's just part of it, Rob," I said tiredly. "I'm tired of spending all my Sundays with your family. I just don't get along with...well, you know. It's stressful."

Rob paused in thought then admitted, "You know, we never spent every week together before I left South Dakota. I guess Mom is glad to have us all close to home again but, to tell you the truth, I'm tired of it myself. I'd rather spend the time studying or with you but I hate to hurt Mom's feelings."

"You can go every week if you want," I offered. "I don't want to cause trouble for you."

"No, no," Rob said quickly. I could hear alarm in his voice. "Mike doesn't come every week and nobody yells at him. I guess it's because he lives in Sioux Falls. Well, it's my problem and I'll deal with it. I just wish you'd talked to me first instead of telling our business to strangers."

This from the man who told his mother about our difficulties! "I told you all this but you don't seem to hear me, Rob," I retorted. "Besides, Leslie isn't a stranger. Thank God she interfered; if she hadn't we probably wouldn't be talking now."

So we made a deal; I offered to cheerfully attend one Sunday dinner a month with the Andersons. Rob matched my offer by volunteering to show me more consideration. He added that he'd cut down his own appearances at the family functions.

"Only if you want to," I said cautiously. "How are you going to explain this to your mother?"

"I don't know," Rob admitted. "But I'll think of something. When are you coming home?"

"Well..." I said hesitantly, making him wait. I didn't want to sound too easy. But I didn't want to sound too tough either. "As soon as this commercial is done," I said abruptly. "I want to see what winter is like." When I hung up Leslie sidled back into her living room, Peter in tow.

I smiled, relieved. "He wants me to come home."

"Of course he does," said Leslie. "Anything else?"

223

"He said he had a horrible time skiing. Isn't that great? I'm going home as soon as this commercial is in the can." I smiled at Leslie. "You get your place back day after tomorrow. Guess I better pack and book a flight."

Peter offered to call the airline and Leslie said happily, "We'll have to go out tomorrow night to celebrate," she said.

"Yeah, I'm finally getting out from underfoot," I snorted.

"That's not what I meant."

"I know. But I have been a pain. I stayed too long and picked my emotional scabs most of the time. You're a saint for putting up with me." I looked up at her. "I never thought I'd say this to anyone but thanks for interfering. Tell you what, let me treat you and Peter to that Italian place. I promise not to barf this time."

I found it interesting that as happy as I was to come to Los Angeles I was even happier to be going back to the Great Plains. When the nasty director started screeching about his technical problems again I coldly told him to quit yelling at me; the only thing I was responsible for was a line reading and if he didn't like the way I performed he should take it up with the client. I wasn't taking crap from nobody, no how, no more. We exchanged stares but he blinked first. If I'd had a revolver I'd have blown the smoke from the barrel.

That night the restaurant was charming, the food was wonderful, Peter's lecture was interesting and I ignored the drooling and pawing going on across from me. I didn't even blanche much when I got the bill. I just swallowed, smiled, and pulled out a credit card. One more night and I was Outback bound.

I was in such a hurry to get home I tried pushing the plane with my butt as it took off. When it landed in Sioux Falls I had to take a moment to compose myself. I didn't want to look too eager. I coolly walked into the terminal to see Rob waiting. *He was a lot better looking than Peter,* I thought critically as I approached him, then quit thinking when Rob grabbed me and swung me around in a fierce hug. The undemonstrative natives watched us curiously but Rob didn't seem to care.

"Don't you ever leave like that again," Rob ordered. "If you get mad, tell me, we'll work it out somehow. I'd rather you threw something at me than walk out on me."

It wasn't the abject apology I was thinking I should hold out for but it was better than nothing. "I'll keep a supply of books handy," I promised.

We held hands as we waited for my luggage then Rob shepherded me protectively to the Buick. He seemed to be back in love. *If all it took was a week off I'd leave more often,* I thought as I stared out the car window. The Christmas snow had melted and the landscape was brown and unappetizing. But the sky was clouding up and Rob told me a storm was on the way. I smiled in anticipation.

Pudgy woke up briefly when I climbed into the trailer and I scratched her ears before she crankily readjusted herself for sleep. I looked around philosophically. It wasn't my L.A. condo but it wasn't a life sentence either. I could stand a few more months of it.

I went into the bedroom to unpack and got solid proof that Rob had missed me; ten days worth of laundry was piled high. No wonder he wanted me back; he must have been running out of underwear. But I was philosophical about the laundry issue, too. This was just one more problem we'd iron out together. Pun intended.

chapter 18

When I woke up Sunday morning a gale force wind was rocking the trailer on its foundations. A blizzard is a whole different animal from the gentle snowfall I'd enjoyed at Christmas.

"Good thing I got the plastic on the windows," Rob commented from the other side of the bed.

I had to agree. The plastic may have looked like hell but it kept the wind from blowing unimpeded into the bedroom. I just hoped it didn't get blown off. Problem was I couldn't see outside and I was curious. I padded to the living room and opened the front door a crack to peek outside. The wind almost ripped the door off the hinges and the glimpse of swirling white I got as I wrestled with the wind to close the door chilled me to the bone. I crawled back into bed to get warm.

"No way am I going anywhere today," I announced firmly and wrapped myself around Rob.

Rob screamed briefly then arranged the covers around us. "We're both in for the day," he agreed. "There isn't any point to shoveling until the snow stops."

Other people probably would have made love in a situation like that. Well, we did that, too, but then we got to the important stuff; we talked money. I told Rob that my condo tenants wanted to buy the place but he agreed that I should wait to sell until things were more settled with us.

"We'd have to buy other property in a year to avoid the capital gains," Rob said. "Who knows where we'll be in a year. Better not start the tax clock until we have to."

I told him about the spokesperson job. "Even if I just get holding fees, with my other commercial jobs, it'll still ensure my SAG benefits for the next year. Oh, and I added you to my medical insurance. It's free because you're my husband. So we're both covered."

Rob blushed. "I think I'm still covered under my dad's policy."

"Well, if you want to stay with that..." I interrupted hurriedly, afraid I'd overstepped myself.

"No, this is better," he said. "It's just that I'm supposed to be taking care of you not the other way around." He brooded for a minute. "I should have been the one to worry about insurance. I'm not a little kid anymore."

I squirmed. I'd agreed to the auditions because they were a good excuse to run away from home, the insurance was just a side benefit, but I couldn't tell him that so I smiled uncomfortably. "I guess we both need improvement."

"No, I'm at fault here."

"No, no, no, we've both made mistakes."

We did our wretched Warner Brothers rodent routine again: "No, no, no, after you, I insist! Oh no, no, no, after you!" And smiled at each other affecttionately.

"How about if I make pancakes for breakfast," Rob offered.

Not being a complete idiot I took him up on it. "If you do the cooking, you get to pick what we watch on TV," I said, just to be fair. Of course, Rob decided on football. It was the playoffs, for God's sake, whatever that meant. "You'll have to explain the game to me," I warned.

"What don't you understand?" he asked.

"Everything," I said. "You can start by telling me what a down is."

He looked at me like I'd come from another planet. "You don't even know what a down is?"

"Nope."

So he went into a long, involved dissertation about yardage and punting and scrimmage. I didn't understand any of the jargon but he was having such a good time pontificating I didn't interrupt. He lectured while he made pancakes, while we ate pancakes, and while we cleaned up. And it made absolutely no sense to me.

"Just watch," he finally said. "You'll catch on."

I doubted it but I curled up next to Rob on the couch. The action

227

was the usual unintelligible mess but by halftime I was starting to put things together.

"I think I've got it," I said to Rob. "Each team gets four chances to go ten yards and each chance is called a down. Is that right?"

"That's basically it," Rob agreed, pleased. "I must be a pretty good teacher."

I humphed. My great brain should be given the credit not his garbled explanation. As a woman, I was capable of solving all sorts of mysteries without much help—sometimes I even made up mysteries just to keep in practice. Rob was pretty lousy at communicating which I considered a guy thing but I didn't tell him that. He was happy with his nonexistent power of articulation and I was learning that sometimes it's better not to insist on the last word even though you think you might pop.

The blizzard had blown over the next day and the sun was out—from what I could tell through the plastic. I was eager to be out and about. The semester had started and I had places to go and things to do, for a change. My classes met on Tuesdays and Thursdays but I needed to organize my office and meet my colleagues. No more hanging out at the public library for me.

I turned on the radio as I made toast and juice to get a handle on the day and was informed that the temperature outside was twenty degrees below zero.

"Did you hear on the radio that parents shouldn't let kids run outside?" I asked Rob when he sat down at the kitchen table and poured himself some cereal. "Is this some new form of Protestant repression?"

"No," said Rob with strained patience. "If the kids run when it's this cold their lungs will freeze and they'll get pneumonia." He gave me a patronizing look.

"I knew that," I mumbled around my mouthful of toast.

Rob looked at me skeptically but didn't take time to argue. He chugged his juice, stuck toast in his mouth, grabbed his parka and looked at me. "You ready to go?"

"Just need to get my coat," I said and ran to the bedroom to get it. I checked myself out in the mirror before Rob's impatient bellow hurried me along. I made a fetching appearance in wool slacks, a short ski jacket, a cashmere scarf, and leather gloves; little treats I'd gotten myself while in California. Rob took one look at me and said firmly, "I'm not letting you out of the house dressed like that."

"What's wrong?" I asked, too startled by the comment to be hurt.

"You'll freeze to death," he explained. He rummaged through the closet until he found one of his old parkas, a knit cap, and heavy gloves. He let me keep the cashmere scarf.

He bundled me up and stood back to inspect his work. "You look like Nanook of Los Angeles," he grinned, "but you shouldn't get frostbite. Make sure you don't run now."

"I can hardly walk in this getup," I mumbled through the layers but I kept them on. I'd never been in sub-zero weather. Rob was a native; he might for once know what he was talking about.

We went out in the blazing sunshine and brisk wind to our respective cars. The Buick roared to life instantly but the Miata didn't even turn over. My little sports car was frozen solid. Rob graciously took full blame for that.

"I should have checked the antifreeze and rigged an outlet. I'm sorry, Stevie," he said, chagrined.

"An outlet? What are you talking about?"

"The battery freezes," Rob began his explanation happily. Two lectures in two days! Rob must have been in guy heaven. I didn't understand much of what he said but I'll paraphrase as closely as I can. There was something about a volt charger that attaches to the battery and must be plugged in. I just nodded along, shivering, until he was done. Then I asked the important question.

"So what do we do now?" I asked.

"I'll work on your car this weekend," he said. "We better get some snow tires, too. You'll just have to ride with me 'til then."

Man, you had to be tough to live in this climate. I gladly got in the heated Buick and out of the wind. I thought about Heather's cracks about my weight and smiled grimly. I may have been fat in Los Angeles but here my little size five body didn't have enough padding to withstand the bone-chilling cold no matter how many sweaters and coats I put on. I'd need an extra layer of blubber just to survive.

Rob dropped me off at the Speech and Theatre Building and I trotted inside to warm my hands on a cup of coffee. The rest of the staff was assembled for a "welcome aboard" meeting. Dr. Torgeson took the floor, introduced me, and explained that I'd just gotten back from Hollywood (wink, wink) and would everybody stand up and introduce themselves? The staff stood up to say their names and tell what they'd done over Christmas vacation. I listened carefully, smiled dutifully, and promptly forgot all the names. Dr. Torgeson I knew of course, but there were eleven full-time professors and ten graduate assistants. All members were equally divided between the Speech discipline and Theater/ Film arts. They were equally divided gender-wise, too, which I thought was pretty egalitarian. The department secretary, Margy, a cherubic, middle-aged lady, was shared by everybody.

I was surrounded by friendly faces so I smiled and nodded pleasantly. Then Dr. Torgeson told me where my office would be.

"As everyone knows," he started, "we have limited office space. Our grad students are already doubled up so you'll have to share office space with a teacher. I knew Miss Fennig wouldn't mind sharing so we've put a desk in her office for you. After all," he finished jovially, "we all know how you girls like to talk. I'm sure you'll enjoy each other's company."

I winced at the 'girls'. He'd been doing so well, too. I looked in the direction of his pointing finger and the wall of friendly faces parted to expose Miss Fennig. She was a large young woman with long highlighted blond hair and wire-rim glasses. If she'd been wearing Birkenstocks and had hairy legs—and for all I knew she did; she was wearing pants so it was hard to tell—she'd have fit in perfectly at Berkeley. Or Woodstock. Dr. Torgeson's assumption that she wouldn't mind sharing her office with me appeared erroneous; those granny glasses were shooting death bolts at me.

Dr. Torgeson concluded the meeting and escorted me to 'my' office. The room was divided down the middle. Our respective sides each had a desk, an office chair, a visitor's chair, and an empty bookcase. Miss Fennig's stuff was piled and jumbled on her side but my side was virgin territory. I was faintly surprised not to see a yellow police line running down the center of the room.

Dr. Torgeson, blithely unaware that anything could be wrong, wished me luck and left me alone to organize my books and plans. I was twirling around in my chair taking stock of the situation when Miss Fennig stalked in. She slammed her books down on her desk and flounced into her chair. I knew she was mad, I'm not stupid, but I did my best to ignore her. She knew that I was trying to ignore her so she redoubled her efforts to display displeasure. She opened her desk drawers and slammed them shut. She picked up books and dropped them.

"Something troubling you?" I asked innocently.

She slammed another drawer, glared at me, and growled, "You're damn right something's troubling me. This is my office. I worked hard to get it. I'm working on a PhD! Do you have a PhD?" I shook my head. "I didn't think so," she said cuttingly. "Just because I'm a woman and I'm the newest member of the staff I have to give up my office. You're not even full-time. And you teach acting! Acting, for God's sake! That's the most ridiculous, useless thing I've ever heard of."

She ranted on but I tuned her out to give this problem some thought. If I were in her position I'd resent sharing my office, too. Not only was it inconvenient but it made her seem inferior to her peers. I'd felt sorry for her until she started flogging me and that last crack really pissed me off. Sharing her office hadn't been my idea, after all, and there wasn't anything I could do about it. Yelling at me was not only counter-productive; it was dumb.

"You have a problem, take it up with Dr. Torgeson," I said evenly, trying to hold on to my temper.

"Oh sure. Like he's going to listen to anything I say. He thinks you're a movie star. That's all he talks about. He thinks it's a big deal that you've been on TV. Like that's important."

Shooting a few commercials might not be up there with winning the Nobel Prize but I was the only person allowed to denigrate my accomplishments. I opened a desk drawer and slammed it to get her attention. "Miss Fennig. I'm sorry I have to share my office with you," I started.

"It's my office. You're sharing with me," she corrected nastily.

"Whatever. You have no idea how sorry I am to be here with you. But it wasn't my idea. If you have a serious complaint take it to someone who can do something about it. I'm not interested in your tantrums." I grabbed one of my books and jammed it in my bookcase for emphasis. "And I'll tell you another thing; I'm not interested in your opinions about my subject and qualifications either. I have an MFA. That's a Master of Fine Arts. We have to actually perform, not write silly, boring dissertations that are only read by other silly, boring people." Uh oh, I was treading on shaky ground here. I didn't want Miss Fennig telling the other professors that I thought they were silly and boring. I reined myself in and got ready for a grand exit. I stood up and pushed my desk chair out of my way. "And before you start trashing my profession let me ask you this: When was the last time a speech teacher became President?"

Okay, it was weak but I hadn't had time to prepare a real crusher. I swept out. Unfortunately, I didn't have anywhere to go. I wandered out to the lobby and inspected the bookshelves.

"Everything all right?" Margy asked helpfully from her station.

"Not really," I said back as cheerfully as I could. I didn't want to go back into my...oops, our office until Fennig left, I couldn't hang out in the lobby forever, and I wasn't sure where the bathroom was. I didn't have any classes scheduled today and I didn't quite know what to do with myself. "I think I'll go home and get some boxes of books," I finally said to Margy. "Here's my phone number if anyone wants me."

I worked my way into my cap, scarf, gloves, and parka. Rob had the car and I didn't want to pull him out of class even supposing I could find him. Oh well, the walk in sub-zero weather would probably cool me off.

I almost froze to death. Every block I had to stop at a store or gas station until I got feeling back in my toes. At my fourth stop a laconic gas station attendant looked at my teary eyes and commented, "Cold, ain't it."

I agreed heartily and stamped my feet. The attendant watched me for a minute then said. "Bobby shouldn't let you walk outside like this. What with the wind chill and all, it's about eighty below."

I looked at him in surprise. "You know who I am?"

"Yup, seen you on TV. I went to school with Bobby." I guess he figured that his name was unnecessary because he didn't bother to tell me what it was. He took a good look at my red nose and wet eyes and said, "Too bad I'm alone here. I'd drive you home."

"That's okay," I said. "It's only a few more blocks."

"Well, you tell Bobby not to let you walk on days like this."

I thanked him for his concern and trudged on. By the time I got to the alley my cashmere scarf was stuck to my face by frozen snot. It was barely nine o'clock and already it'd been one bitch of a day. I cleaned the bathroom so I didn't feel like it had been completely wasted.

Tuesday was better. I had the Buick and dropped Rob off instead of the other way around.

"You shouldn't have been walking in such cold," he remonstrated when I told him my sad story.

"Some guy at the corner gas station told me to tell you that."

"Must have a been Lyle. I went..."

"Yeah, yeah. You went to school with him," I finished for him wearily.

I'd gotten to the office early and had my bookshelves full and papers scattered around my territory before it was time for my first class. Fortunately, my classes were in the building so I didn't have to wander around like a lost soul looking for my students.

"Good luck," Margy called out as I headed upstairs. I smiled a distracted 'thank you'; I had a bad case of stage fright.

Twenty kids had registered for Acting 101 and they were a real mixed bag. I had four football players who explained that they were Physical Education majors and needed an easy A to fulfill their liberal arts requirement; a cultural "jock" course, as it were.

There were two serious theater types who wore unrelieved black and supercilious expressions. The girl, Joan, even wore black fingernail polish. I imagine Andrew, the boy, would have worn polish, too, if he hadn't been afraid of getting beat up. I wondered if I should tell them that Jack Keruoac had died years ago and perhaps it was best to let him rest in peace.

Joan coolly informed me that she and Andrew had discussed the possible value of my class. "We heard that you were a Hollywood actress and everybody knows all the true artists are in New York," she patronized me and Andrew nodded his Byronesque head in agreement. "But we decided that maybe we could learn something from you."

I smiled evilly at her. I thought about telling la faux Bernhardt that most of those noble New York types bust their butts to get to L.A. once they get a union card so they could get some money but decided to save it for later. I knew one thing for sure; these little shits were going to have to work their artistic asses off to get a grade in my course.

The rest of the class were the blond, blue-eyed, passive specimens I'd grown used to, not a spark of intelligence or curiosity apparent in the bunch. How the hell was I going to loosen these kids up? I found out later that South Dakota students, for the most part, were like army privates; they never volunteered or drew attention to themselves until you earned their respect and trust, then they bloomed like little flowers in the sun. Unfortunately, the sunshine of my brilliance had not filtered down to them yet.

I made a little speech about course requirements, the text they would need, the number of scenes required for class presentation, essays to be written, etc. I also told them that they would have to audition for University productions; being cast wasn't required but they had to try. And that I'd be at the auditions to make sure their efforts were sincere.

The biggest football player raised his hand. "My advisor told me there wouldn't be any written work," he said plaintively.

"Your advisor was wrong," I said.

"But nobody said anything about auditioning for a play!"

"If it's too much for you drop the class. Better now than later, don't you think?"

He looked unhappy but stayed in his seat. I wondered if I'd ever see him again.

I spent the rest of the period teaching them theater games. We pushed the chairs against the wall and walked in a circle imitating animals. We played horsy, we played doggy, we played frog. The point of the exercise was to loosen them up and laugh a little. Acting was supposed to be fun, after all. Joan never cracked a smile.

We got to chimpanzee and Joan's chimp looked like it had misogenated with a stork. "C'mon Joan, lighten up," I urged.

"Theater is supposed to be serious," she said with dignity.

What this girl needed was a pie in the face.

My reluctant gridiron hero, Brian, was surprisingly good once he got into the spirit of the thing. He seemed to have a tremendous sense of humor. If he stayed with the class I'd try to develop that.

We finished with 'Mirror' and I gave the assignment for the next class. I told them to pair off and start looking for scenes. "The library is a good place to start but if you're having trouble my office hours are posted," I announced as the bell rang.

My virgin cruise was over and I was unsunk. Miss Fennig wasn't in 'our' office when I returned so I rattled around aimlessly before going to the Student Union for lunch. The Union was on the other end of the campus so I bundled up and trudged across the great frozen waste. The temperature outside had reached its high of 0 degrees and I mentally cursed the local population for building out not up. That's what happens when you have wide open spaces to spread out in. You do. Spread out, I mean.

I ate my salad and observed the usual tall, blond types. Then I opened my eyes and my mind. I saw some black students, some American Indians, Asians, older people…I don't where these folks came from but they seemed perfectly comfortable. I quit feeling like a foreigner.

My afternoon class was a repeat of the morning, minus my two art farts. I wasn't as nervous and things went well. I was going to enjoy teaching again.

I went back to my office to find Miss Fennig writing busily. I looked at her warily and sat at my desk facing her. She looked up from her writing and I braced myself for an onslaught. She surprised me by smiling and extending her hand.

"Hi, my name's Linda. I was awful to you yesterday and I want to start over."

I shook her hand. She didn't have a joy buzzer. "I'm Stephanie O'Neill."

"I know," she said impatiently. "Listen, I want to apologize for the way I acted. I was a real bitch."

Did she expect an argument? I pushed a legal pad around on my desk and Linda smiled wryly. "Thanks for not agreeing with me," she said.

Ahhh man, I suppose now I had to forgive and forget. "Well…I can understand why you were upset. You're staff and I'm just part-time help. I'd resent having to share an office, too," I offered and mentally polished my halo.

Miss Fennig…Linda smiled gratefully. Funny, she no longer looked like a Woodstock throwback. Her glasses winked warmly and, damn, she really had pretty hair.

"It's just so shitty for women. We get paid less, we have to work harder, and when there's a sacrifice to be made, who do they come to? 'Us girls'," she mimicked with bitterness. "I haven't had a roommate since I was an undergrad."

"We can eat fudge and talk about boys," I suggested brightly.

"Let me buy you a beer instead. I'll fill you in on everybody in the department."

I remembered I had Rob's Buick and didn't know how to reach him. "I'd love to," I told Linda, "but I have my husband's car. He's supposed to meet me here to get a ride home."

"Leave the keys with Margy," Linda suggested. "I'll drive you home myself."

That's just what I did.

"We have a pretty decent bunch in the department," Linda began once we'd settled in a downtown bar. "Dr. Torgeson is really one hell of a nice guy despite what I said yesterday. He keeps slipping up and calling us 'girls' but it's a generational thing, not political. I'll say one thing, if you get into trouble you can count on him to go to bat for you. And he's doing his best to equalize the salary issue. I feel bad about sounding so snitty about him..." she trailed off but I just shrugged. "I know Torgeson can't help the lack of space; the Speech Department isn't very important to the Regents," she continued, "but his assumption that I wouldn't mind sharing irritated me. And being called a 'girl' on top of it..." she waved her hand. "But on the whole, you couldn't ask for a better department head," she concluded.

"And the others?" I asked.

She shrugged. "They're mostly decent people. Oh! Be careful around Dr. Muehler. He teaches the TV courses and he's got a reputation for being pretty 'handy'." She waggled her fingers at me.

I made a face. "There's one in every bunch. Has he bothered you?"

"Are you kidding? I'd break him in half! No. He specializes in the pretty female students."

I was shocked. "That's terrible! Why don't they get rid of him?"

Linda sighed. "This isn't California, Stephanie. If a girl ever complained she'd probably be branded as a slut and expelled. And nothing would happen to Muehler. Oh, maybe the Elks would throw him a breakfast and feel sorry for him."

"Linda, that's terrible!" I repeated.

"The kids protect each other. There's one hell of an undergrad network here. Not many girls take his classes and those that do travel in pairs. And word of Muehler's shenanigans have filtered up to Dr. Torgeson. Margy told me she overheard Torgeson tell Muehler that if there were any more rumors of student affairs, Muehler would have to take an early retirement and sell aluminum siding. If you ever want to get filled in on something, ask Margy. She knows everything."

"An office gossip. Neat," I said derisively.

"Margy's on our side. She only told me about the Torgeson/Muehler meeting because she's afraid that Muehler will go after me now that students are off limits. I'm telling you because you're even more of a target than I am; you're pretty, you're part-time, and you're an actress. Reputation for looseness, you know. You want another beer?"

Over a second beer we worked out office hours so they wouldn't conflict and Linda condescendingly offered to give me some teaching tips. The beer had mellowed me considerably so I just grinned at her. "I've had a couple years teaching experience. I don't think I need any advice," I said.

Linda had the grace to blush. "I didn't mean..."

"That's okay," I interrupted. "Listen, I better get home. The old man'll be wondering what happened to me."

We drank up and Linda drove me home. She dropped me off at the mouth of the alley and Rob opened the door as I trudged up the steps.

"You didn't walk home again, did you?" he asked, concerned.

"Linda Fennig and I went for a beer. She dropped me off on the street. Have you eaten yet? How about soup and a sandwich? I'm not very hungry after two beers."

"Is this the colleague you wanted to murder yesterday?" he asked as he hovered over the sandwich preparation.

"That's the one," I agreed. "We got our differences straightened out. And my classes went pretty well, too."

I gave him a detailed description of my day as the soup heated. Rob laughed and frowned in all the right spots. Either I was more entertaining than usual or, could it be, was it possible...?

"Did you miss me today?" I asked as I tripped over him.

"Well...yeah," he admitted. "It seemed, oh, kinda empty not to have you here when I got home. Like when you went to California."

The moral of this story is: Men can't miss you if you don't go away; absence makes the heart grow fonder; men appreciate you more if they have to wait for their dinner or make it themselves. Whatever. Pick one.

chapter 19

It was only the third week in January and there'd been two more blizzards followed by bone-chilling cold. I didn't know which was worse, the storm or the clear cold days. I'd wanted to experience winter and I had. I was ready for spring.

"This won't last much longer, will it?" I asked forlornly.

"Until March," Rob said.

"Oh man," I moaned.

At least my car was back in service. The battery had been thawed and snow tires had been installed. I got a little lecture about winter driving.

"Make sure you wash your car at least once a week," Rob instructed. "The City" (Brookings a City? Talk about illusions of grandeur!) "salts the roads."

"Salts?" I asked skeptically.

"Yeah, it melts the ice but it'll destroy the paint on your car. Wash the car or it'll get leprosy."

I was suffering biblical punishments for no good reason. Not only was the climate unpleasant I found out that, contrary to all Rob's assurances, the family situation remained unresolved. I discovered this when Alice called Saturday afternoon to ask about my health.

"How's your cold, Stephanie?" she asked, concern in her voice.

"Cold?" I repeated and looked sharply at Rob. He'd looked startled when I picked up the phone and greeted his mother, now he positively cringed. I decided to have pity and cover for him. "Oh, my cold, it's much better," I lied smoothly.

"Good. We missed you at dinner last Sunday. I just wanted to make sure you could make it tomorrow."

"Mmmm," I murmured neutrally and changed the subject. When she finally hung up I looked accusingly at Rob. "That was your mother. She expects us for dinner after church tomorrow."

Rob positively squirmed. "Well, you said you'd go once a month."

"You haven't talked to her, have you?"

"Well, she cries…"

"I'm going to have to tell her, aren't I."

Rob smiled at me shamefacedly. "Would you mind?"

It was finally sinking into my thick skull that Rob felt caught between his mother and me. I wondered what I'd do if my mother had lived to put the screws to Rob. I'd probably have told her off but let's face it, Rob and I were different people; and he had a living mother whereas I just had a marker. He probably should be nice to her while he could. Okay, I'd be the bad guy. The only problem I had was when and how. Timing and tone are so important.

I was mentally preparing my big announcement during the church service when Alice stood up to pray for my improving health. At least that's what I hope she was referring to. "Now that my daughter-in-law Stephanie's back from California let's all pray that she feels better," she prayed loudly.

There're all sorts of ways you could take that prayer. I looked at her suspiciously but she just beamed down at me.

"Lord hear our prayer," the congregation droned.

Dinner was almost a repeat of my first supper with the Andersons. Marilyn wanted to hear all about the commercial I'd shot, the restaurants I'd gone to, the clothes I'd bought. I looked around the table and could tell from looks on the faces of Rick and Nancy that they wanted to hear about the disappointments and dangers. I refused to give them any satisfaction…so I lied. I told Marilyn that everything had been wonderful; the days I hadn't been fawned over and feted I'd gone to the beach and luxuriated in the sun (nobody noticed my lack of a tan). For the benefit of the envious ill wishers I said that everything in Los Angeles had been perfect and that I missed it already. The reactions to my monologue were predictable. Marvin, Tom, Mike, and Rob ignored everything going on around them and ate determinedly, Alice ran and fetched, Chris watched her plate silently, Marilyn drank in every word, Nancy interrupted periodically with snide remarks about "women selling their bodies", Rick sat at his end of the table looking envious, and the kids screamed from the kitchen. I kept my intestinal fortitude by repeating to myself that this was the last supper—for at least three weeks—and lied like a rug until dessert.

"I wish I'd gone with you instead of the Hills," Marilyn said enviously. "I guess you heard how that turned out." She turned to glare at Mike who hunkered over his food.

"If L.A.'s so wonderful, I'm surprised you didn't stay," Rick commented nastily.

I smiled. Rick was making my withdrawal from this loving family circle too easy. I glanced at Rob to see how he was taking this across-the-table sniping but he was concentrating on his plate like it was a life preserver. Well, this was my fight, not his. I could and would handle this in my own way.

I made my declaration of independence as we women were cleaning up. The men, as usual, were comatose in the living room with a football game blaring on the TV. I was washing dishes, Marilyn was drying, Alice was putting away, Chris was sitting silently at the kitchen table, and Nancy was chasing her sons out of the kitchen.

"Don't set a place for me next Sunday, Alice," I announced casually. "With my new job and everything I'm getting sort of backed up. I need the time to catch up."

I thought my opening gambit was a marvel of tact but Alice looked like I'd punched her.

"But what will you do? What will you eat?" she stammered.

I smiled at her. "Alice, I have a kitchen, too."

"I'm cooking anyway, why can't you come here?" she continued, starting to look panicked.

"Besides, Sunday's the time for family," Nancy contributed piously.

I'd tried tact and that didn't work so I decided to try honesty. I took a deep breath. "Alice, I can't take all the insults and abuse on a weekly basis."

Marilyn grimaced and nodded in agreement but Alice looked honestly bewildered. "But who's insulted you?" she asked.

Marilyn and I exchanged a disbelieving glance. Hadn't Alice just been at the same dinner table with us? I was back in the *Twilight Zone*.

"Didn't you hear Nancy and Rick?" I demanded.

Nancy puffed herself up self-righteously and stated, "I didn't say one thing that wasn't true."

Alice waved her hand to quiet her. "Oh, that was just you kids squabbling. You can't take that seriously. Now I won't hear any more of it. I'll set a place for you and Bobby next week same as always."

"You can set the place but I won't be here," I said evenly. Alice started to expostulate but I stopped her with a soapy hand. "I'll be happy to come once a month but that's the best I can do. I mean, if you even want me once a month," I amended.

The tension of our standoff must have floated out to the living room and cut off the TV reception because I finally noticed all the men crowded into the doorway watching silently.

"Stephanie doesn't want to spend Sunday with us anymore," Alice announced tragically.

"I don't want to spend every Sunday..." I started to explain when Nancy interrupted.

"Don't you worry, Mother Anderson. Tom, the boys, and I will still be here," she said virtuously.

Alice just looked at her. Then she started to cry and ran to her bedroom. Her reaction was so unexpected I stood frozen with my hands in dishwater.

"You made Mom cry!" Rick said accusingly.

"I didn't mean to..." I stammered. I felt terrible. No wonder Rob hadn't wanted to broach this with his mother. An old lady's tears are devastating.

Rick was trembling, his fists were clenching spasmodically, and he seemed to be gathering himself to defend his mother when Marvin said calmly, "Mother cried because she's tired. These weekly dinners take a lot out of her. She's not as young as she used to be although she'd never admit it. She likes having her boys around and she's gotten a little too used to getting her own way." Marvin looked at Rick. "It's the German in her. Hard-headed people." Then he turned to me. "You call her up tomorrow after she's gotten some rest and talk to her then. Everything will be fine."

"Well, okay...I guess I better go," I said uncertainly and wiped my hands.

"Yeah, we better go," Rob said, abruptly joining in. "We both have a lot of work to do. Thank Mom for dinner, will you, Dad? Tell her we'll see her in a few weeks."

We grabbed our coats and scurried out. We passed Chris and the look she gave us was one of pure envy. But she didn't break her silence.

The ride home was quiet. We parked, plugged the car in, ran inside, and unbundled. I grabbed Pudgy and flopped down on the couch, waiting for Rob to yell at me for upsetting his mother. "Well," I started, "that appears to be that." I figured I'd save time and get the fight on the road.

Surprisingly, Rob flopped down next to me. "Yes," he agreed. "It would appear so."

"I didn't mean to make your mother cry," I said cautiously.

"Dad's right, she's just tired. The thought of having just Nancy and Tom around every week is probably what set her off. I know I'd cry if I was faced with them every week," Rob grinned.

"Well, I'll call her tomorrow," I said, still cautious.

"That'd be nice," Rob grunted amiably and settled back with the remote control.

I watched the TV distractedly and stroked Pudgy. "You didn't have to leave with me, you know," I said. "You can still go every Sunday if you want to. I won't be mad."

"I couldn't let you walk home in this cold. And I told you, I need a little distance from them, too. I see Rick for lunch on campus every now and again and that's enough."

I decided to explore the depth of Rob's surprising partisanship. "Do you think Rick's attachment to your Mom is a little weird?" I said.

"Stevie, please don't start in on my brother. He's always been the closest to Mom and they both feel a strong family connection is important. I'm not so sure they're wrong. He was just upset today because Mom was crying. He doesn't mean any harm," Rob sighed. "I stood up for you today; can't you be happy with that?"

This ex-Marine hadn't done anything except follow me out of the house like a scared puppy! I thought about telling him just how limp I considered his imagined support to be but I swallowed and repeated to myself that I didn't really know much about family dynamics, especially between brothers, for obvious reasons. I guess he'd done what he could under the circumstances. At least I had my weekends back. Now all I had to figure out was what to do with the resentment I felt.

I found the perfect outlet the next day. I was in my office, minding my own business, when Muehler, the co-ed coercer, knocked lightly on my door and stepped in without waiting for acknowledgment. I warily watched as he wandered around the office, looked at the notices on the bulletin board and stirred papers around on Linda's desk, all the while asking inane questions like how did I like Brookings? and was I settling in?...stuff like that. I had notes to organize so I pointedly answered in monosyllables and did my best to ignore him. He finished his tour behind my chair.

"Starting in the middle of the year is stressful," he said casually and put his hand on my shoulder. "You're so tense. Let me rub that knot out for you."

Oh man, his come-on was so lame. I coolly plucked his hand from my neck and dropped it. "I prefer not to be touched," I said. My quiet tone seemed to make him think he could bully me.

"I was just being friendly," he blustered, moving in again.

I pushed my chair back and stood to face him. "So was I," I retorted. "You notice I moved your hand, I didn't break it. Now get out of my office, I have work to do."

He was such a putz; I wasn't even mad, just contemptuous. I think that bothered him more than anything. His other victims had probably been frightened and conciliatory; my disdain was unexpected...and I think he found it threatening. He back-pedaled quickly. He huffed that women were always misunderstanding gestures; he'd just meant to be friendly. He puffed that he didn't think I was all that attractive even if everybody else did. I had to stifle a grin at that; if he'd meant to insult me, it backfired.

He concluded with the classic crusher of the loser male, "You're probably a lesbian anyway."

I've stood off armed robbers in my career as a woman. I certainly wasn't going to take shit from a pot-bellied, middle-aged letch.

"You old fart, how dare you waltz into my office and try to paw me! You show your ugly old face in here again and I will break your arm," I said scathingly. Muehler looked skeptically at my five foot five frame. "Well, if I can't, I bet my husband can," I amended. Rob was the biggest pacifist I'd ever met, which is kind of funny considering he's an ex-Marine, but this guy didn't know that. I advanced on Muehler with my stapler in my hand. "Now get your useless carcass out of here. And if I hear of you bothering any women again I'll slap you with a sexual harassment suit so fast it'll leave your bald head spinning!"

He fled leaving me with triumphant possession of the field. *Take that, Rick and all the other assholes of the world*, I said to myself as I sheathed my verbal sword. *Sexual harassers of the world beware; there's a new acting teacher in town*, I proclaimed in silent congratulation.

Of course, everybody in a two-block area heard the entire exchange. And the male professors made the assumption that I was hell on wheels and tended to avoid me for a while although Linda told me the women were behind me 100%. In the battle of the sexes I had moral superiority, righteous wrath, and the X chromosomes on my side.

I didn't tell Rob about my confrontation but he heard about it anyway. "Is it possible you overreacted just a bit?" he asked quietly over dinner.

"Would you rather I waited for him to fondle me?" I asked sarcastically.

"No, no," Rob said hurriedly. "But I know how hot-tempered you are. Maybe you misread the situation."

"I don't think so," I said coldly.

Rob dropped the subject and I fumed. He didn't even ask me what had happened. He just assumed that I'd been in the wrong. I wondered who he'd heard the story from. Probably from one of the 'gentlemen' I worked with. The guys always stuck together, even against their wives. They only got mad when their mothers were involved.

Connie and Gail had heard about the contretemps with Muehler—my God, gossip traveled fast in this town!—and agreed that I'd acted appropriately. They praised my forthrightness and guts when we met to exercise.

"Rob thought I overreacted," I said bitterly.

"Surely he didn't," Connie said.

"Yup, he told me I was hot-tempered and that I probably misread the situation," I said. I didn't think I was misrepresenting Rob. When some man puts unwelcome hands on you anything short of whole-hearted agreement that the SOB should be horsewhipped can be construed as a negative judgment, consequently, a betrayal. "I think he's getting back at me because I told his mother I wouldn't be spending every Sunday with them."

"Really?" Gail asked curiously. "What'd Alice do?"

"She cried. I felt terrible," I admitted.

We wiped our sweaty faces and I ruefully commented that marriage was a lot more complicated than I'd ever thought it would be. I still thought Rob should have been more supportive of me in the Muehler matter but, as Connie tactfully pointed out, not too many women around here had my confrontational style. Rob was probably still getting used to me. She recommended I try to make allowances then changed the subject.

"You know that Chris won't be working out with us anymore," Connie finally said.

"No, I didn't," I said. "I've been under orders to stay away from Chris and she's avoiding me. She didn't even talk to me last Sunday."

Connie digested that for a minute then added, "She also mentioned she was closing the shop."

"Is the pregnancy that hard on her?" I asked.

"It's not the pregnancy, it's the husband," Connie said darkly, her eyes clouded behind her glasses.

"Yeah," agreed Gail, "she's got a bad case of the browbeaten blues." She started to put on her sweat suit. "Chris has got to learn to stand up for herself."

"Rick can't make her give up her shop. She loves puttering with her pots," I argued. When I didn't get any agreement I scoffed, "What can Rick do? Beat her up?" Still no comment. "C'mon. Rick's a domineering asshole but he's not that big a jerk." I thought about Rick trembling with anger and clenching his fists when he thought I'd offended his mother and asked doubtfully, "Is he?"

"We're not exactly sure. There are rumors," said Gail.

Wow. Rumors about Rick and Chris. I wondered if Rob had heard *those.*

"I'll tell you one thing," stated the normally phlegmatic Connie hotly, "if my husband ever raised a hand to me he better kill me the first time because he'd never get another chance."

Gail nodded grimly. "If my husband ever tried something like that he better never fall asleep when I'm around. His kneecaps would be history!"

I was amused by her outburst. "What would you do?"

"I've got a baseball bat; I'd cripple the son-of-a-bitch," she said stoutly then caught herself. "Of course, my husband would never do anything like that, he's a decent man." Then she added after a moment, "But I'd know what to do if he ever did."

And I thought I was a tough. Rob was lucky I wasn't into team sports. I didn't add any bloodthirsty comments about what I'd do if Rob ever raised a hand to me. I would have had to admit that I raised a fist, well, fingernail, in anger first.

"We don't know anything like that's going on," Connie said after Gail subsided. "I think he's just playing mind games. But mental abuse can be just as bad as physical abuse." Connie ruminated for a minute. "She shouldn't close the shop. It's the only outlet she has. Granted, she doesn't make much money from it but at least she gets out of the house. Now she'll be stuck out on that farm all by herself. I don't envy her when the baby comes."

"Well," I said and shrugged helplessly, "I feel bad for Chris but I really don't know of anything I can do."

Connie sighed unhappily. "I know. There's not much any of us can do. Maybe my husband could…but no. That's not his job. Maybe Bobby…?" she trailed off hopefully.

I shook my head. "I don't think Rob would take any suggestions about Rick from me kindly. And I'm pretty sure Rick wouldn't listen to him anyway. Rob's the baby of the family, you know."

"Oh, well," Connie said and shrugged, "I just hate to see Chris isolated like this."

"There's nothing we can do until she asks for help so we might as well put it out of our minds," Gail said firmly. "I think Bobby's right; you stay out of it, Stevie. I've heard that Rick's got a mean streak. You don't want to get on the wrong side of him."

I grinned at her. "I told you, I'm separated from the Andersons except for one Sunday a month. I'm not likely to get on any side of Rick, let alone the wrong one." Gail looked unconvinced so I added, "Don't worry about me. Haven't I proved I can take care of myself? These guys can't touch me."

I laughed at my own cockiness but Connie and Gail exchanged a troubled look. I thought they were being a melodramatic. I knew Rick was petty but there was no percentage in going after me; he'd just hurt Rob and I'd had it made abundantly clear to me that the Anderson brothers were supposed to stick together—although when that happened I didn't know. They all talked about the importance of family but they only got together when their parents dictated they do so. I'd see Rick once a month, we'd probably be civil to each other for Alice's sake, and that would be it. Sort of like getting my period; bloody, unpleasant, and unavoidable.

chapter 20

By the end of January the in-laws were pushed on the backburner because my life became positively hectic. I was assigned to assist Caroline Inqvest who was directing the upcoming student production, *The Rainmaker*. I liked Caroline; she taught a playwriting course, two speech classes, and the Shakespeare courses.

"I know the play's old but I wanted a Midwestern theme and a manageable cast. Besides, I've always loved it," confessed Caroline. "I don't know if Dr. T told you but this is my first shot at directing a big production so I really need an experienced person to help me. I asked for you specifically."

Maybe she did request my services but I think she was just being kind, I'm pretty sure she would have gotten stuck with me anyway. I don't think any of the men directors wanted me around because of my skirmish with Dr. Muehler; I scared them. But I was happy to work with her because, contrary to Caroline's assumption, I had little directing background. Hopefully, she'd use me for something other than gofer chores and I'd get some real hands-on experience. We'd muddle through together.

Over two hundred young hopefuls, including all of my acting students, auditioned for *The Rainmaker*. Joan and Andrew automatically assumed they'd play Lizzie and Starbuck. Unfortunately for them, Caroline wasn't tuned to their wavelength. After two nights of auditions and discussions, Caroline posted her casting list. I was pleased that out of all the available talent she'd selected three of my students; two earnest young Ag majors to play Noah and Phyle, and Brian, my linebacker with the comic flair, was cast as Starbuck.

"Miss O'Neill," (he couldn't seem to get his tongue wrapped around Ms.) Brian protested to me during office hours, "I can't do this!"

"Why not? Mrs. Inqvest and I think you can," I replied calmly.

"I've never done anything like this before!" he yelped.

"College is filled with new experiences," I droned wisely.

"But all those lines! How will I remember them all?" he asked and dramatically slapped his forehead.

"It's not tough. It'll teach you discipline," I argued, amused.

Then the real reason for his reluctance came out. "What'll the guys think?" he wailed.

Such lamentation from a 6'4", 250-pound male was novel. "Who cares what they think? It's not like you'll be in tights or anything," I said, unmoved. Then I softened when I saw how truly upset he was. I'd have to come up with a pretty big carrot to lead this ass.

"Brian," I asked thoughtfully, "do you have a girlfriend?"

He hung his head. "No."

"Is it tough for you to meet girls?"

His face went red. "Yeah, sober ones," he admitted.

"Well," I said briskly, "not only will you get to know one of the prettiest girls I've seen on this campus, you'll be able to kiss her every night for a month. Does football practice offer benefits like this? I don't think so."

Brian brightened at the thought of the girl we'd cast as Lizzie, Jane Vanhoek. Jane was a truly lovely young woman and she almost didn't get cast because of that; Lizzie is supposed to be plain, you know. But Jane was so darn good Caroline figured we could ugly her up a bit. Besides, when Lizzie gains confidence from Starbuck and turns pretty, the transformation would be really dramatic.

I felt a little sleazy using the poor girl as bait to get Brian but I wanted him to play Starbuck. Unfortunately, pimping Jane hadn't convinced him, he was probably recruited into the athletic department the same way, so I upped the ante.

"Brian, don't you know everybody loves an actor?" I wheedled. "You watch, you'll be an overnight campus sensation."

That seemed to sway him. "It'll be a lot of work," he hedged but I could feel him coming my way.

"So's anything worthwhile. And you might enjoy it," I coaxed.

Brian nodded. "Okay, if you think I can do it."

"I know you can," I assured him.

One crisis was settled but another one reared its ugly head an hour later.

I'd gone to the bathroom to wash out my coffee cup when I heard sobbing in one of the stalls. I didn't know whether to sneak out or offer assistance. I dithered for a minute before finally deciding to put my oar in and offer aid. I knocked softly and asked hesitantly, "Ahhh, do you need help?"

"No. Go away," said a muffled voice I recognized through the tears.

"Joan? It's Ms. O'Neill. Are you sure you don't need help?"

The sobbing subsided and the door slowly opened. Joan stood there smiling wetly. "I'm fine, really," she said. Then the tears started rolling again to contradict her statement.

She was my student, I felt responsible for her, so I mopped her up and led her to my office. I sat her down, closed the door, and handed her some Kleenex. She sobbed awhile and I tried to figure out what to do. Something truly awful must have happened to make Joan cry like this. But did I have any right to pry? Not really. Okay, I wouldn't pry, I'd just offer to listen and help if I could. She could take it from there.

"Joan, I don't know what's wrong but if it's anything you want to talk about, I'm here," I said encouragingly.

Her watery eyes met mine. "It's too late. But I'm sure you did everything you could."

Oh dear; somehow or other I was involved in this. Well, at least that precluded pregnancy or death in the family. I had to find out if my sin was one of commission or omission so I asked her directly, "Joan, what's wrong?"

"I didn't get Lizzie!" she howled and the waterworks started again.

How stupid of me. I should have known Joan would have had her heart set on the Lizzie role even though her interpretation would have been closer to Lizzie Borden. At first her grief struck me as silly; all these tears because she didn't get a part. Then I remembered that there were only four major productions during the school year, and one of them was a musical. The schedule made for limited opportunities. And for someone as apparently dedicated to theater as Joan, this lost audition must have been a crushing disappointment. I had to handle this tactfully.

"Joan, I know how disappointed you must be. I've been there myself," I consoled her.

Her sobs had turned to hiccups and I had to stifle a grin. She could dress up like a corpse all she wanted to but she was still just a kid. "Wasn't I any good?" she asked, black mascara running down her face.

I handed her another Kleenex. "You were fine, Joan. It's just that Jane was better for Lizzie."

"No, she isn't," Joan said vehemently. "She's pretty. I'm plain. You don't know how awful that is. But Lizzie and I do."

Plain? Joan bore a marked resemblance to Lily Munster but I certainly wouldn't have called her plain. "Joan, where did you ever get the idea you were plain?" I asked.

"Oh, I've always known it. (hic) All my sisters were cheerleaders and homecoming queens. I was always mousy and well...just sort of weird. I never had any dates. I just read books. My parents always seemed disappointed."

She was describing the plight of the budding intellectual in a sea of pompoms and dairy products.

"This isn't even my real hair color," she continued. I looked at her dyed black hair and nodded. She noticed my glance and smiled bleakly, "It's really mousy brown if you're wondering." She looked down and twisted her Kleenex. "I don't fit in anywhere. My dad thinks I'm a mutant. I thought I'd found a place for myself in the Theater" (theater was said with a capitol T and an elegant hand gesture) "but I guess I can't even do that."

She softly hiccupped and blew her nose; that gave me time to get my thoughts together.

"Joan," I started, "you are not plain. You're bright and you have a certain...style. Although, personally I think it's a bit overdone."

She bristled at this. "I was making a statement with black. I'm showing my contempt of conventional mores and my grief at the death of the earth," she explained haughtily.

Lord, give me patience. Was everybody back here preoccupied with death? I thought of Marvin contentedly tending his future grave. I guess I could understand where he was coming from; he was pretty old and death wasn't too far off. But this kid glamorizing death? She didn't know what she was talking about. Death was real and death was permanent so you better enjoy life while you can. Wafting around like Dracula's daughter didn't help anything. I think I was a little sharp with her.

"Joan, the earth isn't dead yet and it seems to me you'd be better off spending your time trying to save it than polluting the water with black dye. You're what…maybe twenty? You're a little young for a death fixation. You want to protest something? Write a letter to your congressperson. Get involved. But don't take yourself so seriously. And lighten up on the black. Honestly, you look like Gloria Swanson in *Sunset Boulevard.* It's inappropriate for your age and you're limiting yourself with the look. If you want to be an actor you have to be versatile and that includes physical versatility." She looked resentful and I could see I wasn't getting through to her. "Joan, were you planning on a career in the theater?" I demanded.

"I'd hoped to but now…" she slumped dejectedly.

"Well, the first thing you have to understand if you're serious about this is…Look at me, Joan." She raised her head and I said very distinctly, "You're not going to get every part. Out of twenty-five auditions you'll be lucky to get one job. Sometimes the odds are even worse. Acting is a profession for the eternally optimistic or the brain damaged. You'd better understand that right now or you'll be jumping off a bridge in ten years. You can't go to pieces every time you don't get a part." She was starting to look scared so I changed tactics. "On the other hand, there'll always be another chance. The problem as I see it is that there aren't very many opportunities here but I have an idea how to fix that."

Joan still looked miserable but the hiccups had stopped and she was listening intently.

"What's your idea?" she finally asked.

"I think there's some money in the department budget for student productions," I said. I hoped there was anyway; I thought I'd read something about that in the department manual. "Why don't you direct something? Or get one of your buddies to direct and you can act in it. More productions mean more opportunity. And you can get extra credit for it. I'll help you write the proposal for funding; it'll probably have to apply to next year but it'll be something to look forward to."

The idea intrigued her. Life came back into her eyes along with hope. I promised her I'd see what information I could dig up and what the requirements were. I'd find the necessary forms and try to have something to tell her in a week. She nodded, wiped her face one more time, and left. I dismissed her with my benediction of "Go and cry no more" but she barely smiled. Serious art-farts tend to be pretty humorless. At least I didn't think I had to worry about her committing suicide. That was a relief.

Having successfully played Mrs. Chips, my thoughts turned to the home front.

Rob and I had fallen back into the "I'm in school, the pressure's on again, I'm tired so don't bother me" rut. I was just as guilty of neglect as he was. Now that I had friends and professional obligations I was preoccupied, too. We'd touch base at dinner and then he'd disappear into "our" office or go back to campus and I'd go to play practice. Our sex life was going from perfunctory to non-existent. See, when you're married the desire for intercourse loses its urgency. You know your partner is going to be there tomorrow, the next week, hopefully the next month, and you're tired anyway so you yawn, kiss, roll over and go to sleep. You start taking each other for granted.

The problem was the only glue keeping Rob and me together at the moment was sex so it behooved me to keep the glue fresh. But how?

I discussed the problem with Connie and Gail. The minute the word "sex" came up they both blushed but Gail produced a stack of old women's magazines.

"I think you'll find some helpful hints in these," she said quietly— and then winked. Good ol' Gail, she wasn't as pure as she pretended. Maybe that's why she was still happily married.

So I read articles. To rev up a man's libido, according to the magazine people, lingerie was the way to go. And they weren't talking jockey shorts either. The itchier and more impractical the attire, the more erotic the result. It seemed worth a try.

Which led to another problem. I was embarrassed to go to the local J.C. Penny's to check out the undies. What if somebody saw me? And in this small town, everybody knew me, that had already been demonstrated. I finally called Frederick's of Hollywood for a catalogue.

I made my selections, had them mailed to me, and chose Valentine's Day for a test launch. I made reservations at a downtown steak house and, since their customers made do with beer and mixed drinks, I arranged a corkage fee so I could bring my own bottle of cabernet. It was to be an evening of unalloyed but classy lust.

Fortunately, Rob wouldn't get home until six o'clock so I had plenty of time to prepare. And I needed it. I'd been living in slacks because of the cold weather and shaving hadn't been high on my list of priorities. From the waist down I looked like Magilla Gorilla. It took forty-five minutes to shave everything that needed to be shaved and I spent ten minutes picking bloody Kleenex bits off my legs before I could get into my costume and make-up.

I'd bought a black, push-up bra, matching G-string, garter belt, and stockings. I put on black heels and checked myself out in the mirror. I looked like a whore and felt like a fool. Thank God I'd been dieting; an outfit like this could drive a person to anorexia. That miserable G-string rubbed funny (what do women with hemorrhoids do?) and my butt looked like two moons rising. This better meet Rob's idea of a fantasy and lead to connubial bliss. I sighed and covered my Valentine's surprise with a sedate dress, finished my make-up, and rehearsed my lines. According to the magazine, I was supposed to wait until we got to the restaurant to tell my man, in my sexiest voice, about the visual delight that was in store for him. If all went according to plan, Rob's end of the table would rise and his anticipation would make the resulting lovemaking electrifying.

Unfortunately, Rob hadn't read the article.

The evening started well. Rob surprised me with flowers and a card. I was pleased with the flowers and presented Rob with a card of my own. He smiled over it and put it away without further comment. He said he was hungry and what did I want to do about food? My Valentine's Day gift of a steak dinner seemed to be greatly appreciated.

We got into our coats and struggled out to the car. We'd just had another blizzard and the drifts around the trailer were three feet high. Rob had to carry me through the snow to the car because of those dumb heels. And the draft that went up my backside! The magazine didn't mention frostbite in my nether regions.

We were seated in a booth in the restaurant, eating our salads and toasting each other with the excellent cabernet, when I presented my bombshell.

"I have a surprise for you, Rob," I purred in what I hoped was an alluring voice with an appropriate facial expression. I hadn't practiced this in the mirror so God knows how it came out.

"Hmmm?" asked Rob as he stuffed lettuce in his mouth.

"Underneath my dress I'm wearing a G-string, a garter belt, and a push-up bra. They're black, they're lacy, and they're all for you." I smiled smugly and sat back to watch his reaction.

"What!?" Rob gasped and choked on his salad.

So far, so good. Per instructions from the magazine I moved closer to him in the booth and raised my skirt to show the lacy top of the stocking with the garter attached.

"Happy Valentine's Day, Rob." I leered at him.

He glanced at my leg and…yanked my skirt down. "God, we're in public, Stevie! What if somebody sees?" he hissed frantically and subsided as the waitress passed.

This was not going according to plan. "I thought you'd enjoy a little eroticism," I whispered.

"At home, not in public," he whispered back.

I glared at him. "Oh, relax, Rob, it's not like I flashed everybody in the restaurant."

"But talking about G-strings and garter belts. How am I supposed to enjoy a steak with that going on?" he asked rhetorically, looking around nervously.

"You're not," I said, annoyed. "You're supposed to get all hot and bothered and tear my clothes off."

"Here?!" he asked incredulously.

"No, not here," I said crossly, "at home. Later."

He studied me. "Where do you get these crazy ideas?"

"*Cosmopolitan*," I admitted.

"Explain. Quietly."

So I did. Rob listened intently while he finished his salad.

"So, if I did A, you were supposed to do B," I finished, not looking at him. I was embarrassed too. "The magazine said it'd be a treat for you." I shook my head. "We've got to start reading the same literature."

The waitress brought our steaks, which gave Rob time to frame a response. He poured more wine for both of us after she left and raised his glass to me.

"I appreciate the gesture. You just caught me by surprise," he said.

"It was stupid," I admitted, totally embarrassed. "And uncomfortable!

This stuff itches! And you wouldn't believe the drafts I've been putting up with. My thighs are solid goose bumps! It was a bad idea." I changed the subject to salvage what I could of the celebration. "So, how was your day?"

Rob laughed and listened to me babble about play rehearsals as he ate his steak. He seemed distracted, though. He'd interrupt with little questions, like, "Black, huh?"

"And itchy," I confided.

We finished our meal and when our waitress asked if we wanted coffee and dessert Rob didn't even consult me.

"Just the check, please," he said abruptly. "We have to get home." He seemed to be in a hurry.

On the way to the car he stopped to plant a passionate kiss on me. The wind howled up my backside but I didn't care. I was pretty sure Rob would warm me up when we got home.

Which he did. But first I had to model my new duds for him. I even performed my version of a striptease. Having never seen one, I had to rely on my imagination and daytime talk shows to achieve a close proximity of the real thing but I must have done pretty well because Rob went nuts. Pudgy left the bedroom in disgust. She kept getting knocked off the bed by loose hands and feet.

Afterwards, we cuddled up together. "Silly underwear works," I grinned goofily.

Rob tucked my head more firmly in his neck. "Yeah," he said, sounding surprised. "Where'd you get it?"

"I ordered a Frederick's catalogue," I confessed. "Don't worry. Nobody in town knows I have it. It was even mailed in a plain brown wrapper."

Rob patted me absently then asked. "Do you still have the catalogue?"

"Mmmhmm," I said drowsily.

"Do they have one of those corset things? I wonder what you'd look like in one those," Rob mused.

I raised myself on one elbow to look at him. "You hypocrite! After yelling at me at dinner about showing you my stockings you want me to order more underwear?"

"Hey, you caught me flat-footed. This has never happened to me before; I didn't know what to do. But I came through, didn't I?" he defended himself.

"Well, yeah," I agreed and tucked myself in again.

"So, do they have those corset things? I want to see the catalogue," he persisted.

Rob's a little slow but he catches on eventually.

"Tomorrow," I said and snickered. "And do me a favor, will you? Let's not order anything new until spring unless it's flannel. It's cold out there."

What women have to go through to keep the marital fires burning.

chapter 21

February blew out with a blizzard but March came in like a lamb. The temperature rose, the snow started to melt, and the end of winter seemed to be in sight—which was the only encouraging thing in my life at the moment.

Pudgy had been lethargic and losing weight since Christmas so I took her back to the doctor. At my insistence the vet tested her for leukemia and feline infectious peritonitis. All the tests came back negative.

"I told you before, she's just old," he finally said. "She's lived out her life."

"But she's only thirteen! There must be something we can do," I said, too stunned to accept this death sentence.

"Just love your kitty while you can," he said. My frantic eyes and quivering chin seemed to unnerve him. He tried to usher me out of his office. "I'm sorry. There's really nothing I can do for her."

"How about some more vitamins? They helped last time," I suggested desperately.

The vet shook his head. "I'm afraid I'd just be wasting your money," he said.

"It's my money," I said tightly.

He reluctantly gave me some more vitamins and said, "If these work, fine, but I don't think they will. When the time comes just bring her in. I'll make it easy for her."

"Time comes for what?" I asked stupidly.

"Well, uh, to put her to sleep. You don't want her to suffer, do you?" he asked uncomfortably.

Of course not, I was suffering enough for both of us. I cried all the way home. I couldn't accept the thought of Pudgy dying. My parents had brought her from the pound when she was just seven weeks old and barely weaned. My father had called her 'the shark' because her little tail stuck straight up and looked like a dorsal fin when she was circling his ankles for food. She'd eaten so much Mom had called her Jaws until she grew into her current name. She'd been with me through my parents' death, through the lawyer hassles, college—sometimes she'd been my only friend through the years we'd been together.

Rob found us huddled on the couch when he came home. I was holding her close as I dropped tears on her fur. She'd lift her fuzzy little head and lick them off my face. I don't know if she was trying to comfort me or the teardrops annoyed her. It didn't matter. She was breaking my heart. Rob listened sympathetically to the dismal prognosis.

"Hey, the vet was wrong before, maybe he's wrong now," he said when I finished. He pulled Pudgy and me into his lap. "I told you, he's a cow doctor, for God's sake."

"Do you really think so?" I asked tearfully. I knew I was probably grasping at straws but I needed some hope.

"The vitamins worked before. We'll dose her and pray he's wrong," Rob said stoutly. He scratched Pudgy's head and said to her, "You get better now, you hear? Stevie needs you."

Pudgy purred and I felt a lot better, too. Maybe the vitamins would work. I'd pray for a miracle.

I spent the next couple of days hovering over Pudgy and stuffing pills in her. Sometimes I'd have to wake her up to do it. She started crawling under the bed whenever she saw me coming. I think she found my attempts to fix her extremely annoying. She finally got some relief from me when I remembered I had a life. I had classes to teach and play practice to supervise. I tried not to feel too guilty about leaving her for a few hours each day; she was sleeping most of the time anyway. Sometimes I found it hard to put on a smile and be civil. If Joan had mentioned death to me I'd have socked her.

Mike Hall, one of my colleagues, invited the entire department to his house for a St. Patrick's Day party. I tried to beg off because I wanted to spend the time force-feeding Pudgy but Margy told me I had to put in an appearance.

"You're the only person of Irish descent we've got," she explained as she handed me a map to Mike's house.

I pried Rob away from his books and made him act as my escort/driver. Mike's wife directed us down to the basement, which had been decorated with green crepe paper streamers and cutouts of shamrocks. Margy handed out nametags that read "McHall, O'Inqvest" and the like. I had the only name tag that didn't need to be doctored. Mike handed me a glass of beer that had been dyed green with food color. I inspected it doubtfully; I thought it looked like a specimen from a diseased kidney. My dad would have been horrified. As a true Irishman he was amazed that Americans polluted perfectly good beer this way but what the hell. I murmured "Erin go braugh" in honor of the day and chugged it.

The male teachers seemed to have gotten over their leeriness of me. When Rob and I first appeared at the party the other men had surreptitiously checked him out for damage but he assured them I was basically harmless. Margy also ran interference for me.

"I told all of them what really happened between you and Muehler," Margy confided to me. She'd obviously had a few pints and was having trouble focusing her eyes. "I heard it all, you know. I told them as long as they behaved themselves like gentlemen around you there wouldn't be any problems." She smiled beatifically and lurched off.

I was playing darts at the far end of the basement with Linda, Mike, and his wife when Muehler crossed the room to get a beer. He caught my eye and glared threateningly at me. I raised my head and positively sneered back. No words were spoken but the mutual animosity drowned out all other conversations. The room went silent. Muehler tried to stare me down but that was something the old goof was never going to do. I stared insolently with raised eyebrow and curled lip. Muehler abruptly turned away and the noise level returned. When I refilled my glass with specimen I saw him making his excuses to Mike and walk up the basement stairs. Linda and I smiled grimly at each other.

I hadn't noticed Rob for a while and decided to search him out. He'd never shown up for a party with my colleagues on my turf before and I didn't want him to think I'd abandoned him. He'd joined a group singing *Danny Boy* around the piano. Of course, the sad song reminded me of Pudgy so I watered my beer with a few tears. Everybody assumed I was suffering from Irish sentimentality and let me alone. Rob knew the tears were because of the cat, not booze-induced nationalism, so he didn't even lecture me about drinking when we drove home.

Pudgy continued to sleep and Caroline and I managed to get through final dress rehearsals without any noticeable desire to murder each other. On opening night we enjoyed the surprising success of *The Rainmaker*. I was particularly proud when Brian, my no-neck football player, got the most applause. He deserved it; he was wonderful.

As the director and designated adult, Caroline threw a cast party. She served soft drinks and chips—I think she wanted to make sure everybody stayed sober and in shape for the next performance—but the kids didn't seem to mind. They danced enthusiastically and toasted each other's ability. Brian was flushed and excited as he accepted congratulations from a whole new social circle. He blushed when I added my kudos. "You did good, kid," I said as I shook his hand.

"Yeah, I did all right, didn't I," he agreed modestly.

"I hope it was worth your time," I added archly.

Brian nodded and took me aside. "I've been thinking," he said furtively, "I've always been a screw-up, you know, class clown?"

No shit, I thought to myself, before he continued in a rush, "Do you think I could do stand-up comedy? I mean, it can't be much tougher than what I just did."

I stared at Brian in amazement; it appeared I'd created a monster. "Brian," I said without further hesitation, "you can do anything you want to. Anyway, you can try."

His face lit up. "That's what I thought. But I don't know where those guys get their jokes. Do you?"

I wasn't exactly sure where the jokes came from. "They write them themselves, I think. Maybe they buy them," I said trying to be helpful.

"Oh." Brian's face fell. "I can't afford to hire anyone. And I don't know how to write. I thought they got a book or something."

"Of course, you can get some ideas from a book, I guess. But what do you mean you don't write? You're always telling silly stories. Why not use them?"

Brian stood quietly, deep in thought, then he smiled at me ingenuously, and asked, "Would you help me?"

261

I didn't know anything about writing comedy routines but how could I refuse to help? I was the one who'd gotten him interested in performing, after all.

"Sure. Why not?" I said nonchalantly.

Brian happily trotted off to his adoring public and I looked around for Rob. I was afraid he'd be bored by the theatrical types and was holding up a wall someplace. I found him talking to Caroline who seemed smitten. He excused himself to get me a soda and Caroline whispered to me, "I see why you followed him back here. He's cute."

I stood back and looked at Rob objectively. Yup, he was cute all right. *My man, I think I'll keep him*, I grinned to myself.

Now that I didn't have to devote time to play rehearsals I made sure my other prairie flower, Joan, was blooming. She'd taken my suggestion about directing a play seriously but we had a difference of opinion about her selection of material. She wanted to direct *The Trojan Women*.

"That's epic theater. Isn't that a little ambitious?" I asked her dubiously. "Don't you think you should start with something a little less…monumental?"

"I want to show the degradation and violence that women are subjected to," she pontificated.

"This is tough stuff, Joan," I argued. "Don't you think you should learn to walk before you run? Honestly, I don't even feel qualified to advise you on this. Why don't you try a comedy? Isn't Neil Simon writing anything socially relevant?"

I talked her into staying in the twentieth century and she decided on *The Effect of Gamma Rays on Man-in-the-Moon Marigolds*.

"It's an all-woman cast," she explained earnestly. "That speaks to me."

Thank God somebody did. We got her proposal ready and shipped it off. Then I worked on a comedy routine with Brian. We'd meet in empty classrooms, sometimes the student union, and one Friday afternoon when Rob was busy we met in a bar over a beer. Brian didn't really need me to write material for him. He just needed a sounding board for his ideas. I think what he really appreciated was the approval of someone who'd been in the Business. I didn't begrudge the time I spent working with Brian; I needed the diversion of humor. The vitamins weren't helping Pudgy.

I was getting so depressed over her sad state that Rob insisted I take a Saturday afternoon off to attend a baby shower for Chris that Alice was hosting. I questioned even going considering my history with Chris and Rick but Rob said I had to get out of the house. I wasn't doing Pudgy or myself any good. Gail and Connie agreed. They said I could hide in a corner with them if I chipped in to buy one of those high-tech, yuppie strollers. Gail went to Sioux Falls to buy it and the three of us sacrificed an exercise period putting it together.

"Well, that's done," said Gail, as she looked at the assembled stroller with satisfaction. "All it cost was ninety dollars and two fingernails."

"I think we did pretty well considering we got instructions for a Patriot missile not a buggy," Connie commented wearily.

"And we did it all by ourselves. We didn't have to ask any men for help," was my smug contribution.

"Who needs men?" asked Gail flippantly.

"In order to have a baby shower you have to have a man in the picture somewhere," Connie pointed out in her earth motherly way.

"Yeah," I quipped, "the last time there was an immaculate conception was two thousand years ago and look what a fuss that kicked up."

We all cackled together. It was so good to feel something besides depressed.

Alice had invited her church ladies, her neighbors, her daughters-in-law…she must have included every pair of X chromosomes in a five-mile radius. Her living room was packed with femininity. We played stupid games like "pass the orange under the chin" and "pass the lifesaver on the toothpick". I was surprised that such normally reticent, reserved women would play such physical contact games. I worried about offending with my breath or body odor. My closest teammate didn't worry about offending. She should have.

"I hate kid games, especially physical contact ones," I whispered to Marilyn.

Marilyn grinned. "The last shower I went to was for a cousin named Pam. You remember that old song *Tammy*? One of Pam's friends sang 'Pammy, Pammy, Pammy's in love' to that tune." My grimace of dismay made her laugh. "If you want sophistication you won't get it at a shower."

Chris exclaimed with delight over her shower gifts. She really liked the stroller, she said.

"I was going to give you a Louisville Slugger for your husband," said

Gail responding to Chris' appreciation. The ladies all laughed. "That wasn't a joke," she said aside to me.

We ate cake and drank punch and Chris made a speech thanking everybody. "I really appreciate everything you've done for me," she finished tremulously. "It's nice to know I have such good friends. And I'm sure everything will be just fine when the baby gets here."

Such a cryptic ending to a supposedly happy speech! The younger generation of women exchanged troubled looks. Nobody knew what to say. Then Gail piped up. Thank God for her and the mouth she was developing.

"Yeah, you'll be able to fit behind a steering wheel again and drive far, far away," she joked which broke the uncomfortable silence. The party broke up on a laugh.

Alice and her friends got busy with cleanup. They didn't seem to need any additional help and I wanted to get home to be with Pudgy so I went to the kitchen to make my excuses.

Rick was drinking coffee at the kitchen table. He just couldn't stay away from anything having to do with the two women in his life. I acknowledged his existence with a cool nod and spoke to Alice.

"I'm sorry I have to go so soon, Alice, but I really need to get home." I didn't explain why. I didn't want to give Rick an opening.

Alice looked at me kindly, dried her hands, and kissed me on the cheek. That was the second time Alice had ever kissed me. "I know, Stephanie. Bobby told me about your cat. It's too bad pets don't live longer, isn't it?" she asked sympathetically.

Now, I can take snide comments, I can even handle physical threats, I know how to fight that sort of thing. But kindness just kills me. My chin quivered, my eyes filled up, and I couldn't speak. All I could do was nod agreement. That's when Rick butted in and saved me from making a bawling ass of myself.

"For Christ's sake, it's just a cat," he said in disgust.

My eyes dried up and my chin stopped quivering. My resentment toward Rick had been simmering ever since Rob told me he'd accused me of alcoholism and abortion mongering. I'd been continually offended by his domineering treatment of Chris although I'd kept my promise to stay clear. But enough was enough. I may not have been able to save Pudgy but this I could fight. "Fuck you and the horse you rode in on, you son-of-a-bitch," I snarled at him. "You can make Chris' life a living hell if she'll let you, but you keep your dirty, fucking mouth off me from now on."

The room went absolutely silent, except when one church lady dropped a plate.

"Stephanie, such language!" Alice protested.

I continued to glare malevolently at Rick but I directed my words to his mother. "I'm sorry, Alice, but you're going to hear worse than that if you don't keep this bastard away from me or teach him some manners!"

I finally wrenched my attention back to Alice who looked like I'd slapped her. I guess I had, verbally, and I felt bad about that. After all, she'd shown me kindness and understanding and I'd unloaded on her in a backhanded way. Technically, Rick wasn't a 'bastard'; Alice had been married when he was born. And saying 'son-of-a-bitch'! How come I'd chosen epithets that reflected badly on women? I wished I'd just called him a prick and been done with it.

"I really am sorry, Alice," I apologized, sincerely this time. "I'm just upset right now. I guess I'd better go."

I turned blindly and ran into Nancy. She sniffed at me and pursed her mouth. She seemed to be getting ready to join in with a bitchy comment. I felt surrounded by enemies.

"Nancy, for Christ's sweet sake, would you blow your nose? I'm so tired of that sniffing I could just scream," I hissed, barely in control of myself.

Nancy quit sniffing, Rick glared, and Alice stared. The church ladies didn't move.

"I have to get out of here," I muttered. "I'm not fit to be around right now."

I turned to leave and Rick said at my back, "That's for sure."

I stiffened but Alice hissed at him, "You hush. Stephanie has enough trouble now. She doesn't need you making it worse. Now just hush."

I had never heard Alice scold any of her baby boys before. I couldn't believe she'd done it on my behalf. I sighed wearily. Rick would have something else to hold against me.

I went home to Pudgy.

Well, Pudgy never got any better. She just got thinner and thinner. And weaker and weaker. When I skipped exercise class to watch over her Connie called to see how she was and suggested that maybe it was time to take her to the vet. She offered to come with me.

"She's not ready yet," I told her. But it was me who wasn't ready.

Pudgy finally got so weak she couldn't jump in my lap. She tried her best to follow me around the trailer like she always had but she couldn't seem to summon the strength. I spent my time holding her and crying. She did her best to comfort me. Just like she always had.

"I guess I should just take her to the vet and get it over with," I finally told Rob. "I can't stand the thought of her suffering. But I can't stand to watch her die either. And I have to be there for her. I can't let her go into the dark alone. I don't know what to do," I said and wiped the tears off my cheeks.

Rob stroked Pudgy's head gently. "I don't think she's in any real pain," he said. "I think we should let her die at home. You know how she hates the pet carrier. Yeah, I think it would be best for her to let her die at home in her own time."

I don't know if that was best for her, I sure hope so, but it was best for me. It gave me a chance to talk to her about all the years we'd had together; well, I'd talk and she'd meep at me. At least we were together.

She went into a coma on a Friday night. It was a gradual thing. She'd been deteriorating all day so that evening I put her on a blanket next to the couch. I sat next to her, stroking her and telling her how much I loved her, what a good friend she'd been to me, and how much I'd miss her. I stayed with her, my hand on her paw, and fell asleep after midnight. Rob shook me gently the next morning.

"It's over," he said. "I'm sorry."

I looked down at what had been a beloved friend. Pudgy's eyes were half-open but unseeing. Her little body was limp. I stroked her fur. She was gone.

Rob found a box for her body and we discussed where to bury her. Rob had the only acceptable solution. "I talked to Mom and we think it would be nice if we buried Pudgy in the backyard, maybe under the cottonwood. Is that all right with you?"

We drove to the Anderson house with our little cardboard casket. Rob had already alerted Alice so she was ready with a doily.

"I thought this would be nice to wrap your pet in," she said simply. I nodded. I couldn't speak.

Marvin and Rob dug a grave and we buried Pudgy under the cottonwood that spring morning. The cottonwood was putting out buds and the breeze was gentle.

"Good thing we had the thaw," Marvin commented as he and Rob filled in the grave. "I wouldn't want to have to pay for a backhoe and the freezer's full."

I stared at Marvin in horror when comprehension of what he'd said sunk in. But Marvin hadn't meant anything bad; he was just being practical in the way of country people. Then I snorted through my tears. It was funny in a macabre way.

Rob took me home to drink wine and reminisce. I couldn't believe it; ten o'clock in the morning and he was encouraging me to drink.

"It's an Irish wake," he explained.

I did most of the drinking, most of the talking, and all of the crying but Rob was there for me. He told me I still had him and that me cry a little more.

Another blizzard blew in that night. I didn't think winter would ever be over.

chapter 22

Winter ended. It had to, I guess, or the entire population of Brookings would have been lined up at the Campanile to jump off and I'd have been first in line. The snow melted, the trees grew new buds, and when I drove past the dairy unit I noticed cows with calves. But I knew winter was officially over when Rob took the plastic off the trailer windows. I was so caught up in the renewal of spring I even suggested planting flowers on Pudgy's grave but Alice had already sowed grass seed. She'd been as kind as it was in her practical nature to be about Pudgy's death. She wasn't about to turn her backyard into a formal pet cemetery.

She was bothered by the continued animosity between Rick and me and used the Easter season to try and make peace between us.

"I'm sure Ricky didn't understand how much your pet meant to you," she said. "I've spoken to him and he'd like to apologize. Won't you have a little talk with him; see if you two can't be friends?"

The thought ran through my mind that if I didn't do what she asked she'd dig up Pudgy. Then I dismissed the thought as unworthy. After all, she'd donated a doily as a shroud. It wouldn't hurt to listen to what Rick had to say, especially if he wanted to apologize. Alice was pleased when I agreed to talk to Rick after Easter dinner.

Rob and I celebrated the resurrection with the Lutherans. The choir outdid themselves and the flowers on the altar were beautiful. The Protestants can put on a pretty good show when the mood strikes them—and it doesn't cost too much.

I made a bunny cake as my contribution to the familial feast. I cut up a chocolate cake, covered it with white frosting and coconut, and used candy for the eyes and whiskers. Rob thought it was weird but I was proud of it.

"I thought you made pies," he said, eyeing my cake dubiously.

"I'm expanding my repertoire," I retorted loftily.

Alice was delighted with my cake. "You're so creative! Where did you get the idea?" she exclaimed.

"I got the idea from a magazine. I get lots of good ideas from magazines," I said with a sidelong look at Rob who choked on the piece of candy he'd filched from an unguarded Easter basket.

I was hanging up my coat when Marilyn grabbed me and whispered, "Garage. Five minutes. Bring a glass."

It seemed a little early for the garage but Marilyn had been sitting with Nancy and Chris when I arrived. No wonder she seemed so eager for a sedative. I had some jitters about my proposed 'talk' with Rick; a little liquid courage probably wouldn't hurt. I grabbed one of the wine glasses I'd given Alice off the table and followed Marilyn.

"I miss Wilma a little bit," I said as I swirled the zinfandel Marilyn had provided in my glass.

Marilyn snickered and pulled a pack of Carltons from her pocket. "Cigarette?"

I declined but she lit up. For Alice's sake we opened the garage door. The spring breeze was brisk but pleasant. She smoked and we sipped in companionable silence. I was really beginning to like Marilyn. Ex-beauty queens can be all right. Maybe Marilyn thought the same thing about ex-actresses.

Mike appeared in the doorway with a glass. "Is this a closed party or can anybody join?" he asked.

Marilyn and I shared a glance, surprised at his appearance. I shrugged and Marilyn poured him some wine. Mike lifted his glass to us and smiled.

"I don't want to sound like you're not wanted but…to what do we owe the honor? Is the TV broken?" I asked him.

"No. Just nothing on," he said honestly.

"Oh. How flattering," I said dryly.

Rob showed up in the doorway with a glass. "I heard this was where the party was," he explained.

I regretfully watched as Marilyn poured him the last of the wine.

She noticed my expression and said, "Don't worry, I've got another one."

It's hard to dish properly with men around so we talked about the weather. Which led to summer. Which led to Marilyn's lake cabin.

"You haven't been out there yet, have you, Stevie?" Marilyn asked. "We'll probably have a family barbecue when it warms up." She crossed her eyes.

"If you ever want to get away for a week just let us know," Mike offered. "We usually only use it on weekends."

"For a small fee, of course," Marilyn amended.

"Marilyn, she's family," Mike protested.

"I should charge her double then," Marilyn snapped back. She turned to me and said, "It's nothing against you personally but Mike's brothers would be out at the cabin every damn minute of the summer if I let them. The deal is: If I offer, no charge. If you demand, it'll cost you."

"But honey," Mike objected.

"I bought that cabin with money my grandfather left me, Mike. If your family wants use of it, they can help pay the bills," she said firmly then turned to me to explain apologetically. "See, I had Tom and Nancy for practically the whole summer when I first bought it."

"He's my brother," Mike said weakly.

"He's not mine!" riposted Marilyn.

"But you're a member of our family now," Mike bleated.

"Mike, I have my own family if case you've forgotten. You wouldn't have that nice job at the bank if it hadn't been for my father. Your parents may buy that "self-made man" crap but you and I both know that you married up." The confident, bluff banker-brother shriveled before my eyes to a chastised boy stirring his toe in the dust. Rob watched the transformation in amazement then turned to stare at Marilyn with disapproval. She met his look unflinchingly. Rob turned to me uncertainly but if he thought I'd help his brother and him out he was sadly mistaken. I gazed at Marilyn with respect and amusement.

She took a deep breath to calm herself. "I've said too much," she said, "but if I don't speak up for myself no one else will. And I'm tired of Mike acting like my time and property is his to give away. I'm not his servant! Or his brothers'."

"No problem," I assured her. "I know just where you're coming from."

"I think I better go inside," Mike said uneasily.

"Me, too," agreed Rob. They both retreated.

"Score one for my side," Marilyn said after they'd closed the door. She sounded very satisfied. "I've been mad about that cabin situation for a long time. It's about time I said something."

"In vino veritas," I murmured.

"Yeah. Should I open the other bottle? I'm on a roll."

"Later. I promised Alice I'd have a talk with Rick after dinner. I better keep my head clear."

Marilyn was aghast. "Why in the world did you promise that?" she demanded.

"Alice was really nice to me when my cat died. I owe it to her," I defended myself. "Besides, what harm could it do? Alice said Rick wants to make peace. Since he's Rob's brother, shouldn't I try to get along with him if possible?" I asked reasonably.

"I don't think it is possible. Look what he does to his own wife. I bet Alice tells Chris he's just excitable and misunderstood." Marilyn cogitated. "Maybe I'll offer the cabin to Chris. You know, if she ever needs to get away. She looks just sick." I shrugged noncommittally and Marilyn sighed, "It'd probably just make more trouble for her." She shook a warning finger at me. "You just make sure you don't end up an Anderson casualty, too."

I was troubled by Marilyn's vehemence but maintained that a mere conversation wouldn't be that bad and if we could stop all this sniping and niggling...well, that would be wonderful. Marilyn kept shaking her head 'no'. Her negative response to my arguments daunted me. "Maybe he'll forget all about it," I finally said weakly.

"Maybe," Marilyn said dubiously. "I suppose we ought to go in and tote that barge and lift that bale."

"I suppose. Say, with no football on do you suppose the men'll do the dishes?" I asked hopefully.

"In your dreams. They seem to think their hands will shrink if they touch dishwater. Maybe we should suggest that Tom wash dishes with his gut. He could stand a little shrinkage in that area," Marilyn snickered.

The wine-tasting club broke up and we giggled our way through the

271

serving process. The meal and cleanup—done exclusively by us women, as usual—was uneventful.

The dishes had been put away when Rick appeared in the doorway, a look of saintly forbearance on his face. "I'd like to borrow Stephanie for a little bit. I think we need to have a talk," he announced. "Would you take a short walk with me, Stephanie?"

Rats, the cup hadn't passed from me. Marilyn shook her head frantically at me but I sighed and agreed to walk and talk with Rick.

"Good," Rick beamed, "I'll just get our coats."

As I left the kitchen Marilyn whispered, "I'll have the wine waiting when you get back."

Rick and I walked a block without speaking. I was waiting for him to open and set the tone. I was also girding myself for whatever came.

"Now, Stephanie," began Rick with an expression of saintly patience on his face, "I want you to hear me out before you say anything. Can you do that?" I nodded. His angelic aspect threw me off momentarily. I'd forgotten Lucifer was an angel, too.

"Good. Now, you and Bobby have been married, what? About eight months? Umhmm, umhmm. Well, you know Mom asked me to speak to you." He paused for a minute to collect himself before dropping his bombshell. "I'm sorry to have to say this but…well, frankly, we don't think you fit in as a member of our family. Now, you promised to hear me out," he said and raised a cautionary hand which was unnecessary; I was speechless. He continued, "We've had nothing but trouble ever since you came here. We're a very close family and you're causing a big schism in it." He paused again, I suppose to see how I'd reacted to his opening salvo, but I clamped my jaws together. I'd promised I'd listen to him and, by God, I'd honor that promise.

Rick nodded in satisfaction at my silence and started in again. "We find your sense of humor inappropriate. You're too irreverent and glib. Your language is appalling. I don't think my mother had ever heard such vulgarity from a woman when you swore at me at the baby shower. And you're encouraging unacceptable behavior in other members of the family who should know better." He shook his head sorrowfully. "I'll tell you frankly, I would never have married a woman like you and I think you're making Bobby's life miserable."

"Did Rob say that?" I asked as calmly as I could through gritted teeth.

"No, but I'm his brother and I know what he's thinking. Now let me finish. This acting business is also unacceptable. The women in our family don't run around the country; they stay home where they belong." Then came the clincher. "That commercial that you left Bobby for last January didn't even show, did it?"

Not yet it hadn't, but that's the nature of the business. Sometimes you get holding fees and sometimes the commercials never show at all. It's a big crapshoot. But I certainly never expected to have a failed job thrown in my face. My jaws were beginning to ache.

Rick continued. "You obviously don't put much store in our family. You never even took Bobby's last name, did you? I guess what I'm trying to say," he concluded, smiling jovially which contrasted weirdly with his speech, "is that you have to change. And that means controlling your mouth. Nobody's interested in your opinions and jokes and certainly not your obscenity."

He stopped again. My molars were almost ground to dust. "Is that everything?" I asked evenly.

"For the moment. If I think of anything else I'll let you know. I'm sure you'll take steps to modify your behavior for Bobby's sake, if not your own." He smiled again, very satisfied with himself. "I feel much better, don't you? Aren't you glad we had this little talk? I think it cleared the air."

Having finished his speech, he turned to go back to the house. He was done. I was not. I planted myself in front of him. I was damned if I'd let myself be turned into a Stepford wife without an argument.

"No, Rick, what you had was a monologue. I have a few things to say, too. And I think you owe it to me to listen."

He clearly wasn't happy but he stayed put. I took a deep breath to calm myself. *Don't lose your temper*, I reminded myself.

"First of all, I wouldn't have married anyone like you either, Rick. But that's what makes the world go round. You know, different strokes and all that? Secondly, I know you don't like me. And that's okay, too. I don't like you either. But I don't think you speak for everybody." I was starting to get excited so I took a moment to calm myself again. I held my hand up to stop Rick from interrupting. "Please just hear me out. Now, if I'm making Rob's life miserable, it's up to him to tell me, not you. And frankly, I don't think you know what Rob wants or likes. From what I can tell you Anderson brothers avoid each other. You all talk togetherness but you don't practice it unless someone else is around to run interference." I stopped for another calming breath before continuing. "If you find me an unacceptable member of your family, that's fine, Rick. I married Rob, not you. I have no intention of changing; I think I'm just fine the way I am. If you can't live with that, that strikes me as being your problem, not mine. Now do we understand each other?"

I finished my speech with my own personal version of a saintly smile. Apparently, it had the same effect on Rick that his had had on me. He got all red in the face and spit was coming out of the corners of his mouth. I think peace was the last thing he had on his mind.

"I knew you wouldn't see reason," he finally spat out.

"I won't be bullied," I countered.

Surprisingly, his eyes filled with tears. Frustration, I suppose. "Our family is falling apart and it's all your fault," he bawled at me.

"Your family is not falling apart," I said disgustedly, "you're having marital problems. I suggest you look in a mirror if you want to know the cause."

He glared at me and I glared back. He was clenching and unclenching his fists but I wouldn't back down. I could see that he wanted to slug me but even Rick knew he couldn't get away with that. He abruptly made an end-run around me and stalked back to the house with me trailing slowly after. But I'd kept my promise to Alice. I'd listened in the hope of peace. The fight, if there had been one, had been all on Rick's side. Of course, I didn't have any back teeth left but they were a small sacrifice. I needed crowns anyway.

By the time I got back to the house Rick had ordered Chris into her coat and they left immediately. Marilyn raised her eyebrows at me and suggested that we repair to the garage. I agreed with relief and ran the whole scene down to her over a fortifying glass of wine.

"God, what a jerk," was Marilyn's only comment when I finished.

"But I didn't scream or yell or anything. I told the truth as I saw it. Can I have another glass of wine?" I asked shakily, reaction setting in.

She poured. "Wait'll Bobby hears about this," she said gloomily. "Listen, you can have the cabin if you need to get away. No charge."

"Why would I need to get away? I didn't do anything wrong," I asked, puzzled.

"You poor child," Marilyn smiled sadly. "I keep forgetting how new you are to all this. The only truth the Anderson men will accept makes them all out to be heroes."

Her attitude seemed a little overwrought but I chalked it up to booze. Rob was not Rick, or Mike for that matter. I didn't put much stock in the fact that he came from the same gene pool.

Rob asked about running the gauntlet with Rick when we got back to the trailer. I ran through it for the second time expecting applause for my self-control and forbearance. Rob listened without expression.

"That's hard to believe," he scoffed lightly when I finished.

"What?" I asked. I was too surprised to be hurt or angry.

"It sounds like you two had another misunderstanding. I know Rick resents your faculty status and I think he's still mad about the talk you had with Chris but this is over the top even for him. Sometimes I think you both deliberately hear what the other says wrong," Rob said dismissively. "Well, I've got work to do. Better get at it."

I watched him as he set up his books at the kitchen table. Did he just call me a liar? I think he did. I concluded that Marilyn was right when she said the Andersons stuck together. Alice had set me up and Rick and Rob had knocked me down. The next question was: Who in their right mind would put up with this crap? I was at a loss as to what to do next.

I didn't have much to say to Rob the rest of the day but he didn't seem to notice. He had the attention span of a sparrow and once away from his family anything they did or said was forgotten. I wasn't that lucky. The more I thought about Rick's 'apology' the madder I got. *I bet he was speaking for the whole family*, I snarled to myself. I rattled around the trailer, alone with my anger. I didn't even have Pudgy to comfort me.

Alice called the next day. "Did you have a good talk with Rick?" she asked cheerfully.

"You bet," I returned coldly. "He got your message across loud and clear."

Alice seemed puzzled by my tone. "That's nice then. These misunderstandings just cause trouble down the road."

This was too much. "There won't be any more misunderstandings," I snarled. "Well. Gotta go. Bye." I hung up.

I was too furious to sit in the trailer by myself. I had to get out. In the back of my mind was the dark thought that I might not be in

South Dakota much longer and I better see what I could while I could. I decided to go for a drive even though Rob had told me to stay off the highway when I'd mentioned that my car made a funny humming noise.

"It's the snow tires," he told me. "Don't drive too much until I get the regular tires on. You'll just tear them up on the asphalt." He'd patted my hand. "Don't worry about it. That's why you have me."

Maybe I'd become hypersensitive but I found the remark and hand pat patronizing and condescending. This was behavior worthy of Rick. But it didn't seem worth fighting over. I just listed the gaffe in the 'Rob's sins—continued' category. That's what I'd come to, collecting crimes to be screamed about later. I had to remind myself that tire changing was Rob's expression of love—not that it would do him any good when the dam finally broke.

I didn't spend much time on asphalt anyway. I'd selected Oakwood State Park as a destination and the only way to get there was on a gravel road. Ordinarily the trip would have been dusty but at this time of year the road was still wet. When I got out of the Miata to appreciate the view I was amazed at the amount of real estate it'd managed to collect. At least the tires didn't hum in the mud.

The park was lovely so I decided to keep going. I rebelliously got on the highway and hummed past another lake before driving through a little burg called Castlewood. I drove slowly down the main street. There wasn't all that much to look at. The town consisted of a post office, a bar, a gas station, a cafe, and a junk shop called Knuth's Antiques. I decided to check out the antique shop; maybe I'd pick up a bargain.

The old, bearded proprietor watched me suspiciously as I wandered around his shop. I smiled at him but he just squinted his eyes at me. He obviously thought I would shoplift some of his junk. It was time for lunch anyway so I walked across the street to 'Myrtle's Café'.

Three men in overalls and Dekalb Seed caps sat at the counter chatting with the middle-aged waitress who had painted-on eyebrows and red, red lipstick. Her white uniform bulged with too many years of hamburgers and french fries and her peroxided hair was teased up in a bouffant style.

The conversation came to a halt when I walked in. The waitress called out, "Just sit anywhere, hon. Coffee?"

I nodded and slid onto a stool on the other end of the counter. The men didn't resume their conversation; they just gave me quick glances from under their cap visors. I guess they didn't see too many new faces at their watering hole. They didn't seem hostile, just curious. The waitress walked quickly over and poured some thin brew into a crockery cup. She moved fast for such a heavy woman.

"Menu?" she asked. I nodded again and she slapped one on the counter in front of me. "The special today is meatloaf, mashed potatoes with gravy, and canned peas. But you probably won't want that. I know you college girls are always watching your weight. I watch my weight, too," she smiled cheerfully. "I watch it go up." And she laughed. Her laugh came from her feet, rippled across her stomach, up her bosom, and emerged as she threw her head back. She had an earthquake of a laugh that was very infectious. I grinned along with her and glanced at the menu.

"I'll have a BLT," I said. "Light on the mayo."

"French fries?" she asked briskly.

"No thanks."

"I'll get you a square of Jell-O instead. And how about a nice glass of milk? Skinny's nice but you have to stay healthy, too," she coaxed.

I agreed and she hurried off. Apparently, she was cook as well as waitress. I read the nametag that was riding high on her ample breast as she breezed by: Myrtle. This seemed to be a one-woman operation.

I was left to myself so I looked around. The cafe was old but it was clean. Myrtle had framed pictures on the walls of the local football team, the high school marching band, a few school pictures of young girls, a wedding portrait, and an enlarged picture of a pretty, bouffant cheerleader circa 1965. Myrtle hadn't changed much in twenty-five years—except for the padding, of course.

I twirled my stool toward the farmers sitting at the other end of the counter. They'd been peering at me but when I turned to them their eyes went back to their coffee cups. As I twirled back to the photo gallery I heard some titters and snickering. I wished I'd brought a book to read.

The tittering and my discomfort had peaked when Myrtle came back with my order. She placed the BLT and Jell-O in front of me, tsked that she'd forgotten the milk, promised to be right back with it, and grabbed the coffee pot again. "More coffee, hon?"

I shook my head and she called out to the farmers, "You boys want more coffee?" She took their incoherent snuffles for assent and charged off. Honest to God, that woman could pour coffee from three feet away and not spill a drop.

"I'll make another pot and get that girl's milk," she announced and strode to the back room. The minute she left the snickering started again. I felt the sandwich catch in my throat. I tried to tell myself I was being paranoid, why in the world would those men be talking about me? They were probably just telling off-color jokes.

Myrtle came back with my milk and a filled coffee pot. She heard the giggling and looked sharply at the trio. She glanced at me sympathetically. So, it wasn't my imagination. I just hoped things didn't get ugly. If this were L.A. I'd be getting ready to run. But Myrtle handled the situation.

"You boys leave off that giggling," she scolded. "You sound like a bunch of little kids. You're going to hurt this poor girl's feelings. She doesn't know you're harmless." She turned to me. "They're only brave when there's a bunch of 'em. You should see them on Saturday night at the VFW. They're too scared to ask a girl to dance. Aren't you, Ole?" she challenged the middle farmer, the apparent ringleader. "And if a pretty girl asked you to dance you'd wet your pants. Now you three just drink your coffee and behave yourselves. Why aren't you out in the field anyway?"

Chastened, the three mumbled that it was too wet to be in the fields yet and they sure hadn't meant anything, mumble, mumble, blush.

Myrtle nodded at them and started passing out fresh, weak coffee, finishing up with me. "Sandwich okay?" she asked.

I nodded, my mouth full. Myrtle cut her eyes at the farmers and said to me, "Don't you pay any attention to them. They're good boys but there's a reason they're bachelors." She looked into my face more closely. "Say, I've seen you before, haven't I? You look familiar." She swiped a stray piece of hair from her eyes. "But that can't be. You're not from around here, are you?"

I swallowed. "I'm from Los Angeles," I said and had a sip of milk.

Myrtle's eyes got wide. "I knew you weren't from around these parts. Los Angeles! My, isn't that interesting!" she exclaimed.

I smiled sourly. "That old guy across the street didn't think I was interesting."

Myrtle sniffed. "Gilbert's just an old maid in pants. He hates everybody and everything. If his mother hadn't left him money he'd starve. So, are you just passing through?"

"I live in Brookings now."

"I knew you were a student!" she said, shaking a finger at me.

"Actually, I'm a teacher," I admitted.

"No! Well, my goodness. Either teachers are getting younger or I'm getting older. Hard to tell which!" Her laugh rolled from her toes to her nose again. Then she settled down to interrogate me. I told her I was born and raised in California; that my ancestry was Mexican and Irish; that I was I newly married to a South Dakota native. We even discussed Rob's relatives and where they came from. She wanted to know why I was in Castlewood and I explained that I was playing tourist. After she'd pried everything out of me, she was generous with information about herself. She pointed to the pictures of the cheerleader and the bride on the wall.

"I was a pretty girl, wasn't I?" she asked unselfconsciously. "And that's me and my husband Kenny. We had a farm around here. Had three kids." She paused, smiling at the memory of good times then continued matter-of-factly. "Kenny got cancer and died. I had to sell the farm to pay the hospital bills."

"No insurance?" I asked delicately.

"We were farmers. We couldn't afford insurance. And ten years ago, that's when Kenny died, things weren't too good for farmers. A lot just went under. Well, after the bills were paid I had enough left to buy this cafe. The kids all worked their way through college and we're all making out just fine."

There was no self-pity in her tone. I murmured some idiocy about government agencies that might have been helpful at the time but Myrtle snorted.

"Government agencies help themselves," she scoffed. "No, I got two arms and a strong back. I don't need no government agency to take care of me. And I raised my kids the same way. We'll help our neighbors if they're willing to help themselves but we don't expect no handouts and we don't give 'em!" Myrtle was quite emphatic on that point.

"How about your family?" I asked. "I imagine they helped out?"

"My family expected Kenny to take care of me and the children. I guess I did too. Well, he did his best but he was just a man. Taken all the way around, they're kind of a pitiful bunch. No, women have to take care of themselves. I learned that the hard way."

"So you wouldn't remarry?" I asked.

"Who would I marry?" she demanded. She tossed her head at the three farmers cowering at the counter. "Them? No thank you."

Myrtle seemed to have a pretty good handle on the world I found myself in so I asked her casually, "Did you ever have any in-law problems?"

The question set off the earthquake. "Honey, God made in-laws to keep us from getting too comfortable. Of course I had in-law problems. My Kenny was an only son so I had his parents on my back until the day he died. That was the only good thing about Kenny passing. At least I got rid of them." She laughed herself out and gave me a sharp look. "In-laws giving you a hard time?"

"Yeah," I admitted.

"Better get used to it. If you're married, you've got in-law problems. Just learn to ignore 'em," Myrtle advised. "That's all any of us can do. Now eat up."

I was dutifully finishing my Jell-O and milk when Myrtle asked me if I'd been out to Lake Poinsett (pronounced Ponset) yet. She said it was a real pretty spot and I'd probably like it. I tried to find it on the map but didn't have any luck until Myrtle spelled it out for me.

"It's French, isn't it?" Myrtle said. "Never could wrap my tongue around those French words."

It was the unidentified lake I'd driven past. I promised Myrtle I'd stop on my way home, thanked her, and paid my check. She poured the "boys" some more coffee and walked out to my car with me. Myrtle shook her head in amazement when I unlocked the Miata.

"That's one of those fancy foreign cars, isn't it?" she commented.

"Well, it's not so fancy…"

"My grandfather drove Fords, my father drove Fords, I guess I'll stick with Ford as long as they keep making 'em. Imagine me in one of those little bitty seats!" And her laugh rolled up again. I promised to stop in again when I was in the area and drove away, waving to Myrtle and smiling at the thought of her in this little bitty seat. Myrtle was too much woman for this car.

I drove down another gravel road and parked on a small hill overlooking Lake Poinsett. I listened to the ice crack and watched the clouds blow by. After hearing Myrtle's recitation of her calamities I didn't feel so sorry for myself. I realized that we were pretty much alike, give or take fifty pounds. We'd both survived death and destitution. We both had in-law problems. I'd been acting like Joan, taking my problems much too seriously. I'd return to my policy of Anderson avoidance and forget about Rick's denunciation. I still wasn't sure how mad I should be at Rob for not believing me. This was the second time he'd told me I was stretching the truth. Where had he gotten the idea I was a liar? I'd have to give that some more thought. I hummed home.

chapter 23

——

I could ignore the Andersons as long as a few blocks separated us but it's pretty tough to be oblivious to people when you're in the same room with them. I was ordered to put in an appearance when Chris gave birth to a boy on the first of June.

"I just get into trouble when I'm around Rick," I declared. "I'm not going."

"You have to," Rob insisted.

So we went to the hospital to ooh and ahhh and deliver a baby gift. We counted Baby Anderson's fingers and toes with Grampa and Gramma and reported to Chris that all parts were present and accounted for.

Chris was radiant. I hadn't seen her so happy, confidant, and unmashed in months. Maybe losing that mountain of weight on her stomach had something to do with it.

"Isn't he gorgeous?" she asked raptly.

Personally, I thought the baby was a little, red, wrinkled thing that could have been improved with a cool iron but I lied and agreed that the baby was gorgeous. Chris told us that her parents had been in to see the baby and that it had been so good to see them. She told us her father had started a savings account for the baby's education.

Rick walked in and I tensed up. We hadn't exchanged a word since our Easter confrontation and I would've been more than happy if he'd scheduled his visit after I left. Oh well, no hope for it now; I'd be as unobtrusive as possible.

Rick strutted and puffed like he'd done all the work. "I've got a fine boy, don't I," he congratulated himself. "I'm going to name him Marvin after you, Dad."

Marvin smiled, quietly pleased, and Rob and I exchanged an amused look. Marvin was a nice name for an old man but for a little boy?

Giving birth must have given Chris backbone because she actually disagreed with Rick. "I think my father would like it if we named the baby Joseph, after him. Personally I think Joey would be sweet," she said nervously.

Rick got red in the face and I waited for spit to show up in the corners of his mouth. "He's my son," he began.

"He's my son, too," Chris interrupted, starting to get teary, "and I'm not naming him Marvin! No offense, Marvin."

"None taken," Marvin murmured and looked to Alice for help. I expected her to jump in on Rick's side but she just looked flustered. The atmosphere was getting pretty thick. I was so uncomfortable I started babbling even though I knew it was the worst possible thing I could do.

"Maybe a new name might be appropriate," I said brightly. "I've read that it's bad luck to name babies after living people. Don't either one of you have any dead heroes in your families? That'd be a nice compromise."

The assembled Andersons looked at me. Now froth appeared on Rick's lips.

"Or maybe not," I backpedaled.

"Stay out of it," Rob hissed at me.

"Yes, you should mind your own business," said Rick, his color going back to pre-stoke hues. "I'd say you have enough problems in your own life to have time to interfere with decent people." And he gave me a queer, triumphant look. Alice asked for details of the birth to change the subject.

"What was that last crack of Rick's supposed to mean?" I asked Rob as we drove home.

"I don't know," said Rob tiredly. "Just stay away from those two."

"If you remember you twisted my arm to get me to the hospital," I snapped. "And, honestly, all I did was make a suggestion about a name. I don't know what Rick got so mad about."

"You were interfering," Rob said.

"I was making a suggestion. God, can't I even talk anymore?" I asked rhetorically.

Rob acted like he'd be perfectly happy if I didn't open my mouth for the rest of his natural life so I gave him the silent treatment for a week. Unfortunately, he was studying for finals and didn't notice.

Crazy Eddie, the old man at the end of the trailer row, died. When he failed to clean up the bar one Saturday night, his boss commissioned the college boys next door to knock on Eddie's door and check on him. When the boys didn't get an answer they called the police who broke in the door. The old guy must have been dead for a week. The policemen came rushing out of Eddie's trailer, choking and gagging.

We were a solemn group as we watched Eddie's body being brought out in a bag.

"It looks like a Hefty bag," I murmured to Rob. "Will he be buried like that?"

"Maybe the county will have him cremated," Rob said. "Nobody ever heard of any family. It's really sad."

We all nodded at that statement. It was really sad, living for the bottle and being removed in a bag. The boys left to have a beer in Eddy's memory but Rob and I continued to watch as the ambulance drove off. Rob got that patient, saintly, Anderson look on his face and began a little, well-intentioned lecture. Funny how much like Rick he was getting.

"See, families are valuable," he said. "At least there's someone around to take care of you so you don't die alone and forgotten."

I hate lectures, even well-intentioned ones. I pointedly looked in the garbage can filled with empty bottles and said in my best nasty-nice voice, "Maybe it was his family who drove him to drink."

That started a fight but it was better than silence. If I'd had to be quiet much longer I'd probably have ended up on the water tower with a rifle. Screaming for half an hour got the worst of my crazies off but it didn't ease Rob much. He still seemed to have something on his mind—not that he was willing to discuss it with me. He didn't even seem interested in a wild romp in the hay to cement a peace treaty. I had to dig out the itchy underwear to get him interested.

The last week of school the Theater Department had an awards banquet for the student performances. It was sort of a collegiate Tony

Awards and Brian had been nominated for Best Actor, quite a coup for the first time out. In honor of the occasion, Rob and I got gussied up.

"I don't know why I have to go," Rob grumbled as he struggled to get his tie even.

"Because I need an escort and that's part of your job description," I retorted as I put on my earrings. "Hurry up. We're going to be late."

I'd selected a rather low-cut cocktail dress for the evening. If I do say so myself, I thought I looked pretty foxy. Rob apparently agreed with me. As I was preening in the mirror he put his arms around me and nuzzled my ear.

"Let's see if we can cut out early, okay?" he murmured.

Why did he only think of sex when I was in a hurry? I slapped his hands away with distracted irritation. "Let's go make like authority figures."

The banquet fare was the ever-popular rubber chicken. Sometimes I think banquet food is what pulls this great country together. No matter where you go the menu is rubber chicken and dehydrated peas. In Brookings a green square of Jell-O at each place was included.

The presentations and acceptance speeches were the usual unsuccessful attempts at humor. It made for a long evening but I was pleased when Brian won. So was Brian; he charged through the crowd of well-wishers and back-patters to give me a hug. He lifted me off the ground and twirled me around which was easy for him because he was a foot taller and about a couple hundred pounds heavier than me. Then he gave me a big smacking kiss.

"I won, Miss O'Neill, I won!" he crowed as he put me down.

"You sure did," I agreed, grinning. "Congratulations. You earned it."

Rob stood next to us, looking annoyed. I turned to include him. "Brian, you remember my husband, Rob Anderson."

"You bet," Brian said. His red face beamed happily as he wrung Rob's hand. "Your wife's the best teacher ever. Honest to God!" Brian assured him enthusiastically.

"I'm sure," said Rob.

Rob's tone chilled Brian a little. "Well, guess I better go. Thanks again, Miss O'Neill." And he charged off, scattering art farts in his wake.

I looked at Rob curiously. "You weren't very gracious," I said.

"I didn't like him pawing you like that," he said shortly.

"He didn't paw me, he hugged me. He was excited," I explained.

"I still don't like it."

A light went on in my head. "Why, Rob Anderson, you're jealous!" I accused, amused.

"I am not. I just think that as a teacher you should maintain some distance," Rob said stuffily.

"He's just a kid!" I scoffed.

"He's a very large kid," Rob retorted severely.

I was a little disturbed by his attitude. Brian was a like a puppy; a kiss from him was nothing more than a slurp. But from the judgmental look Rob was giving me I knew I was going to have to break out the underwear again. I was even more disturbed when I noticed other staff members watching the scene covertly. A hug from a student didn't justify all of this attention. What was going on?

The semester ended with no indication from Dr. Torgeson whether my part-time services would be required next year or not—and Dr. Torgeson was always too busy to talk to me. I tried waylaying him in the hallway once but he said "he'd have to get back to me, he was in a hurry" and scurried off. I didn't know if the department was out of money, if my teaching performance was unsatisfactory…what? I also noticed Muehler giving me the same queer, triumphant look I'd gotten from Rick although he was careful to stay away from me.

Maybe I'm paranoid but the strange looks were starting to bother me. I asked my officemate Linda if she'd heard anything.

"Not really," she said evasively, then offered, "Why don't you ask Margy? She knows everything that goes on."

So I invited Margy out to lunch. Over salad I described the weird stares I'd been getting.

"So," I concluded, "Linda says you know everything that's going on in the Department. Why's everybody looking at me so funny? Why won't Torgeson talk to me?"

Margy put her fork down and said uncomfortably, "Well, I hate to be the one to tell you but…" she hesitated and finished in a rush, "word is that you're having an affair with one of your students."

I leaned back in my chair, flummoxed. "Any student in particular?" I asked.

"The football player, Brian."

Of course! Everything made sense now. My stomach started churning and I had to fight for control. "Do you know how the rumor started?" I asked, as calmly as possible, which is tough when all you want to do is throw up.

"Muehler's been spreading it around the Speech Department. But I'm pretty sure it didn't start with him…" she paused.

"Who started it?" I said through my teeth.

"I really don't want to be the one to tell you," she repeated and she really did look unhappy, "but I think it's better you know. I'm pretty sure your brother-in-law Dr. Anderson is behind it. I guess he saw you with Brian in a bar. You know his office is in the next building over and it was easy for him to get together with Muehler. The campus isn't that big; we all know each other." Margy paused again. "It isn't true, is it?" she asked delicately.

I'd been pushing the remaining salad around on my plate but her question brought me up short. "Of course not," I said hotly. "How could you even think that?"

Margy squirmed but argued, "You do spend a lot of time with Brian…"

"I was helping him write a comedy routine!" I said impatiently.

"And that kiss he gave you at the banquet…"

"He was excited. I'm his teacher!" I exclaimed.

"He's young and good-looking," Margy said and looked me in the eye. "And so are you."

I just stared at her. At least five years divided Brian and me and I considered them an unbridgeable canyon. But to middle-aged people… oh man.

"I didn't really believe it," Margy continued, "but when your own brother-in-law starts something like that…" she trailed off.

Yeah, when your own brother-in-law starts something like that…I felt even sicker. "Why didn't anybody ask me about this?" I demanded.

"You know Dr. Torgeson doesn't like confrontations. Besides, it's such an ugly subject," Margy said apologetically.

It sure was. And almost impossible to counter, especially when the source is "your own brother-in-law". I thanked Margy for the information, drove her back to the office, and went home to vomit.

By the time Rob came home I'd gotten myself calmed down enough to talk to him about it without screaming. We sat down at the kitchen table across from each other and I laid out the whole sordid thing. I don't know what I was expecting from Rob; rage, maybe denunciation of Rick, certainly support.

"I couldn't get hired in Hollywood because I wouldn't take my clothes off. Here, I'm accused of moral turpitude. I just can't win," I finished bitterly.

Rob said slowly, "Rick told me there were rumors about you and Brian. He said Muehler told him you'd been spending time in your office with the door shut. I told him I didn't believe anything was wrong."

I smiled wanly. "Thank you. I know there's only a few years difference in age between Brian and me but, honestly..."

"But then I saw Brian grab you," Rob interrupted, sounding harassed, "and...well, I don't know what to think. I know you don't get along with Rick but he's my brother. Why would he lie to me? Especially about something like this?" He shook his head in confusion and looked at me helplessly.

I quietly digested his statement. Rick had spread filth about me and Rob wouldn't believe his brother would lie, ergo I must be at fault somehow. I'd given up a comfortable lifestyle for this yahoo, I'd put up with a lot of crap from his family, but this was too much. It was time to go ballistic. So I did. I yelled, I paced, I raged, I shrieked, I waved my arms in the air, I threw books...I had a fine tantrum. I howled my frustration and anger to the universe—and at Rob, of course. I did everything I'd promised I'd never do again; the son-of-a-bitch had it coming. And it felt g-o-o-o-d.

And what did Rob do? He walked out and slammed the door behind him.

It's not very satisfying to shout when nobody's there to listen. So I drove to the liquor store, bought a nice bottle of wine, and crawled into it, just like Eddy. I bawled into my merlot and finally passed out on the couch.

I woke up the next morning alone, still on the couch, stiff, and miserably hung over.

"God, Pudge," I whispered, "my mouth tastes like I cleaned out your litter box with my tongue. Pudge? Pudge?"

Oh yeah. Pudgy was dead. Lucky her. I'd have to get better to die. I looked at my watch; eight o'clock. Good thing I didn't have classes anymore; I'd've been late. I stretched and licked my lips. Between the exertion of the tantrum, the wine, and the tears, I was feeling seriously dehydrated and my head hurt. I washed down four aspirin with a Diet Coke and took stock of my situation. I was alone and apparently had been since last night although I could have been wrong about that. The bed was unmade but that didn't mean anything—it always was. Alice had tried brainwashing me into seeing the value of daily bed making but it hadn't took. Screw it, who cared if Rob had come home or not. I took a shower and brushed my teeth to clear my head.

So. What options did I have? Not many. I guess I didn't have a job at the University anymore so what could I do? Well, there was always acting. I decided to give ol' Heather a call. My last commercial hadn't shown yet but maybe she could get me some interviews in the near future. It was a ray of hope. I'd go back to bed and call her at noon.

"Well, Stevie," said Heather waspishly when I got through to her, "I'd pretty much given up on you. You can't just call up whenever you feel like coming to town and have everybody waiting for you. The Business just doesn't work that way."

God, she sounded so happy to tell me off. My head was still throbbing and my stomach was upset and I was not in the mood to be cut off at the knees by Heather; I'd been worked on by experts.

"Heather," I snarled quietly so as not to disturb my head, "you can be such a bitch sometimes."

"I'm an agent, it comes with the territory," she retorted. "If you want to work, fine, move back to L.A. and I'll break my butt for you. But until you do, don't waste my time." She hung up.

The hits just keep coming, I moaned to myself.

I briefly considered moving back to Los Angeles. I could just pack up and go...where? I couldn't get into my condo. If I tried to camp out with Leslie again she'd probably run screaming into the Pacific. I couldn't bear the thought of staying in the trailer. What to do, what to do.

Then I remembered Marilyn's offer of her lake cabin. Maybe she'd let me rent it for a week or two until I got my head together and could think clearly. I'd be out of the trailer but close enough to be in contact with Rob to discuss whatever needed discussing—like divorce. I reflected ruefully that it was a hell of a lot more trouble to get out of a marriage than it was to get into one—more painful, too.

I called Marilyn, gave an abridged version of my sad story, and asked to rent her cabin.

"Just tell me what you want and I'll mail you a check," I told her.

"Don't worry about money," she said. "I'll be glad to let you use it. When do you want it?"

"Today okay with you? I really need to get out."

"Fine. I always leave a key under a rock out there."

She gave me directions to the Lake Campbell cabin and the security rock. I packed what I thought I'd need, left Rob a note telling him where I was and why, and left.

From the way Marilyn talked I'd assumed the cabin would be a pleasant home-away-from-home on the lake; it turned out to be a two-room shack. The key under the rock fit the padlock on the back door. I almost broke the key struggling with the padlock but it finally opened. The hinges screecked as I pushed the door open into an unfinished room that had an old refrigerator, a sink, a double hotplate, a table, and four chairs. A thin wall separated the kitchen/dining area from a bedroom that had four stripped cots. There was a toilet, sink, and shower in a closet but the water was turned off. So was the electricity. There was no telephone, TV, or even a radio. I couldn't find a furnace anywhere. It was cold, musty, and dank.

I went outside and walked around the cabin. Well, there was a lake anyway; Marilyn hadn't lied about that. There was even a wooden dock standing in it. And a locked building with a pulley sticking out of the roof that I assumed was a boathouse. I walked out on the dock and knelt down to test the temperature of the water with my fingers. Maybe I'd swim a little tomorrow.

I finished my cruise around the cabin and found the electrical main switch. I forced the switch and went inside to test the lights. I smiled when the overhead fixture glowed and the refrigerator hummed. Next I turned on the water lines. Rusty water gushed out of the kitchen faucet. I waited for a minute or two to see if the water would run clear. It did. Unfortunately, it never warmed up. The hot water heater must be off. I found that in a lean-to but it had to be at least a hundred years old and I had no idea how to light the pilot—or if it was safe to do so. My headache was coming back which was really starting to piss me off. I don't understand why booze hits me so hard. *Other people can drink without getting deathly ill*, I thought. Why, in most modern literature the heroine would have a couple before-dinner cocktails, a bottle of wine with dinner, and an after-dinner brandy just to aid digestion. Then she'd close a major corporate deal or track down a murderer and beat him up. Not me. One bottle of wine and I'm sick for a day or two. And I gain about three pounds.

Well, there didn't seem to be another soul around for miles, which gave me a chance to recover from my hangover and my heartache. I'd have to set in some supplies, though. I drove to a bait shop I'd passed earlier. I bought Diet Pepsi, bottled water, some Twinkies, a bag of Nacho Cheese Flavored Doritos, and a couple of paperbacks.

As he rang up my purchases the man at the register told me that the lake was dead until the weekend. "There's some retired folks across the way but around here it's pretty much weekenders. Nah, there's not much to do. The bar next door opens up at about five if you want to drop by for a beer. It's mostly local boys who drink there but I'm sure they wouldn't mind if a pretty girl wanted to join them."

My stomach turned over at the thought of a beer. I went back to the cabin, used a wadded up sweatshirt as a pillow, my jacket as a blanket, and curled up with my water, Doritos, and a paperback. I'd never been in such quiet before. Every rustle in the grass was magnified into the stealthy approach of a rapist. I just knew Charlie Manson was loose and banging on the screen. Nope, just a moth. I missed my television. Damn Rob for making me live in this misery. Ever since I hooked up with that jerk my living conditions had gone from bad to worse. I finally fell asleep to the soft lapping of the lake with the lights on and the bugs knocking to get in.

After a breakfast of Twinkies and Diet Pepsi the next morning I was sitting on the end of dock plotting how to get a TV, a radio, and some bedding out of the trailer without being caught by Rob when I heard a car stop by the cabin and a cheery, "Yoo-hoo, Stevie?"

It was Marilyn and her two kids, Tiffany and Ryan. "I hope you don't mind if we join you," she called sunnily.

I trudged up to meet her. "It's your cabin," I said. "Besides, I could use some company. I've been getting lonely out here all by myself. Where's Mike?"

Marilyn waved a hand at me. "He won't be coming," she said airily and walked around to the trunk of her Cadillac. "I brought our summer stuff and a few groceries. We'll have to do a major shop later."

She opened the trunk and I saw a tiny TV, a VCR, some tapes, a radio, a clock, appliances, blankets…she even brought a cellular phone. Stuff! I had stuff again! I helped her haul everything into the cabin. We unpacked the groceries and moved two cots into the kitchen.

"The kids can sleep out here," Marilyn decided. "Or they can set up the tent and sleep outside. They like that."

She showed me how to light the pilot on the water heater. "I see you figured out the lights and the water," she said approvingly. "That's more than Nancy ever did."

We made the beds. Then she instructed the kids to go jump in the lake. Literally.

"I'm going to have a beer," Marilyn announced. "Want one?" She uncapped a bottle with one swift twist and toasted me with it. "Here's to freedom. You're not the only one who needs a break. See," she said confidentially, "Mike and I got into a big fight over you and Bobby. I told him his brothers were idiots and I was on your side. So, here I am!"

Marilyn looked delighted with herself but I felt like the Typhoid Mary of marriages, spreading dissolution wherever I went. Marilyn took a healthy swig of her beer and added, "Mike didn't believe that Rick would start a story like that about a family member but I told him Rick would kill his grandmother if she crossed him. Sure you don't want a beer?"

Life was getting too complicated for me. "Oh sure, why not," I said. Marilyn uncapped a bottle for me, which gave me a moment to think.

"Listen, Marilyn, I don't want you and Mike fighting over me," I began after we toasted each other with our bottles. "Don't get me wrong, I appreciate the sympathy" (I really did. I didn't feel quite so alone in the world. Somebody believed me.) "but this is between Rob and me. You shouldn't have to pick sides."

"Of course I do. I even called Alice and told her what Rick said to you at Easter and she was shocked. She said she'd just told him to make peace. He made the rest of that other stuff up," Marilyn said. "And don't worry about me and Mike. If we weren't fighting over this it'd be something else. I've decided to stand up on my hind legs and I like the view. I'm tired of him and I'm really tired of his brothers—they're all a bunch of hogs, Bobby included. I, for one, am tired of slopping my

292

hog. So I just left a note, like you did, and split. We can stay here until those two men come to their senses."

"What if they don't?"

That prospect didn't even faze Marilyn. "We'll worry about that later," she smiled and dismissed the idea. "In the meantime we'll have a vacation. Too bad I had to bring the piglets but I am their mother and Mike certainly wouldn't look after them. So here we are."

We toasted and drank. Maybe the beer was finishing off what was left of my liver. Maybe I was facing divorce. It was hard to worry with Marilyn so buoyant.

Marilyn assigned cooking, cleaning, and babysitting chores. "This is great," she exclaimed. "No men around, giving orders and refusing to help with anything. It's like living in a commune!"

Marilyn may have felt liberated but I had a few reservations. Tiffany and Ryan were noisy and probably even more work than Rob had been but how could I complain? It was her cabin. And taking care of the kids kept me from thinking too much.

"I'm going to put the boat in the water and gas it up," Marilyn announced after lunch. "Who wants to go waterskiing?"

Tiffany and Ryan shrieked enthusiastically and loped down to the boathouse. Marilyn lent me a bathing suit and we followed the kids.

I was curious about waterskiing. I'd never tried it. Marilyn drove her powerboat competently and I sat next to her, intently watching Tiffany and Ryan. They were terrific on skis; they slalomed, they balanced on one ski, they made it look so easy I decided to give it a try. Marilyn stopped the boat, the kids helped me put on the skis, and gave me instructions. I struggled and struggled to rise but I couldn't seem to get my dead butt out of the water.

"I don't understand it," I spluttered after I'd plowed the water with my face for the fifth time. "I exercise, my legs are in shape, what am I doing wrong?"

"You're trying too hard," Marilyn said. "Have another beer."

The beer was probably part of the problem but I had one anyway. Floundering around with huge wooden things on your feet burns up a lot of calories.

Two days went by with no contact from the outside world. I was damned if I'd unbend to initiate a dialogue with Rob. He knew where

I was. I was right and, more importantly, he was wrong. It was up to him to make the first move. Why in hell didn't he make it?

"Uh…Marilyn," I asked hesitantly as we made supper, "does your phone work?"

She picked up the receiver, punched a button, listened for a moment, and said, "Sure. Why?"

"Doesn't it seem odd to you that nobody's tried to call us?"

"Like who?"

"Well…Mike, for instance. Or Rob."

"Nah, they're too busy pouting. And they're waiting us out. One thing you'll learn about Midwestern men is that they're great pouters and waiters. They'll hold off as long as they can."

I listened to Marilyn's kids bickering over the Gameboy and asked, trying to keep any desperation out of my voice, "What if they hold out for a month?"

"They won't," Marilyn said confidently. "They'll give in when they run out of socks. Or when they get sick of eating out."

"Won't Alice do their laundry and feed them?"

"Not Mike. He lives too far away," Marilyn said calmly. "Besides, what do we need them for? We can entertain ourselves. Wait'll this weekend! That's when the fun starts."

We were outside roasting hotdogs that evening when a pickup pulled up next to the cabin. Chris climbed out of the cab loaded down with her baby and a diaper bag. She called out, "I heard you two were out here. Do mind if I join you?" Then she burst into tears. And I do mean burst. She shook so hard tears flew off her. She looked like a sprinkler.

Marilyn and I looked at each other and shrugged.

"The more the merrier," Marilyn yelled back.

"You want a hotdog?" I shouted hospitably.

Marilyn yelled at her kids to help Chris with her luggage and we watched as they unloaded the pickup and dragged Chris down the path to the cabin.

"It would appear that another in-law has seceded from the Anderson union," I commented bemusedly. "You don't think Nancy's going to show up, do you?"

"That would be the one thing that would chase me back home," Marilyn snickered. "Let's find out what's wrong with Chris."

The baby started howling from the cabin. Marilyn listened for a minute, made a face, and looked at me. "Maybe we should have our hotdogs first," she suggested.

The howl went up an octave. I agreed.

chapter 24

Marilyn spent the rest of the evening cooing and clucking over Chris and the baby and getting her story. I didn't talk much. I'd learned the hard way that Chris twisted what I said.

"Rick insists we call the baby Marvin and I just hate that name. I want to call him Joe," Chris sobbed. "We can't even arrange the baptism and Alice is upset with me about that."

"So that's why you left? Over the baby's name?" asked Marilyn. "Why don't you just name him Richard, Jr.?"

"Yeah," I snorted, "call him Dick. His father's one."

My snide crack went right over Chris' head. "That was just one of the reasons." Chris looked at me and sniffled. "I think what Rick did to you was terrible, Steph. You have some weird ideas but you're not immoral and I told him that. Well, Rick started yelling." The waterworks started again. "I don't know why he keeps yelling at me; I didn't do anything."

"Neither did I," I commented dryly.

Chris cried for a minute then said, "I gave up my shop for him when he told me I should. I did everything I could to make him happy, except name the baby Marvin and I can't do that for the baby's sake. It's a horrible name for a child!" She rearranged her progeny's blanket protectively. "Thanks for letting me and the baby stay here. I didn't know where else to go. I just couldn't tell my folks how bad things are."

Chris sniffled some more but I wanted one thing clarified.

"How'd you know we were out here?" I asked Chris.

"Bobby came out to the farm and said you'd left for the lake. He wanted to know if Rick started that awful lie. Rick said he was just repeating what he'd heard. Then he started yelling that he'd seen you with that football player at The Lantern. He said where there was smoke there was fire and you should probably go back where you came from. That's when Bobby left."

"When was this?" I asked.

"Yesterday. And Rick's been yelling at me ever since. I just couldn't take anymore."

Marilyn comforted Chris but I had to think. So. Rob must agree with the smoke/fire deduction or he'd have been out here to apologize. I guess I knew where I stood in the scheme of things.

"Is this a community property state?" I asked Marilyn.

"No," she said as she patted a bawling Chris, "but you don't want a divorce."

"Maybe I do," I said.

She waved that comment off impatiently. "You just need a vacation," Marilyn declared. "We'll do some waterskiing, go to some parties... Have another beer!"

"Not for me," Chris sniffed. "I'm breast feeding."

"Marilyn, this isn't summer camp," I protested.

"Of course it is," Marilyn said. She left off comforting Chris to pat me instead. "You're just tired. Things'll look better after a good night's rest."

Marilyn decided we should all go to bed early. She unrolled a sleeping bag in the floor of our room for Chris and put the baby in a laundry basket next to his mother. It's quite possible Marilyn was right about a good night's rest but little Joe/Marvin/Dick did his best to make sure nobody got one. Tiffany and Ryan gave up early and went outside to sleep in the tent. Chris finally got up and sat with him in the kitchen so he could slurp whenever he liked. It was a haggard group that ate pancakes next morning.

I spent the day reading on the beach and watching the kids paddle around in inner tubes. My sleepless night was catching up with me and I was starting to get seriously depressed.

Marilyn joined me. "You okay?" she asked.

"I've been thinking everybody would have been a lot better off if I never came here," I confessed.

297

"All the blow-ups would have happened sooner or later, it's just that with you around they happened sooner," Marilyn said with a smile. "I probably wouldn't have told Mike off about the ski trip if you hadn't refused to go. If you'd been there to share chores I'd've been mad as hell but I'd have put up with it. And it wasn't right, expecting the women to do all the work. Chris would probably never have had the nerve to stand up to Rick if you hadn't led the way. And let's face it, she really needed to stand up to Rick." Marilyn paused then looked at me admiringly. "You were an outsider who refused to put up with stuff we all accepted as normal. You got us thinking. You're not a problem, you're a catalyst," she concluded thoughtfully.

Catalyst? Such a big, complex word for an ex-beauty queen! I raised an ironic eyebrow at Marilyn and she grinned at me. "I'm not a complete fool," she said. "I was a psychology major in college. No," she continued seriously, "you didn't cause all these problems. The men did."

"Leaving Mike seems a little extreme," I said.

She shrugged that off. "He's got the idea that because I stay home with the kids, and he's a business success, he gets to make all the decisions. And I just went along with it. I'm not saying he doesn't do a good job for the bank but he wouldn't have even gotten it if it hadn't been for me. I taught him how to dress and how to behave in that sort of social circle. And the money he's invested is money I inherited. So I think it's time he started appreciating me—and consulting me. We'll just see how long he lasts on his own. Besides, I needed a vacation."

"What about Chris?" I asked.

Marilyn sighed. "She's been in trouble for a long time. Rick blames her for everything that goes wrong with his life. If he had a dog he'd probably kick it. I think the main problem is that he's always competing with his brothers—and losing. Tom got the hardware store and Mike makes more money. The only brother he was more successful than was Bobby. And Bobby came home from the Big City with you." She smiled. "You're better educated than Chris, you're better-looking, and Alice told me you've got money. Baby Bobby married better than he did. But brotherly code prevents him from resenting Bobby so he punishes Chris. And now you, too."

I nodded thoughtfully. "Then explain this to me: Rob told me that Chris told Rick that I tried to get her to abort the baby," I said, told

Marilyn what I'd really said, then asked, "Why would Chris make up something like that?"

Marilyn's eyebrows climbed. "Probably to take the heat off herself but throwing you to the wolves is an awful way to do it. What a pair of liars. Maybe she and Rick deserve each other. Now I'm sorry I let her stay here. I was too surprised to do anything else when she showed up. We've never had anything in common; I thought you liked her. Well, too late now." She paused then added, "Although with her here Rick doesn't have anyone left to push around. He's probably going nuts." She grinned. "Serves him right. He's always dominated Bobby, you know. I really noticed it at my wedding. Bobby must have been only fifteen or so and Rick ragged at him constantly. I felt sorry for him but Alice thought it was wonderful that Rick 'took care' of his little brother. I wondered if that wasn't one of the reasons Bobby went all the way to California. I was glad that he brought a hell-raiser like you back with him."

"All you're saying is that I am the cause of all the trouble," I concluded, exasperated.

"Of course you aren't," Marilyn said impatiently. "Rick is. Weren't you listening to me at all? You just encouraged the slaves to revolt. Like Spartacus. Did you see that movie on cable? God, Kirk Douglas was a hunk."

"Yeah, I saw it," I said sourly. "Spartacus got crucified."

"There's a downside to everything," Marilyn admitted.

We sat quietly, absorbed in our own thoughts. After a few minutes, Marilyn lifted her head and listened. There was nothing to hear. "The baby's quiet. We should grab some sleep," she suggested. "Our neighbors are coming in from Sioux Falls tonight and there'll probably be a party. You'll love these people." She smiled in anticipation.

The neighbors, a collection of doctors, lawyers, and bankers, appeared after supper and the weekend turned into one long party, most of it spent on the water. I tanned dark bronze and Marilyn said enviously as she slathered on sunscreen, "I wish I could tan like that. I just burn and peel."

"It's my inheritance from my mother," I explained. "My father was a melanoma waiting to happen."

"Whatever. You look great."

I must've. I was getting a lot of unwanted attention from husbands and glares from wives. When the flirtations and glares got too onerous

I tried hiding out in the cabin but that wretched baby would start to howl as soon as I walked in and I was driven back outside. Like father, like son, I thought crankily.

The parties stopped when Marilyn's friends went home Sunday night. "They'll be back next weekend," Marilyn said as we waved them off. Then she asked briskly, "What do you want to do tomorrow?"

I'd worry about tomorrow when it came. Right then I wanted to go to sleep, I was exhausted. But with Joe/Marvin/Dick around that wasn't going to happen any time soon.

The next day Marilyn decided Tiffany and Ryan needed to explore their pioneer heritage so she packed the three of us in her Cadillac and drove over to a tourist attraction/pioneer museum called Prairie Village to get us educated. I'd never even been on a farm before so I was fascinated with the antique tractors and other equipment although Marilyn had to explain to me what everything did.

"This stuff would probably still do the job but people like bigger and better equipment. My uncle just got a tractor with air conditioning, TV, and stereo in the cab. It cost over $100,000," she said. "It's a status symbol. It's like driving a BMW instead of a Model T."

We moved on to the restored main street of a town. I particularly enjoyed the beauty parlor and the permanent-wave machine. "Now I know where Nancy gets her hair done," I cracked.

We inspected a replica of a sod hut. Marilyn made a big deal about how miserable it must been to survive a Midwestern winter in such a drafty little thing but I thought the hut resembled my trailer; all it needed was a shag rug and some plastic on the windows. Then Marilyn pointed to the outhouse in the back. I guess I had been lucky; at least I'd had indoor plumbing and running water.

I gained a lot of respect for the pioneers, particularly their wives, that day. I also regained some perspective. I thoughtfully thanked Marilyn for taking me to the museum but her attention had already moved on.

"Hey, you want to go shopping in Sioux Falls tomorrow? You need a new bathing suit and there's a great little boutique that just opened up…" she burbled.

Marilyn chattered happily about shopping all the way back to the lake cabin. She called out to Chris, "Hey! You want to go shopping with Stevie and me tomorrow?"

Marvin/Joe/Dick was attached at the moment so Chris just smiled, nodded at her lustily sucking infant, and said, "Better not; he doesn't travel so well yet."

"Of course," smiled Marilyn. "You know, Steph, you and Bobby will probably have kids one of the these days. Will you breast feed? It increased my bust line, you know. Personally, I think breast feeding saved my marriage. Mike is really boob oriented. I think he was breast fed and never grew out of it..." she chattered on. Marilyn seemed to be having the time of her life.

We went shopping, we barbequed, we swam, we skied. I spent so much time in the water I turned into a brown prune and I got so tired of having fun I could have cried. I missed Rob and I hated him and I found the ambivalence exhausting. I quit washing my hair and shaving my legs.

"Did you know that stubble acts like Velcro?" I asked Marilyn as I moodily threw a dust bunny against my shin and watched it stick.

"God, Stevie, either shave or sweep," Marilyn replied in disgust.

Us Anderson outlaws were starting to seriously get on each other's nerves.

"B.F. Skinner, you know, the behavioral psychologist? Well, he forced a bunch of rats to live in close quarters and they cannibalized each other," Marilyn expounded after a tense lunch.

"Please don't lecture," I requested with a barely concealed sneer.

The final blowup was about Chris' baby. Little Dick/Marvin/Joe seemed to spend all his time crying, which was really driving everybody nuts. Breast-feeding shut him up as long as he was attached but the minute his mouth was free he used it to howl. And, boy, did he howl. Thank God the neighbors weren't around. They'd have called the police.

Marilyn finally snapped. "Can't you shut him up?" she asked with barely controlled ferocity.

"I don't know what's wrong with him," Chris said distractedly.

"Does he have diaper rash?" I asked. My experience with babies was nil but I'd heard about diaper rash. It seemed to be the infant version of jock itch.

"No, he's fine. Maybe the other kids are bothering him. Could you ask Ryan and Tiffany not to make so much noise?" Chris asked Marilyn.

"Yeah, they're even starting to get to me," I contributed helpfully.

"No, I cannot," said Marilyn shortly. "They're kids. They make noise. Get used to it. That baby is just going to have to learn that the universe doesn't revolve around him."

"But he's just a baby," protested Chris.

"And he's already just like his father. Has to have his own way all the time," Marilyn retorted.

"Don't you criticize my baby," Chris flared.

"I'll criticize him whenever I want," Marilyn shot back. "And, by the way, when are you going to name that damned kid? You have three choices. Pick one!"

Chris dissolved into tears and the baby wailed even louder.

"Maybe you should lay off Chris," I uneasily suggested to Marilyn over the wailing.

Marilyn wheeled on me. "You shut up, too! Until you have some kids don't you criticize mine! I wouldn't be in this mess if it weren't for you!"

"You shouldn't blame Stephanie," Chris interrupted with a sniffle.

"Hey, nobody asked you to come," I yelled at Marilyn. "You offered your cabin, I took you up on your offer. You and your two screaming kids weren't included in the deal!"

"I was trying to support you!" Marilyn bellowed.

"Well, you're doing a great job, aren't you!" I roared back.

The situation deteriorated from there. Fortunately, Ryan and Tiffany were out by the boathouse and didn't get to witness our display of sisterhood in action. After enough hurtful comments had been exchanged, we separated to lick our wounds. I retreated to the end of the dock to let the mosquitoes finish me off. At least I was alone. I slapped, flapped, and swore for half an hour until Marilyn joined me. She sat down next to me and handed me a bottle of Avon's Skin-So-Soft.

"Are you implying I have a tough hide?" I asked.

"Peace offering," she said. "It's mosquito repellent."

"Oh. Thanks," I said gratefully and rubbed some on my arms. "I didn't know mosquitoes got this big."

"Us Midwesterners just call them our state bird," Marilyn said calmly.

We sat silently and breathed in the scent of Skin-So-Soft. "Uh, sorry about the things I said back there," I started hesitantly.

"Me, too. I already apologized to Chris," Marilyn said.

"It wasn't supposed to be like this," I said, morosely. "I thought we had a *Lysistrada* thing going."

"Lysis who?" Marilyn asked.

"*Lysistrada*. It's a play by Aristophanes," I said with a slight shrug. Marilyn's exhibitions of erudition had irritated hell out of me. I didn't want to irritate hell out of her.

"Who's that?" Marilyn asked blankly.

"Ancient Greek comedy writer," I explained diffidently. "He wrote about a bunch of Athenian women who got tired of the constant war with Sparta so they all hid in a temple and refused to have sex with the men until they ended the war."

"Did it work?"

"I never finished reading the play," I admitted and reflected on the last day or two. "The women probably killed each other."

"Probably," Marilyn agreed then said briskly, "Listen. I have to make a quick trip home. Would you watch the piglets?" I nodded. "I'll be back in a few hours. Just don't let the kids murder each other," she said by way of instruction then jumped up, patted my shoulder, and left.

It was a long afternoon. I probably should have appreciated the quiet time after the last week but I got bored. I tried to interact with Ryan and Tiffany but they obviously considered my attempts at babysitting ineffectual and condescending. Except for a little intra-family warfare the kids were pretty self-sufficient so I finally let them alone to splash around in the lake in their inner tubes and wandered up to the cabin to see what Chris was doing. I was so desperate for diversion I asked Chris about her clay pots. It was her favorite subject and she was able to give me an uninterrupted dissertation because Dick/Marvin/Joe was plugged into his food source and thankfully quiet.

By the time Chris had gotten to the glazing of pottery my eyes had glazed over, too. When I heard tires crunch on the driveway I grabbed the excuse to leave by saying, "That's really interesting, Chris, but I think I hear Marilyn's car. I better see if she needs help with anything." I hope my relief wasn't too obvious as I ran out the door.

It was Marilyn all right. "Hey, you need any help?" I was yelling when a familiar Buick pulled up and parked behind the Cadillac.

"Look who followed me home," Marilyn called out cheerfully. "Should we keep him?"

Rob climbed out of the Buick and waved at me nervously. I glared at Marilyn, turned on my heel, stalked back into the cabin, and slammed the door. Of course, that set off that miserable baby. Marilyn followed me and grimaced at the decibel level.

"Would you mind taking him into the other room?" she shouted to Chris over the noise. "I need to talk to Stevie."

Chris took one look at my face and silently carried her howling infant into the bedroom.

"What's he doing here?" I snarled at Marilyn. "Is this your idea?"

Marilyn was unimpressed by my show of anger. "Partially."

"Well, I'm not even going to talk to him," I taunted.

Marilyn shrugged. "I can't make you if you don't want to, I guess. But aren't you even little bit curious to find out why he's here?" I just glared at her so she wheedled, "C'mon, Stevie, you could at least talk to him. It won't kill you."

"He had his chance a week ago. Now I'm not interested in anything he has to say."

Marilyn sighed. "You've both had a cooling off period; now it's time to make up and go home. This cabin is fine for a weekend but anything more than that…whew!" She waved off the stink of that thought. "Besides, you probably still have some sort of feeling for him. You wouldn't be this mad if you didn't." As she talked she took my arm and gently propelled me toward the door. "You know, I've always been curious about what you saw in Bobby. I mean, he's cute and all that but it'd take a lot more than cute to get me to give up an acting career in California."

"Well, the sex was good," I muttered, distracted. I let myself be coaxed outside.

"Really. Well, well, well, wait'll I tell Mike his baby brother's a sex machine. Maybe he'll ask for pointers." By this time Marilyn had steered me through the door. Then she gave me a push toward Rob who was leaning against his car. "Now be a good girl and go yell at your husband. It's his job to take abuse and he's earned it."

I nodded and started the long lonely trek toward Rob. When I hesitated momentarily I felt a poke in the back. I turned to see Marilyn right behind me. "I wouldn't let you go alone," she explained in response to my questioning look. "Besides, I'm dying to find out how this'll end." She grinned and gave me another poke. "Go on."

I didn't have much choice so I marched up to Rob, stuck my chin out, and looked at him right in the eye.

"Marilyn says you want to talk to me," I challenged and Rob looked alarmed.

"I hoped we could talk alone," he stuttered.

"Not until I know what you want."

Rob seemed so nonplussed that I momentarily felt sorry for him. Then I heard the echo of a screaming baby over the lapping of the lake. I'd had a week of aching eardrums and Rob hadn't. He didn't deserve any pity.

"Well," he started hesitantly after exchanging a look with Marilyn, "we're having a family conference and I came out to get you."

"What, you need someone to throw rocks at?" I scowled at him. "Sorry, I'm not interested. You'll have to find another victim."

"No, no," Rob was starting when Marilyn interrupted him.

"We'll all be there," she said calmly. "It's about you so you have to come. And don't worry, nobody's going to pick on you."

I looked at Marilyn narrowly. "Did you set this up?"

"Nope," she denied sturdily, "but I agreed with Marvin and Alice that we need a family conference. You can go with Rob." I shook my head rebelliously until Marilyn added, "Unless you want to ride with me and the kids. I'm also taking Chris and her howler. You can sit in the backseat with them."

I shuddered. "I'll go to this meeting if you think I should," I said, "but I'm taking my own car. I'm not getting trapped anywhere." I directed this last comment at Rob with a glare.

He nodded with resignation. "Do you mind if I drive in with you?" he asked quietly. "I'd like a chance to explain a few things."

Marilyn didn't even give me a chance to be nasty. "What a great idea!" she exclaimed. "You two go ahead. I'll meet you in Brookings as soon as I get the kids rounded up." She hurried off and left Rob and me looking at each other silently.

"I have to get my purse," I muttered. "I need my keys and stuff."

I sauntered to the cabin and took my sweet time getting my purse. I did it to annoy him but when I returned he just walked over to the passenger's side of the Miata. I was a little surprised; normally, he assumed that he'd drive whatever vehicle we had, wherever we were going.

I didn't say a word as I navigated the gravel road up to the highway. If he wanted to talk he'd have to start on his own. He'd get no help from me.

As I hummed along with the tires on the asphalt Rob cleared his throat and began.

"I guess I better start by saying that I'm sorry. I should have believed you." Out of the corner of my eye I could see him peering at me expectantly.

I glanced at him and sneered slightly. "That's it? That's all you have to say?"

"Well, I said I was sorry. Isn't that enough?" He wasn't being sarcastic; he seemed honestly puzzled.

"No, it's not enough!" I flared and accelerated to emphasize my point. "You called me a liar. You implied I was a whore. You walked out on me. Saying you're sorry seems a little chintzy, don't you think?"

He hung his head and blushed in shame. "I went to the folks to sleep that night. If it makes you feel any better, Dad told me I was acting like a damn fool and to go home where I belonged. But you were gone by then."

"I left you a note. You knew where I was," I said coldly.

"Yeah, but Mike called and told me to give you some time to cool off. He said Marilyn would be out there with you. Besides, I wanted to check things out. You know, get the truth?"

I took my eyes off the road to look him in the eye and declare, "I told you the truth."

He nodded unhappily in agreement. "Yeah, well, I know that now. But you have to understand, Rick's my brother…"

"What am I? Chopped liver?" I interrupted.

"Well, no, but…" he waffled.

"You better shut up before you say anything stupid. Oops, too late!" I said mockingly.

He obliged me by sitting hunched over in his seat silently. I started to hum along with my tires again.

"Why are you humming?" he finally asked.

I thought about ignoring his question but figured if I answered him I might find an excuse to be snotty again. "Can't you hear the tires? I like to hum along with them. It's calming," I explained.

"You're still driving on the snow tires?" he asked in dismay. "Why didn't you get them changed?"

"I don't even know where the other tires are. You stored them somewhere and I didn't worry because you said you'd take care of it," I retorted and gave him my nasty-nice smile. "Remember?"

"Oh yeah. Sorry," he said.

We made the rest of the trip without further conversation. I filled the silence with humming just to annoy him. I think it worked.

chapter 25

I refused to go into the Anderson homestead until Marilyn arrived so Rob went in alone. I didn't have to wait long before the Cadillac pulled into the driveway behind my Miata. Marilyn distractedly ordered the kids to play in the backyard and not to destroy anything or each other.

"We've got enough to worry about besides broken arms or windows. Well, you ready for this?" she asked me brightly. "I think you're going to get some nice surprises."

I eyed her suspiciously. "How do you know?"

Marilyn reached into her purse, extracted her cell phone, and waved it under my nose. "I've got long distance capability. Every time you hogged the bathroom or went swimming I did a little business. Chris, you okay?" Chris struggled out of the back seat, got a good grip on her wrapped-up baby, and nodded. Marilyn grinned. "Then let's go. Court is in session."

She led the way to the dining room where Marvin sat at the head of the table facing Rick who was placed at the foot. Rob sat next to Marvin and Alice sat between her sons. She was holding a handkerchief and sniffling quietly, Marvin and Rob looked like their shorts were pinching, and Rick looked pugnacious and trapped. Three empty chairs faced Alice and Rob; Marilyn motioned me to the center chair. She placed Chris next to Rick and she sat between Marvin and me. I stuck my chin out and looked at the Andersons across from me stonily. I proudly thought us outlaws looked like the three Fates sitting in judgment—or maybe the three Furies. Then I glanced briefly to my left at

Chris who'd released a breast and attached her kid, and to my right at an interested, grinning Marilyn and decided we probably looked more like the Three Stooges. I was reattaching my chin to my face when Marvin cleared his throat.

"Well," Marvin began heavily, "it has been brought to our attention that Rick has been spreading vicious rumors about Stephanie and one of her students."

"Hey, I saw her with this kid," Rick interrupted desperately in a last ditch effort to justify himself.

"She was tutoring him. You should have talked to Stevie before spreading it all around that she was sleeping with him," Rob countered. "She didn't get her job for next year, did you know that?"

"The department probably ran out of money. I can't do anything about that," Rick retorted. "Besides, are you sure the story isn't true?"

"Rick!" Alice said, sounding shocked. "This is your brother's wife!"

"Muehler said she and this kid were meeting a couple times a week, sometimes with the door closed. And I saw her at a bar with him. Female teachers don't go to bars with football players, not decent ones anyway," Rick continued. "What do we really know about her? She's just somebody Bobby dragged back here. She doesn't belong and I think we'd all be better off without her."

Rick was finally out in the open. I shot a 'see?' glance at Rob but he ignored me. He was gripping his hands together so tightly his knuckles were white. Then he released his hands into fists and brought them down on the table.

"You've been mad ever since I outgrew your hand-me-downs and bought new pants," he began. His voice got louder as he gained momentum. "You keep saying that family should stick together but you don't know what that means. You've never been a brother to me. All you ever did was order me around. And I took it, I guess because you were so much older than me..." Rob's voice was trembling slightly. I knew first-hand how hard emotional stuff was for him. He stopped to swallow, then began again, "Our family is more than just Mom, Dad, and us boys. It's our wives, too. And ever since Stevie got here you've been after her. The only thing I can figure is that you know you can't take me because I'm bigger than you so you pick on her. And it stops now. I know Stevie can be a pain in the ass (excuse me, Mom) but she didn't deserve this. If you've got a problem with me you come to me. You don't go after Stevie. Not this way." Rob unclenched his fists with effort and laid his hands flat on the table. Then he stared directly at Rick, his blue-gray eyes were cold and implacable. "She's my wife," he stated flatly. "She's not going anywhere unless I go, too."

My Knight was scrambling back on his horse. Of course, I didn't appreciate that he excused himself to his mother and not me. I used worse language than he did but that was beside the point. And I wasn't that big of a pain in the ass. Was I? My ruminations were interrupted by my father-in-law.

"That's enough now," Marvin rumbled at Rob. He glanced at me then stared stonily at his third son. "I've listened to you say mean things to Stephanie and I've watched you browbeat your own wife but I didn't say anything; I knew Stephanie could take care of herself and I didn't want to interfere in your marriage. But spreading a deliberate lie about your sister-in-law to dirty her reputation and cause trouble between your brother and his wife…Well, there's no excuse for that. Do you know I've even had people come into the store and ask me if the rumor is true? I'm ashamed to have to admit that my own son is a liar and a bully." Marvin paused and the Andersons took a moment to stare at Rick in condemnation. "Now, your mother and I have been discussing what you can do to make up for the harm you've caused."

"Aww, Dad…" Rick whined.

Marvin raised an admonishing hand. "We think Bobby's right about Stephanie's little job." (Little job? Thanks.) "So the first thing you have to do is admit to Dr. Torgeson that you made up this ugly story. If he has any reservations about Stephanie's moral fitness…well, we can put his mind at rest. We'll do that right now. Stephanie, you need to come along for this."

I was a little nettled at Marvin's peremptory tone but how many chances would I get to watch Rick eat humble pie? You just bet I'd go along.

"Next we come to Bobby," Marvin continued and looked sternly at his youngest son who hung his head. "You should have stayed with your wife instead of running home to your parents. You're a married man, you have your own home, you stay there and work out your problems. Your mother seems to think you're still five years old and lets you run back here but I know better. I should have sent you right back to your wife where you belong. We've all handled this situation poorly. So you tell your wife what you will do to make it up to her."

I looked at Marilyn to share pleased surprise but there was no surprise to share; Marilyn seemed to know exactly what was coming. It finally dawned on me that this whole scene had been carefully scripted and I was the only one in the audience. I sat back and waited for Rob's next line. It was a dilly.

Rob looked at me and took a deep breath. "I know you've hated the trailer ever since we moved in," he started. "One of my professors, Dr. Swenson, is leaving on sabbatical for a year in Saudi Arabia and he wants to take his family with him. He just built a new house and needs someone to make the payments and take care of it. It'll cost a lot more than the trailer of course..."

"But Marvin and I will help make up the difference," Alice interrupted. "It's the least we could do, Stephanie. But you know, dear, it was unwise of you to meet with a young man especially with a closed door. You know how people talk. But I'm sure you've learned your lesson. And if you have a problem about taking our money you can always move back here. I've always said that you could have the basement..."

Fortunately, Rob nipped that train of thought in the bud. "Uh, maybe we better go see Dr. Torgeson."

Marvin announced that Rick, Rob, and I would ride over to the University in his Buick. I think he was making sure that Rick couldn't ditch. "Mother, you wait here with the girls." He looked sternly at Rick. "We're not finished yet."

Marvin herded us into the Speech building. Margy took a break from her typing to smile at me and wink. This was a good sign; after all, Margy knew everything.

Dr. Torgeson was cordial to the assembled Andersons. He listened to Rick's confession and apology with disapproving murmurs and head shakes, then turned to me and said, "I understand you've been wondering about next semester?"

No shit, I thought sarcastically. Rob was standing behind me and must have felt my body tense up for a brisk comeback; he squeezed my shoulder to remind me that I didn't have any lines yet. I nodded.

"I should have gotten back to you earlier," Dr. Torgeson apologized, "but you've been on vacation? Feel all rested up? That's good. Well, I'm happy to inform you that the Department is in the position to offer you a full-time job. You'll have to teach some fundamental courses along with your acting classes and I think the Television Production people have something for you. You'll assist the Oral Interpretation team. And one of your students has been approved to direct a production next semester; I think you should supervise. How does that sound?" He sat back in his chair while he and Marvin exchanged smiles.

I just gaped at him stupidly. Wow, a full-time job! I'd never had a full-time job before. I bet I'd even have benefits! I wouldn't have to worry about getting acting jobs to get medical insurance!

Then I got hold of myself. "What about the budget?" I asked suspiciously. "Last year you didn't have the money for additional full-time staff."

"Dr. Muehler has decided to take an early retirement," Dr. Torgeson said after exchanging another look with Marvin. Then Dr. T, Marvin, and even Rob turned to beam at me.

I was flummoxed. "I'm not sure what to say," I stammered.

The three of them looked disappointed; I'd finally gotten a line and apparently I'd blown it. Dr. Torgeson recovered his aplomb quickly. "Let me know before the end of the week," he said. "We have to fill the position if you're not interested, you know."

Rob was exasperated with me as we drove back to the Anderson home. "Why didn't you just say yes?" he demanded.

"How come Muehler took early retirement?" I parried.

"He wasn't given a choice," Marvin said. "Dr. Torgeson has been looking for a reason to get rid of him for a long time because of his history with students. He mentioned to me at Kiwanis that he'd like to use this incident with Stephanie and I told him to go ahead. I didn't see how you could be more embarrassed than you are. Tackling the subject head on seemed to be the best way to go."

"Does Muehler get a pension and everything?" I asked Marvin.

"I suppose so," he said.

"That's doesn't seem right," I said mulishly.

"The man worked for thirty years. I can't see taking his pension away from him. He'd probably fight his dismissal then. And this is cheaper than a lawsuit," Marvin said firmly. "Muehler abused his position but it's better we handle it without getting lawyers involved."

I must have looked like I was going to argue so Rob hurriedly suggested, "What about the house I told you about? Don't you want to see it?"

Marvin had parked in his driveway. "Mrs. Swenson's expecting you but hurry back when you're done. We haven't finished the family business yet." He shepherded Rick into the house.

Rob refused to explain Marvin's comment as he drove me to the Swenson's. "It's between the folks and Rick," he said. "I don't know any more than you do."

Rob and I toured the Swenson house which had a living room, a formal dining room, a large master bedroom, two smaller bedrooms, and a large kitchen complete with dishwasher, microwave, garbage disposal, wall oven, gas stovetop, and a refrigerator with a water and ice dispenser. There was a sliding glass door off the breakfast area leading to a deck overlooking the large backyard. I touched the refrigerator reverently.

Rob pointed out that the house had two full bathrooms. "You could have your own toilet. We could both get stomach flu and not need a bucket," he whispered.

I'd been trying to act cold and unimpressed but his comment caught me off guard; I snorted so hard a snot bubble formed on my left nostril. I had to excuse myself to find a Kleenex.

The Swensons were pretty normal but nice. Mrs. Swenson had probably made a lot of Jell-O in her time. She discussed decorating as the men toured the backyard.

"Your husband tells me you have your own furniture so we'll be storing our things in the basement. But if there's anything of mine you'd like to use feel free," she offered.

I declined politely but mentally approved of the beige walls and carpet. My earth-tone chairs and couch would work nicely. I could have all my stuff back. Thank God for people who play it safe when it came to color. Makes it so much easier for renters.

Mrs. Swenson watched me kindly. "If you change your mind just let me know. I'd like to help if I can. I always thought it was strange that the men get away with lying and cheating but women always have to live under a cloud."

"Does everybody in town know about my 'student affair'?" I asked, dismayed.

Mrs. Swenson patted my arm. "Well, you know small towns. And it's worse if the woman is young and pretty. I know just how awful this must have been for you. So if there's anything I can do to make your life easier, tell me. I'm happy to help."

From the way Mrs. Swenson was talking it sounded like she had her own skeleton rattling in a closet but the men returned and led us to the attached garage before I could find out any more. Dr. Swenson explained that they'd be leaving their cars at his mother's so we could park both of our cars inside. Mrs. Swenson pointed out the glass storm windows.

"Your husband will to have to put these up," she said. "We usually wait until after Halloween. It doesn't really get cold until then."

A microwave, two bathrooms, and no plastic flapping on the windows; I wouldn't even have to plug my car in. I was being led into temptation. Hell, I was way past being led; my anger toward Rob was draining away with each step I took.

We moved on to yard care and the lawnmower. "I hope your husband likes to mow," Mrs. Swenson said jokingly.

He'd better, I thought. I sure wasn't going to do it. But I'd worry about that problem when…wait a minute, *if* it came up.

Dr. Swenson didn't have a joke in him; he came right to the point. "We won't be out until mid-August. Can you wait until then to move in?"

I wasn't even sure I was moving at all so I just said coolly, "We'll have to let you know."

Dr. Swenson looked disconcerted but Mrs. Swenson patted my shoulder. "You take your time," she said.

Rob and I drove back to the Andersons' for the third act. Everybody sat in his/her assigned chair in the dining room, except for Chris who stood in the doorway. It appeared that she and Rick had been arguing because he was red in the face and she was tearful.

Marvin rumbled in a 'Dad' voice, "Mother and I have already told Rick how disappointed we are in him but now that doesn't seem to be enough. He deliberately tried to drive out a member of our family and he has to be punished." This was beginning to sound like *The Godfather* with a Midwestern twang. I swallowed a nervous giggle and Marvin continued. "Mother and I have decided that Rick will not be allowed to attend family gatherings at least until the end of this year. He'll have to go to his own home for lunch. He will not spend Thanksgiving or

Christmas with us. We will not loan him money or help him in any way. Unless it's an emergency, of course."

Rob sucked in his breath as an awed silence descended over the room. I half-expected Marvin to stand up, rip the buttons off Rick's shirt, and break an imaginary sword. Rick started to sniffle. Apparently, this was the worst punishment Marvin could have inflicted on him. But I was not impressed. I'd been trying for months to avoid the Anderson get-togethers. Banishment wasn't a punishment; it was a reward.

Alice looked woefully at me and said, "I'm so ashamed. I tried to raise my boys right but I must have done something wrong. I'm a bad mother. I'm so sorry, Stephanie."

I looked at Alice in disbelief. Rick screws up and Alice thinks she's to blame? Was she nuts?

Marvin patted Alice on the back and said tremulously, "Now, mother, it's not your fault. Rick's a grown man. He should have learned right from wrong by now. Don't you take this on yourself."

At Marvin's words, Rick buried his head on his folded arms and just bawled. But if he was looking for sympathy he didn't get it. Another unforgivable sin in the Anderson code was making Alice cry.

I even felt terrible. I'd momentarily forgotten Marilyn's lecture about Rick bringing this on himself. I was again thinking that Rick was right; if I hadn't shown up none of this would have happened. I was assuming my share of guilt in the whole miserable affair, just like Alice. Then I mentally slapped myself. All I'd done was marry Rick's brother and treat his wife like a person. Rick had been getting his own way for a long time and crushing anyone who didn't submit. He just went too far this time and got caught.

Alice wiped her eyes and blew her nose. "Stephanie, Marvin and I have decided on Rick's punishment," she said quietly. "But you get to name your own penalty." She looked at me expectantly.

So did everybody else. I was on the spot. Marvin and Alice had had days to work on their speeches, I had to adlib. Let's see; I could make a blistering recap of the wrongs I'd suffered but that would be stupid. Everyone knew Rick's crimes and screeching about them would be counter-productive and boring; I'd just lose my audience. What to do, what to do.

"Maybe he should make a public apology?" I suggested.

Marvin shook his head. "This family's been embarrassed enough.

We'd like to clean our dirty laundry out of the public view." He glanced at Rick and added pointedly, "For a change."

Rick cringed. I enjoyed the sight for a moment and thought some more. "Well," I began, "I don't think it's right for you and Alice to pay for anything. If anybody should pay damages it should be Rick. If we move to the Swenson house, make him pay the difference."

"He's got a wife and baby to support," Marvin objected. "He can't afford it."

I didn't need his money anyway. The only thing I wanted was for this jerk to be publicly humiliated and I wasn't going to get that. How could I hurt him? My gazed landed on poor, forlorn Chris standing in the doorway. *Can't afford it with a wife and baby,* I repeated to myself. *Ahhhh,* I mentally sighed.

"You're going home with Rick, aren't you?" I asked her. "I mean, you married him, you had a kid by him, you must see something in him, although what it is is beyond me." I couldn't resist the zinger though it made me sound petty. I modified my tone. "How about this; Chris gets her gallery back and anything she earns she gets to keep for herself. That'll give her some independence," I started reasonably then had an inspiration. "And...Chris gets to name the baby," I concluded triumphantly.

I was pleased with myself. I wasn't doing this for Chris, I didn't owe her any favors; I did it to look like a hero at Rick's expense...and maybe the baby would thank me someday. Rick looked pure hatred at me and but his glares didn't bother me one bit. Oh, I had the knife in and I was twisting it.

Chris raised her head. "Is that all right with you, honey?" she asked Rick anxiously.

"Doesn't matter if he likes it or not," Marvin said, looking sad but very determined. I guess you're never done trying to instill virtue in your offspring.

"Rick, is it okay?" Chris persisted. The damn fool was going to throw her advantage away. Rick looked at his father then at his wife. "Yeah, it's okay," he said with no grace whatsoever. Once an asshole, always an asshole. But he was Chris' problem not mine, thank God.

"We've done everything we could to rectify the difficulty Rick put you in," Marvin said to me. "Are you satisfied?"

I looked at Rob levelly and said, "I need to talk to Rob."

Rob gulped but Marvin accepted my statement and court was adjourned. Marilyn and I walked outside.

"I have to take Chris back to the lake so we can pack up. I think we should have one last party before we go home," she was saying as Rob slowly trailed after us.

"Uh, can I ride back out with you?" he asked me hesitantly. "I left my car, you know. And maybe we could hash this out."

"Sure," I said shortly.

"Bring a swimsuit," Marilyn told him. "We're having a party tonight."

"I'll go get one," he said and turned to go.

Marilyn watched him walk into the house then said to me, "You going to make it hard on the poor guy?"

"Yup."

"Do you really think he thought you were screwing that kid?" Marilyn asked after a pause.

"I don't know," I said slowly. "He sure wasn't much help."

"It's pretty hard to believe a brother would make up something like that," Marilyn commented.

"Are you taking Rob's side?" I asked, ruffled.

"No, I'm just trying to see things from Bobby's point of view. Geez, relax, will you?"

I subsided. "Rob should have believed me," I muttered.

"Yeah, he should've. He screwed up. But he's human; he makes mistakes. Can you say you haven't made any mistakes in the last year? I thought not." Marilyn paused again and took a deep breath. "I'm probably way out of line but Stevie, try to put yourself in Bobby's place. You waltz out here and tell Alice that her life is stupid and she should make Marvin help with the housework." I stared at Marilyn in surprise. "Yeah, I heard all about that. Sometimes the brothers talk to each other; I guess Bobby was asking for advice. Mike told me Rick was livid over that. And remember the wine episode? When you backed up Chris?" Marilyn dug her keys from her purse and smiled at me. "And I've got a piece of advice for you. Never recommend abortion. Not here."

"Oh, c'mon, I didn't 'recommend' it," I made quote signs with my fingers, "I just offered it as an option. And I don't understand the big deal. It's legal. Marvin told me he didn't have a problem with it."

"I doubt he was referring to his grandchildren," Marilyn said dryly.

"I think you should cut Bobby some slack. Do you have any idea how much crap he took from his brothers because of you? Rick told him in the Hills that he'd better start acting like a man and learn to control his wife, about how awful you were and how Bobby could have done better. You know, I'd never seen Bobby talk back to Rick about anything until Rick started badmouthing you. He probably didn't tell you about that, he wouldn't, but he defended you." Rob came out the front door with a small bag. "Here he comes. Guess you better make up with him. I'm closing up the cabin." She walked off and smiled back to take the sting out of the ultimatum. "See you out at the lake!"

Rob walked around to the driver's seat of the Miata. I guess he'd had enough of being a passenger. I didn't mind; the strains of the day had worn me out. I sat back and closed my eyes. We didn't speak on the short drive to the lake.

Rob parked next to the cabin. I pulled myself out of the car, walked down to the end of the dock, and sat. After a moment Rob followed me. We dangled our feet together in silence.

"Lake isn't very high this year," Rob said conversationally.

"Ummm," I said disinterestedly.

"My dad said I should apologize again," said Rob. "He said I was a horse's ass. I guess I was. So, I'm sorry."

I nodded but I wouldn't look at him.

"Did you hear me? I said I was sorry again," Rob persisted.

"I heard you."

"So?"

I looked at him and raised a sardonic eyebrow. "That's it? You were a horse's ass and you're sorry?"

"I've done everything I could to make up," Rob said. "What more do you want?"

I said indignantly, "I want a lot more than that piddly little apology. I was thinking more in the line of you walking on your knees over ground glass...say, for a mile or so."

Rob studied me intently for a minute then he started rolling up his pant legs. "If you can find a mile of ground glass, I'm ready to walk on my knees," he said, determination in his voice.

I looked at Rob, irritated. I wanted something more than a simple "I'm sorry" but the ground glass request had been purely rhetorical. I knew it and, dammit, he did too.

"Oh, leave your pants alone," I said with disgust. "You know I was kidding about the glass…More or less."

He quit fiddling with his pants and said simply, "Stevie, I messed up. I'll do whatever you say to make it up to you. I miss you and I want you to come home. I love you."

And, of course, that made me bawl. "I'm so sick of this lake," I snuffled, then added accusingly, "Chris said you knew the truth days ago. Why didn't call me then?"

"It took some time to fix things. I didn't want to talk to you until I had something to offer."

That made some sense. I snuffled again and he gallantly took off his shirt and offered it as a handkerchief.

"Thanks," I muttered. "I'll wash it for you. I hate crying. My eyes always puff up and get all red. I must look like hell."

"You're always beautiful to me," said Rob, then ruined the compliment by adding, "although I have seen you look better" and had the temerity to grin at me.

"Ohhh!" I breathed. "I'm still so mad at you I could just scream! And you have the nerve to tease me? I'd like to slap your face off your head!"

My veneer of civilization fought with my need for violent physical expression. As usual, the violence won. I pushed him off the dock.

Lucky for him the lake was low. When Rob stood up the water only reached his chest. He blew water from his nose as I smiled at him in grim satisfaction.

"That make you happy?" he asked.

"Sure did," I said savagely.

"Good." Rob abruptly reached up and pulled me in with him. I spluttered to the surface. The water came up to my chin.

"Water's nice, isn't it," Rob commented and splashed water in my face. "You've been needing a good fight," he flicked water in my face again, "so, c'mon, fight." He splashed me one more time.

"You son-of-a-bitch," I screeched and tried to splash back. Of course, I was at a severe disadvantage being buried in water the way I was. I flailed around for a while but couldn't get any purchase. I swam in a few feet. Now I could splash effectively but Rob was too far away to hit.

"You coward," I yelled, "come in and fight like a man!"

For the first time in our marriage Rob did as he was told without an argument. He waded in and we splashed each other until I used up all my anger-generated energy. It was fun, too, although I would never have given him the satisfaction of admitting it.

We finally crawled up on the beach together, gasping and laughing. Marilyn must have been watching our little performance because she suddenly appeared with towels and a couple of beers.

"I figured you needed these," she said then looked at me meaningfully. "Don't forget, we have to finish off the food and booze before we all go home tomorrow."

I stopped laughing and looked sidelong at Rob. "We haven't even begun to settle anything yet," I said.

"You will," Marilyn said cheerfully. "And even if you don't settle everything today the vacation's over. You'll have to fight it out in your own home." She directed her attention to Rob. "We're having steaks tonight. Want one?"

"If that's okay," he said cautiously.

"We need you to pick on," Marilyn assured him. "Now you two make up. We all want to enjoy our last night." She went back up to the cabin.

This was the first intimation Rob had that Marilyn was going to throw me out and I mentally cursed because she'd probably blown my only bargaining chip. Rob just checked his pants pockets for his keys and wallet, sighed in relief when he found them, and took off his shoes. "I'm glad I wore old shoes today," was all he said.

I couldn't stand it anymore. "I may go back to the trailer because I don't have anywhere else to go," I said sullenly, "but I'm still not happy about being called a liar by my own husband."

"No, you're not a liar." Rob's tone was getting a little testy.

"You didn't believe me," I said doggedly. "You thought I was a liar and God knows what else and I didn't do one thing to deserve any of it."

"I don't think you're a liar!" Rob said loudly.

"Don't you yell at me. You don't have anything to yell about. I'm right and, more importantly, you're wrong! Admit it!" I said self-righteously.

"Okay, okay, you're right and I'm wrong," Rob said and started rolling up his pants legs again. "Where's the ground glass? A mile on my knees would be easier than this," he said, exasperated.

"Don't you dare play martyr with me!" I scolded.

"I'm trying to make up," Rob retorted.

I looked sidelong at him. "We can't make up until I'm done being mad."

"How long will that take?"

"I don't know. I've spent a week surrounded by two screaming kids, a crying baby, a depressed doormat, and a landlady. Maybe a week of yelling at you will just about balance things out," I said.

Rob studied me. "How about the house and the job? We have to give people an answer soon."

"I'm thinking about it."

"God, Stevie," Rob exploded, "the whole family's done everything possible to fix this mess. I'm even willing to walk on my knees! What's there to think about?"

I looked Rob dead in the eye. "Actually I'm pouting," I explained.

"You've been pouting for a week!" Rob said, exasperated again.

"I was depressed for a week," I corrected. "Now I'm pouting. I think I've earned it."

Rob looked at me narrowly. "Do I have to stay around for the pouting?"

"Of course. I'll need you to yell at when I'm done," I said reasonably and Rob sighed. "Don't sound so miserable," I warned him. "You don't want to stay around to take your lumps that's fine with me."

Rob threw up his hands. "Whatever it takes to make you happy. Dad'll kill me if I don't come home with you. When'd you get to be such of pet of his, anyway?" he asked.

"I didn't know I was," I replied.

"I haven't seen him this mad since Mike wrecked his car on the way home from a kegger," he commented then shook his head in frustration. "You know, I'll never understand you."

"Yeah, well, right back at you. Double," I retorted.

He nodded and shook out his pant leg. "I wish I'd packed some dry clothes. Can we go home after dinner?"

"No, I think I'll spend the last night with Marilyn and Chris. I feel like I owe it to them. You know, solidarity? Besides, I have to help clean up. You can go if you want."

He hesitantly picked up my hand and kissed it. This was his one graceful little gesture and he was good at it. "If it's all right with you, I'd like to stay too."

"I share a room with Marilyn," I warned him. "And it's a single bed."

"I don't mind if you don't."

I reflected on my tour of duty in the henhouse. I'd had it with cold feet but I didn't want to capitulate too easily. There were principles involved. Oh hell, I'll take comfort over principle any day. I looked at Rob and said grudgingly, "I guess it's all right. You want to kiss my hand again?"

Rob had obligingly given my hand a smooch or two and he was starting to work his way up when Marilyn's kids came barreling down to get the boat. Marilyn followed them down part way and called out to us.

"No fair kissing, Stephanie. You're the only one here with a man. And we still have some wine to finish up. Bobby, you better have a glass and get mellow because I'm going to pick on you all night."

We went up to the cabin to make dinner. Rob didn't get picked on, although we made him do K.P. It was only fair; us 'girls' had paid for the food and cooked.

The children were sent to bed and the adults sat down to finish up the wine. The only one who didn't have much fun was poor Chris. It's hard to have fun around a bunch of lushes when all you can drink is orange juice. Personally, I don't think she was looking forward to going home. She sat isolated and subdued. I wish the same could've been said for the baby. He cried most of the evening.

Marilyn volunteered to spend the night in the tent with her kids so we could be alone. When Rob and I were spooned together cozily in the single bed, his hand on my breast, Dick/Marvin/Joe started howling again.

"God, what's wrong with that kid?" Rob asked. "He sounds like he's being burned alive."

"Nothing, he just cries," I explained. "I think he does it to annoy people. He couldn't be more like Rick if he tried."

The baby's crying stopped abruptly; Chris must have plugged him in. Rob fell asleep with his arms wrapped around me. I stared at the wall for quite awhile before I finally dropped off. I still felt used, abused, bruised, and confused. And I was afraid I was surrendering again.

chapter 26

After coffee and aspirin the next morning, we packed the dirty laundry and leftover food, swept the floor one last time, and locked up.

As we walked to our respective cars Chris said, "Thanks for letting me stay with you guys. I'd die if my folks knew Rick and I were fighting. And, Stevie, I probably won't open the shop until the baby's older but it'll give me something to look forward to. Thanks for being such a good friend." She climbed into her pickup and drove off in a cloud of dust.

I snorted. I was pretty sure Chris would never open another shop. In future I'd save my favors for someone who wouldn't waste them. Oh well, maybe she'd at least give the kid a name.

Marilyn and I silently watched the pickup disappear over the hill. Then Rob and I helped Marilyn load up her Cadillac. She slammed down the trunk hood, dusted off her hands, and said, "Next time we come to the cabin I'll leave the kids with Mike. Or maybe my mother. She isn't totally gray yet. Sound good?" I half-heartedly agreed and she bawled to her children, "Okay, everybody into the car. Your dad can't wait to see you."

The Cadillac spun out in the gravel and Marilyn waved an arm briefly before disappearing in her own dust cloud.

I followed Rob's Buick back to Brookings. "Why don't I take your car and get the tires changed while I'm thinking about it," he said as he hauled my bag up the steps of the trailer. "I'll leave the Buick with you in case you need to get some groceries or anything."

He whistled as he left; the little woman was home where she belonged and he had a car to fix. As far as he was concerned everything was settled. But I still needed to think this through. I ran through my list of confidants. There was always Leslie but she was probably at work. Besides, I needed someone who knew all the players. I finally called Connie.

"Do you want to have coffee or something?" I asked her plaintively. "I need an outside opinion."

"I'm making a batch of chocolate chip cookies," she said. "Why don't you come over?"

Fresh cookies? She didn't have to twist my arm. I took a slight detour to buy a half-gallon of ice cream on the way. I rationalized the calorie overload by telling myself that I'd need the fat and sugar to keep my strength up as I searched my soul.

I sat at Connie's kitchen table idly reading the cross-stitched Bible platitudes on the wall as Connie took two trays of cookies from the oven, handed her sons each a hot fistful, and banished them to the backyard. She put two more trays of cookie dough in the oven, poured me a cup of coffee and listened as I began my tale.

Of course, she already knew about Rick's ugly little fiction. "I heard about it a couple weeks ago. It was all over the Ag Department. My husband asked me if there was any truth to the story. I told him it was just vicious gossip," she said.

"You didn't think to tell me?" I asked, miffed.

"Gail and I discussed it but we didn't think it was our place. But we set everybody who asked straight. Let me tell you, my husband isn't very impressed with your brother-in-law right now. What'd Bobby do?"

So I filled her in on Rob's desertion, my week in the cabin, and the Anderson-instigated solutions to my difficulties as I stuffed cookies in my face.

"Oh, my. You have had a week," Connie said when I finished.

"No kidding," I agreed and contemplated the cookie plate. I really shouldn't have any more but they were so good…Oh what the hell, I'd suffered enough. I grabbed another cookie, then asked, "Tell me, is my in-law situation normal?" I made an encompassing gesture with my hands being careful not to drop any crumbs.

"Of course not," Connie said. "Oh, fighting is normal, I have some in-laws I go a few rounds with myself, but nobody goes to the lengths Rick did. Say, you want some of that ice cream?" I nodded.

As Connie got out bowls and spoons I asked, "So what should I do?"

"About what?"

"The job, the house, the relationship. Should I stay or should I go?"

Connie seemed to be having trouble following my thought process. "Go where?" she asked.

"Los Angeles. California."

"Why in the world would you go to California? Bobby can't go right now."

"That's just it. Should I leave him?"

Connie frowned. "That's a little drastic, isn't it?"

I smiled wryly. "I had a friend in L.A. tell me not to do anything drastic when I told her I was coming here with Rob. I seem to have come full circle."

Connie smiled then said, "I've always wondered how you two got together. Would you mind telling me the story?"

Nobody's ever had to ask me twice to talk about myself. As she dished out ice cream I gave her an abridged version and finished saying, "I guess I had abandonment issues and getting married seemed like a good idea at the time." I stuck a spoonful of ice cream in my mouth.

Connie's mouth was hanging open. "That's either the most romantic story I've ever heard or the nuttiest."

"It sounds nutty to me. I had no idea what I was in for." I sighed. "You know, life sure wasn't like this on *The Waltons*. Rob should have warned me what I was in for."

"He probably didn't have a clue that you'd have so much trouble. You two come from such different backgrounds. And, Stevie, you can't blame Bobby for not preparing you, you should have asked," she scolded lightly. "You two are a couple of babies. You both rushed into this marriage and the minute anything goes wrong you both go tearing off in different directions and jump to crazy conclusions without even talking to the other person. I'm your friend, Stevie, and while I applaud your gumption, sometimes I think you need to take a time out. For your own good I'm going to give you some constructive criticism and I don't want you getting mad and flying off the handle." She put her hand on mine, to hold me down I guess, and gave me the impulse control speech. Then, when I looked crestfallen, she gave me another cookie.

"So should I cancel out the impulsive marriage with an impulsive divorce?" I asked.

"That's exactly what I'm talking about. I think you truly love Bobby and still you're ready to take off without even talking to him. Don't you think he loves you?"

"Well, Marilyn told me he stood up for me against his brothers when I ran back to Los Angeles. And I actually saw him tell Rick off at the family conference. He said if I went, we went together. That was a first time I ever heard him say anything like that. And when he remembers he takes care of my car. I guess in his guy way he does love me."

Connie laughed and refilled my coffee cup. "If the universe were perfect, men would be bodyguards with ATM machines in their stomachs. But they come with baggage and no coping skills. Women have to help them learn and it's a difficult process. After the year you put in you're further along than most newlyweds. Taking off now seems like a waste of perfectly good suffering."

I pushed a cookie crumb around the table with my finger. "If we were just talking about the summer, it wouldn't be so bad," I said slowly. "I'd take a chance I'd get over feeling, well, violated. What if I don't get over it?"

Connie helped herself to a cookie. "You'll survive. As a matter of fact, you're the only person I know who could benefit from this sort of experience."

I looked at her dubiously. "How could I possibly benefit from this?"

"Think about it: You got a full-time job, you got a decent place to live. Any influence Bobby's brothers had over him is gone. And it'll be a lot easier for you to leave when Bobby graduates," Connie said calmly.

"But I'm being pressured to sign contracts today and if I do I'm stuck for a whole year. Isn't that being impulsive again?" I asked doubtfully.

Connie said thoughtfully, "You said you can't get into the house until August. Why don't you sign the contracts and put Bobby on probation for the summer? Get to know each other as adults and if, by the end of the summer, you don't think you'll make it together, well, then rent an apartment and Bobby can get roommates for the Swenson house. You won't lose the year because the University job will look great on your resume. And if you do decide to stay with the marriage you'll have a decent place to live. You can't lose."

I ate a spoonful of ice cream. Maybe she had something. Then I smiled sourly. "How about my little scandal? Am I going to have to wear a big scarlet A on my shirt?"

"I wouldn't spend too much time worrying about it," said Connie comfortingly. "There's always been a lot of gossip about you. You know, being on TV? And you're one of the few women in Brookings who doesn't have to shop for large sizes. There will always be talk about you." Connie patted my hand again. "You didn't do anything wrong so I don't think you'd get more than a C. But we'll make it red if that makes you happy." I had to laugh and Connie smiled with me. "Your friends know the truth and will defend you, Stevie. And you've got tremendous leverage against your husband. An opportunity like that doesn't come around too often."

I nodded. It was slowly dawning on me that there was no unalloyed bad thing. "Maybe you're right..." I said uncertainly and smiled hopefully into Connie's kind round face framed by the halo of curly blond hair. I should have asked for her advice a long time ago. Just because she wore the biggest under-wire bra and had the tightest perm didn't mean she wasn't smart.

We finished our ice cream and Connie gave me some cookies to take home. "Bobby's basically a good guy. He'll get his degree and find a job in a city. The only thing he can do here is teach and I don't think he'd be satisfied doing that. And you'll have an amusing story about your frontier adventure to tell your city friends on your silver wedding anniversary."

"What do you mean, 'frontier adventure'," I asked. "You make me sound so..."

"Effete? Superior?" Connie offered. I frowned at the unflattering assessment and Connie added, "You were pretty insufferable when you first got here. You acted like a missionary. No, that's not right; more like you were Margaret Meade and we were the Samoans. But I guess any big city person would act like that. Look at how the movies and TV show us! No wonder people think we're all a bunch of yokels. Oh well," Connie sighed. "I didn't hold it against you because everybody acts strange when they're alone in a new environment. Personally, I'd like to see you stay. You got me motivated to exercise. If I keep it up maybe I'll lose a size or two." She looked pointedly at my grease-stained sack of cookies. "But not today." She walked me to my car and shook a stern finger at me. "Take the job and the house. And you and Bobby start approaching this marriage like grownups. Start talking to each other," she instructed.

"I'll try," I said, daunted, and drove home. I parked the Buick behind the Miata and was met at the door by Rob. "I got the tires rotated," he reported. "And I changed the oil and checked the plugs while I was at it."

"Looks like you washed it, too. Thanks," I said and handed him the sack of cookies.

"Well, it seemed the least I could do," he said, digging a cookie out of the bag and munching. "Who made these? They're good."

"Connie. I talked to her about our problems. I told her that I still feel crappy about what happened, and she had some ideas. Rob, maybe you should sit down."

He dutifully sat at the kitchen table after pouring himself some milk to wash down the cookies and listened as I laid out Connie's suggestions.

Rob didn't look particularly happy when I told him of his probationary status. "I thought I'd already done everything I could to make up with you."

"And I appreciate it," I said hurriedly. "But Connie has a point, we don't know very much about each other. The only thing we have in common is sex. Sometimes I don't think we even like each other."

"I like you," Rob said simply.

"Well, we'll use the summer to learn to communicate and decide if we have a future together."

Rob said reluctantly, "I guess I don't have much choice, do I."

We left it there; neither one of us had a clue as to how we were supposed to go about 'learning to communicate'. We spent the afternoon being polite and getting on each other's nerves and we knew from experience how deadly that was. We finally ordered a pizza for dinner and Rob got a six-pack of beer to wash it down. We watched TV and had two beers each. One thing led to another and we had a romp on the squeaky bed. At least we still had sex working for us.

I slept like a log in the baby-free silence and woke up refreshed and relaxed. Rob delivered a cup of fresh-brewed coffee and massaged any residual stiffness out of my neck. Then he volunteered to deal with the Swensons and delicately suggested I call the Speech Department. I didn't argue at all; I picked up the phone and punched the buttons. Margy cheerfully put me through to Dr. Torgeson and I announced that I'd be delighted to take the job. He seemed pleased at my acceptance then added, "It was suggested that maybe you'd be interested in working with our summer stock program. We all feel bad about the unfortunate misunderstanding and would like to include you. There'd be a small salary, of course..."

I smiled to myself. Being a victim was turning into a goldmine. Besides, summer stock sounded like fun; I'd get paid to work on sets and coach the kids. I also let myself get coaxed into taking a leading role— just to help out, you know. I played Elaine Navazzio, the adulterous wife in *The Last of the Red-Hot Lovers*. It seemed appropriate somehow. And it was a gas. I was back in the theater!

Unfortunately, summer stock meant I was busy twelve hours a day and didn't have time to do much of anything outside the theater— including housework and communicating. Of course, Rob was busy with summer school, too, but he didn't bitch when he had to do the laundry. He was taking his probation more seriously than I was. But he was adamant about what domestic jobs he'd perform. He ignored the bathroom and refused to dust but he'd run the vacuum without any nagging. He also took over most of the cooking chores—he would have starved if he hadn't.

We barely saw each other so we didn't waste time arguing about attending family dinners. I was so busy I was happy to go; they were becoming the only decent meals I ate. And Alice tried hard to keep the meals pleasant. She even turned the July dinner into a birthday party for me. She made a big chocolate cake and the Andersons sang to me. I was slowly coming to realize that Connie was right; my public embarrassment was turning out to be a private blessing. My in-laws had never treated me so well. Rick was in exile but I didn't lose my edge; I still had Nancy to fight with.

Summer stock ended with a big cast party. I went to bed late and woke to see Rob packing a bag.

"Do you want to go to church or on a honeymoon?" Rob asked. "I made reservations at Custer State Lodge in the Black Hills if you're interested in the honeymoon."

I goggled at him. "What if it's like Minneapolis?" I said. "All we did was fight."

"We'll probably fight this time, too," Rob said cheerfully. "So? You want to go?"

And skip church? I packed.

I was excited about going to the Black Hills. I was particularly interested in seeing Mount Rushmore; I'd seen *North by Northwest* about ten times. Unfortunately, to get there we had to drive for eight hours through central South Dakota, which is probably where Tolkien got the idea for the Desolation of Smaug. I thought the landscape was depressing but Rob rhapsodized about all the space; a man could breathe, he said. *Maybe a man could breathe*, I silently jeered, *but this woman thought a tree or three wouldn't be out of place. Just for contrast.*

I got plenty of trees in the Hills. I even got to see a herd of buffalo. "These are twice the size of the buffalo on Catalina Island," I marveled as we drove past them to the Lodge.

"This is their natural habitat," Rob explained. "I don't think buffalo appreciate ocean breezes."

"Could you stop the car so I can get out and take a picture?" I asked, excited by the proximity of the real, genuine wildlife. "Leslie will never believe this."

"I'll stop but you can't get out," Rob objected. "Didn't you see the signs? Those animals weigh over two thousand pounds and they're unpredictable. If they charge they could easily knock the car over. At least one tourist a year has to get scraped up off the road because they left their car."

I wasn't sure whether Rob was worried about damage to me or the Buick but I obediently took my picture through the window. We checked into the hotel and the next day, at my impatient urging, we spent the afternoon at Mt. Rushmore, which is awesome. This is not valley-speak; the monument is truly awesome. I was admiring the faces and the engineering prowess that went into sculpting them when a middle-age couple next to me started commenting in loud East Coast voices about how quaint South Dakota was, how provincial the denizens seemed to be, and how funny the local accent was. I scowled at them. Were they deaf or did they think I was?

Then the man asked loudly, "I recognize George and Martha but who's the other couple?"

I started to giggle until he turned and stared at me, offended. Good Lord, he'd been serious. I thought about making some nasty comment about the ignorance and bad manners of tourists but I uncomfortably remembered Connie's comments about my own early behavior. I'd probably acted just as awful as these people one short year ago. Well, I'd be as charitable to them as Connie had been to me. Besides, I was supposed to be on a belated honeymoon; it was time to make love not war.

I wandered off to find Rob. Some of the paperbacks I'd gotten for the drive had a few ideas that sounded promising. One book described getting naked and running through the trees like wood nymphs. Well, we were in a national forest and after consultation, Rob agreed it was worth a try. We hiked through the woods until we found a pleasant clearing and got down to business. But it was no good; insects chewed on us, pine needles poked us, and the boulder we selected was hard on Rob's knees and my backbone. And vice versa. We gave up, toured the Crazy Horse Monument, and went back to the Lodge to finish the job in bed.

"Sorry about the wood nymph thing not working out," I murmured during our after-intercourse recess.

"I'm always willing to try anything new," Rob said. "Keeps life from getting boring."

"That's true," I agreed and sighed contentedly. "I'm probably going to have one hell of a bladder infection from all this sex."

"Just have to get you back in shape," Rob said and started all over again.

We went out for a steak dinner afterward. Rob needed the protein.

"We're coming up on our first anniversary," Rob announced casually over salad.

I dropped my fork. "I forgot all about it," I said blankly.

"You've been busy," Rob said, unperturbed. "So. Am I off probation?"

"I hadn't given it much thought," I dithered. "We didn't learn to communicate the way I planned. Did we?"

"You have to make up your mind. If you don't want to live with me I have to find some roommates," Rob said matter-of-factly.

"Yeah, I know," I said, thankful that the waiter brought my steak to cover my indecision.

"We haven't had a fight in two months," Rob pointed out after he'd been served.

"We haven't had time," I retorted.

"We had time the last few days," Rob argued.

"We kept busy," I said, and smiled.

"Maybe we could stay busy for the rest of our lives," Rob suggested with a gleam in his eye.

I'd have to invest in a case of K-Y jelly, I snorted to myself, but the offer had appeal. I gazed at Rob speculatively. The summer had been quite pleasant. And even if the only thing we had in common was sex, well, it seemed to me that sexual compatibility was worth a lot. We could still concentrate on communication and there was a world of literature we could explore while we did it. But the rest of our lives? I don't think I was ready for that just yet. I leaned forward on my elbows and made Rob a counter-offer. "How about if we agree to stay together for, say, a year. We can really work on some basic marriage skills and next anniversary we can decide if we want to re-up. What do you think?" I leaned back in my chair and waited for his reaction.

Rob looked at me like I'd lost what was left of my mind. "You make it sound like the Marines."

"Well…" I agreed slowly, "our first year seemed like boot camp to me."

Rob smiled grimly. "You've learned caution."

"It's called impulse control," I corrected.

Rob stared at me. "It's not exactly what I wanted to hear but I don't want to break in another roommate." He abruptly held his hand out to me. "It's a deal. I'll re-up for a year if you will. Shake?"

I looked at his outstretched hand doubtfully. "Don't you want me to sign something?" I asked. "I mean, is a handshake binding?"

Rob studied me for a moment, spat it on his palm, and grabbed my hand. "This'll make it stick," he said and grinned. "Deal?"

I was totally grossed out and tried to pull back my hand but Rob wouldn't let go. Our struggle was starting to draw attention. "Okay, okay, you've got a deal," I hissed. "Let me go."

I hid a smile as I carefully wiped my hand on my napkin to make sure all the spit was gone; we were stuck with each other for one more year. On the whole I was pleased with the decision. Maybe next anniversary I'd get flowers.

*****

We moved into the Swenson home a week later. I spent two days packing; all the boxes were taped, labeled, and ready to be loaded. Rob was in charge of finding cheap transport. The morning of the move the temperature was ninety degrees and the humidity stood at eighty-five percent. By eleven o'clock my T-shirt was soaked with sweat and sticking to my body. I was sitting on the steps waving my sweaty face with newspaper when Rob pulled into the alley driving the hardware store's delivery truck loaded with all of the furniture I'd stored in his parents' basement. He was followed by Marvin and Alice in Chris' pickup.

"Dad and I'll load everything if you want to go on ahead," Rob said cheerfully. "Chris is already lining the kitchen shelves for you. You can sit with a cool drink and supervise."

That sounded like my kind of job so I agreed happily. Marvin suggested that Alice and I buy some beer while he and Rob loaded. "We'll need to replace fluids so we don't get heatstroke, won't we, son," he said, deadpan, then winked at Alice.

I looked at Alice warily. Since Rick's Kangaroo Court I'd avoided any time alone with her and I didn't have a clue what to say. Maybe if we didn't have any conversation...

"I'll put the top down on my car," I said brightly and busied myself with the ragtop before she could object. Alice sat silent and tense on the way to the liquor store. I don't think she'd ever ridden so close to the ground before and she wasn't at all comfortable with it. And she fretted that the wind messed up her hair. I took pity on her and put the top up again after we bought the beer.

Alice seemed more relaxed in the enclosed space as I drove over to the Swenson house. "Marvin and I saw your play," she said. "We were very impressed with your ability!"

"Maybe the part I played was, well, not in the best taste," I said uncomfortably, "considering what happened and all..."

"We were real proud to tell people you were a member of our family, Stephanie," she said with dignity.

"Alice," I said impatiently, "I wish you'd call me Stevie."

Alice covered my hand on the gearshift with hers and gripped firmly. "I have enough sons. I need daughters," she stated quietly, and then added, "I know Bobby never gave you an engagement ring. My mother had a garnet ring I'd like you to have."

Was she saying she wanted to adopt me? I snuck a peek at Alice's profile. Her eyes were serene but her jaw was set. I didn't know what to do. Nobody'd volunteered to be my mother since my own died. I'd spent my teen years fighting the legal system for my freedom and inheritance. The shark-like qualities required for those battles didn't prepare me for the mother smother I could anticipate getting from Alice. Well, the poor old girl was surrounded by men; I guess I could understand wanting a little backup estrogen. And it's not like she'd asked me for money; all she wanted was the dubious pleasure of my company. She seemed to be offering me a bribe to get it. Oh hell, she'd exiled one of her sons for me, I guess I owed it to her to be a part-time replacement. I was going to get the smothering anyway; I might as well get the ring, too.

"Okay, Stephanie it is," I conceded. "You want us at dinner after church tomorrow?"

"That'd be nice. I'll give you the ring then," Alice said and I pulled into the driveway.

We were met at the front door of the Swenson house by Connie and Gail. "Surprise!" Connie called out. "We came to help."

"Oh good, you brought beer. Is it hot enough for you, Alice?" Gail asked as she pulled us into the house.

I heard Marilyn's voice from the kitchen, "Is she here? Can we start the party?" She walked through the living room, followed by Mike, carrying a plastic wine goblet. "I wish the guys would get here with the kitchen boxes. I hate drinking out of plastic. You want some wine?"

"Isn't it a little early?" I asked with a sidelong glance at Alice.

"If Alice roped Nancy into helping she's probably been drinking vodka out of a paper bag and sharpening her tongue. I intend get mellow and stay that way. Chris is in the kitchen if you want to say 'hi'."

That's about all I got to do before the pickup arrived. Connie and Gail had to finish lining the kitchen shelves with paper; it was feeding time for The Babe and Chris got sidetracked. That's right—The Babe. After all this time Chris still hadn't settled on a name and everybody'd gotten so tired of referring to him as 'the baby' or a combination of names, we'd started calling him Babe. Poor kid. I knew he'd probably end up in therapy for having such an awful nickname foisted on him—

unless he became a successful Major League baseball player. I'd always wondered where those horrible nicknames came from. Now I knew.

By two o'clock all the furniture had been unloaded and the boxes unpacked. Alice even had the beds made (I had my king-sized bed again!). I played lady of the manor and gave directions. The only time I lifted a finger was to turn up the air-conditioner.

"This move is a lot easier than the last one," I commented to Alice as she bustled by.

"Mrs. Swenson is a good housekeeper," Alice said which was high praise from her.

All that remained was to set up the TV and stereo systems. The men helped themselves to beers and started puttering. We women settled ourselves in the living room to supervise.

Alice disappeared and returned with a wrapped package. "For your new home," she said.

"Presents, too? Cool," I said and unwrapped some doilies.

"They're runners for your bedroom bureaus," Alice explained.

I smiled. I was going to have my own dandelion explosion.

"I have a housewarming present for you, too," Gail said. She pulled a small package from her purse. "Actually, it's from Connie and me."

I opened the package to find a gaudily embroidered red C on a white background. "It's your scarlet letter," Gail explained and giggled. "You only get a C because even the characters you play never get any action. What are you doing wrong?"

Connie waved a contemptuous hand. "Stevie's old news. Didn't you hear that Sandy at the grocery store ran off with the man who had the body shop behind Kmart? She even left her kids with Bear. Now that's worth an A!"

I smiled and admired the needlework. "I think I'll get a letter sweater and show this off."

The women laughed and I pinned my C on my shirt. The comments were getting pretty ribald for this prim crew when Alice excused herself and went into the kitchen. The hilarity stopped.

"It was supposed to be a joke," Gail murmured. "And it was Connie's idea, I just did the embroidery." She glanced at Marvin uncomfortably.

Marvin didn't say anything, which wasn't surprising. Nobody seemed to know where to look or what to do. Well, it was my house and my party. I unpinned my C and said, "I'll go talk to her. Can I get anybody a beer while I'm up? No? Okay."

Alice was straightening drawers. "Aunt Sarah sent some nice hand-embroidered pillow cases to give to you as a belated wedding present," she said as I watched her fiddle. "I'll make sure you get them when you come tomorrow."

"That's nice," I said, trying to figure out how to make Alice feel better. "You know, the letter is just a joke. As far as I'm concerned, whatever happened is forgotten."

Alice looked at me gratefully but she didn't say anything. She just moved to another drawer. Obviously, something was still wrong.

"I bet you miss Rick," I ventured finally.

"Of course I do. But he has to be taught." Her mouth was a determined line as she spoke. I never realized before that sometimes punishment was worse for the parent than for the erring child. I was on my second beer and feeling charitable. Maybe it was time to temper justice with mercy.

"You know, Alice," I said hesitantly, "it's alright with me if you want to shorten Rick's sentence. I think he's probably learned his lesson. Maybe he deserves time off for good behavior."

And if he didn't, Alice sure did, I thought to myself.

Alice's face softened and she smiled at me. "You're a good girl, Stephanie. Maybe you're right. I'll talk to Marvin about it." She closed the drawer.

"Ready to rejoin the party?" I asked hopefully. "It sort of fizzled when you left."

She shook her head. "Our work's done. I think it's time we all went home. You and Bobby need some time to yourselves. I'll go get Marilyn and Mikey." I trailed after Alice as she routed all the partiers from the living room. "I still have work to do and I'm sure the rest of you do, too. Marilyn, you and Mikey better come take a nap before you go to the cabin. I don't want you driving right now."

Marilyn made a face behind Alice's back but let herself be herded out with the rest. Connie was the last one out.

"I'm glad you decided to stick it out," she whispered to me and smiled. "From what you've told me, I think God would strike you dead if you really tried to leave Bobby."

I blinked at her. Was she seriously suggesting that Somebody was micromanaging my life? I hadn't heard anything like that since I was a kid and I wasn't receptive to the idea then.

When I was ten my mother made me go to Catechism and the nun, Sister Mary Frances of the mustache and combat boots, told us about Little Suzy who always held the door open for her guardian angel and said, "After you, guardian angel." One day Little Suzy got flattened by a truck and the guardian angel met her at the Pearly Gates saying, "After you, Little Suzy." That apparently was Little Suzy's reward for being so polite. I told Sister Mary Frances that I thought the guardian angel should have kept Little Suzy from being flattened by the truck in the first place. She sent me home with a note.

I was tempted to scoff at Connie but then I remembered all her kitchen platitudes. I didn't want to be rude. And I thought about all the times I tried to leave Rob or he tried to leave me, and the strange series of events that kept us together. What the hell. Connie's explanation was as good as any. I accepted her good wishes, thanked her for her help, and then Rob and I were alone.

"I have to get my car," he said. "You want to look at the old place one more time?"

"Sure." I grabbed a six-pack of beer to take along.

Rob drove the Miata and parked it behind his Buick. The boys next door came out to say good-bye and I handed out beers. We sat on the steps and the guys sipped quietly.

"I'm going to miss you two," one of the boys said. "You had some great fights."

Rob and I exchanged a glance. Yeah, we had some great fights. They almost finished us.

We shook hands all around and Rob and I went inside the empty trailer. "Remember how dirty it was when we first came?" I asked.

"Yeah, how come you cleaned it up to leave?"

"I think your mother's rubbed off on me more than I'd like," I said. "Do you think the owner will notice that?" I pointed to a small dent in the paneling caused when I threw a book at Rob and missed.

Rob grinned. "Nah, there're so many other dings he'll never notice."

"I hope you're right." I looked around. "We've been through some times here, haven't we?"

"We sure have."

I pointed to a corner. "That's where Pudgy died."

"She was a good cat."

"The best," I agreed before my throat closed up and my eyes teared.

Rob began hesitantly, "I asked the Swensons about pets. They said they had no objection to a cat. And one of Mom's neighbors has a cat that littered last June. A couple of the kittens look a lot like Pudgy. If you want to go over and look at them, they're ready to leave the mother." He stopped when he noticed my lower lip quivering. "Of course, if you don't want a kitten that looks like Pudgy we'll find something else. There's never a shortage of kittens…"

"No," I quavered, "I'd like one that looks like Pudgy. Thanks." I was full of booze and sudden affection. I threw my arms around him. "I love you, Rob!" I snuffled into his neck.

He hugged me back. "I love you, too."

"I'm not normal without with a cat in the house. You know what? Maybe we should get two cats. Just think how normal I'd be with two!" I burped.

"We'll just have two weird cats," Rob said rolling his eyes. "But anything you say. Well, ready to start phase two of our marriage?"

I snickered. "After you, guardian angel."

"What?"

"Nothing. Let's do it."

We locked the trailer and drove our respective cars away from our first home to our second. I drove very slowly.

Where I Ended Up

Mrs. Nelson quit whispering about Mrs. Olafson when she saw she couldn't interest me in her gossip so she went back to something tried and true. "Now, you take this weather. It'll go over a hundred degrees tomorrow, you wait and see. I don't know how this fat old lady will survive it. Guess I'll just stay inside in the air-conditioning and try not to melt. Fritz says the heat is good for the corn but I'm no stalk of corn!" She had another big belly laugh and I grinned in agreement. "But bad as it is it must be better than where you come from," she continued after wiping her face. "I've heard that Los Angeles is just a pistol."

We'd begun the closing ritual. "Well, it's dry heat. Doesn't seem so bad."

Kyrie eleison.

"But the smog! I've seen pictures where you can't see your hand in front of your face!"

Christie eleison.

"It's not as bad as it was. There're only a few really bad days a year anymore."

Kyrie eleison.

"Well, as long as it's not humid. You know it's not the heat it's the humidity."

Christie eleison.

"You bet."

Kyrie eleison. Lord have mercy. I retreated into the house with my tomatoes. I had to walk carefully around the two kittens that were underfoot angling for more food, their little dorsal fin tails sticking up.

I'd name them as soon as I got to know them better. The only thing I was sure of so far was that they were hungry all the time. I'd seen a pig feeder down at the hardware store. It'd be perfect for dispensing dry food for my new little sharks.

I put the tomatoes in the sink and wandered around the house restlessly. I'd been so peaceful on the step before Mrs. Nelson got me. Now I was stuck in the house. I returned to the kitchen, started to wash the tomatoes, and peered out the window; Mrs. Nelson had returned to her garden and was watching my house. She waved happily and I waved back despairingly. One of the other wives on the block told me to keep my drapes pulled; Mrs. Nelson had a pair of binoculars and had already reported the goings on between Bob and me in our house. No wonder Mrs. Swenson had been so sympathetic about baseless gossip. I was probably going to have to put plastic on the windows just to keep the old biddy from peeping in. Damn, and I'd been so pleased with my views. There may be no unalloyed bad thing but there's no unalloyed good thing either.

I retreated to the living room, turned on the TV, and channel surfed. Nothing on. I turned the TV off and looked at my new phone in desperation. I'd already called just about everybody I knew. I'd even called Heather in Los Angeles. She was her usual fractious self.

"I suppose you think you can waltz out here again and have everybody fall all over you because you've got that hair commercial running," she said when I finally got through to her.

"It's running?" I asked, pleased. "I haven't been watching TV much lately. When do I get a check?"

"It's in the mail. So what's on your mind?"

"I got a new phone. I'll give you the number if you want it."

"I told you, you can't conduct an acting career from South Dakota," Heather said threateningly.

"I know," I said. "But I'm here for awhile anyway. So, thanks a lot, it's been nice knowing you, but you might as well pull me from your files."

My announcement was met with stunned silence. I smirked to myself; this was the first time I'd ever shut her up.

"You're kidding me," she finally said.

"Nope."

"But there's nothing there but buffalo and Indians! I saw *Dances with Wolves*."

"Living in a tepee isn't so bad once you get used to it."

"A tepee!?" she squawked. "You're kidding me!"

"Yeah, I am," I said impatiently. "It's not that bad, Heather. Do you know I have the same radio in my car that I had in L.A.?"

"Are you kidding again?"

"Nope. And I take walks all by myself. At night. I've gotten some whistles but that's it. I haven't seen any graffiti in months."

"Aren't you bored? What do you do back there?"

Boredom hadn't been one of my problems the last few months but I didn't want to go into my personal history with Heather so I ignored the first question and jumped right to the second. "I've got a full-time teaching job, I just finished a season of stock, I've got friends, a husband, a house…I'm pretty busy. Do you know I'm even learning to water ski?" I said.

There was a moment of silence then Heather said enviously, "Marriage must be wonderful."

I wasn't ready to go that far so I said, "It has its ups and downs. Well, I just thought I'd call and let you know…"

"I won't do anything yet," Heather interrupted. "You still carrying that extra five pounds?"

"Yeah, and I might put on another five just to keep warm this winter. Do you know how much fun it is to eat anything you want?" I teased her.

"Don't you dare! I might get another call for you and I can't sell flab. And keep your union memberships current. I bet by January you'll be ready to spend a couple weeks out here."

I'd called Heather to tweak her and here she was being…well, not nice, but not mean. "Why, Heather, I'm touched," I said sincerely.

"Don't be. You're a pain in the ass but you're good. I can probably still make money with you."

"I won't take my clothes off," I warned her.

She sighed and said, "I'll only send you out for Disney auditions. Maybe the Christian channels. They don't pay much but it's better than nothing. So don't think I'm getting soft or anything."

"Heather, you'll always be a bitch to me," I assured her.

"I'm an agent; it's my job," she'd said and hung up.

That call had been a hoot; who else needed my new number? You know, I don't think I'd spoken to Leslie since before the big blow last June. I'd gotten the feeling she'd gotten a little bored with my upsets and complaints. And our lives weren't exactly going in the same direction. Funny how quickly you can lose touch with a friend. Well, I wanted to talk and she was the only person who didn't have my new phone number. Of course, it was only five o'clock her time and she was probably at work but I called anyway; I could at least talk to her box.

Leslie picked up on the second ring. "Stevie! How are you? Nah, I'm fine, I'm taking a mental health day. Should I get the guest bedroom ready? The last time I heard from you you were talking divorce! I was afraid your in-laws had murdered you!"

I tucked the kittens around my feet comfortably and gave her the saga of my summer; the fights and the resolutions, summer stock...I yakked nonstop for twenty minutes. I concluded with, "I'm not looking forward to another winter but at least I have an excuse to eat pizza. I need the body fat." I didn't hear anything on the other end of the line. "Leslie, are you there? I didn't put you to sleep, did I?"

"I don't know what to say. It sounds like a soap opera," she finally said.

"Nah, you can change the channel with a soap opera," I corrected. "I shook hands on staying with this show for a year. See if the ratings go up. And Bob and I are making progress. I refused to take his parents' money for anything so Bob has no choice but to let me pay half the rent. That makes me a financial equal. He's had a few vestigial problems about not being in control but it won't kill him."

"How come you call Rob Bob?"

"He's evolving. He decided he wasn't a Rob; that was his bachelor persona. Everybody around here calls him Bobby and he hates that, too; he says that's his baby name. So he's going to try Bob for a while and see if that fits. I hope so, his middle name is Alfonse."

"Oh." Les sounded bewildered. "So are you Stephanie?"

"Only to my parents-in-law," I said, admiring my antique garnet ring. "But I'm evolving, too. Marriage does that to you. I've started using Anderson instead of O'Neill. It's easier than explaining my marital status all the time. I'm keeping O'Neill as my stage name."

"I thought you hated acting."

"I love acting. I think it's a little weird that I had to come to South

Dakota to do any but I had a great time this summer. When I get back to the city I think I'll join a company if anybody'll take me. And if I need money I can always do commercial work. Right now I'm teaching full-time. Did I mention that?"

"Yeah. I can't believe they actually fired that guy and hired you. People must be more enlightened back there than I thought."

I'd agreed with that sentiment until I helped Linda move into Muehler's much larger office. She listened to me expound on truth, justice, and the Midwestern way until we'd move all her boxes. Then she wearily set me straight.

"Stevie, this Department is getting a full-time staff member for approximately half what Muehler was costing. And Torgeson finally got rid of a liability. I appreciate the fact that you think we're so enlightened back here in the boonies but it's enlightened self-interest."

"I make half what Muehler did?" I repeated stupidly.

"You're a woman and untenured. Don't look so disappointed." Linda had laughed at my crestfallen face. "Torgeson could just as easily have hired a man. And the extra money will be used on student productions. Where do you think Joan got her grant?"

I guess if you want pure altruism you have to hire Mother Theresa. And she died, didn't she? So I smiled at Les' comment and murmured, "Something like that. Anyway, one more winter and I'm coming home."

"So you are planning on coming back to Los Angeles," she said. "From the way you were talking I got the feeling you were settled in the Outback for good."

"Bob won't stay because of all the gossip about me. Besides, L.A.'s the land of opportunity for a water expert. Which in a way is too bad; if I were planning on having kids I might consider it," I said. "But we're taking it one year at a time; we haven't even discussed kids. And I'm ready to take on Los Angeles again. Bob'll pretty much go wherever I want and he won't even bitch. The finger pointing and whispering doesn't really bother me all that much" (*except for Mrs. Nelson and her binoculars*, I thought to myself) "but he feels guilty because his brother caused it. His whole family does. Remember how his mother used to order me around all the time? She doesn't anymore. As a matter of fact she takes my part against Bob. I think she's giving him an ulcer but better him than me. I could probably burn down a barn and she'd back me up. It's great."

"Funny how things turned out," Les murmured.

"Yeah," I agreed remembering Connie's comments about a higher power. I'd light a candle if the Lutherans had them.

Leslie interrupted my musing with, "I've got news too. Peter and I are getting married!"

"Are you nuts? After what I just told you?" I asked incredulously.

"Peter and I've put a little more thought into it than you two did," Les said loftily and gave me the details. Peter had proposed last week, he'd bought her a rock as big as a toaster, they were planning on a New Year's Eve wedding in Philadelphia, and Leslie was flying back East soon to meet his parents.

"I've already talked to his mother on the phone and she sounds just lovely," Leslie finished happily. "I'm sure we'll get along beautifully."

I remembered the look on Peter's face when his family was mentioned and I was pretty sure Leslie was being foolishly optimistic. At least she'd have the advantage of a three thousand mile buffer.

"Can you be a bridesmaid?" Leslie interrupted my thought. "My mom's lining up a bunch of cousins but I'd like to have at least one friend. The dress will probably be ghastly but you've never been to Philadelphia, have you? It could be fun. Maybe Rob...er, Bob could be usher or something so he doesn't feel left out."

"I'm sure he'd love to," I said, crossing my fingers. "I'll ask him."

She babbled on about her wedding—about invitations and flowers and menus. I listened patiently. God knows, it was her turn.

"Any words of advice?" Leslie concluded.

My first thought was "Run!" but she obviously wouldn't do that. "I can give you some good Jell-O recipes," I joked feebly.

"No, I'm serious. Any wisdom you want to pass on?" she pressed.

Any wisdom? Was she kidding? I felt like a bloody veteran returning from the front lines trying to explain to a raw recruit what war is like. And she sounded like she wanted it in twenty-five words or less. I suppose I could quote Connie's impulse control speech but I'd probably just offend Les. That was a speech for me, not her. Let's see, what sampler saying had been embroidered on my soul that I could pass on? I hurriedly riffled through my memory of Connie's collection of kitchen art/advice. Nope, nothing apropos there either. I'd have to improvise.

"Leslie," I said smiling ruefully into the receiver, "enjoy your wedding because what comes after is work. But if you hang in there your life with Peter will probably make sense eventually. Just prepare yourself because," I paused for emphasis then finished with a sigh, "the first year is a bitch."

CPSIA information can be obtained at www.ICGtesting.com
Printed in the USA
LVOW13s2134030214

372193LV00003B/164/P

9 781462 012633